Millie Myerson and the Prince of Wales

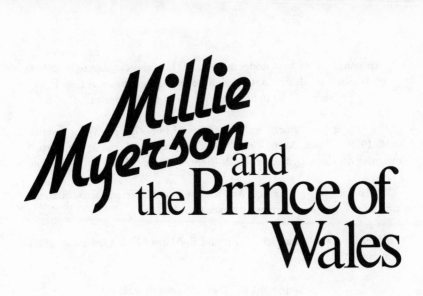

Millie Myerson and the Prince of Wales

Penina Spiegel

St. Martin's Press
New York

Copyright © 1982 by Penina Spiegel
For information, write: St. Martin's Press,
175 Fifth Avenue, New York, N.Y. 10010
Manufactured in the United States of America

Library of Congress Cataloging in Publication Data

Spiegel, Penina.
  Millie Myerson and the Prince of Wales.

  I. Title.
PS3569.P477M5   813'.54   81-21531
ISBN 0-312-53242-3   AACR2

10 9 8 7 6 5 4 3 2 1

First Edition

To Willard Goodman,
the original Phil Tovman

Millie Myerson and the Prince of Wales

Prologue

The Prince toyed with his breakfast juice, absently running his finger over the coat of arms etched into the thin crystal. A copy of the morning edition of the London *Times*, neatly folded in quarters, lay unopened next to his place mat. The edge of the newspaper and the edge of the linen mat were perfectly aligned. In his grandfather's day, palace copies of the *Times* had been printed on special, heavier stock; today, his was an ordinary newsprint copy, albeit extraordinarily crisp and immaculate. The pressure of his thumb on the moist glass made a small, squeaky sound that was somehow satisfying.

He looked up as his wife entered the room. Tall and leggy and blonde—a type he was reputed, with some justification, to favor—she moved with an endearingly coltish grace.

"Good morning, darling," she said, leaning down to kiss him. "Sleep well?"

"Yes, thanks. And you?"

"I shouldn't kiss you," he said to the laughing, dark-haired girl in his arms. "You'll catch my cold."

"I held you all night long. Did you know that?"

"I knew," he said softly. "I knew."

The window at his left looked out over the palace grounds; manicured lawns, green and sparkling with moisture, their riotous color-splashes contained in neat, orderly beds. The Prince stared unseeing at their sharp brilliance, his vision unaccountably filled with an image he had kept from his mind for almost two years.

No. Exactly two years, he realized with surprise. The beginning of June. So that's why . . .

. . . He saw her as clearly as if, once again, he had awakened before her in the room filled with the luminous undersea translucence of dawn light filtering through pale curtains. She sprawled on her stomach, her dark, tousled curls brushing his shoulder, and, under the light sheet that covered them, her foot was negligently hooked around his ankle.

He was swept with a sharp impulse, as painful as it was irrational, to lift the sheet away and run his hand down the curve of her back, newly tanned, to the rise of her buttocks gleaming whitely with the outline of her bathing suit.

His wife said something, and, guiltily, the Prince turned his attention to her. She wore a Wedgwood blue dress the exact shade of her eyes, and he thought, as he did almost every morning, how pretty his wife was, how very lovely. She is so *young*, he thought with a pang. I wonder if she knows.

He replied to her question and then did not know what she had asked or what he had answered.

But we've been happy—are happy, he corrected swiftly. And admitted, because he was at his core an honest man, that his wife, who had been giggly and lighthearted when they married, was now most often silent, perhaps in echo of his silences. And then, maybe not, he defended. After all, she's not a schoolgirl anymore. She's a wife and a princess and a mother.

But, still, I wonder if she knows. I wonder if she knows that nothing she has to say interests me. I wonder if she knows that it takes an effort of will to keep my eyes from glazing over when she speaks to me.

I hope not. I most sincerely hope not.

His wife poured a cup of coffee and handed it to him. The graceful, bare-armed gesture pleased him; he smiled at her, then quickly looked away. Her eyes were fixed on his face; her answering smile glowed with a pleasure too intense for him to bear with comfort.

The Prince turned a little in his seat, a very little, not enough to give offense. There had been so many women. But not, he thought, and repressed the grin that threatened his courteous demeanor, so many as was commonly believed. And perhaps, when you came right down to it, there had been only one. Only one who counted. And even that— If I hadn't had my own peculiar . . . requirements in a wife, I probably would have married long before, and that other thing would never have happened at all. My father married at what? Twenty-five? Twenty-six?

"James," said his wife louder, but without sharpness.

"I'm sorry. What did you say?"

"James!" said the girl, her brown eyes snapping with laughter. "I'm too old to make love on the floor."

"Rubbish," said the Prince, and proceeded to prove it.

"I said the baby has got to learn to sleep through the night. She can't keep waking every few hours expecting to be fed."

"Every two hours, James? I'm getting sore."

"Nonsense. A warm bath will fix you right up."

"Well, you know best, Your Royal Highness."

"Good morning, Your Royal Highness. Good morning, ma'am." The tall, serious-faced man inclined his head and shoulders briefly, then stepped into the room.

"Good morning, Peter. Won't you join us?" said the Prince's wife, as she always did.

"I've had my breakfast, but I never say no to another cup of coffee," said the equerry, as he always did.

Two pairs of eyes looked at the Prince expectantly. "Well, sit down then, Peter," he said. His wife poured the coffee, handling the delicate china with precision. The equerry opened the black leather folder he carried and cleared his throat. In a practiced voice, between sips of coffee and bites of a buttered roll, he read aloud the day's program for the Prince and Princess of Wales.

He was back in the shining luminescence of the bedroom three thousand miles and two years away. He looked down at her face, relaxed and childlike in sleep. One dark curl dangled rakishly over her forehead. Unable to resist, the Prince blew at it gently. She turned and snuggled into his chest, licking soft licks at an apparently preselected spot on his midriff, in the hollow between his ribs. Then, like a jungle cat who has staked out her territory, she dropped a kiss on the moist spot she had left on his skin and grunted with satisfaction. James swallowed his laughter so as not to wake her. He knew that she slept deepest in the hours closest to dawn and woke slowly, making the transition inch by inch, moment by moment.

With an unconcerned movement she flipped over on her other side. She buried her head under the pillow and snuffled in her sleep, unaware, and uncaring, that her rounded bottom was now angled invitingly toward him.

The Prince put his hand between her thighs and groaned softly, as he felt the dampness that was always there for him.

". . . then, as long as you're in the neighborhood, as it were, you may wish to visit the Royal Pediatric Clinic and see how they're coming along, sir."

"Right." The Prince shifted a little in his seat and arranged the damask napkin to cover the indecorous stiffening in his trousers.

The Prince gave in. He took the sleepy girl in his arms and swiftly satisfied his need—torn between pleasure and rue. He wondered if she would be angry when she woke up—if she remembered this at all, and found, to his delight, that he couldn't predict her response. Then he smiled, as, in her sleep, she said, in a cool, distant voice more suited to the drawing room than the bedroom, "Thank you very much, James. Now go to sleep."

The Prince, since he was not a man given to useless might-have-beens, banished the image and returned his attention to the schedule that awaited him. But, just before he did so, he granted himself one small indulgence.

What the hell, he thought, it's spring, and brushed an imaginary kiss on the forehead of the girl who had slept in his arms in another country and another June.

Chapter I

JUNE

Millie Myerson was dreaming. A glowing red sunset enveloped her in rays of warmth, sweet and sensual. The music, faraway, drifted closer. Millie relaxed into the strains. "See the pyramids along the Nile, watch the sunset on a tropic isle . . ."

The burnished sunset was a part of her, vivid, crimson shot with gold. Safe, enclosed, aroused, yearning, she floated on the dream. ". . . Just remember, darling, all the while—"

A harsh clanging broke inside her head. Then it stopped, and was instantly forgotten. Millie snuggled closer into her Eden. ". . . You belong to me . . ."

The clanging came again. Then she heard a voice. It spoke in her ear, very close. Slowly she drifted away from the glowing color, reluctant. Someone was talking in the dark, very near, in her bedroom. Befuddled, she realized it was her own voice. The answering machine had picked up on the second ring, and she could hear her own message. "Leave your name and number, and you'll get a callback. Start right after the beep tone."

She groped for the phone and found it on the floor beside her bed. Millie fumbled the receiver to the vicinity of her ear. "Who is it?" Her voice came out thick, in a half-whisper.

"Rise and shine, lotus blossom. Happy Monday!" The bright, wide-awake voice of her friend Gerald sang in her ear. "The sun is shining, the birdies are singing. As a matter of fact, I think I'll knock their little blocks off, all that stupid chirping and—"

"What time is it?" she broke in, dazed.

"It's six-thirty, and you have a seven-thirty call. Let's go, rise and shine."

"You already said that," she pointed out crankily. "What do you mean, I have a seven-thirty call. I'm not booked for today."

"Yes, you are. I just booked you. Hey! You fall back asleep again?" he shrilled into the phone."

"I'm up, I'm up," Millie answered, only half lying.

"Consider yourself lucky. I left you for last, since you live so close. I've been waking people up since five-thirty. That's how I earn my living. And, speaking of which, remember how you earn yours? Stopwatch, tick-tock, script supervisor, big book with itsy-bitsy notes . . . Stop me when something rings a bell."

"What's the product?"

"What do you care! Just put your little tush into your little designer jeans and bring it over here. Stage Five. I got work to do." He hung up with a click.

Forty minutes later, Millie stood on the corner of Broadway and Sixty-eighth, looking about hopefully for a cab. Laszloed, Tatianaed, tush obediently jeaned, she took a deep breath of the sparkling, sunshiny air, and promptly choked on the exhaust of a passing bus. Springtime in New York, she thought, coughing.

She spotted a cab heading in the wrong direction and she sprinted across four lanes of traffic against the light, ignoring the halfhearted, reflexive cacophony of honking. "Fifty-fourth and Tenth," she told the cab driver, feeling in her capacious tote bag for a cigarette.

"Hey, lady, ain't you seen I headin' uptown?" the driver snarled. "I headin' uptown and you wantin' to go downtown. What're you? Somkinda tourist?"

"Good morning, Mr. . . . Melrose," Millie replied, sweetly, leaning over to read the name on the license clipped to the dashboard on the driver's right. "It's a beautiful day, and I hope you are well. I also hope the taxi commissioner is feeling very well this fine morning."

The cab driver acknowledged her offhand inquiry into the health and welfare of the gentleman who signed his hack license, which license required him to convey any passenger anywhere he or she wanted to go within the city limits, with a muttered "cunt" under his breath. He salvaged his masculine pride by making an illegal U-turn, cutting off three cars, a van and a bus, with only a casual swipe at an early-rising bag lady crossing Broadway on the diagonal, discoursing animatedly to her Henri Bendel shopping bag.

Millie settled back against the seat and lit her first cigarette of the day. The dream was still with her, vivid, erotic. The strains of the tune she hadn't known she knew played in her head. "See the pyramids along the Nile, Watch the sunset on a tropic isle . . ."

When people told the slender, dark-haired, diminutive Millie she was cute, she pretended to be annoyed. "What's cute? An I.Q. of one thirty-five and people think I'm cute!" Actually, she was less annoyed than she appeared to be. She figured her choice wasn't between cute and Lauren-Bacall-sleek; her choice was between cute and okay. And cute is better than okay.

When she looked in the mirror, all she saw was the slight irregularity of her features. Her tawny skin and merry brown eyes held little charm for her. She missed the vivacity, humor and warmth that others saw and remained unconvinced of her idiosyncratic appeal.

She wore her short dark hair in a curly, tousled, windswept style, which nevertheless required the monthly donation of handsome sums to the coffers of her hairdresser. Her brown, almond-shaped eyes had just enough slant to them so that people often thought, mistakenly, that she was Eurasian or Hawaiian. Although her resemblance to her mother and sisters was strong, she alone had that vaguely exotic look, proving, she told her friends, that someone among her sedate, pious Eastern-European ancestors, had been fucking where they shouldn't have been.

The cab pulled up in front of the unprepossessing glass doors of the CC&G studios. Millie paid the driver and got out. Just after she had safely slammed the taxi door shut, she leaned over and smiled at the driver. "Prick," she said sweetly, and watched with satisfaction as the cab screeched away from the curb.

Millie turned and walked into the building, carefully pushing open the glass door, which for as long as she could remember, had had a wide, horizontal crack across its surface that someone had taped over with gaffer tape.

Cohen, Cohen and Gilhooley, known to production people in New York as CC&G, was the largest television commercial house in the city. Also the cheapest. They paid only union minimums and nitpicked over every fifteen minutes of overtime. They had both film and videotape facilities, and, aside from commercials, portions of feature films, entire television programs, and a major, long-running soap opera were shot there. The New York film production community earned a good portion of its annual income at CC&G, bitching all the way.

Millie rode up in the creaky elevator, miraculously working for once, and hit the fourth floor, which contained Stages 4, 5 and 6. She turned down the narrow corridor, unaccountably painted a virulent shade of internal-organ pink, and, ignoring the three-piece-suited stranger standing to one side, pushed open first one, then the other, of the pair of consecutive heavy, cast-iron doors that opened into Stage 5.

The cavernous room was empty, except for a knot of people gathered in the far corner around the coffee urn. Millie dug into her tote bag for the bright red sweater she'd stashed there and tied it over her shoulders. Sound stages were always kept at freezing levels for the comfort of the cameras and equipment; that of the humans was completely incidental.

As she headed for the coffee, Millie passed Buddy Morrison, one of the younger grips, moving toward the door. "I love cold rooms," he leered, staring meaningfully at her small round breasts, nipples erect from the cold, stretching the thin fabric of her pale blue T-shirt.

Millie ignored him and kept walking, wondering why someone who made as much money as he did didn't get his missing two front teeth replaced, and have something done about their rotted neighbors while he was at it.

She joined Grace, the middle-aged, stocky, black wardrobe mistress, standing in front of the trestle table loaded with sickly looking, greasy donuts. Grace turned and greeted Millie with delight. "Good morning, lambkin. How *are* you?"

"Hi, Gracie," Millie responded warmly. She stared down at the unappetizing array. "Have you ever wondered who it is who goes from production to production squeezing the jelly donuts so the red goo oozes out all over everything?"

Grace laughed. "I know what you mean. I don't think I've ever seen a whole jelly donut on these tables."

"With all the fruitcakes running around this business, maybe somebody gets their jollies violating jelly donuts," Millie speculated.

"It wouldn't surprise me a bit," Grace agreed, putting her arm around Millie's shoulders in an affectionate hug.

Millie poured herself a styrofoam cup of coffee and wandered over to the set. Peering through the semicircle of standing lamps that surrounded it, Millie saw the standard CC&G library/study set. An island of eight square feet of black-and-white-tile flooring ended abruptly at the grimy concrete of the studio floor. Two book-lined walls met at right angles, enclosing a heavy mahogany desk. A verdant Boston fern stood on a brass plant stand, next to a red-leather desk chair.

The entire set, when viewed on camera, would give the illusion of being but a small portion of a much larger room, which in turn was just one of many in an elegant mansion, the home of some moneyed Brahmin. The set looked as if it had been patterned on the morning room of "Upstairs, Downstairs," but Millie knew that it long predated that program.

This set had served as the background for innumerable white-coated actors who came out from behind the imposing desk to confide, "Nine out of ten doctors prefer the ingredient in Anacin," or to discuss, in an *entre-nous* tone, the painful itch of hemorrhoids.

It was also used in political spots and had already been the study from which a governor, several senators, and a clutch of would-be mayors had denounced their opponents' programs, some of which programs had been announced from behind this selfsame desk.

Millie also knew that the book-lined walls were false fronts, with only a few real books at eye level, in case the speaker needed to reach up and pull down a "practical" or working book. The Boston fern would be dead by evening, killed by the hot lights, and the cracks in the red leather seat were mended with gaffer tape painted to match the leather.

In the few seconds that Millie spent musing, the hands of the studio clock hit seven thirty, and activity picked up. Lights were snapped on, bathing the set in a hot, electric glare that seemed to crackle with intensity. Technicians wandered around, and one of their number dropped into the vacant red-leather chair to stand in, i.e., let the camera people and video men adjust their machines to the tones of real flesh, for which there is as yet, happily, no substitute.

Millie eyed the assistant electrician who had been impressed into stand-in duty with dislike. His name was Micky Hyams. His hair hung in lank, greasy strips to his shoulders at a time when even that last bastion of the affluent counterculture, Geraldo Rivera, had cut his short. His moustache bristled unkemptly on his upper lip. He was tolerated because his father was a respected, old-time member of the stagehands local. Micky got his union card as a sort of primogeniture, an unwritten tradition, which assured that sons of members were not put through the almost insurmountable trials for membership that kept out other, less well-connected newcomers.

Millie watched him with disgust, as he shoved a finger up his nostril in an elaborate, histrionic display of nose-picking. "Whaddya think? They'll gimme a SAG card?" he chortled, convulsed by his own wit.

"Asshole," someone breathed in Millie's ear.

"Who, me or him?" she inquired, turning around.

"Him, of course," Gerald grinned at her. "You haven't given me any reason to call you an asshole yet this morning. However, the day is young . . ."

Millie jabbed him playfully in the ribs, and they embraced in an affectionate hug. "Watch my coffee," she warned, steadying the cup in both hands behind Gerald's waist. She kissed his freshly shaven cheek and caught the scent of his after-shave.

Gerald had a narrow, bony face atop a lanky body, and a look, quite without reason, of someone who is chronically underfed. His dark, shiny bangs flopped over his forehead much in the style favored by the young John-John Kennedy. Millie's frequent pleas that he get a grown-up's haircut had so far met with no success.

Gerald was several years younger than Millie's twenty-eight. Also a "son," a second-generation production person who had gotten his first break by virtue of his father's prominence, Gerald differed from the others by having genuine talent. While the other "chicklets"—as they were called, contemptuously, by people who had broken into the business through persistence, guts, and a stubborn unwillingness to accept defeat—were distinguished primarily by a glassy-eyed devotion to dope, Gerald had an almost manic energy and an organizational ability that made things work. He was also very funny.

Millie, who was one of the unconnected ones, valued her friendship with Gerald and regarded him with only occasional envy. Doors that she had banged her head against, futilely, for years, opened before him as if on oiled hinges. Now he hiked his creased jeans and looked at her lugubriously. "So this guy goes to the doctor," he said, conversationally, "and he says, 'Doctor, you won't believe this, but I've got five penises instead of one!' 'Really?' says the doctor. 'How do your pants fit?'"

"'Like a glove, doctor,'" Millie finished the joke in concert with Gerald. "That's old," she said, with mock contempt.

"Okay, it's all I got right now," he replied, unhurt. "See you later." He started off, then halted in midstep. "Hey! Call the job into your union, will 'ya? I didn't get a chance."

"What's the product?" she called after him.

Gerald turned and walked back to her. "Prince James," he said with a grin. "Prince James and the crown jewels."

Millie looked at him disbelievingly. "Then *you* call the job in, if you're so funny."

"I'm not kidding. Prince-fucking-James is here. Right here in our tenement. He's doing a half hour on the Magna Carta. He brought it with him, too. I don't think he brought the crown jewels, though." Gerald hitched up his errant pants once again. "Don't you read the papers? He's in dressing room D right now, with about five guys that came with him—"

"So *that's* who I saw loitering outside the stage," Millie interjected.

"Bingo. Secretaries and guards and things that sound like they belong on a horse . . ."

"Equerries," Millie supplied.

"Yeah. I wonder if they do dope. Should I go in and offer some around? After all we're the hosts, and he may not have brought his stash with him."

"Are you telling the truth?" Millie glared at him suspiciously, ignoring his dilemma.

"Cross my heart. Or doesn't that work for Jews? What's the matter? Do I detect a glimmer of interest in my little Millie's eyes?" He pinched her cheek in a grandmotherly manner, giving it a painful, un-grandmotherly tweak at the end.

Millie slapped his hand away. "Cut it out!" She was notorious, and secretly proud, of her reputation for never, ever going to sneak a peek at some famous star who might be shooting in the same studio. The one exception she had made had been for Lillian Hellman, who was doing spots for her latest book. Millie had gone, gladly, to shake the woman's hand and had judged, quite correctly, that half the people at CC&G had no idea who Ms. Hellman was, and the other half thought her first name was Julia.

"I think you probably fried your brains beyond repair," she glared at Gerald.

"No, really. I got home last night about two. I was down in Chinatown with Max and Sandy, and when I got back there was this thing on my machine. Old princie is doing some friends-across-the-sea bit, and, whatever it is, he was supposed to do it at NET, but they shifted it over here. So I've gathered you all here today, dearly beloved . . ."

"What happened at NET?"

"Beats the shit out of me. All I know is, I got the word, and I came down here, and I haven't been to bed in thirty-six hours. But with a little help from Frosty the Snowman—Hey, meatball!!!" he yelled suddenly across the stage. "Just because you were born stupid doesn't mean you have to stay that way! That goes back on Stage Three for the dog-food shoot."

Gerald took off after the errant stagehand, who had "liberated" a piece of equipment from another stage. Millie looked after him for a moment, laughing, then headed for the payphone. She shoved a dime in the slot, dialed, and listened, as the voice on the other end said briskly, "Script Supervisors, good morning."

"Hi, Carol? It's Millie Myerson. I'm at CC&G and I'm working on—"

"I know, I heard, you lucky thing!" Millie marveled at the movie business grapevine, on which the fabled native jungle telegraph had exactly nothing. "What time is lunch?" Carol asked. "Business agents are required to inspect working conditions for their members, you know."

"When was the last time you were inspired to inspect conditions at CC&G?" Millie laughed into the phone.

"It came over me just this morning," Carol giggled. "Do you think he likes married ladies with three kids? I'd leave Paul *and* the kids in a minute—"

"MILLLIIIEEEEEE!" someone bellowed from across the stage. "Gotta go," she said into the phone, cutting off Carol's speculations as to the sexual and romantic predilections of the Prince of Wales. "They're screaming for me." She hung up and crossed to the set.

A group of men filed in from the narrow corridor that led from the dressing room. They were dressed formally, in dark suits, vests and ties. They look like the spokes on a wrought iron fence outside an East Side townhouse, Millie thought, with an inward giggle—slender black poles topped with round balls. Then she recognized the one in the middle. Prince James.

You look just like your stamp, she thought irreverently, ignoring the frisson that went through her. Millie saw a slender, handsome man, looking a little younger than his thirty years. His hair waved crisply from an immaculately straight part, and he had a light tan. He was dressed in a charcoal-gray glen plaid suit with a thin pattern of maroon and navy stripes, a white shirt and a navy tie with maroon and gold stripes running on the diagonal.

He alone of his companions did not wear a vest. He wore no jewelry except for a small gold signet ring on the little finger of his left hand. He toyed with it nervously, sliding it up to the knuckle and back again in a rhythmic movement.

James Nicholas Andrew George, Prince of Wales, Earl of Chester, Duke of Cornwall, Duke of Rothesay, Earl of Carrick, Baron Renfrew, Lord of the Isles, Great Steward of Scotland, had arrived at work.

The room was suddenly silent. The Prince looked up, aware of the hush that surrounded him. Millie thought he flushed, slightly. It must be awful, she thought, to walk into rooms where everybody stops dead and stares at you.

The Prince cleared his throat. "Good morning," he said, into the general silence. There was a mutter of sorts around the room, some of which could have been answering "Good mornings."

His face was strict, reserved, his lips set in a firm, straight line. But he looks . . . vulnerable, Millie thought. I don't know what it is, but something sort of gives him away. What a strange thing to think.

"I'm sorry to have gotten you all up so early, and I thank you for coming," he continued.

"That's okay, Prince. We get paid for it," a voice yelled from the back of the soundstage. The ensuing laughter, in which the Prince joined, broke some of the tension in the room.

The director, Bob Jones, a hack known as much for his pompousness as his tremulous cowardice, introduced various producer types to the Prince and was in turn introduced to his entourage, as Millie dropped into the canvas chair reserved for her to the right of the camera.

She didn't even bother to wonder how Bob Jones had pulled this particular plum. Movies, television shows, and commercials are often made in spite of the director, not because of him. Millie, and the others who knew their craft, simply played the hand they were dealt and tried to work around those whose incompetence impeded, rather than aided, the progress of a shoot.

Millie's job was immensely detailed and required enormous concentration. The script supervisor, a nomenclature preferred over the more common "script girl," by both the women who performed the job and the occasional man, keeps track of every line of dialogue, prop, camera angle, lens, wardrobe, etc., while timing every take to the second.

Millie opened the large, leather-bound looseleaf notebook that accompanied her from job to job and started to fill in the ready-made forms. As she worked with her varicolored felt tipped pens, she half-listened to the familiar production litany: "Camera one, frame up please."

"Let's see bars. I want bars. Today, sometime. Thank you."

"Camera one, get out of two's way."

The group around the Prince had dissolved. His entourage had gathered off the set, around the coffee urn, leaving him alone, sitting at the desk under the hot lights.

The first shot was simple, Millie noted. Oddly enough, in an art form where most scenes, even the most harrowingly emotional, are, for reasons of economy, shot out of sequence, and thus bear no relation to the one immediately preceding or following, the first shot this morning, in an excess of logic, would also be the first shot of the program.

Prince James, sitting at the desk, would introduce himself, express his pleasure at visiting the United States and his eagerness to share with its citizens some of the history of the Magna Carta, which document was, for the first time, conveyed out of its native land to one that had once been a possession of his ancestors.

Millie stole a glance at the Prince. She had, as all script supervisors do, the best seat in the house, about six feet away from the Prince's desk on the set. For it was her job to detail the action so carefully and so meticulously that the scene could be re-created if need be, in exact copy, from her notes.

The Prince looked a trifle apprehensive. His hands busied themselves with the papers on his desk, which were, in fact, simply props. He, as an experienced television performer, for this was not the first such program he had done, would glance down at them occasionally, as if he were absorbing a dozen paragraphs in a single, superhuman glance. In fact, he would be reading off the teleprompter, which was placed, as it should be, very close to the lens of the camera. Thus the Prince would be looking his audience directly in the eye. Had Richard Nixon learned this simple technique early enough, John F. Kennedy might today be president of a small college in Massachusetts.

While Millie watched, a prop man wheeled in a metal trolley carrying a mahogany cabinet with a glass top. Inside was the venerable Magna Carta, foundation of whatever is free in our society.

The prop man positioned the trolley to the right of the Prince, while Millie jotted down the technical term, "Camera left."

Camera right and left are, by convention, one's right and left as one faces the screen or the set. To further confuse matters, stage right and left are from the point of view of the actor facing the audience, that is, the exact opposite of camera right and left. This distinction confuses even professionals and has been the basis of more than one screaming fight.

The cabinet, with its priceless contents, would be out of the establishing shot of the Prince talking to camera and would be picked up with a dolly movement as Prince James rose and walked over to it.

The prop man sauntered off, joining his fellows at the side of the set. Millie overheard a crack about toilet paper and hoped against hope that the Prince's hearing was not as acute as hers. She looked over at him, sitting at the desk in the hot light, and saw that his face was perfectly blank.

The assistant director's voice came over the PA system. "We're ready for a take. Let's make one. Very quiet now, please. Slate it."

The Prince looked up as if something was bothering him. "Just a moment, if you will. I hope that this . . . er . . . this suit won't strobe."

Millie cracked up internally, stifling any outward manifestation of her laughter. So the Prince knew his videotape jargon. She heard the reassurance from the video operator that the suit would not, in fact, strobe, an effect that is caused by the way certain stripes or plaids "read" on television, making them appear to vibrate in a dizzying manner.

They made the first setups with no problems, everything moving routinely. Millie was busy, and time passed quickly. It was close to one o'clock before she had a moment to look at her watch, and she knew that, with a seven-thirty call, they would be broken for lunch by one-thirty at the latest.

There was a short lull, as they prepared for the next setup, which would be the Prince, leaning over the cabinet and pointing out salient features of the document within. Millie concentrated on her paperwork, until someone thrust a styrofoam cup in her field of vision.

She looked up and then leapt out of her seat, throwing her book aside and enfolding in her arms, as best she could, the very large man who stood in front of her. "Morty! I didn't see you. I didn't know you were on this job!"

He hugged her, lifting her off the floor. Morty Aronson, an old pro, the best gaffer in the business, and an all-around nice guy. "How are you doing, Morty?" she asked, from the depths of his bear hug.

"I'm just fine, honey. Be a good girl, and I'll let you rub the Jewish Buddha." He leered at her with mock intensity and indicated his large, rotund stomach. Millie threw back her head and laughed at the standing joke between Morty and pretty girls.

As she did so, she caught a glimpse of the Prince, watching them, a small, almost wistful, smile on his face in echo of their laughter.

Morty pulled up a vacant chair next to Millie's and dropped his bulk into it. "I thought you could use a cup of coffee about now," he said. Millie turned her attention to him, thinking that he was one of the sweet ones. She thanked him, and they exchanged industry gossip for a few minutes, while Morty kept a watchful eye on his minions, moving lights about the set. Every now and then he called out to one of them in a quiet tone that was instantly obeyed.

The disembodied voice came over the PA. "We're going to make this shot, then lunch." A cheer went up from the far reaches of the stage.

Morty stood up. "I have to go see what the boys are doing."

"Thanks for the coffee," Millie smiled at him. They both, for no reason at all, looked over at the set, where the Prince sat, riffling the prop pages of his speech.

He looks isolated, Millie thought, although what was odd was not the fact that he stayed on the set during the short break, but that he sat there alone. Normally, however glossy the superstardom of the actor sitting in that seat, someone would have wandered over to share a coffee and a moment's banter.

Morty's thoughts must have been running along the same lines as hers, for he looked at her questioningly. "Have you met him yet? Go over and talk to him. He's a nice guy." Morty grinned at her. "They could use a nice Jewish girl in Buckingham Palace. At least, it couldn't hurt." He laughed and Millie laughed with him.

"What? And have *her* for a *machateynesteh?*"

"She could do worse for a daughter-in-law. You're okay, Millie." Millie reached up and kissed him on the cheek, recognizing praise of a high order when she saw it. Morty turned to go. "Besides, a nice girl like you should be married, already," he observed, in the obligatory afterthought.

The disembodied voice said, "We're going in for a take. Quiet everyone. PLEASE!" and Millie was back in her familiar world of concentration, clicking her stopwatch, jotting seemingly illegible notes in her notebook. It seemed just a moment till she heard "Lunch. One hour!"

Millie stayed in her seat as the room emptied, filling in the notes she hadn't had time to do under pressure. She knew that, the second she stood up, it would all be out of her brain: camera angles, lenses, durations, camera movements, talent movements, each little notation in its alloted slot on the page.

She was only vaguely aware of the people moving out of the

soundstage, headed for one of the many dinky coffee shops in the area, or in some cases for one of the equally seedy bars, for a quick one, two, or three before returning for the afternoon.

Millie worked for a few minutes in the eerie quiet of a deserted soundstage. She realized she was freezing and shrugged into her sweater. The temperature dropped very quickly once all the heat-generating bodies left the stage. She heard the massive doors open and looked up to see Gerald coming across the empty stage toward her. "You might as well take lunch. If you put in for it, I won't okay it," he called.

"You buying?"

"Only if you eat fast. I have to be back here in . . ." he consulted his watch, "thirty-five minutes."

"Deal."

Wang's Deli, on Eleventh and Fifty-fifth, is possibly the only Korean-owned Jewish deli in the world. Wang's would have been patronized merely by virtue of being open for business in the far reaches of the West Side of Manhattan where the film studios were clustered. Soundstages require enormous vastness of space. The low-rent district in which they were therefore located was a no-man's-land at night. By day, the limousines that ferried stars and celebrities on their way to film, tape, loop or voiceover were generally unmolested.

Wang and his smiling wife were sympathetic to pleas for emergency corned beef sandwiches and jokes about his name betrayed the neophyte.

Millie and Gerald shared a back booth. Millie, disregarding the fact that she had eaten no solid food that day devoured a pastrami on rye, along with several very sour pickles. She watched Gerald languidly spoon up his soup and wondered if his stomach was troubling him again. Gerald, of the blithe spirit and carefree air, suffered from a nervous stomach, a fact he made known, with a complete lack of self-consciousness, only to a select few, which few included almost everybody he met.

Millie noticed for the first time that the T-shirt he wore depicted Donald Duck in a transcendent act of masturbation, the end products of which were flying all over the yellow cotton background. "Nice T-shirt," she commented, into the silence.

"It's funny, that's what he said."

"Who he?" Millie asked, knowing full well.

Gerald shot her a contemptuous look, in wordless disparagement of sudden, unbecoming coyness. A thought struck Millie. "Where's he going for lunch?"

"What do you think?" Gerald returned, interested.

"I don't know. The Four Seasons? Cote Basque? Lutece?"

"Wrong on all counts," Gerald said gleefully. "Dressing room D."

"How come?"

"How come, you ask? One of those assistant guys asked me to send up 'a light repast.'" His voice put the phrase in quotes. "So I did. Gefilte fish, stuffed cabbage, pastrami, potato knishes, kasha knishes, lots of sour pickles, and cherry cheesecake for dessert. Catered by Wang's, just like us. Oh, and Dr. Brown's Cel-ray Tonic."

Millie dissolved in mirth. "You did not!"

"I did too." He nodded sagely at her.

"He probably never ate food like that before."

"That's the idea. It's about time he learned what's good."

"However, if he spends the entire afternoon in the men's room . . ." Millie speculated.

"Then you get another day's work out of it. C'mon. Let's go." Gerald stood up, digging into his jeans for his wallet.

They walked the two long blocks back to the studio, enjoying the sunny outdoors, bickering amiably over whether Elizabeth Taylor or Sophia Loren had caused the greater stir at CC&G when they shot there. Millie, feeling good, strode along, swinging her heavy tote bag by its straps.

"You weren't there the day Elizabeth Taylor did that public service spot," Gerald insisted. "Walter Hough practically set up camp outside that little dressing room over in the corner on the fifth floor where they put her. Every time she stuck her nose out the door, Wally shoved his face real close to hers . . ." He demonstrated by pressing his face right up against Millie's, ". . . and said: Elizabeth *Taylor!* E*liz*abeth Taylor!"

"What did you do?" Millie asked, convulsed.

"What did I do? What I did was I told Walter I had a hot tip in the third at Hialeah, and he flew out to his bookie at the newstand on the

corner with a fifty in his grimy little hand. By the time he got back—"
Gerald broke off in midsentence. "Oh, oh. Look at that."

Parked, or more correctly, reposing, in front of the entrance to
CC&G was a gleaming Rolls Royce Silver Cloud. Its shiny chrome-
work collected the sunlight and sent it back, enhanced for having
bounced off such a worthy reflector. Attached to either side of the
windshield was a miniature flag, on the left the Union Jack,
counterbalanced on the right by the Stars and Stripes. Next to the
Union Jack was a rectangular banner Millie had never seen before. As
it lifted in the spring breeze, she caught a glimpse of gold lions against
a crimson field and a flash of white and royal blue.

Gerald circled the Rolls, admiring. His action did not in any way
disturb the composure of the uniformed worthy posted next to the car,
in whose conscientious charge the vehicle evidently rested.

Gerald's tour of the car brought him face to face with the
uniformed chauffeur. Brought up short by the man's steely stare,
Gerald looked manfully into the watchful eyes. "Nice car you got
there," he confided.

The personage looked at him, unsmiling. "How do you feel
about test drives?" the irrepressible Gerald inquired. The gentleman
stared back at him, impassively. "Not good. I can see that," Gerald
concluded hastily. "Well, it's been swell and all that. Gotta go now.
Loved talking to you," he threw over his shoulder, as he caught up
with Millie. Together they entered the building, laughing.

It was dead quiet on Stage 5, and at first glance appeared to be
empty. The initiated knew, however, that on every piece of stored
furniture lining the room, under the piles of drapes, padded quilts and
ratty, unidentifiable material, lay a sleeping crew body.

Millie headed for the wardrobe room and a chat with Gracie,
while Gerald split off for the control booth, saying darkly that he had
to "knock some heads."

The wardrobe room, on the outer periphery of the building was
one of the few that had natural light and unfiltered air. Green plants
on the window sill lent it a further air of homey domesticity. As Millie
entered, the PA system crackled, and the director's voice was heard,
whispering, "Should I do it now? . . . Oh, am I on? Attention
everybody." The amplified sound of paper rustling carried over the
mike. "A confidential memo from George Gilhooley . . ."

Millie looked at Gracie and saw her own brimming amusement mirrored in the black woman's eyes.

"Today we have the honor of working with an illustrious . . ." Jones's voice stumbled a little over the four-syllable word, ". . . personage, His Royal Highness, the Prince of Wales.

"The Prince is to be addressed at all times as 'sir.' 'Your Royal Highness' is also correct. He is not to be called 'mister' or 'prince.'

"No one is to approach His Royal Highness or speak to him unless he speaks to you first. If he *should* happen to speak to you, please answer politely and briefly.

"Since we are all, I can safely say, American, we are not required to curtsy or bow. However, it is perfectly correct to do so, if you think you can do it gracefully."

"He's forgetting something," Millie breathed, through her giggles. Grace nodded, pursing her lips to restrain her laughter. She was far too polite for the open ridicule that came so easily to Millie.

"I know I can rely on you all to be on your best behavior," Bob Jones exhorted in Gilhooley's name. "Let's surprise Prince James, and show him that the English aren't the only ones with gracious manners!"

This was too much for Gracie's self-control. She burst out in helpless guffaws. "If we can hear Gilhooley's announcement . . ." she wheezed between gusts of laughter, ". . . so can the Prince!"

"Please remember," the confidential memo continued, "each and every one of you is a representative of CC&G and the United States of America. Thank you."

"I guess that's it," Millie said regretfully. "Show's over."

"I'll tell you something, though," Grace said when she had recovered, "I've been working around him all morning, and he's just a joy. 'Please' this and 'thank you' that, and just as nice as he could be."

Millie looked at her, thinking that if Count Dracula walked into the wardrobe room, Grace would find it in her heart to say something nice about him. Maybe his well-brushed teeth, Millie speculated. Aloud she said, "I guess he comes from a good family—well brought up and all that." The thought threatened to send them off again. Their laughter by now had a life of its own, and the joke needn't be all that funny for them to enjoy it.

Gerald's head appeared in the doorway. "We're in," he said, and went off to convey the same message to all the nooks and crannies of the studio. Lunch was over, and the clock had started again. "I gotta go," Millie said, jumping up from her chair.

Millie planted a quick kiss on the wardrobe woman's cheek and headed back to the set. As soon as she opened the heavy doors leading onto the soundstage, she spotted Denise. And realized that Denise had spotted her quarry.

The bleached-blond, skinny makeup girl, woman, or artist, depending upon one's politics, was headed directly for the Prince of Wales, who was entering the stage from his dressing room. The irresistible force and the immovable object met on neutral grounds—the desk area on the set. Millie hurried so she could get to her chair and eavesdrop.

She watched Denise's long-fingered hands with their crimson, inch-long porcelain nails sketching in the air between the two. The Prince listened courteously, his face giving away nothing.

Millie caught Denise in mid-sentence. ". . . so I thought it would be just great, y'know, if you could visit a typical American family, except I guess we're not so typical since Jack and I split up, but they do say that single-parent families are, y'know, becoming more and more typical in this country, anyway . . . I don't know about yours . . ." Denise rambled on. The Prince listened, attentive, expressionless.

"Anyway," Denise continued, the lack of encouragement impeding the flow only slightly, "I'll give you my address, and you can drop over anytime. Whenever your *shed*yool permits," she said, giving the word her interpretation of a British pronunciation.

"I'm sure I'd be pleased to take you up on your kind offer," the Prince replied. Unaccountably, Millie's heart sank. "If my schedule permits, that is," he continued.

"Yyyyyyaaaaaaayyyyyyyy, Prince!" Millie applauded silently. And screw you, bitch, equally silently, aimed at Denise.

Denise, undaunted, continued to enumerate the delights of her husbandless abode, while the Prince's eyes scanned the room. "Excuse me," he called. For a wild moment Millie thought he was talking to her. "Are you Gerald?"

Millie swiveled her head and saw Gerald, halted in his habitual half-run. He switched directions and approached the Prince. "Yes, I am," he admitted, warily. Millie could see him thinking, Trouble I don't need from this yoyo.

"I understand you're the person who organized my luncheon." Gerald nodded, carefully. "I wanted to thank you. At home I rarely get to eat pastrami. Have to send to Blum's for it."

Millie could have sworn the Prince was repressing an inward grin. For what reason she couldn't say, since his face was unfailingly polite and bland. Gerald looked at him, nonplussed. "Well, thank you . . . uh, sir. I'm glad you, uh, enjoyed it." Pulling himself together, he looked around for a way out and found it in the hapless Denise. "You're supposed to be on Stage Three," he accused.

"What the hell for? All we got on Stage Three is dogs. And they don't need makeup," she responded angrily.

"For because we're paying you to be on Stage Three, that's what for," he snapped. This economic logic had its effect on Denise. She turned and headed for the exit, hips swiveling with outrage. Gerald turned back to the Prince. "Excuse me. I have things to do . . . uh, sir."

"Thanks again for lunch."

Gerald headed toward the other side of the stage. Millie put her book down and joined him. "He knows you set him up," she said, skipping a little to keep pace with Gerald's long strides.

"What, set him up? I got him a good lunch!"

"You got him food that was unfamiliar and that very possibly he couldn't eat." She looked at his stone face. "A lot of New Yorkers can't manage pastrami and all that other stuff," she pointed out reasonably. "Anyway, I could have sworn he got a kick out of the whole thing. And he doesn't seem to be the type to run complaining to Gilhooley and get you into trouble. And even if he does, you won't get fired."

This last, unkind, reference to his father's position brought a cordial "fuck-you" from Gerald. He quickened his pace and left Millie behind.

She turned back to her seat, cursing her mouth that ran away with her and got her into trouble. She berated herself for hurting Gerald needlessly. You don't know when to shut up! Millie sank back into her seat, picked up her book, determined to concentrate all the more in penance.

She stole a look at the Prince and caught him looking at her. Their eyes met, and for a moment there was a triumphant gleam of pleasure on his face, the look of a little boy who has put one over on his fellows. Then it faded. The Prince's face resumed its look of alert responsiveness, and Millie turned back to her work.

The afternoon proceeded, but not smoothly. Somehow all the production glitches had found their way to Stage 5. The atmosphere of lighthearted professionalism that had marked the morning faded, and in its place came a strained tension that seemed to communicate itself to the machines. First a tape machine broke down, then one of the cameras lost color and had to be replaced. The rhythm was broken, and it became an uphill climb.

The afternoon wore on. Tempers frayed, and production people took on the familiar, wild-eyed look of panic suppressed. If the take was okay for camera, the audio didn't work. If the audio was just dandy, the lighting director found an errant boom shadow that he swore hadn't been there in rehearsal.

The evil genie that twists the tongues of actors settled on the Prince, and he blew one short sentence, take after take. He invariably reacted without temper and calmly picked up the speech from an earlier point.

Late in the afternoon they were doing an insert shot, in which the Prince would get up from his chair, turn, take two steps over to where the Magna Carta had been in the earlier establishing shot and, looking into the camera, say his line. Millie overheard the director instructing the Prince to turn to his right and look to his left. She knew instantly that was wrong.

She walked over to the two men and said, calmly, "Excuse me, Bob. Could I see you for a moment?" The two of them walked a couple of paces away from the "talent." "He's got to turn left and look to his right to match that shot," she said quietly.

Any director worth his viewfinder would have relied on his script supervisor's information. Many a director's butt had been saved by a timely word from the script, averting a disaster in the editing room when the footage wouldn't cut. Most of them knew it and were grateful. Bob Jones didn't and wasn't. "I'm sure it's the right." He looked at her obstinately. Since the trolley carrying the Magna Carta had been moved around every which way since the shot they were trying to match, it was his memory against hers.

"Look, I'm paid to know these things. Trust me. The shot won't match that way. He's got to turn left and look to his right." Millie showed him the page in her book with the notes describing exactly where the Magna Carta had been during the establishing shot, and wondered why she was fighting to save this moron's ass.

"Goddamn son-of-a-bitching—" he exploded.

"Goddamn son-of-a-bitching *what!* I'm telling you it's to the *left.*"

"I know it's to the right, and don't tell me different," Bob Jones shrilled, unleashing his repressed petulance.

Millie's temper blew. "It's to the left, and you can stuff it up your ass!"

"One moment, please," the quiet voice with its clipped accent interjected, cutting off what was shaping up as a full-scale brawl. "Can't we check the tapes and see?" the Prince inquired mildly.

Millie seized on the idea. "Let's do that."

Jones hesitated. "No. We'll do it your way. He'll look to the left, and, if you're wrong, it's your ass." He stalked off.

"But I'm right, and you know it," Millie said softly, under her breath.

The answer came, equally soft. "And still, the earth moves around the sun."

She looked at the Prince, surprised. "Galileo Galilei," she replied, showing off.

"Fifteen sixty-four to sixteen forty-two," the Prince shot back, just as quickly.

"That, I didn't know," she admitted. "The exact dates, I mean."

"I have a mind for trivia. And I can't remember exactly, but I think you *were* right."

"I know I was right. It's in my notes."

"Insert Three, Take One," came the disembodied voice over the loudspeaker. They separated, each to his appointed task. Millie sat down in her seat, happiness bubbling up in her throat. Inexplicably, the song from her dream played in her mind, and for a moment she was back in the heat, the sweet excitement. Then she wiped her mind clean and concentrated on her book.

But now Millie was so aware of the Prince, and of his eyes on her, that she felt as if she were as much on stage as he, except that *everyone* stole covert glances at him, while she, occasionally, surprised him looking at her, and suspected him of tuning in on her conversations during the setups, while he stared off into space, or busied himself with the papers on his desk.

Along about eight o'clock, Gerald dropped into a seat next to her. "This is just too much for a one-day shoot," he said morosely. "We're already into overtime, and, if I don't break the crew for dinner soon, we'll be into penalty. Triple time."

Millie looked at him, seeing his tension and weariness. "Do you think we'll run over into tomorrow?"

Gerald shook his head. "Can't. Princie has to finish up today."

"Can't you cater dinner, and we'll work straight through?"

"Yeah, we can. But we have to have everyone on the crew agree. And there's one asshole standout, as usual."

"Who?" Millie asked, then answered her own question. "Jim Malone."

"You got it. At this rate we'll never get out of here."

"What's his problem."

"His problem is, and I quote: 'I am not a pack mule. I want to sit down and eat my dinner like a human being.' End quote. We're in for a long night, tiger lily."

"Do you want me to talk to him?"

Gerald looked at her in disbelief. "Nah, Morty and Ken White and Steve Cunningham are strong-arming him right now. What do you think, you'll bat your eyelashes at him, and he'll cave in?"

"You never can tell."

"I can tell. Feminine wiles won't work. Beating his brains in will." He disengaged the leg curled under the arm of the chair, straightened his lanky body, and, with an offhand "See ya," he was gone.

Either strong-arm tactics or sweet reason prevailed, for the trestle table was set up with a spread from the deli, and work continued.

"The Magna Carta was signed in 1215, and re-ratified in 1216, 1217 and 1225. They kept at it till they got it right," Prince James smiled engagingly into camera. "For the first time in recorded history, it contained a clause which stated that, if King John were to breach the terms of the charter, a Council made up of twenty-five barons could join to wage war against him. Thus there is an unbroken thread between the Magna Carta and the articles of impeachment, which were recently issued against one of your presidents."

Millie stretched her neck to ease the stiff muscles and looked at the studio clock. Ten-thirty, and she'd been working steadily since seven-thirty that morning, with only a short break at lunchtime.

She contented herself with a yogurt for dinner. Pastrami was nice, but twice in one day . . . She was amused to see the Prince's equerry loading a plate with generous helpings of *kasha varnishkes*, stuffed cabbage, and other examples of Wang's expertise. *Abi gezunt*, she thought. I bet they don't serve food like that in Buckingham Palace.

Just as she was spooning up the last of her yogurt, the PA system squawked into life. Gerald's voice announced "That's a wrap everybody. We'll finish tomorrow. The call is 8:30. Sharp!" The powers that be had decided. "This is a hot set," Gerald added. That last phrase was both whipped cream *and* the cherry to the tired stagehands. It meant that the equipment did not have to be wrapped, or put away, but could be left standing where it was overnight.

The studio emptied faster than a leaky lifeboat.

The night air was cool on Millie's face, refreshing after the canned, overconditioned air of the studio. She was tempted to walk the mile uptown, but gave that thought up in the interest of preserving her body in its as-yet-unmugged state.

Millie's apartment was called, in real estate parlance, an "alcove studio/sep.kitch." The entire apartment consisted of a long "L" shaped room about the size of a suburban living room. The confined space didn't really bother her. She was used to living, eating and sleeping in small, defined areas. The adaptability of New Yorkers is never-ending.

The thirty-story building itself was part of an enormous complex just north of Lincoln Center. The neighborhood had once rivaled Hell's Kitchen for ferocity. After the establishment of Lincoln Center brought culture to the West Side, the slums had been razed, their inhabitants shuffled off to a barrio somewhere else, and in their place rose rows of white towers guarding well-tended patches of lawn. Health food stores, restaurants, antique stores, and emporia devoted singlemindedly to bathrooms, kitchens and bedrooms followed in their wake, like the pilot fish who feast on the leavings of the great white shark. Grimy streets that had once echoed with the violence of flashing knives now sparkled with rows of outdoor cafes interspersed with hip boutiques, like the spoor marking the passage of the giant Bloomingdale's bird.

When Millie opened the door, she thrilled, as always, to the sight through the knee-to-ceiling windows that made up the far wall. The lights of the buildings across the way hung before her, lanterns in the dark sky, looking somehow theatrical, like a stage set arranged for her pleasure. The wood parquet floors reflected gleams of light that vanished as she switched on a lamp.

A cheerful, chintz-covered couch and two matching easy chairs clustered in front of the window. Next to them, a plant-, record- and book-filled wall unit separated the living area from the six-foot-square sleeping area, filling out the short arm of the "L." A glass-topped dining table with two wicker chairs near the entrance pretty much completed the furnishings. The entire effect, however, was warm, inviting and comfortable.

Millie debated the idea of having a drink and decided she was too tired. She ran a bubble bath instead and climbed in, sighing as her taut body unwound in the soothing warmth.

She lay back and contemplated her polished toenails resting on the faucet. A strange day, she thought. In this business, you never know what the hell the next phone call would bring. Prince James had a sweetness about him, yet he seemed . . . closed. Although he appeared relaxed, affable, his ease seemed studied, and, underneath, Millie sensed a vigilance, an alert watchfulness. He appeared spontaneous, yet his spontaneity had a very careful quality to it. She laughed out loud as she recalled his deadpan face, thanking Gerald for "organizing" his lunch, and remembered the mischievous twinkle buried deep in his eyes.

She wondered what he was doing right this minute, then quickly dismissed the thought. That way lay insanity. She was too cynical, and too bruised, to harbor thoughts like that.

The dearth of eligible men with an emotional capacity greater than that of a kindergarten child is well-known, and Millie suffered from it more than most, for she had an unerring ability to spot phoniness, and a complete lack of tolerance for stupidity.

The last affair she had had, with an actor, had ended badly, and that was almost two years ago. The trouble with actors was that they had seen all the movies, played all the romantic leads. They knew the right moves and the right things to say. After all, they played love scenes in the mirrors of their mind, time after time.

Yet underneath was a grasping, infantile, unslakeable thirst for continual applause that grew tiresome after a while. Millie and John had had endless conversations about how, in an ideal affair, each partner would take turns being cossetted and cared for by the other. But somehow it had never been Millie's turn to be babied. John's hungers, John's needs always took center stage.

As the years wore on, and Millie's twenties turned inexorably toward thirty, she had grown used to solitude and more or less resigned to extended periods of lovelessness.

Melancholy settled over Millie like a pall. She touched herself, feeling silk and soapsuds under her hand, moved briefly, and was comforted.

Chapter II

She slept badly that night, dreaming shapeless specters and nameless fears, and woke to the inanely chipper voice of the newscaster on WINS, feeling groggy and out of focus.

Perversely, everyone at the studio was cheerful and up. It was often like that on the second day of a shoot, sort of like the second day of the new term at school. You know who's sitting next to you and where your locker is.

Prince James looked alert, crisp, with that brisk virility men have when they are freshly showered and shaved. He was dressed, correctly, in the same suit as the day before. He exchanged cordial good mornings with the people near him and settled himself at his desk.

He looked over at Millie. "Good morning," he called, his voice pitched just loud enough to cover the seven or eight feet between them.

"Good morning," she replied, and then congratulated herself on the cleverness of her repartee.

Neither of them seemed to know where to take it from there, and they each looked away, intent on objects of consuming interest in the opposite direction.

During the first setup of the morning, the Prince was reading a rather long speech off the teleprompter when a lamp overhead blew, with a retort that sounded exactly like a rifle shot in the enforced quiet of the room. Everyone jumped, startled.

Millie had been watching the Prince carefully, as was her job, and she noted with interest that he didn't miss a beat. He didn't flinch, and, except for the briefest of flickers in his eyes, nothing betrayed the shock he must have felt. The guards and equerries leapt from their posts on the sidelines and stopped short, just outside the circle of light, realizing that whatever it was had not affected the Prince, who was calmly reading his lines. Millie wondered at his iron control. She had seen that kind of discipline before, but only in the most gifted of actors. Coleen Dewhurst had it, and Robert De Niro. It was unexpected in a civilian.

At midmorning, while they were setting up for the next shot, Millie went to get herself a cup of coffee, feeling sullen and disagreeable. She deflected several attempts to engage her in conversation and ignored a coarse speculation on the desirability of her ass put forward by one of a group of stagehands, which she overheard, as was intended.

On her way back to the set, she looked over and saw Morty Aronson engaged in animated conversation with the Prince. James was sitting on a corner of the desk, one leg resting on the floor and the other swinging free. Morty stood in front of him, his rotund belly encased in a bright yellow turtleneck. The two of them were laughing, and the Prince looked easier than Millie had ever seen him. Wondering if Morty could possibly be sharing one of his extensive store of off-color stories, Millie hurried closer, intending to eavesdrop if she could. The next few minutes were, mercifully, never very clear to her.

Moving quickly toward her seat, Millie's foot caught in a cable. She went sprawling, landing on her knees and the palms of her hands, skidding on the concrete floor. She saw, in slow motion, the coffee cup describe an arc in the air, turn over and spill its steaming hot contents all over the Prince's lap. The bulk of the scalding brown liquid landed in the vicinity of his crotch.

Someone helped Millie up. People gathered around, brushing her off. Gracie was dabbing at her leg. Millie looked down and saw a jagged rip in the knee of her white jeans, the edges of the tear staining with the blood that flowed from a gash in her leg. Everyone seemed to be talking at once, their voices coming from a great distance.

"Oh Jesus Christ! Who the fuck did that?"

"Honey, what happened?"

"Where's wardrobe? Does he have a double for that suit?"

"Why the fuck not? This is going to cost us!"

"How'd she do that? Is she hurt?"

"She tripped?"

And Morty, yelling in a great roar, "I told you motherfuckers to get some worklights in here!"

She answered no one. Someone repeated over and over: "Get a doctor. We need a doctor." Millie wondered, dazed, if the doctor were for her or for the Prince or for someone else. A momentary gap in the crowd allowed her a peek at the set. It was empty. No one sat at the desk where the Prince of Wales had been a moment ago.

She looked up and saw Gerald. She became aware that he stood facing her, a hand on each shoulder, and was shaking her gently. She thought he had been talking for some time. "I'm going home," she said, cutting off whatever he was saying.

"Are you sure you're all right?" Millie saw the concern in his eyes.

"I'm fine. I'm fine. I've just got to get out of here."

"Are you *sure* you're okay?"

"I'm sure. I just want to get home." She was functioning on automatic pilot, knowing she had to say something to satisfy these worried faces.

"Get a P.A. to put her in a cab," she heard Morty say and blessed him. They were going to leave her alone.

"I'll do it," Gerald said. "Tell everybody to take five."

Millie never remembered getting home. She remembered remonstrating with Gerald as the cab pulled up in front of her building, and, to prove she was okay, she sailed past the doorman with a queenly air, ignoring the torn jeans and the blood seeping brightly against the white fabric.

She reached the haven of her apartment. The sunlight streamed in through the great windows. Millie stripped off her T-shirt and jeans, dropping them on the polished floor, and, dressed just in her underpants, looked down at her leg. The blood was congealing. I should wash this off, she thought, and crawled into bed.

She lay, not sleeping and not waking, curled into a ball. The rest of the day passed in a haze, while she concentrated on keeping her mind a blank, forcing herself into the twilight sleep of misery suppressed.

The answering machine went off at intervals. "Hi, Millie? This is Carol at Local 161. I heard what happened, and I hope you're okay. Let me know if you want to file Workmen's Comp. I sent Barbara Baker in, so don't worry about a thing. Bye."

Several other people called, their words expressing concern, their voices dripping curiosity. The news was certainly brightening up dreary workaday sets all over the city.

At five-thirty the doorbell rang, insistently. She pulled on her dark-green, terry-cloth robe and went to answer it. Manuel, the Puerto Rican handyman stood in the doorway. She looked at him blankly. "You forget, lady? I come to do windows today?"

It took her a moment to remember. Once a month Manuel came after work to clean the enormous double windows that made up one wall of her apartment. He performed the identical service for other tenants, under the aegis of the building office, for which they paid at a rate that would earn them a fifty-minute session with a Park Avenue psychiatrist, while Manuel received the minimum wage. Millie paid him eight bucks, of which the IRS would undoubtedly remain in blissful ignorance, and they were both happy. It was part of the widespread economic underground that secured the city's financial viability. It had its own rules, its own pay scales, and worked like a charm.

Millie quickly explained that she was sick and he should come back another day—any other day. He took his leave, but not without offering to get her something from the Chinese restaurant on the corner. Chicken soup, he advised politely, would undoubtedly clear up whatever ailment she suffered from.

Millie closed the door behind him, cheered a little, marveling at the universal esteem in which the curative powers of chicken soup were held. Her grandmother, raised in a *shtetl* in Russia, and Manuel's, in the *barrios* of San Juan, evidently had a lot in common.

She had just crawled back into bed when the doorbell rang again. Her fleeting kind thoughts about Manuel were rapidly transformed into a muttered "shit" and a strong wish for his early demise. Irritably, she flung open the door, expecting Manuel and his chicken soup.

Gerald pushed past her into the apartment. "I come bearing pizza and grass. Which do you want first? God, you look good," he commented, eyeing her tousled hair, swollen eyes and rumpled robe.

"I don't want anything. Just go away and leave me alone."

"Of course! Heat the pizza and smoke a joint while it warms. A wise choice. I see you have much experience with fine dining. Oh, *Gourmet Magazine* will want to hear about this!" He chortled at his witticism, busily taking the pizza out of the cardboard box and, careful not to tilt the toppings off, shoving it into the oven.

His culinary responsibilities discharged, he settled himself on the couch and lit a joint. "So we have this preproduction meeting on that shampoo shot," he said conversationally, ignoring Millie's sulky face. "And there's our star, Sherry Twigs . . . know who she is? That blonde model with the hair and the teeth? And her husband, Dan Raguzi, who's going to direct this opus. He got busted for coke on his way into Cannes for the film festival, so already, how smart could he be?" Millie smiled, diverted despite herself. He passed her the joint, and she inhaled, feeling the harsh, hot smoke fill her lungs.

"There must have been more coke going into Cannes than there is in all of Colombia," Gerald mused, "and he gets busted! Anyway, he calls her 'Twigsie,' she calls him 'Ragsie,' her assistant is 'Babsie,' and *his* assistant, everybody immediately calls 'Fagsie.'"

Millie laughed out loud, then sobered, remembering her own tribulation. "What happened on the other shoot? How come you're through so early?"

"No problem. We finished that one up after lunch."

"Do you realize that with a little more effort I could have spilled coffee all over the Magna Carta?" she asked bitterly. "Eight hundred years old, and they bring it to America for Millie Myerson to demolish."

"Not to mention the Prince. Why'd you want to keep him from having kids? Huh? He seems like an okay guy," Gerald cheerfully twisted the knife.

Millie shot him a truly dirty look. "What happened to him? How is he?"

"He's okay. He's fine. Grace took care of his pants, and I loaned him my jockey shorts. Just kidding," he added, as he caught Millie's baleful glance. "No, really, nothing happened. We lost half an hour, but we didn't have a full day to do anyhow."

"Did he . . . say anything about me?" she inquired, looking

casually out the window. The pinky-beige stone buildings across the way basked in the late afternoon sun.

"Sure. He asked how you were and did you get home okay and all that polite shit. He's really a nice guy."

"You sound surprised."

"I am. I expected him to be a royal pain in the ass—" Gerald broke off, dissolved in mirth. "God, am I funny. No, I expected him to be a real *kvetch*. Gimme this, bring me that and how"—his voice took on a querulous tone—"can I drink my Perrier without a twist? But he's not. He's a lot nicer than some of the other talent I had to deal with. So, if I were you, I'd just forget the whole thing."

The doorbell rang again. Gerald looked at her inquiringly. "Whoever it is, I don't want any," Millie said crankily. Gerald went to the door and returned with a long silver rectangular box.

"Pour madame," he said. "I hope you appreciate I tipped the delivery boy out of my own little pocket."

Millie wasn't listening. She opened the shiny box to find an armful of tawny, long-stemmed roses, the most perfect she'd ever seen. Peach and apricot tones shaded into honeyed orange at the throats of the extravagant blossoms. "Oh, they're gorgeous," she breathed.

"Not bad," Gerald allowed.

Millie found the attached envelope, textured vellum with an embossed gold crest on the triangular flap, where a return address would normally go. She opened it carefully and took out a matching card, folded in two. The front flap said, in flowing calligraphy, "With the compliments of H.R.H., the Prince of Wales."

Millie opened it and read, "I hope you are feeling better. I'll call this evening to see how you are." And the scrawled signature, simply, "James."

She handed the card to Gerald and busied herself finding a vase, filling it with water.

"I'm impressed," said Gerald. "The guy makes an appointment for a phone call."

"This is such a sweet thing to do." Millie lifted each of the spectacular roses individually and arranged them in the tall crystal vase, the only good one she owned. "I've never seen flowers quite like this. And when you consider that I—"

"Just about scalded his balls off. I think it's *real* polite of him."

"You're nice, you're really nice, you know that?" Millie kissed him happily on the cheek and dropped down on the couch next to him. Together they smoked the rest of the joint and lazily started on the pizza, catching the drippy strings of cheese and licking their fingers. The elegant, expensive flowers lent a touch of the Ritz to her studio apartment on the West Side of Manhattan.

They sat in companionable silence, Millie curled up in her long robe, Gerald's feet stretched out on the coffee table, listening to the sweet sounds of Benny Goodman, with occasional forays into Sinatra and Jobim. Millie dozed, her head on the arm of the couch, her bare feet in Gerald's lap.

The doorbell rang, loud in the quiet room. Millie raised her head. "Oh, fuck! This place is like Grand Central Station. Where the hell is the doorman?"

Gerald stood up, negligently tossing Millie's feet aside. "The young, spacy one is on. You could drive the whole fucking Rose Bowl parade through the lobby, and he wouldn't notice. Answer the doorbell, morning glory, it's your turn. I'm gonna take a piss."

With that he disappeared into the bathroom. Millie headed for the door. "That's elegant," she threw over her shoulder. "*Please* let me know when nature calls. After all, I *am* interested!"

Laughing, she opened the door and turned to see the Prince of Wales. He wore a light-blue, button-down, Ivy-league shirt, open at the throat, and casual, well-cut gray slacks. He looked at her from under a tweed newsboy's cap, the brim shading his eyes.

Millie's stomach dived down to the floor, then swooped up and around before settling somewhere near her throat. She stared at him, immobilized with shock.

He glanced over at the stocky, formally attired man who accompanied him, then looked back at Millie. She stared up at him, dumbly. "Good evening," he said quietly, his face somber.

Millie managed a return through dry lips, then glanced down at her crumpled robe. She ran a hand through her hair.

The Prince echoed her motion, touching his hand to the cap on his head. "My disguise," he grinned at her, sweeping it off.

Millie could think of no response to this. James waited, turning the cap over and over between his hands.

Millie heard Gerald's voice behind her and, following the Prince's gaze, turned just in time to see Gerald cross the living room, blithely zipping up his fly. "I said, 'Who is it?' Is that too difficult a question for you?" She opened the door a little wider and Gerald saw the Prince. His mouth dropped open.

James merely looked uncomfortable. "Nice to see you again, Gerald. I hope I haven't come at an inconvenient time," he said, talking to Millie, but looking steadily at Gerald.

Millie pulled herself together. "No. No, not at all. Please come in." She turned and led the way into the apartment.

The Prince and his companion followed. "Perhaps you didn't get my note," James said, eyeing the flowers, which held pride of place on her coffee table.

"Oh, I did! I got your note. And I thank you so much. It was a lovely thing to do." Millie and James looked at each other, confused. Gerald watched them both, his insouciant tongue stilled for once. "You said you were going to call," Millie pointed out.

"Quite right. And so I have."

Millie looked at him uncomprehending. Her quick brain had turned to jello. She wondered briefly if her phone was out of order.

The Prince's dark-suited companion cleared his throat into the silence. "Excuse me, sir, if I may." He spoke with a marked Scottish brogue. "Judging from what I recall of American slang, from the cinema, you know . . ."

The answer hit Millie and the Prince at the same moment. She saw it dawn on his face, and she burst out laughing, her gaiety released by the ridiculousness of the mistake. She wasn't going nuts after all. James caught her laughter, while the Scotsman grinned from ear to ear, pleased with himself.

"What is it? I don't get the joke," Gerald complained, looking from Millie to the Prince to the stocky stranger.

"It's the language," Millie explained, between giggles. "We don't speak the King's English anymore."

"I should say not," James interjected. "You see, in England, to call means—"

"Here it means to telephone," Millie interrupted.

"There, at home," the Prince continued, "to call means to pop in, you see—"

"Just to drop over," Millie finished. "Haven't you ever read any P.D. James?" It suddenly occurred to her that, unlike the friends that frequented her apartment, these people were going to stand around all night unless she said something. "Why don't we all sit down?"

"I'll be just a moment, if you don't mind, miss," the Scotsman said.

The Prince, too, abruptly recalled his manners. "Miss Myerson, may I introduce Chief Inspector Ian MacCrae. Ian, Millie Myerson. And this is Gerald . . . er . . ." He searched for the last name.

"Rubin," Gerald supplied. "Hi," he said to MacCrae, "Just call me Gerald, never Jerry, and we'll be cool."

MacCrae smiled at Gerald as they shook hands and turned to Millie. "May I?" he inquired. Millie nodded. Whatever it was he wanted, she wasn't going to argue.

MacCrae moved briskly around the room, glanced out the windows, walked through the bedroom area into the adjacent bathroom. She heard him pull the shower curtain aside. Then he stepped out. "Everything seems to be in order, sir. I'll leave you now. Goodnight, miss. Goodnight, Gerald. A pleasure meeting you both." He bowed slightly and walked purposefully to the door, dusting his palms in the gesture of a job well done.

Gerald sprang into action. "I'll go with you." He caught up with MacCrae in three loping strides. "See ya, folks."

A wave of the hand, and he was gone. Millie and the Prince were alone, standing as if rooted to their places. The awkwardness that had been dissipated by their laughter returned. "Please sit down. Can I get you something to drink?"

The Prince looked at the couch, then dropped into the armchair which stood at right angles to it. "Whatever you've got on hand would be fine."

Millie grabbed the pizza paraphernalia off the coffee table and headed for the kitchen, praying that she had some white wine in the fridge. Praise the Lord. There was. She rummaged hurriedly through her utensil drawer, looking for the corkscrew, wondering all the while if she could excuse herself for a few minutes while she shaved her underarms, a chore she had sadly neglected for the past few days.

She dismissed that idea. In her current state of mind, she'd probably cut a vein out of sheer nervousness. Millie returned to the living area carrying a tray with wine, glasses and some hastily assembled cheese, crackers and peanuts.

The Prince stood when she entered the room. "Here, let me have that." He took the tray from her and set it on the coffee table.

He sat down, then deftly inserted the corkscrew into the cork. Millie settled herself on the couch, sitting primly, ankles crossed.

She looked down and saw that her feet were bare. What the hell, she thought.

"This is a lovely flat. You've got it fixed up very comfortably," he said, twisting the corkscrew. He pulled out the cork, deftly, and poured the wine.

Millie watched his hands, strong, long-fingered, able. He wore a businesslike, gold watch on a plain, black-leather strap, but Millie wasn't fooled. Its wafer-thinness spoke eloquently of Cartier. I've always been a sucker for men with nice hands, she thought. "It must seem very small to you," Millie said, looking around with a critical eye.

"Not really. It's a good-size bed-sitter." His smile flashed, briefly, almost shyly. "And the view is just spectacular."

Well, spectacular is a bit much, Millie thought. The tenth floor is really too low for one of those panoramas you see in the movies. "Where do *you* live?" she asked, and then wondered if it was a stupid question.

"Lots of places. But mostly I have a flat, a self-contained flat, in Buckingham Palace." He looked at her intently. She sensed his urgency. There was an intensity about him, a determination to speak the truth, hear the truth and cut through the bullshit. "Is your name actually Millicent? Mildred?" He looked at her over his wineglass.

"No, just Millie. You see my parents were immigrants to this country, and my mother thought that Millie was a glamorous American name. My sisters are Gladys and Edith." James smiled slightly, in acknowledgement of the fact that she saw this as humorous. "I'm the youngest," she added.

"I'm the eldest," he returned gravely.

Millie laughed. "I know." Then, after a moment, "What am I . . . would you . . . I mean, what do I call you?" She kicked herself for stammering.

"I'd like it very much if you would call me James. At least in private. I'm very much afraid that in public it has to be 'sir.' People never know what to call me. I've often thought it would be simpler if they just said 'You, there!' " He grinned at her. The teasing light was back in his eyes.

Millie laughed and relaxed a little. She settled back on the couch, tucking her feet under her. She sneaked a glance at him. He was watching her speculatively. She had the feeling that he missed nothing.

"What does your father do?" he asked.

"He used to . . . he had a small Jewish gift shop. He sold Hebrew books, magazines, all kinds of Jewish-oriented *tchachkes* . . . things," she amended. "Chanukah menorahs, yarmulkes, mezuzahs, silver kiddush cups, bar mitzvah presents . . . odds and ends . . ." She trailed off, wondering how to describe to Prince James the kind of small store that was so prevalent in any good-sized city in the country. James nodded, unfazed by a list of items offered for sale, very few of which could have been in any way identifiable to him. "And then the neighborhood changed, and the younger people moved away, and the older ones didn't have much money, so the store more or less failed. And he retired."

"I don't think I've ever really known someone up close who was Jewish, seriously Jewish, I mean. There's a lot I've missed in some ways." The Prince looked embarrassed for a moment, then resolute. If it was true, he wasn't going to apologize, or take it back.

A wave of emotion swept over Millie, fueled perhaps by grass and wine and excitement. She felt the familiar clutch in her pelvis where sex always started for her. "I have to tell you I think it took a lot of courage to do what you did . . . send the flowers, and then follow it up and come here. To see someone you'd like to . . . be friends with . . . know better, and not . . . let it go, fade away, but have the guts to do something about it . . ."

Millie flushed, realizing that, as always, in the grip of strong emotion or nervousness, she was babbling. "I don't want to make too much of this," she said, cursing her mouth, which often ran on of its own accord, taking her into uncharted waters. She stole a glance at the Prince and thought that, somehow, he was relieved. Then she realized how much of an admission she'd made. And knew it wasn't lost on him.

A smile lurked in his eyes. He got up and paced around the small living area, directing his words more at the light-studded vista out the window than at her. "I don't want you to make too little of it, either."

A rush of excitement coursed through Millie's veins. He turned to face her, leaning back against the window. "You see, I'm well aware that often, when I go places, it's the nicest people that I don't get to meet. They sort of . . . hang back. They don't want to appear to be sucking up. The ones who do push themselves forward are often . . . exactly the sort I don't want to know."

"Like Denise."

"Exactly like Denise," he laughed. "Wherever I go, there are lots of Denises, but very few people like you . . ." He looked at her for a moment, then added, "And Gerald and the others. I sometimes wonder," he reflected idly, "what they think. The Denises, I mean. I half-expect them to turn up wearing a T-shirt that says 'I fucked the Prince of Wales.' Sorry," he apologized quickly.

"Look. Let's make a deal right now. You don't apologize for using words that not only have I heard before, but have been known to use on occasion myself—"

"And you stop thinking of me as a creature from outer space," he challenged. "Deal?"

"I don't think of you as a creature from outer space. It's just that we're so very different." They stared at each other. They were crossing a bridge, and they both knew it.

After a moment, the Prince glanced away. "And I'm trying very hard," he said to no one in particular. He crossed over to the couch, sat down next to her and, after a brief moment, moved back to the chair in which he had sat previously. "Tell me about your job," he said abruptly.

"Well, I don't really have a job. I freelance, go from job to job as they come up. It's called 'continuity' in England. What I do, I mean."

"I know. Is it hard? The instability? Not knowing where you're going from day to day."

"You get used to it. After a while you build up a reputation, and you sort of know you'll get enough work. There *are* jobs that last for several months—feature films. And it's interesting. You get to meet all kinds of people . . ." She grinned at him impishly. "I can't think of any way I'd rather earn my living. Tell me about you."

"Well, I'm sort of a civil servant, you might say. I have an office in Buckingham Palace, where we administer the Prince of Wales Trust, among other things. We use the funds to encourage worthwhile efforts on the part of youth, artists, scientists, all sorts of deserving people. I sit on committees—I'm patron of the Royal Anthropological Institute—you should see the work they do, it's fascinating. I won't sit on committees or boards or such if they just mean to use my name. If I can't get involved and stick my tuppence in, they can't use my name. "And I help administer the Duchy of Cornwall, which I . . . which belongs to . . ." he faltered. "I'm the Duke of Cornwall," he explained diffidently. "And I'm colonel in chief of several regiments. *And* I visit schools, plants, hospitals, wherever a bit of encouragement and a bit of show might do some good. I declare things open. I declare things closed. People hand me things, symbolizing the Spirit of Man, or Eternal Hope, or Perpetual Motion, for all I know." He grinned at her. "And I accept them, with thanks. I'm grease in the wheels. I keep things moving, as best I can. It's sort of social work, really, on a different scale. We call it the 'Family Firm.' My father calls Buckingham Palace a 'tied house.'"

Millie looked at him blankly.

"He means it comes with the job," the Prince explained. "Lose the job, lose the house."

"Oh, I see," she laughed.

"There's one big difference. I know where I'm going to be every single day for the next six months. And the six months after that are penciled in." He looked at her steadily, his gaze attentive.

"Do you ever feel trapped?" she wondered.

"Not trapped, exactly. It's more . . . dedicated. I mean, this is what I want to do, what I've trained to do. And I want frightfully much to do it well."

He crossed over and sat down next to her. "But I don't have much time." He leaned over and kissed her, his mouth soft, searching. "Which is not to say that you don't deserve all the time in the world, my dear Millie," he said softly. He jumped up and resumed his pacing. "Which is also not to say that my problems are your problems. I don't want them to be."

Millie watched him in silence, sipping her wine. She sensed his intensity and didn't trust it. He turned to her abruptly.

"Are you related to Bess Myerson? I met her last evening—no, two evenings ago. Interesting woman."

"No. I don't think I'm related to any Myersons. You see that wasn't my father's name at all. When he came to this country from Lithuania, either he changed it or it got changed for him."

James looked at her inquiringly. "You see, often when immigrants arrived at Ellis Island, if they said something unpronounceable when the customs man asked them their names—if the customs guy heard something he couldn't say, he changed it to something he *could* say. On the spot. I don't know what my father's name was—he won't talk about it—but I know it got to be Myerson at Ellis Island."

"Did your father come to America because of the war? Hitler?"

"No. He came way before that. 1930. He was fifteen. I don't know why he came. I don't know how he managed it. I've asked him, but he won't say. He's the only one of his family who left Europe—and the only one who's still around."

"You don't talk to each other?"

"No, we don't. He's sort of . . . not there. Someone once said about him that he's not really living in America at all. His body is here, but his soul is in the great yeshivas of Eastern Europe—that don't exist anymore."

Millie's voice took on a bitter note. "Once, when I was a kid, I went shopping with my mother for school clothes, and I came home all excited, and I ran to my father and yelled, 'Daddy! Daddy, look! I have a new dress.' And he looked at me and, with genuine confusion on his face, said, 'But you already *have* a dress.' It's not that he begrudged us. When it was explained to him, that in America little girls have more than one dress, he accepted it without complaint. Just one more example of the craziness of the New World."

Millie stopped short, appalled at herself. "You *can't* want to hear this!" Why on earth was she filling the Prince of Wales's head with this? You sure have a knack for appearing glamorous and sophisticated, she assured herself. *Meiselach* from your childhood, he doesn't need.

"I want very much to hear it." He shifted his hips lower on the seat and lounged, relaxed, his long legs stretched out in front of him. "And your mother?"

"My mother! Now that's a word that sets me off." It was Millie's turn to jump up and pace the small living room, her turn to stare out the window. "My mother is a pisser. There's some excuse for my father. When he was a kid, he was the youngest of God knows how many children, nine or ten or something, and he was sent away at an early age to yeshiva—sort of a Talmudic boarding school."

The Prince nodded his understanding. "Go on."

"Very possibly because his parents couldn't afford to keep him. I don't know exactly how I know this. He never told me. Anyway, these little boys, seven, eight, nine years old, slept on the benches in the *beis midrash*—the study hall—and they ate, by rotation, at different homes in the *shtetl*. The people were literally dirt poor, and it sounds to me like they ate mostly potatoes. There's an old joke: When a Jew eats a chicken, one of them is sick."

Millie looked at James, to gauge his response to the bitter witticism. His eyes were steadfast, undaunted, with a suggestion of sadness. "Go on," he said quietly.

"Anyway, if the woman he was assigned to that night or that week or whatever, if she was . . . loving, then he got a smile with his dinner. And if not, not."

"And your mother?"

"Most mothers," Millie began slowly, "want their children to have more than they did. My mother wants us to have less. No, not less, exactly the same. And not a droplet more. My mother keeps a close eye on the world, to make sure that nobody has something she doesn't. And, since she didn't have much, the rest of us are in a lot of trouble. She has yet to admit that anything I've done is any good . . . the scholarships, the cum laude degree, nothing. She refuses to this day to believe that I freelance. Every time I finish a movie, she asks 'So why did they fire you?' And I go, 'Ma! They didn't fire me! Everybody, actors, cameramen, makeup, wardrobe, props, sound men, *everybody!* is out of a job.' And she says, 'So what did you do wrong that they fired you? You can tell me.'"

James laughed, as he was meant to. That's me, Millie the wit, she thought. Some folks turn lead into gold, I turn pain into a good story.

"It doesn't sound very . . . encouraging," James said. "What I don't understand is, how did you turn out to be so . . . sweet, and funny, and brave." The ache under the humor had not escaped him.

"Brains," said Millie, and grinned at him. "I went away to college at sixteen. Scholarship. I took a look around me, and I said I'm getting out of here. I don't want to live like you folks. I made myself up. What you see I did all by myself." She swept her arm in a majestic, slightly tipsy gesture, indicating herself, the apartment, and somewhat inaccurately, the view.

"And now you don't need anybody else?" the Prince inquired, in the tone of someone who seeks enlightenment on an unarguably small, but vital point.

Millie returned his gaze. "When I was a kid," she answered, somewhat elliptically, "I thought, that if only I could hang on until I grew up, then I'd live in a Hollywood movie. Smoky nightclubs, romance, tiny satin hats with swooping feathers, beaded evening gowns, one true love—all with appropriate sound track, you understand. But I'm not a kid anymore. Now I'm all grown up, and I know you have to be very careful or—"

"Or you get hurt," he put in gently.

She raised her chin and looked at him, defiant, challenging. "Or you get hurt. I'm not in the market for anymore hurt. Thank you very much, I pass."

James ignored the challenge in her eyes and her out-thrust chin, and watched her steadily. Slowly, her defiance melted. "I have a pretty good life now," she said quietly. "No Prince Charming is going to come riding up with his little white horse and screw it up." She had spoken without thinking, and when she heard her own words, she started to laugh.

James smiled. "My name is *James*. And I'm afraid I'm fresh out of white horses. I do have a lovely bay mare, if that's any help," he supplied diffidently. "Her name is Whiskey, because that's exactly the color she is. I always thought Charming was a bloody stupid name. Never could understand why his parents named him that."

He reached across and took her hand and held it. His hand felt warm and dry and sheltering. She looked down at her small hand with its polished fingernails nestled in his tanned, long-fingered one, and decided to leave it there. For the moment.

"I really admire you, you know," James said. Millie searched to either side and lifted the pillows of the couch, searching for the object of his admiration. He smiled in response to her clowning, then continued, undeterred. "I've tested myself in many ways. I've flown every kind of plane there is, sub- and supersonic. I've dived sixty feet below the polar ice cap in the Arctic. I've parachuted out of planes. I've stood watch on the bridge in a Force Ten gale." His blue glance, fixed with intensity, remained on Millie. "But the one thing I don't know, that I'll never know . . . is could I have done what you did. Start from nothing, less than nothing, actually, and do it all by myself, with no help at all. I've never lacked—for money, or guidance, or encouragement. I've never *really* been on my own."

"But isn't that true of anybody who's born to wealthy parents? You're not alone in that, surely."

"No. No, it isn't quite the same. If it was just that I'd been born wealthy, I would have been off to South America or somewhere long ago, to see if I could make my fortune, like Puss 'n' Boots . . ." His somber face belied his smile. "I can't disappear from view for half an hour, let alone half a year. The thing that bothers me most is not knowing how successful I would have been had I been able to try."

He looked around the apartment, at the ingenious use of space, the airy chintz, the tender pools of lamplight. "It must be lovely to know that every single thing in this room is here because you chose it. And you earned the money to pay for it. That's true, isn't it?"

"Well, yes, it is, but only because no one ever offered to pick up the tab," she grinned at him mischievously. "I'm not proud. I'll take help from wherever I can get it. But, so far, the kind with no strings attached has been in short supply. So, if I want something, I have to get it for myself. But I have no objection to being spoiled. As a matter of fact, it's one of the unattained goals of my life," she joked.

James smiled back at her. "That's why professionalism has always meant so much to me. Whatever I've done, I've made damn sure that I've met the standards of the other chaps—or bettered them. I've always been aware that some of the men I've come up against, whether at school, or at Cambridge, or in the services, were either on scholarship or supporting themselves, or in some cases, even sending money home to their families. If I bested them, it had bloody-well better be because I *was* better."

He slapped one clenched fist into the palm of the other, then looked down at his hands, as if he had just become aware of their presence at the ends of his arms. He looked over at Millie, then reached out and took her hand again.

"But you can't go through life feeling that you've got to *prove* something all the time."

"I don't anymore. But I damn sure used to. Now I've more or less finished . . . testing myself. I'm reasonably sure I'm a pretty good bloke. I've learned to ease up on myself a bit. I used to be the sort of person who, if I heard that *some* body, *some* where, was crawling into or out of a submarine, I had to do the same—just to see if I had the nerve. Now I've gotten to the point where I say, let's leave something for the younger ones, all right?" He fell silent.

"I've been very lucky," he said, after a pause. Millie looked at him, silently inviting him to continue. "It could so easily have gone the other way. You see, I was the first person, ever, in my position, who . . ." He didn't like the start he had made and fell silent for a moment, thinking. Millie waited, her hand in his.

"The Queen . . . my mother," he corrected, realizing that the formality ran counter to what he was trying to do. "My mother, when she was a child, she wasn't the heir to the throne, most of the time. The early time, that is. So there was no problem." His ordinarily crisp speech and organized sentences faltered as he tried to articulate thoughts he had perhaps never shared with anyone.

"The closest analogy to my position is . . . was . . . the Duke of Windsor. And he had a horrible childhood. His father . . ." Millie reviewed in her mind the procession of recent kings, searching for the right one. "His father once said, 'I was afraid of my father, and my sons will damn well be afraid of me!'" Millie had a mental image of a picture she had seen somewhere, perhaps in a schoolbook, of a stern, bearded, humorless man and his wife, the Queen, of the ramrod back and the steely attitude. It was funny to think that the ancestors of the young man sitting next to her had been in her schoolbooks.

"So, he and the other children, effectively grew up without a home life at all. He *was* terrified of his father. Do you know, he had to bow to his parents every time he saw them—even if they were alone?" James looked at Millie to see how she was taking this very singular revelation. He was not a man used to baring his introspection to strangers. His openness was fragile, conditional. He allowed her to see his vulnerability through an act of will, a disciplined effort that would enable him to achieve his purpose. His confidence was a display of trust, of courage, with the unspoken wish that she would be able to follow on the path he led.

Millie watched him, afraid that anything she said would recall him to a sense of the proprieties and break the gossamer thread of communication between them.

"So, there you had a Prince of Wales who was reared with only one thought, to be molded, shaped, forced into the proper figure of a king. No matter at what cost."

Millie thought of that golden prince and his unhappy end. A life of exile, endless years of boredom and neglect, barred from any commerce with the society that had nurtured him. Perhaps that was why, having found someone to love, and who loved him, he clung with steel talons, prepared to pay any price, even the loss of the only job in the world he could possibly hold. She thought that the hapless Duke had, in a way, done James a great favor. He had shown, clearly, the one, single road James could never walk.

"I've been much luckier," James continued. "My parents made a conscious decision with us, my sisters and me. They felt we'd learn the *job* by osmosis, as it were, from watching them. Just like other kids learn about what their parents do. Their goal was to raise functioning, secure, happy people first, and then the position would take care of itself. I'm very grateful to them.

"I know that people are always interested to know what goes on inside the royal family . . . but, really, we're a family like any other," he said earnestly. "We laugh a lot, we do our work, we row occasionally. The kids go to school. We have our happy times. And our tragedies."

Millie thought of the recent, untimely death of the dashing young Marquess, of an age with the Prince, in a fiery plane crash. "He was your . . . cousin?" she asked gently, not sure what the exact relationship was to him.

"My second cousin, actually. But we grew up together. Went to the same public school. I don't have a brother, you know, just lots and lots of sisters . . ." His face lit with a teasing smile for an instant, then sobered. "But that's what Douglas was, really." His face brightened. "You would have liked him. He was smart and gay and great fun, and he would have adored you. Probably would have tried to cut me out, too! He liked cheeky, bright, pretty girls with saucy tongues."

"Thank you, sir," Millie acknowledged the compliment. That's the first time the "sir" has come naturally, she thought.

"Don't give it a thought, duckie," he said, with an uncannily accurate Cockney accent.

Millie laughed. "But were you lonely, always being different?" she asked.

"There's that word again," the Prince remarked. "Well, the different part doesn't come at you all at once, you know. I mean, you don't sit up in your pram one day and say 'Hurrah, I'm the Prince of Wales!' Which I wasn't yet, strictly speaking. I've cast my mind back trying to pinpoint the one moment when I *knew*. And I can't find it. I don't think there is one. The idea that your life is destined for just one purpose, that the role you will play and the duties and responsibilities that go with it are fixed . . . are waiting for you . . . inevitably, well, that just dawns on you, slowly, in the most ghastly, inexorable way . . ." He trailed off, smiling a small disparaging smile, apprehensive lest he had revealed too much.

Millie smiled back at him, reassuring, accepting. He really has an . . . endearing smile, she thought.

"Anyway," he continued in a brisker tone, "I didn't think I *was* different. I thought everybody was like me. I guess all children do. I thought all five-year-olds had these marvelous soldiers outside their homes who saluted them.

"When I was a kid . . . when I was a kid I was taken to someone's home. I don't remember who, or why I was there, but I looked around, and I could see, bright child that I was, that there was only one bedroom. And I asked . . ." He paused, and Millie could see that, whatever the childish faux pas had been, it was still painful to him. "'Where does the Nanny sleep?' I could see by all the faces that I had made a mistake. And I didn't know what I had done."

Millie ached for the small James, bewildered by the grownups' disapproval, not knowing what his offense was. But she would not demean his painful honesty with easy sympathy. He had accepted her childish reminiscences with a competent calm, not belittling them, and not overpowered by them, either.

"I never forgot that," he continued. "I look at other people and compare, and think myself into their worlds. I've gotten pretty good at it. I'm very aware of a lot of things that I wouldn't have any idea about otherwise," he boasted happily. "Because it's important. Most of the world lives one way, and I live another. And I have to reach out to *them*, not the other way around. It's up to me, not up to them. Do you follow?" Millie nodded.

"I know you do," James said softly. "It takes imagination, and empathy and pretty brown eyes, and a whole lot of other good things," he teased. "But it strikes me," he continued, sobering, "that you were a lot lonelier than I was. True?"

"True."

"You see," James continued, "I fit into my world, admittedly in sort of a unique way, whereas you—"

"I didn't fit into the world at all."

"Not in the world you were in then. You do now."

"But the sense of not fitting never leaves you."

"Like the sense of being different. But you see, I *did* have my family. To this day I'm very close to my parents, and my grand-mother. And the Queen is a very big help. She knows, you see. She *knows.*"

Anything Millie could say would be superfluous. The only person on the face of the earth who truly understood what lay ahead for Prince James was his mother, the Queen.

Millie got up and stood in front of him. He took both her hands in his. "Let's go for a walk," she said impulsively.

"A walk! My dear, I can't. You don't understand! I wouldn't have been able to come here at all if I hadn't had the foresight to divert the press. I canceled all my engagements and told them the shooting would run all evening."

"Of course you can. This is New York City. Put your cap on, and nobody will notice."

James stood up. He took her face between his hands and looked down at her gravely. He put his mouth over hers and kissed her gently. "If you want to, my love, I will try."

Millie looked up at him. She leaned up and kissed him, lightly. "I'll be just a moment."

She climbed quickly into jeans and a shirt and looked at her glowing face in the bathroom mirror. She beamed at her reflection, elated, and blew herself a kiss. He said "my love," she thought. He doesn't toss things like that around lightly.

How do you know that? her reflection answered. Just a cotton pickin' minute here. How do you know that? For all you know he's got a girl in every port. Or whatever the equivalent is for princes. And the English call everybody "luv."

She glanced at the sobered face in the mirror and quickly did a lick and a promise makeup job, hitting just the essentials—blusher, a dash of grey eyeshadow and mascara. She flipped off the light and closed the bathroom door, ready to rejoin her prince. She pushed down the little voice in her head that repeated "my love." They don't call everybody "my love."

The young night-doorman was skulking, as usual, behind the drape at the far corner of the heavy glass wall that made up the entrance to the building. Millie and the Prince crossed the lobby hand in hand and separated only to go through the revolving door.

A nondescript, dark-blue Buick with two men in the front seat waited at the curb. When the Prince followed Millie out of the revolving door, Ian MacCrae leapt out of the passenger side of the car.

"Sir, you should have called for me."

"Don't worry about it. Nothing was going to happen to me in the lift," James smiled at him. "We're going for a stroll."

"Sir, do you think it's wise?"

"Tonight, Ian, I don't think!" James answered suddenly curt.

Millie and the Prince crossed over to Central Park West, walking hand in hand, silently. The street was alive with presence, tree-shadowed, luminous. A cool wind, blowing off the river, played in the branches of the newly leafed trees overhead, murmurous. The lights of the city glowed in the distance.

Ian MacCrae followed, ten paces behind, just out of earshot. The blue Buick crawled along, a car-length behind.

Millie was very conscious of the athletic body keeping pace with hers. Her hand in his felt . . . right. Just a guy and a girl out for a walk, she thought. They passed couples like themselves, arms folded about each other's waists. No one paid them any attention, and, in any case, James's face was shadowed by the newsboy's cap he wore. Anonymity hung over them like a sheltering cloak.

Millie looked down the hushed street. At intervals the street lamps shed pools of glowing light. The darkness between was intensified, mysterious. Across the street, outside the park, a solitary man whistled "Blue Moon," the tune syncopating with the echo of his footsteps.

When Millie had first come to live in Manhattan, she had carried on an ecstatic love affair with the city. She had walked its streets, vibrated to its mood, listened to its silent music. After eight years, the glamor had faded, the sheen dulled.

Tonight, she saw it through a stranger's eyes, and her soul reverberated once again to the city's siren song. She looked at James and saw that he was listening. "How did you know I'd be home?" she asked suddenly.

"It never occurred to me for a moment that you wouldn't."

Millie stopped short, dismayed. He looked at her and took a deep breath. His eyes mirrored his discomfort, his determination to be honest, and his fear of damaging his cause. "How can I say this without sounding insufferably arrogant? It's not . . . taking you for granted. I forgot. I forgot that you were American, and I forgot that you weren't an old friend. You see, I've been rather spoiled. At home, when I do have some time free to see my friends, and I let them know, well, they always accommodate me."

I'll *bet* they do! Millie thought. I can just picture someone telling the Prince of Wales, "No, you can't come over tonight. I have to wash my hair."

"Please don't be angry. In a way it's rather a compliment . . . I felt so close to you, watching you at the studio, that I forgot that the rules were different." His voice was level, but his eyes pleaded. Millie softened a little toward him, and, quick as ever, he sensed it. "Shall we go into the park?" James asked, dismissing the small disagreement from their world.

"Are you crazy? Instant death. No one goes into Central Park at night."

"Pity. In London, everyone walks in the parks at all hours. So I understand." Except me, hung in the air, unspoken.

They were at Columbus Circle and stood for a moment, looking up at the semicircle of skyscrapers that ringed it, their lighted rooms beacons against the night sky, promising excitement, tension and glamor.

Millie and James turned up Broadway. It was a different world. Where Central Park West had been all quiet dreams and chamber music, Broadway was seamy, raw, life set to a jazz theme. Unidentifiable litter blew about the street. The gutters ran with a scummy, viscous liquid. And on this, one of the first really warm spring nights, the street was crowded with people: blacks, Spanish, West Indian, elderly Jews, the fashionably dressed mingling with drunks. Dope deals were consummated outside newspaper kiosks, chic restaurants, pizza parlors. At Seventy-second Street a man stationed himself outside the bank and unpacked an accordion. He tailored his selections to the passersby, switching from "Bei Mir Bist du Schöen" to "That's Amore" to "Sweet Georgia Brown," with impish ease, his music a running commentary on the scene.

In front of the movie theater a black man on bended knee crooned "Mammy" into a giant-size popcorn container he wielded like a microphone. The pedestrians divided into two streams, flowing around him without breaking stride.

Millie watched James eagerly absorbing the vibrant parade, clearly enjoying himself. Two young Puerto Rican boys, about ten years old, separated out from the crowd coming toward them. As they brushed past Millie, the nearest one feinted a grab at her. He snapped his fingers shut in a pinch that just missed closing on her breast. He whispered something in Spanish, which she didn't understand, but his meaning was abundantly clear.

Millie whirled around. The two boys had run a few feet away, then turned waiting to see what would happen. "Why don't you just go fuck yourselves!" she yelled. The Prince looked down at her, startled, and quickly followed her glance. The younger of the boys danced on the balls of his feet in a boxer's motion, his clenched fists feinting and jabbing in the air. He grinned mockingly at James.

"What happened? What's wrong," James asked, bewildered.

Ian MacCrae, moved rapidly toward them, eyeing the boys warily, not sure what, if anything, had happened.

"Oh, nothing," Millie said, suddenly embarrassed. "The little creep just . . . he tried to . . . touch me."

"The bastard!" James exploded. "I'll bash his bloody head in!" He pivoted on his feet, starting after the kids.

Millie grabbed his arm. "Don't! Don't worry about it. It's the warm weather. It brings them out." She looked at his grim face. She could feel the muscles of his arm, tensed, under her hand. "Please? Don't be upset. It happens twice every five minutes. It's nothing to get into a fight about."

"The little bastards! And they're just kids!"

"There are no kids in New York. Just small muggers. C'mon." She coaxed him away from the two boys, who loitered, hoping for a fight.

"Trouble, sir?" MacCrae asked.

"No trouble," Millie answered.

MacCrae looked at James questioningly. The Prince hesitated, then he nodded. "It's all right," he confirmed.

They quickened their steps while MacCrae, watchful, dropped back out of earshot. "This is a first for you, isn't it," Millie said. She looked up at his grim face and knew that he was dwelling on the incident, weighing his handling of it, wondering if perhaps others of her escorts would have avenged the liberty taken with their lady. Poor baby, she thought. He really doesn't know that some things you just have to swallow and forget.

Millie put her hand between his tense shoulder blades and rubbed, gently. "Let's go to Zabar's," she said, looking for a way to distract him.

"What's Zabar's?"

"You'll see."

"All right. But I want to tell you—I have to tell you one thing." He stopped walking, as if to underscore the importance of what he was about to say. "I don't want to appear a worrywart or anything, but there are some things that *you* don't understand. If anything happens in this Zabar's of yours, if I *am* recognized, just get in the car and the driver will take you home. Don't worry about me, just get in the car," he repeated.

"I can take care of myself," Millie said, insulted. "I can get myself home."

"I don't doubt that." He looked at her, amused. "You don't understand quite what kind of circus travels in my wake. If we're seen together, if they catch on to . . . Well, you're just not used to it. You'll have reporters camped on your doorstep. They'll go through your life with a magnifying glass, and before you know it you'll be reading interviews with your greengrocer and dissertations on the kind of toothpaste you prefer. And that's the best you can hope for," he said with grim humor. "Take my word for it. I've had more than one . . . friendship mucked up by the press."

He turned to her. "I don't mean to have it happen to this one. For once in your life, Millie, just do as you're told."

"I still think you're exaggerating. This is New York City for chrissakes. Robert Redford runs around here, and nobody gives a damn. Woody Allen lives across the park, and Dustin Hoffman lives around the corner. Nobody cares." She waved her arms expansively. "And *everybody* shops at Zabar's. I bet Jackie Onassis gets her bagels and lox there."

"What are bagels and lox?"

"Oh, my God! Oh, my God!" Millie whirled around in mock astonishment. "Are you in for a treat!" She laughed up at him. "What a privilege! To feed someone their first bagel and lox!"

"Well, that narrows the field. At least I know you eat it . . . er, them . . . whatever," he laughed.

As always, Zabar's was crowded. The long room, lined on either side with specialty areas, sold delicacies from around the world: smoked fish, sturgeon, scotch salmon, lox, all kinds of salads, sausages of every conceivable ilk, cheeses, both domestic and imported, giant hams, game, both smoked and roasted, and more. The center aisle contained tables piled high with breads, condiments, mustards, marmalades, jellies and pastries: Turkish, Russian, and plebeian Danish.

Cooking utensils hung from the ceiling, pots, pans, steamers, dicers, ricers, strainers, intermixed with sausages tied with white string and hams hanging in netted bags. Coffees from South America, Europe and the United States reigned in their own particular fiefdom, where they were ground to order, and the aromatic scent hung heavy in the air.

Affluent New Yorkers milled about, adding to the confusion. They waited patiently in informal lines at each of the stalls, only occasionally breaking out into disputes over whose turn it really was. The countermen, none of whom had been there for less than a decade, cut even, transparent slices of smoked salmon, laying them onto pieces of heavily waxed paper with almost Japanese precision, measured and ground coffee, sliced bread, dished out potato, carrot, eggplant, Greek and mushroom salads, and offered slivers of "taste" to those customers who took their fancy.

Millie and James stood on one line, inhaling the pungent aromas, while she picked up a dozen bagels. She moved unerringly to the refrigerator section where she got a container of cream cheese. "I know Zabar's by heart," she boasted, laughing up at James. They joined the semicircle of people gathered at the long counter, while she waited for her turn to buy lox.

"Hi, dolly," the counterman smiled at her. "What can I give you tonight?"

"A quarter pound of lox, please. Nova Scotia."

Suddenly, Millie heard a woman's high pitched voice scream: "That's him. I know it! I saw him on TV!"

A jostling, heaving, protoplasmic mass separated Millie from the Prince. She looked over at him, startled, and saw him quickly sweep the cap off his head. She smiled, realizing that, having been "made," as it were, he didn't want to waste the disguise for another time.

"Can I have your autograph?"

"Hey, Jimmy! Look over here!"

"How's your mother?"

"Can I kiss you?"

"He's not the king. He's the son of the king."

"Leave him alone, Angela, you can't go around kissing strange princes!"

James handled the crowd brilliantly. He smiled at each of the shoving questioners and responded to as many queries as he could safely answer. He seemed not to hear those that were a trifle awkward. "I'm sorry, I don't give autographs; I'm enjoying my stay here very much. New York is a wonderful city. Well, of course, I like London, too. One's home is always dear to one, isn't it?" So much for Millie's blasé New Yorkers. They were mobbing him.

Millie watched, wondering. Underneath all the good-humored banter, she saw what she now recognized as his public face. Despite the smile creasing his face and the gregarious twinkle in his eyes, despite his jaunty, hands-in-his-pockets stance, Millie realized that he had looked more open, less guarded, at her house, when his face had been serious, almost grave.

She turned to the counterman. "I'll just take my lox, please."

"What's the matter, lady, a prince come into *your* store every day of the week?" He handed her the white paper package with the price scrawled in black crayon, and she walked to the cash register to pay.

For the first time in her life she didn't have to wait in line at the cashier. Three of the four registers were unmanned, the clerks having joined the crowd around the Prince. At the fourth, a bored, husky young man with a wiry moustache and a respectable beer belly encased in a white T-shirt thumbed through the sports section of the *Daily News*. He took her money without a word, handing her the change and a receipt, looking as if nothing at all unusual were happening, or, if perhaps there *was* something going on, it had nothing to do with him.

Millie watched Ian MacCrae and the driver expertly peel the prince out of the crowd. They dissected the mob away, unobtrusively, in a practiced manner. Millie realized that, while the Prince was still laughing and bantering with the crowd, he was almost entirely disengaged and walked swiftly out of the store.

She climbed into the back seat of the anonymous blue Buick

double-parked in the street. After a moment, Ian MacCrae walked out of the store, moving rapidly. Behind him came the Prince, the driver at his back. James joined her in the back seat, while MacCrae got in front next to the driver, and the car took off. They made a quick right on Seventy-ninth, leaving behind the knot of people gathering outside Zabar's, then an immediate left and headed down West End.

MacCrae turned around to face the back seat. "That wasn't very clever, sir, now was it?" he asked sternly.

James looked at him, deadpan, his eyes dancing. "Zabar's is always like that," he said, in the tone of one imparting privileged information to a novice. Millie giggled.

"It was my fault," she said. "I didn't realize—"

"You're not *supposed* to realize, miss," MacCrae interrupted, admonishing. "His Royal Highness is supposed to know better." He turned his back on them and faced forward.

Millie and the Prince grinned at each other with the conspiratorial glee of children who have been caught being naughty and unexpectedly let go with a warning. James put his arm around her and hugged her, hard. She snuggled happily into the curve of his arm.

The Buick turned into the driveway of her building. The driver stayed with the car, while MacCrae accompanied them across the empty lobby to the elevator. He pressed the button and stood back to allow Millie and the Prince to enter the elevator. James barred the way for him with an arm across the open door. "That will do, MacCrae. We can make it upstairs all right." His tone brooked no argument.

James pressed ten, and, reluctantly, MacCrae stepped back, with a bow, to allow them to go up alone. "Is he going to wait there all night?" Millie asked, then blushed. God *damn!*

"If need be," James answered evenly. "That's his job."

The elevator doors opened, and Millie marched out, her cheeks flaming. They walked down the corridor to the door of her apartment.

"Here, let me help you with that," said the Prince, taking the keys out of her strangely nerveless hand.

In the bright, surgical light of her tiny "work-in" kitchen, Millie sliced bagels, spread cream cheese and topped it with thin, coral slices of lox.

"Why, it's smoked salmon. Why didn't you say so?" James

leaned over from his lounging position against the fridge to swipe a sliver from under Millie's knife. She grinned up at him and lightly slapped his hand away. He's a *mensch*, she thought. He seems just as at home in a kitchen as he would at some stately ceremonial.

She recalled seeing him on television some years ago, robed and solemn, at his investiture as Prince of Wales. His hands clasped between those of the Queen, his mother, he had sworn eternal fealty to his liege and sovereign. "Do you know how to cook?" she asked suddenly.

"Of course, I can cook. I'm a very good cook." He sounded a little insulted. "I do a marvelous quiche, not to mention a perfectly delectable kedgeree. And my toad-in-a-hole is first rate." He winked at her, the mischief alive in his face, knowing the tables had turned. Millie had no idea if toad-in-a-hole was a dish or a joke.

"What's kedgeree," she asked, playing it safe.

"It's lovely. You make it with rice and saffron and codfish. I do it up very well. I'll make it for you sometime," he offered. Millie smiled at him, uneasy. Promises tripped smoothly off his tongue.

They sat on the couch, side by side, munching bagels and drinking coffee. James slipped off his highly polished cordovan loafers and stretched his long legs out on the coffee table. He looked content, at home. Millie was, unaccountably, pleased. The extravagant roses he had sent her leaned elegantly in the crystal vase, and the measured, perfect notes of Andrés Segovia playing Bach partitas paraded about the room.

"I've been very happy here with you tonight," James said, staring fixedly at the flowers on the coffee table. "I knew I would be."

"When did it come over you? Before I spilled coffee on you or after?"

He leaned back on the couch and looked at her somberly, ignoring her misplaced attempt at levity. "Are you having an affair with Gerald?"

So that had rankled. "No. No, I'm not. Gerald is a friend. A very *good* friend. I'm not having an affair with anyone." Not even you, echoed in the room.

James heard it and chose not to listen. He leaned toward her, drawing her to him, and kissed her. Now his kiss was insistent, probing and challenging. Millie felt herself respond, resistance melting in the heat of sensation that coursed through her body.

He leaned down and closed his mouth over her breast through the thin fabric of her blouse. Electricity flashed through her. She sucked in her breath with a quick intake. He raised his head and grinned at her, mischievously, aware. She looked down at her blouse and saw the circle of dark wetness his mouth had left, and her nipple, outlined, thrusting against the tissue silk. She arched her back, pressing her breast against his mouth.

He pulled her blouse out of her jeans and ran his hands up her back to her shoulders, then down her arms to her wrists. He took each of her palms and planted a kiss, first in one, then the other, and then drew her against him, into his embrace.

The moment his fingers found her striving wetness she drew back, alarms of distrust sounding in her brain. She stood up, tucking her shirt back into her jeans. James leaned back against the couch, his arms at his sides, watching her intently.

She turned to face him, her sandaled feet planted firmly, her stance belligerent. "It's all too easy for you. I've seen how it goes. Yes, sir. Quite right, sir. Immediately, sir." Surprise flashed across his face, and something else, that could have been hurt, flared in his eyes, so briefly that she wasn't sure it had been there at all. Then it was gone, and he was composed. "I'm not part of the amenities," she continued, driven. "I wasn't 'laid on' as you so aptly say in your country, as a souvenir of your American tour."

"What's underneath this, Millie? What's this really all about?"

"There *is* no underneath. It's very simple, all on the surface, just as you like things to be." She had no reason to say that, but Millie was past being fair. She felt out of control, angry, and didn't know why. "And I don't take well to being one of a multitude," she added for good measure.

Amusement gleamed in his eyes. "Well, I don't know about that," he said judiciously. "I'm not celibate, certainly, but I don't think . . . a multitude is quite accurate." He stood and crossed over to her, clasping his fingers behind her waist, arms encircling her. He kissed the top of her head, then leaned his cheek against her dark, fragrant hair. "Millie, Millie, how can I make you understand?"

He hugged her close, his body warm against hers. She leaned her cheek against his chest and felt the steady pulse of his heartbeat. His erection pressed against her stomach, and she wondered, miserably, why she was behaving like an ass.

He took her chin in his hand and tilted her face, so she was forced to look at him. "You shan't do anything you don't want to do." He held her tightly for a moment, then released her.

They stood looking at each other for a moment, tensely, separated by a few inches and by a continent. "Would you sleep with me if I were not . . . who I am?" he asked. Without waiting for an answer, he swept his cap off the dining table, and with a formal, "Good evening, Millie," he was gone.

Chapter III

Millie watched the door swing closed behind him. She stood still for a moment, then in a savage motion stripped her clothes off and crawled into bed. She realized she'd forgotten to switch off the lights in the living room and, cursing, went from one to the next, pitching the room into blackness.

Millie pulled the comforter over her head and burrowed under the pillows, determined to get right to sleep and not think at all. After a few minutes, she angrily tossed one of the pillows on the floor and flipped over on to her back.

What the holy fuck is wrong with you? Nineteen million girls would sell their grandmothers for the chance you just threw away. Something good comes your way, and you can't stand it. You have to kill it. When will you learn? Not everything has to be the romance of a lifetime. Everything doesn't have to be so goddamn momentous. There's such a thing as sportfucking, and you know it. You've done it before, so why you suddenly have to come off like the Blessed Virgin is beyond me.

But I usually wind up crying, she answered herself. Besides, I'm not here to entertain visiting royalty. He can fucking well get his fucking elsewhere.

He will, the taunting thought came. He will.

She turned over and, restlessly, turned right back again. She clasped her hands under her head and stared up into the soft darkness. This was not the first time she'd been in this situation. Once before a famous actor had made a big play for her, hitting on her unceasingly all through the picture they had done together. His crinkly, blue-eyed smile set female hearts to throbbing all over the world. And Millie had sent him home, unfucked. She had, of course, never heard from him again.

She never knew exactly why she hadn't seized the opportunity to make love in reality to the man who figured in countless female fantasies. Perhaps it was simply the stubborn sense she had that it was all desperately easy for him. She was sure that he hadn't been turned down by a woman since his first film footage had come back from the lab.

Perhaps she sensed, and couldn't bear, the routine, uninvolved, passionless manner in which he went about getting laid. It had no more meaning than a visit to the barber. And if you're looking for meaning, Honey, boy are you in trouble! she thought. She remembered how casually he had taken her rejection. He'd gone home undismayed, secure in the thought that, while Millie's indisputably delightful body had been denied him, there were many others, equally appealing and more willing. But when he had singled her out, making his preference for her very clear, she had felt this same jumble of emotions, excitement, desire and . . . fear.

She saw, against the dark, shadowy canvas of the ceiling, the green and gold and russet of New England, the campus of the small, select college she had attended. She'd come up by herself, on the train, away from home for the first time. Her mother had behaved as if she were going to reform school rather than college. "A good girl doesn't leave home until she's married. Men don't like a girl who's too smart. If you carry on like this, you'll wind up alone like a stone. And don't forget that I'm the one who told you so."

She hadn't been far wrong, Millie thought. She never let anyone know how lonely she was. She presented to the world the same face she showed her family, cheerful, confident and happy with what was to them, her aberrant lifestyle. She'd die before she'd give her mother—or anyone else—a chance to pity her. I take care of that all by myself, she jeered into the darkness. Come on, Myerson, grow up!

She thought of her father, spending his days serving on countless committees for this yeshiva, that yeshiva, welfare groups for the sons of this or that small town in Lithuania, which no longer existed on any map but the one in the minds of her father and his cronies. Evenings he spent buried in the Talmud, enticed by the pure, intricate, unfailing certainty of its lore. She couldn't remember when he had spoken to her last, except to note, in the bastardized Yiddish-English they spoke at home, that *"Der* tea is *kalt."* He would wait, wordlessly, while the offending glass of tea was replaced with a fresh one.

Millie had once been told by an aunt that her father was indeed proud of his brainy daughter. When she was small he had remarked, "My daughter is so smart that, if she were a boy, she would have been a *gadol hador,"* a student and interpreter of the Talmud so outstanding that there appears but one in a generation. "But she's a girl," he continued, unwilling to comment on the vagaries of an Almighty that endowed little girls, uselessly, with the gift of scholarship.

The word scholarship returned her once again to college. Sixteen years old, utterly naïve, trusting, a head filled with dreams and romantic fantasies, a body surging with unexpressed teenage sexuality. Millie had been one of the few scholarship students, and one of the fewer Jewish girls. She had been the youngest girl in the school, the second youngest ever to attend.

Her roommate had been a buxom blonde named Muffin. Muffin came equipped with a bright red Mustang, dozens of rainbow-hued cashmere sweaters and a clique of girlfriends, all of whom had names like Buffie, Popsie, and DeeDee. They all lived in Manhattan, in the East Fifties, Sixties or Seventies on, or possibly just off Fifth Avenue. They regarded Millie with polite, if distant, curiosity, and she knew that somehow, in their teeny Waspy brains, her smartness was inextricably linked with her Jewishness.

Frederick Cooper III took shape in front of her. She turned over on her stomach and buried her face in the pillow, trying to make the image go away. Fred. Tall, curly-haired, slender. Perfect, right down to the tweedy jackets with leather-patched elbows and the unlit pipe clamped between his teeth. A teaching assistant, he had singled Millie out for special attention from the beginning. He praised her work in class and took her out for long walks, followed by the first beers she had ever drunk. She hated the taste, but swallowed them anyway, anxious not to disclose any more of her differentness than she had to.

The first two months of school passed in a delicious haze. Millie, utterly trusting, her ideas of adult life formed by movies, Jane Austen, and the endless romantic fantasies playing in her head, had accepted

this new love and her unfolding sexuality with delight, as a confirmation of what she had always believed—that if she could just hang
on and survive her arid childhood, her life would be an effortless,
exhilarating upward slide into adventure, achievement and the world
of her fantasies. And here she was, the first time away from home, and
it had all come to her: academic recognition, challenging studies and
Fred. And this was just the beginning!

It was one of Muffin's friends, Bootsie or Tootsie or whatever her
name had been, who had taken it upon herself to enlighten Millie.
Millie had crawled halfway under the bed looking for an errant sock.
The picture was frozen forever in her mind, the last time she looked at
the world with eyes of innocence—the dust balls and the bedspread
hanging down and the slice of beige wall. The sock lay a foot from
Millie's outstretched hand when the girl's voice changed from
conversational to pointed.

"You've been spending a lot of time with Fred Cooper lately. Of
course, you know he's married."

The blood drained out of Millie's head. She froze, her hand in
the act of closing on the sock. The bedspread, the vee of wall, the
floor, the whole picture flew up in a jolting movement and then
snapped back into place. Her outstretched hand shook with the force
of the tremors that palsied her body. It seemed as if hours had passed
when she got out from under the bed, sock in hand, and listened to
her own voice, brittle, elaborately casual. "Of course, I did. We're just
friends, nothing more." The girls didn't seem to notice anything
amiss. Millie left the room, still holding the sock and locked herself in
the bathroom. She was numb. She didn't feel a thing.

And she didn't feel a thing for several months after that. She
went to class, came home, studied, and was in bed by eight o'clock.

Looking back on it, she realized that she had come close to a
serious depressive state—depression, the refuge of angry women, who
would much prefer to kill.

She hadn't thought about Fred in years and wondered why it was
coming back to haunt her tonight. Certainly she'd been over him for a
long, long while. And actually, she thought, it was just what you
needed at the time. A good, solid dose of reality to sweep the cobwebs
out of your brain. It certainly hadn't embittered her or soured her on
men. She'd gone on to have several joyous, loving affairs. She'd just

never committed herself in quite that way again, heart, body, soul, and life's breath. Which is all to the good, she thought. She'd learned to be . . . careful. Heaven doesn't protect the working girl. The working girl protects the working girl.

She realized suddenly that she had no way of getting in touch with James. She had no idea where he was staying, and she'd be damned if she'd call the British consulate cold, asking to speak with the Prince of Wales. Even if she felt like apologizing.

Better that way, she thought. Much better. And drifted off into sleep.

She awoke feeling bleak and for a moment couldn't remember why. Then her hand, dangling over the side of the bed, touched the pillow on the floor, and it all washed over her, draining the color out of the day.

Oh, well. Easy come, easy go, she thought. The phrase was a wry joke between her and her friend Lucy, who admonished Millie with it whenever she was weeping out the end of a love affair or an unfair work setback. My friends hold me together with spit and chewing gum, Millie thought as she waited for the coffee to drip. She glanced at her watch, then dialed Lucy at work.

"ABC–TV," the sterile voice said.

"Lucy Rogers, please."

"Lucy Rogers's office."

"Lucy, please. Tell her it's Millie."

"Miss Rogers is in conference," the implacable voice responded.

"Look, just tell her it's me, and I want to talk to her. Pass her a note or something." Millie wasn't up yet for confrontations this morning. She held on while Muzak played in her ear.

There was a click as the line opened, and she heard Lucy yelling to someone in her office. "Just tell them to hold their horses . . . Because I said so, that's why." Then, in an easier, no less cheerful tone, "Millie? Hi. What's up?"

"Can we have lunch?"

"Not a chance. Not today. I'm jammed." Something in Millie's voice registered belatedly on Lucy. She switched gears without missing a beat. "Sure. Meet you at O'Neals. The one on Fifty-seventh, not the one on Columbus. Twelve-thirty. Bye."

Millie smiled at Lucy's rapid volte-face. They were always there for each other.

"Let me get this straight," a disbelieving Lucy said over their screwdrivers. "You meet this terrific guy, he's single, *straight*, good-looking, and not to mention rich. He takes your part against an asshole director, you spill coffee all over *his* pants, he sends *you* flowers. He behaves like an absolute sweetheart. And you're not happy. Run this by me once again, I must have missed something. Oh, and he's a prince to boot. I forgot that part." Lucy shook her head, slowly. "It's head-examining time for you, sweetie." She picked at her salad, examining a black olive she found hidden under a lettuce leaf.

Millie laughed. Lucy always made her feel better.

Lucy Rogers, tall, elegant, athletic, resembled a younger Dina Merrill. Her hair, expensively streaked with many shades of honey blonde, rose from her clear white brow and fell to her shoulders in a smooth, even curve. She wore large, tinted glasses, more as a prop than an aid to sight. She tipped them down on her nose and peered over them more often than she looked through them, adding to her air of judicious contemplation mingled with deliciously ironic humor.

She was the only pampered daughter of a wealthy, socially prominent West Coast family. Lucy had come East directly from Stanford University, the proud possessor of an honors degree in Clinical Psychology, which, she often quipped, had better prepared her for a career in television than one would have thought. Her calm good sense and unshakable composure enabled her to negotiate with relative ease the frenetic waters of the Big Apple. She observed, with a coolly critical eye, the frantic machinations of her ambitiously cutthroat colleagues, carefully sidestepping the more outrageous maneuvers and, occasionally, instituting some of her own. At present a unit manager, Lucy was well on her way to her first associate producer credit.

She and Millie, despite, or perhaps because of, their extreme dissimilarity of appearance, background and temperament, had been fast friends since the day they had met. They had both applied for the same entry-level, ninety-dollar-a-week, drudgery-guaranteed job. When neither of them was hired, they instantly concluded that anyone so clearly deficient in perception as to fail to recognize the rare combination of talent, intelligence and pure competence that they represented was clearly beneath consideration. They went off to lunch at the Plaza, splitting a tuna fish sandwich, the only item on the menu that they could, by pooling their resources, afford.

"Listen, it doesn't make any sense to me, either," Millie said now. "I have no idea why I'm behaving this way. I think I'm jealous of him."

Lucy halted in the act of spearing a tomato wedge, her fork frozen in midair. "Jealous of him? You mean you want an exclusive on him? Oh, come on!"

"Not that kind of jealous. I mean . . . look, from the time this guy was in diapers, everything has been handed to him on a silver platter—" Millie broke off, realizing that Lucy was grinning at her from across the table.

"When clichés start coming out of Millie Myerson's mouth, I know we've got trouble in River City."

Millie smiled her acknowledgement, then continued, her need for release pressing her to talk. "Everything in his life is ordered for his convenience. He doesn't even *ask* for things—I was watching him at the studio. He doesn't give orders. All he does is *intimate* that he would like something done. And that's it! It's done," Millie said bitterly. "Just like that. Everything for me has always been such a goddamn struggle. It took me three fucking years to get my union card! Three years of politicking and manipulating and begging! And for what? All a union card is in this business is a permit to find your own jobs. It's not like it's a free trip to Acapulco!"

"So?"

"What do you mean, so?"

"So, this isn't the first time you've met somebody who was born to power. And wealth. So what? As I remember, the British royal family works pretty damn hard at what they do. Anyway, didn't Prince James go to University? Oxford or Cambridge or one of those?"

"Cambridge."

"You see!" Lucy said gleefully. "They don't hand out *those* degrees with a stamped, self-addressed envelope and proof of purchase."

"He's done lots of other things, too," Millie said, perversely. "He served in the RAF *and* the Royal Navy. Had his own command, too."

"So what are you telling me?" Lucy said gently. "Anyway, the point isn't what he's got or been given. The point, Ms. Myerson, is what does it do for you? Why don't you just have a good time for as long as he's in town? How long's he here for, anyway?"

"I don't know for sure. He said he didn't have much time." A pang shot through Millie. She pictured James, hands thrust into his trouser pockets staring somberly out the window, his image doubled, reflected by the dark glass pane. "I don't have much time," he had said. "And I'm trying very hard."

"I still don't understand why you didn't go to bed with him. It'll be something to tell your grandchildren about."

"And we have a charming little affair, and next week he's off to Windsor Castle, or Buckingham Palace—or his yacht!—for chrissakes. And a little smile crosses his face whenever he happens to think of me."

"That's right. And you'll have had a good time in bed. What's wrong with that?"

"Nothing. It's just that . . . I'm not real good at that. Somehow I always wind up getting attached to the fuckers and crying my eyes out for six months."

"You know," Lucy said, eyeing her contemplatively. "That's so unchic, they can take away your Bloomingdale's card if they find out."

"I know," Millie smiled wryly. "I don't have a light touch. Do you know I haven't slept with anyone since John?"

"But that was over two years ago!"

"Not quite. Just two years," Millie defended.

"Besides, he was an actor. They all suck."

"There just hasn't been anyone I've wanted to sleep with. Anyway celibacy agrees with me," she joked.

"Bullshit. You know what? I think you have a good case of holiness-of-the-cunt disease. Before you let anyone into your precious pants, you have to have guarantees in writing and violins and God knows what all else. A letter from the Pope maybe. That's plain stupid, Millie. And you're missing out on a lot."

"I want it to be more than just . . . bouncy-bouncy."

"Why?" Lucy asked pointedly. "What's wrong with some nice, juicy, no-strings-attached sex?"

"Nothing. Nothing at all. It's just that this is . . . different."

"Would you have slept with him if he were, oh, a director or a stage manager or something, who you were attracted to? You are attracted to him, I take it?"

"You know, that's just what *he* asked me."

"See! I told you he was smart. Here's this guy with *alleh mey-less*"— she used the Yiddish phrase for perfection, someone with every desirable quality—"and he can't get laid."

Millie grinned at her. "You speak a better Yiddish than any Episcopalian I know."

"I hang out with the right people. As my old boss used to say, 'Dress British, think Yiddish.' Which brings us back to the topic of this afternoon's discussion. What about it? Are you attracted to him?"

"I think that I'm *more* than attracted to him. I think he's . . . I think he's just . . . terrific," Millie said wistfully. "I think—I *know* I would have slept with him . . . if I didn't feel that way about him." Millie busied herself digging the anchovies out of her salad, lining them up neatly, side by side on her napkin. "If you want to know the truth, the only reason I *didn't* was because I'm violently, sickeningly attracted to him. I was just plain too nervous."

Lucy watched her for a long moment. "Well, maybe this is your big chance," she said slowly. Millie looked at her questioningly. "Practice," she said firmly. "Here you have a thing that is absolutely finite. After all, how attached can you get in a few days? Consider it a seminar in Advanced Not-Taking-Things-To-Heart-So-Much."

"You don't understand! I'll never see him again. I blew it."

"All right," Lucy nodded. "Easy come—"

"Easy go. I knew you were going to say that," Millie laughed.

"So forget about it. What else is new?" Lucy changed the subject briskly.

"I had a screaming fight with Bob Jones on the set," Millie said glumly.

"That's good. That's professional," Lucy approved. "Although I will admit the thing about Jones that can drive you nuts is not that he's a hack—there are plenty of those—but that he doesn't *know* he's a hack. He thinks he's Ingmar Bergman. If only he had the good sense to understand that he's a turkey . . ." Lucy laughed.

"It just about killed me. A shmuck like that getting a glorious piece like the Magna Carta to do. The whole time I sat there, I was thinking how I could have made it something special—"

"In between sneaking horny little peeks at Prince James," Lucy interrupted. "But, you know, you'd make a good director if you ever got a shot at it. You have the executive ability and the imagination, and God knows you understand how the whole thing works. Which most of them don't!"

"You're telling *me!* I'm on the set with them all day. At least you get to stay in your nice little office. But I try not to think about it. I have about as much chance of getting a piece to direct as I have of . . ." she trailed off.

"I know. What you need is someone who's willing to give you that first break. Can't you cosy up to George Gilhooley?"

"You know who could direct if he wanted to? Gerald."

"Sure. All he has to do is keep after Daddy, and sooner or later Rubin'll throw him a quick-and-dirty spot to do." Quick-and-dirty was film slang for test commercials, done on the cheap and not intended for wide distribution. They were, therefore, the way in which people often crossed the magic line from "I've never done it, but I'm sure I can," to "I'm a director."

"The funny thing is," Millie said, "he doesn't want to. Gerald doesn't have the slightest desire to direct—or even produce. He's happy doing what he does. And I'd give anything in the world for a break like that."

"Life ain't fair," Lucy said.

As they left the restaurant, Lucy reached down and hugged her much smaller friend. "I love you," Millie said, reaching up to kiss Lucy first on one cheek, then the other, European fashion.

"I love you too, hon. And listen, try not to be so intense about everything, huh?" Millie shrugged. "And about that other thing—it's probably better that way. I don't think the world is ready for Queen Millie the First!"

Millie walked home, cutting through the park, avoiding Central Park West. Staying off the street they had strolled together did not lessen her sense of James's presence. She lectured herself, striding briskly. The words "futile" and "self-destructive" were prominent in her inner monologue.

The day was overcast, and the park seemed to glow with soft grays and refracted light, which normally awoke in Millie a connoisseur's appreciation of the myriad moods of Central Park. Today she moved through its quiet luminescence unseeing.

She could hear the phone ringing from inside her apartment as she fumbled with the keys. As usual, when she either had to pee so bad her teeth hurt, or the phone inside was ringing, the keys somehow did not fit the locks. Finally she got the door open and raced for the phone, breathless. "Hello?"

"Hello, Millie? Is that you? You sound funny. Are you all right?"

"I'm fine, Ma," she said, resigned. She pulled off one earring that was digging into her ear and kicked off her high-heeled sandals. "What's up?"

"Everything's the same here. Nothing is new. I just didn't hear from you for a few days, so I wondered . . . is everything okay?" Her mother's voice fell to a hush filled with foreboding. "A girl living alone, I mean . . ." She trailed off, unable to verbalize the nameless dangers lurking, waiting to attack unmarried girls who left the safety of their parents' abode.

"Everything's fine. I just told you."

"That's all you ever say. You never confide in me like other daughters do. Everything can't be fine all the time. I know that. So tell me. What's the matter?"

Millie's heart softened. Her mother had a point. MS Magazine was full of articles about mothers whose daughters thought they were the last person on earth to accept the realities of life in the eighties. The women who wrote these articles were filled with pleased surprise. Their mothers not only understood, but calmly shared feelings similar in emotional tone, albeit separated by a generation. Sometimes all it took was one good talk. And one of them had to be the first to open up.

Millie took a deep breath. "I was doing this shoot with Prince James—"

"What a nice boy," her mother interrupted. "I saw him on TV. I know he never gives his parents a bit of trouble. Of course, he should be married by now, but with a boy it's different. They can afford to pick and choose."

"Yeah, well, I was in the studio and—"

"What was it? A commercial?"

"No. British royalty doesn't do commercials. It was a piece about the Magna Carta."

"The what?"

"The Magna Carta. It's a very old document. He brought it with him. From England. We did this whole piece on it. It'll be on NET. Channel Thirteen."

"Will your name be on television again?"

"Yes, I guess it will."

"Good!" her mother said triumphantly. "I'll tell Mrs. Plotkin."

"So, anyway, I was walking across the stage, and I didn't look where I was going, and I tripped and spilled my coffee all over him. I felt so bad."

"Were you wearing a brassiere? I *told* you and told you. Men don't think a girl is decent if she doesn't wear a bra."

The building intercom buzzed. "Look, Ma, I've got to go. There's someone at the door."

"Be careful who you let in. Don't talk to any delivery men. And, if they say they're from Con Ed, don't believe them."

"Okay, Ma. I won't. Bye." Millie hung up the phone and pressed the intercom button.

Gerald's cheery voice said, "You're home! Buzz me in, petunia."

"Oh, good, you're dressed." Gerald eyed her green-and-white striped silk dress and the white linen blazer she hadn't had time to take off.

"Dressed for what?" she asked suspiciously.

"The wrap party."

"What wrap party?"

"The Prince James shoot wrap party. If you'd remember to turn on your answering machine, you'd know these things. Your presence is requested, etcetra, etcetra, etcetra. I sound like whatisname—in *The King and I?*" he asked, diverted. "The one with no hair."

"Yul Brynner. Since when do we have wrap parties for a lousy two-day shoot?"

"Since everybody and his bubbeh wants to meet the talent."

"I'm not going."

"Of course you're going. It's too good to miss. They cleaned out Stage Five, finally. Even the rigging. And all this crap came sifting down that's been there since the year one. All this gray dust mixed with horseshit. It was great. Sorry you couldn't see it." The CC&G building was widely rumored to have been a stable when it was first built toward the end of the last century.

"And they've got this big cake," he continued. "It's about two feet square and it says 'Welcome, Prince James,' in blue writing on white frosting. It looks just like a bar mitzvah in Scarsdale. All it needs is thirteen candles and strolling musicians playing 'Hava Nagilah,'" he disclosed gleefully. "What do you mean, you're not going?"

"Just what I said. I'm not going."

"And you'll never guess who they got to cater! Wang's!" Despite herself, Millie burst out laughing. Gerald nodded, approving. "By the time he gets back home, he won't be able to look a pastrami in the face. Look, sweetheart, if you don't show, you'll look like the world's biggest asshole. You have to face these people sometime, unless you've become independently wealthy and plan to retire."

Millie looked at him blankly. Then the penny dropped. "Oh, the coffee business. It's not that. It's *him* I don't want to see."

Gerald looked at her, his normally blithe expression unwontedly intent. "Aha! Another passionate night of love, successfully negotiated by Millie Myerson, Queen of the Sexpots," he chortled.

"Thanks a lot. It's always nice to know you can count on your friends," she said bitterly.

"Princes are for fairy tales. And I don't think Our Miss Millie is ready to play with the jet set."

"What makes you say he's a jet setter?"

"Oh, come *on!* Where are your eyes? That bird flies around the world playing with himself. Or maybe not just with himself," he added darkly. "And if you think I'm telling you this for any fishy motives . . ."

"I don't."

"Good. 'Cause if there's one thing I don't have, it's a fishy bone in my body. Do I have a pun there? Gotta work on that."

"I thought you liked him."

"I do. I got nothing against him, as long as he— Listen, shitface, try to understand. I don't give a fuck who you fuck and who you don't. All I know is, if you don't show your pretty face at this bash, the half the business that drinks will think you fell 'cause you were doing dope, and the other half, that does dope, will think you fell 'cause you were drunk." Millie looked at him, knowing he was right. "That's why I'm here. It doesn't take much to screw up a career. And I figured you might need a strong right arm to shove you out the door. Is any of this registering on your peewee brain?"

He looked at her. It was.

Stage Five had been decorated much in the manner of a high school gym for the senior prom. Crepe paper streamers, red, white, and blue, hung from the rigging. The enormous American flag, used as set dressing in political spots, stood in one corner. Next to it someone had taped a small Union Jack, the kind schoolchildren wave when the Queen passes in procession.

The cavernous room was crowded when Gerald and Millie arrived. Everyone who had the remotest connection to the shoot or to CC&G had wangled an invitation, which it was necessary to have wangled, because the guard at the door required identification before he checked one's name off the list.

They stood for a moment in the doorway. That was a moment too long. Denise snaked her way out of the crowd, looking up at Gerald with limpid eyes. "Have I ever told you you're just the *cutest* thing?" she asked, ignoring Millie. Her crimson talons toyed with Gerald's collar.

"Frequently," he replied, knocking her hand aside.

"I hear Woody Allen is doing his new movie here. Woody just adores me, and I know he would want me to be makeup artist on his shoot. And even though it's ten weeks work, I think I *could* make myself available, seeing as how it's Woody. As a favor to an old friend." She touched her hand to her dangling earring.

"Terrific. As soon as Woody asks for you, I'll be in touch. In the meantime, wait by your phone." He gripped Millie's elbow and half-pushed, half-pulled her into the room.

Millie instantly spotted the Prince across the studio, surrounded by people, all seemingly talking at once, vying for his attention. He looked up, and his eyes met Millie's. And held. His face was impassive, giving away nothing. The intensity of his gaze was compelling.

A flashbulb went off, blanketing the Prince in a millisecond of white glare and he looked away. Millie realized that, mixed in with the regulars, were reporters and press photographers, as well as crews from the three networks, the two local stations plus NET. To her surprise, she also caught, among the print and television crews jockeying for position, smatterings of German, French and the clipped accents of the BBC.

"C'mon. Let's get something to drink. The evening shouldn't be a total waste," Gerald said in her ear. His arm at her elbow urged her toward the bar set up on a trestle table against the wall.

Drinks in hand, they moved out of the traffic flow. "I'm surprised they aren't charging for the drinks," Millie observed.

"Bet you anything they considered it."

"I wonder what paroxysm of good taste prevented them," Millie returned tartly.

"I love those big words you use. And you do it so nacheral," Gerald clowned. Millie jabbed him in the ribs with her elbow. "Hey, watch it! I don't trust you with a full glass in your hand."

Millie glared at him and started away. She took one step and came face to face with Mr. and Mrs. Rubin, Gerald's parents. She turned and moved back to Gerald's side.

Ralph Rubin, short, squat and pugnacious, was the owner of a small but powerful commercial production company. Millie had worked on his shoots a couple of times, and privately referred to him as The Man Who Sits On My Purse. When Ralph Rubin wanted to sit down, he parked his ample rear in the nearest chair, no matter who it belonged to or what might be resting on it, with all the aplomb of Queen Victoria, who, when she wished to sit, did just that, relying on her aides to see that there was, in fact, a chair under the royal posterior.

Since the script supervisor needed to balance her large, unwieldy book on her lap, while she manipulated the stopwatch that hung on a chain around her neck with one hand and her many-colored pens with the other, and since very few people have laps when they are standing up, there was always a specific chair on the set sacred to her.

Once, just for the hell of it, she'd walked up to Rubin, comfortably ensconced in her seat, and said, "Excuse me, Ralph, but I'll need my chair for the next shot." He'd looked up at her with mild curiosity, as if he were deaf and hadn't perfected the art of lip-reading. He didn't say anything, nor did he relinquish her seat.

Now he turned to Gerald and, without preamble, said, "I hear you're doing the Sherry Twigs shoot. You're really too inexperienced to handle a job that size. Listen to George Gilhooley. Do exactly as he tells you, and you'll be okay."

Gerald nodded. "Right, Dad." He turned to his mother. "Mom, I'd like you to meet Millie Myerson. She's a script supervisor who does a lot of work at CC&G. Millie, this is my mom."

Millie looked at the tall, blond woman with the tanned skin leathered by endless tennis lessons. She was dressed in a designer black-silk suit with a high-necked, white-crepe blouse. Her black lizard pumps were Ferragamo and a small Hermes bag dangled negligently from her arm. "Hi, Mrs. Rubin," Millie said. "It's nice to meet you. I've always wondered, does Gerald give you as much trouble at home as he does us here at work?" She glanced at Gerald. His face was suffused with pleasure at her friendly, intimate teasing.

Mrs. Rubin stared at a point above Millie's head. "Nice meeting you, Billie," she said. "If you will excuse us, there are people here we have to say hello to." And they were gone, Mrs. Rubin towering over her husband, a guiding hand at his elbow. Millie noticed that she hadn't said one word to her son. Which might be all to the good, judging from his father's idea of parental encouragement.

"Testing, testing, one, two, three." The amplified voice of Mr. Gilhooley came over the loudspeaker.

"It's working, shmuck, I plugged it in." A carefully unidentifiable voice came from the back of the room. The mass of people turned toward the set area, forming a ragged semicircle many tiers thick. The lights were on over the set, spilling their hot glare for the benefit of the television cameras.

Mr. Gilhooley stood in front of the mahogany desk. On his right was the Prince of Wales, elegantly at ease, hands clasped behind his back, handsome. He wore a double-breasted navy-blue blazer with polished gold buttons, a crisp white shirt and a navy and gold striped tie.

On Gilhooley's left was a small man with a fringe of gray hair around his shiny bald head. His silver-rimmed spectacles threw off glints of light. His tiny body was strangely high-waisted, so that his belt rode over a small, round paunch. A plaid bow tie over an expanse of shirtfront and a bristly moustache added to his elfin appearance.

"Who's that?" Millie whispered to Gerald.

"Don't you know? That's Ebenezer Cohen. Cofounder of this establishment."

"Ebenezer! You've got to be kidding!"

"Nope. That's his name."

"Jesus, the only other Ebenezer I ever heard of was Scrooge."

"Bingo!" said Gerald. Millie giggled, and he shushed her as Mr. Gilhooley started to speak.

"Well, here we are," he began, unnecessarily. He was a man of medium height. His black hair rode back from his forehead in crinkly, oily waves. He wore black, pointed rectangular glasses in a style out of favor for the past fifteen years. There was something oddly out of synch about him. His gestures always seemed to be a beat or two behind his words. He spoke with a puppetlike, jerky effect, as if his strings were being manipulated from somewhere else, badly.

"I want to welcome you all here tonight. It's good to see all these familiar faces." He gazed blankly out at the crowd. Millie was sure he would be hard put to identify ten of those "familiar faces" with any degree of certainty, even though many of them worked for him day in and day out. "But, most of all, I would like to welcome His Royal Highness, the Prince of Wales, Prince James."

There was a burst of applause and a few yells of "Hiya, Jimmy!" James smiled out at the crowd and winked. The applause rose in response to this wordless sally.

"It's not often that we are distinguished by such a . . . distinguishing honor," Mr. Gilhooley continued. "We are a small company. Our profit margin is very modest," he lied. "There are weeks when just meeting the payroll is difficult for us." Automatically, he had launched into his poverty speech, the one he used when negotiating pay raises for the staff.

"But we do it because we feel responsible for all of you. Where would you all be without us?" he asked rhetorically. Ebenezer Cohen nodded his agreement. "You know it, and I know it," he confirmed, soaring majestically into the world of the non sequitur.

Millie looked at James. His face was devoid of expression, but his eyes gleamed wickedly. Gilhooley continued, "So that's why we do what we do. Even though it's a hardship. And we do it so well. So without further ado, let me have the . . . I have the honor to present, er . . . His . . . the Prince, with the following small mementos of his stay at CC&G. Although they are very small, we know that they will be appreciated.

"First—" He held up so that all could see, a CC&G T-shirt. It depicted, in black print on a Halloween-orange background, the CC&G logo: a clumsy silhouette of a tape camera forming one half of a circle, an old-fashioned, anachronistic film camera completing the other half, and underneath, in Gothic letters, "Cohen, Cohen and Gilhooley." It was sold to those employees who wished to purchase it at four dollars over cost.

"I know the Prince will wear this, and I know he'll enjoy it," Gilhooley affirmed. He handed the T-shirt to the Prince, who held it up, then folded it neatly into smaller and smaller squares until he had a very small packet of material in his hand.

"Next, and not least," Gilhooley continued, "I would like to present the Prince with this plaque." He held up a piece of dark-stained wood, carved to look like a scroll. There was a legend burnt into its surface. "And I'll read it to you. Even though we had to rush to get it done on such short notice.

"It says: 'H.R.H. the Prince of Wales taped a television program entitled "Magna Carta: Innovation and Inspiration" at CC&G studios on June 12th and 13th . . .'" His voice trailed off, belatedly, as he realized he had come to the end of the inscription. "Here." He thrust it at the Prince. "And regards to your mother," he added, inspired.

The Prince looked at it, turning it over in his hands. He nodded, then backhanded the plaque to a man standing behind him and a little to his left. The man received it, expressionlessly, while James smiled at Gilhooley.

"And now a few words from Prince James," Gilhooley said, bending to the mike.

James moved closer to the microphone. "First, let me say that I listened with great interest to your remarks regarding the financial straits of CC&G. I'm very glad that the roof seems to be in order," he said with an upward glance, "else I'm afraid you might have asked me to chair an appeal." He smiled radiantly at George Gilhooley. Gilhooley, uncomprehending, smiled back, pleased and proud.

Millie choked. Gerald stifled a giggle, which he quickly turned into a cough, smothering it in his handkerchief. James had a way of saying absolutely antic things, but with such an innocently straightforward demeanor that his intent often went over his audience's head.

"And I would like to extend my thanks to all of you," James continued. "I know that this project was thrust on you without warning and with very little lead time. I do admire all of you for your professionalism and the unfailing good humor with which you went about your labors. It was a great pleasure working with you, and I'm sure the experience was one I shan't easily forget."

There were a few snickers and some heads in the crowd turned to Millie. She blushed and looked up at the Prince. She saw that he hadn't intended the inference, and he quickly resumed speaking to cover it. "It was my very great privilege to get to know some of you, and I'm sincerely grateful for the opportunity. I shall take the warmth of your welcome back home with me . . ." a quiver shot through Millie, "and I will convey your good wishes to the Queen. Once again, I thank you very much, and I hope you all enjoy the festivities."

James started away from the set. Gilhooley caught him by the arm. "The cake. You have to cut the cake," he hissed. James turned back, inquiring. Someone pushed forward the trolley that had once supported the Magna Carta. Now it held an enormous white cake. Millie saw that Gerald's description had been, if anything, understated. It was marvelously ornate, rimmed with roses, vines and curlicues.

James looked down at it. Someone thrust a slightly tarnished cake knife into his hand. He looked at the knife, then back at the cake, hesitating. His eyes scanned the crowd and lighted, fixing on one individual. Millie, in the back, couldn't see who he was looking at. "While I'm very sensible of the honor conveyed to me," James said smoothly, "I do feel that this ceremony could more properly be performed by one of you."

His eyes gleamed with wicked pleasure and he extended the cake knife to someone in the front row. A piercing giggle broke the silence. "Who? Me?" Denise's voice hit every note from middle to high C.

James waited. Denise stepped forward, smirking. Her hand fluttered in the vicinity of her breast. "Why you're just the sweetest thing," she crooned.

She took the knife and delicately, with great panache, cut the cake. Ebenezer Cohen shuffled forward, inch by tortuous inch till he stood next to Denise. The top of his head came up to her armpit. His eyes gamboled in her cleavage.

She smiled down at him and, with a flourish, lifted a gooey slice of cake on the serving knife. Mr. Cohen stretched out his hand, two fingers extended, made a swift pass at the icing, and circled them back toward his mouth.

He licked his fingers. "Good," he said. It was the only word he was heard to utter the entire evening.

Denise turned to the Prince. She extended the same courtesy, and the same piece of cake, she had accorded Mr. Cohen. Millie watched him, certain that under his impassive courtesy, he was convulsed. The Prince ignored the proffered cake and, in a practiced motion, extended his right hand. Reflexively, Denise shifted the cake knife and shook the Prince's outstretched hand. Flashbulbs popped. Denise smiled exultantly into camera.

"Show's over," Gerald said. "Play your cards right, and I'll drop you in my cab."

Millie looked at him quizzically. "What got into *you* all of a sudden," she asked suspiciously. Gerald lived on the East Side, almost directly across town from CC&G, and in the opposite direction from Millie's apartment.

"Don't worry. I'll stick it into CC&G. God knows they've been sticking it to me long enough. C'mon." He grasped her elbow firmly, urging her through the crowd toward the door.

"Do you think we should say good-bye at least?" Millie hung back.

"I thought you already *said* your good-byes." They both looked back toward the set at the other end of the studio, but all they could see was a crush of people. "Feeding time at the Bronx Zoo. Forget it."

Bob Jones brushed past them on his way out. Millie couldn't resist. "Hi, Bob. Did the footage cut?" she asked in an oblique reference to her contretemps with him.

He looked at her sourly. "All my footage cuts," he snapped and stalked out of the studio.

"He's so full of shit," Gerald said. "They haven't *begun* to put that stuff together yet. They haven't even finished coding it yet."

"Yeah, well. If it cuts, it's because he's a genius, and, if it doesn't cut, it's because I'm a moron."

Someone tapped her on the shoulder. "Excuse me, Miss Myerson?" Millie turned to see the man who had been standing behind the Prince, the one to whom he had passed the plaque. Her heart leapt. "Are you Miss Myerson?" he asked again.

"Yes. Yes, I am."

"This is for you." He handed her a small piece of paper, folded in two. It had clearly been ripped out of a pocket diary. Millie unfolded it, her pulse beating furiously.

"Please wait," it read, in a firm, slanting hand. "You look especially lovely tonight."

She looked up, to find that the man had disappeared into the crowd and Gerald was staring at her. "Let's . . ." She cleared her throat and started again. "Let's wait around a bit, okay?"

The crowd thinned out. The television crews had left, and with them the print photographers and reporters. James purposefully worked his way toward them. He appeared unhurried, chatted comfortably and shook hands, yet his progress was sure and fairly rapid. At his elbow was the serious man who had handed Millie the note, and behind him, eyes watchful, was Ian MacCrae.

"Good evening," James said, his voice firm and resonant. "Did you . . . Have you got my note?" He paused and added ruefully, "I can't seem to stop asking that, can I?"

Millie laughed. "Yes, I did. How have you been?" This sounded inane to her own ears. She had seen him less than twenty-four hours ago.

"I'm perfectly splendid," James replied. And stopped. He seemed unsure where to go from there.

"A lot better than you would have been if you had eaten that cake. It looked shitty." Bless Gerald. Whatever difficulties Millie and

James were having making ordinary conversation didn't seem to apply to him. All three laughed.

"Yes, well, I'm often offered things to eat which . . . one would rather not. I've gotten quite good at avoiding them."

"I thought you did beautifully—the whole thing," Millie said.

"Thanks ever so!" James smiled down at her. "It's all in a day's work. I manage to show the flag and keep myself amused at the same time."

"I noticed," she said impudently.

"The trick is not to meet the eyes of anyone else who sees the same joke you do. If one does . . . if I ever did, I'm afraid I'd just . . . dissolve." The trim gentleman behind James cleared his throat, meaningfully. The Prince realized he'd been talking a bit freely. "This is all quite . . . private," he added. He glanced from Millie to Gerald and was reassured by what he saw. "Oh, and I'd like you both to meet my senior equerry, Peter Goldsworth. Peter, Miss Millie Myerson and Mr. Gerald Rubin." They shook hands all around.

Peter Goldsworth was about ten years older and a trifle taller than the Prince. He had wavy, sandy hair, neatly parted, and wore horn-rimmed glasses. He had an air of quiet, restrained competence.

"I was wondering," James continued. "I've got two engagements after this, but, if it isn't too late, perhaps you'd both join me for dinner." He looked inquiringly from her to Gerald.

Gerald knew a cue when he heard one. "I'd love to, but I'm busy tonight."

James turned to him. He rocked back on his heels slightly. "Would it help to unbusy you if I told you that I've found that it's not wise for me to be seen in public alone with a young woman?" he asked understandingly. "I've found that it's much more comfortable to go out with a group of people. That way the press doesn't know for sure just whom one is interested in." He grinned at Gerald.

"Well, if you're going to twist my arm . . ."

"Excellent. It's settled then. Ten o'clock?"

"Fine with me," Gerald said.

Millie spoke up. "Would it be all right, in that case, if I asked one of my friends—a very special friend, Lucy Rogers, to join us?" She felt suddenly that she would need more knowledgeable support than Gerald was able to give.

"That would be super. I'd like that very much," James responded. Millie saw that he really was pleased. "Where would you like to go?"

Gerald and Millie looked at each other. "Wherever you'd like would be fine with us," Millie said politely.

"Do stop that," snapped the Prince testily. "This is your town. You know where you like to eat better than I do." At least this natural reaction was more appealing than the stiff formality under which they had been laboring.

"Des Artistes," Gerald said. "Cafe Des Artistes. It's in the West Sixties."

James glanced at his equerry, and Millie knew that the reservations had just been taken care of. "Splendid. We'll see you all there at ten, then. I'll be looking forward to it." And he was off.

Millie, Lucy and Gerald pushed open the door to Des Artistes and stood in front of the maitre d's desk. All three realized at the same moment that they had no idea how to explain whose party they were with. "You do it," Millie said. "I'm convinced that if I ask him for the Prince of Wales, he'll want to know if I'm the Queen of Hearts."

"I don't give a flying fuck what he thinks," Gerald whispered. He turned to the maitre d'. "We're here to join—"

Ian MacCrae metamorphized in front of them, seemingly out of nowhere. "Good evening, ladies. Good evening, Gerald-never-Gerry. It's nice to see you again." He led them to a table in a sheltered corner. Prince James and Peter Goldsworth stood as they approached. There were introductions all around.

Millie watched, flabbergasted, as Lucy dropped a small, perfect curtsy. "Finishing school," she whispered to Millie out of the corner of her mouth.

They all took seats, Millie at the Prince's right, Peter Goldsworth at his left, with Lucy and Gerald completing the circle. Ian MacCrae had disappeared. They busied themselves ordering drinks, settling in, looking at menus. Millie took out a cigarette, which Peter Goldsworth lit with a small gold lighter. Millie noticed that it bore the same crest as the Prince's notepaper and wondered if it had been a Christmas or birthday present, or some such.

"Are you a native New Yorker, Miss Rogers?" Goldsworth asked.

"No, I'm not. I'm from San Francisco originally. Why don't we drop the 'mister' and 'miss' right now?" She smiled sweetly at him. "I'm Lucy, he's Gerald, that's Millie and you're Peter, okay?" She turned to the Prince. "What do you prefer to be called in private, sir," she asked.

"Well, my predecessor was rumored to have insisted on either 'Sir' or 'Darling.' I find that Your Royal Highness takes too long to say, and when people call me 'Wales,' I get the giggles. So how does 'James' suit you?" He smiled at her. Millie could see that she was entirely charmed.

"Perfectly," Lucy said, and raised her glass in a small, wordless toast.

I'm so glad I invited her, Millie thought. After that conversation flowed smoothly, easily. Peter and James both seemed to have the ordinary person's thirst for inside show-business stories, and Lucy and Gerald were happy to oblige.

Millie, for the most part, was quiet. She passed the evening in a haze, following the conversation only intermittently, conscious every moment of James, sitting next to her. She stole glances at his hands, busy with his knife and fork, toying with his wineglass, deft, competent and strong. The signet ring on his left little finger glinted with his smallest movement.

She breathed deeply, catching his already familiar scent, compounded of clean soap, a brisk, light cologne and something else, that personal, indefinable aura that each of us has. Every now and then he turned to her and smiled. She looked at his sweet, full mouth and felt her stomach muscles contract.

Millie toyed with her food, sometimes remembering to carry the loaded fork to her mouth.

"So George Gilhooley hears that Ella Fitzgerald is shooting on Stage Two," Gerald was saying. "So he rushes up there and runs over to her and says, 'Oh, it's such an honor to have you here! You're such a great star! I'll never forget your performance in *Hello, Dolly!*'" Lucy laughed so hard she choked on her wine. "Ella looks at him. She stares at him like he was a cockroach that crawled out from the wall and says, very dignified, 'You're very kind. I'll tell Pearl Bailey how much you admire her.'"

* * *

Although the story was an old one for Millie and Lucy, their laughter was as loud as that of the Prince and his equerry, who were hearing it for the first time.

They had finished their meal and lingered over brandies and coffee. Lucy picked up the thread. "On this last series I did, the whole thing was a screw-up from beginning to end. The unit moved from town to town. You remember," she said to Millie, "it was that idiot thing about these two cowboys who wander around the country solving crimes and having adventures.

"Anyway, the whole thing was a mess. We had no real shooting schedule, and I hit each town about a day ahead of the company, trying to nail down locations and get everything locked in. I didn't get a full night's sleep for about three months. And I had this assistant, who was wished on me. Melody, her name was. I'll never forget her. Big tits and no brains. The first time we took a flight together, she told me all about how she had psychic powers and was in touch with other planets—frequently, I might add," Lucy said in response to their laughter. "And she spoke to vegetables and plants and had these spirit guides—she called them her Masters—and sent her soul on trips while her body was sleeping. And all the time I'm hearing this, I'm smiling . . ." Lucy demonstrated a grimace through clenched teeth, "and inside, this little voice is going, 'Oh, my God! Oh, my God!'

"Well, there was nothing I could do about it. She was the producer's daughter. Lord knows she wouldn't have been hired if she wasn't—" She looked over at Gerald. "No offense," she said.

Gerald shifted uncomfortably in his seat. "It's nothing," he said, to the Prince's inquiring glance, "it's just that my father is a big shot, and nobody ever lets me forget it."

"I know just how you feel," the Prince returned drily, and smiled at the approving laughter.

Lucy continued. "We rented a car and drove into this Godforsaken town, Yenemsvelt, Tennessee . . ." Prince James and Peter looked a little confused, but they let it pass. Lucy was on a roll and she was too funny to interrupt. ". . . at about five in the morning. And this time, we're not a *day* ahead of the unit, but just a few hours. They're due to arrive in the afternoon, and I've got to set the whole thing up during the morning. We check into this decrepit motel—it looked just like the one in *Psycho,* but I was so tired, Tony Perkins could have stabbed the entire Mormon Tabernacle Choir for all I cared.

"I set the alarm for seven-thirty, figuring I can get a couple of hours sleep, because by this time I'm punchy, and anyway, who can you talk to in a small town at the crack of dawn?

"At six AM my phone rings. I've had exactly forty-five minutes sleep, and I have a hard time just finding the damn thing. Melody is calling. 'Lucy?' she says. 'I just heard the company is going to be here early. They'll be here before noon.'

"Well, the adrenalin just shot through my body. I was halfway out the door, pulling on my jeans, before it occurred to me to wonder how she knew this. I mean, why hadn't they called *me* with this information. I called her back. 'Melody, how do you know that the company is going to get here early?' 'The Masters told me,' she said. I have *never* come so close to murdering another human being in my life."

Millie watched the staid Peter Goldsworth rock with laughter. Lucy is probably the best thing that ever happened to *him*, she thought.

"What did you do with her?" the Prince asked, fascinated.

"I sat her down—not that day, I waited a couple of days, till I could bear to look at her—and I told her that, while I was perfectly willing to listen to anything the Masters might like to share with me of a personal nature, she was never, *ever*, to give me production information from them again!"

"What happened to her?" Peter asked.

"I have no idea. *I* lost her," she used the slang production term for getting rid of something or someone, "and she went on to spread joy somewhere else."

When the laughter had died down, they sat quietly, sipping their brandies, enjoying each other's company. Then Gerald got an idea. "What are we all doing this weekend? Let's go down to Disneyworld. I haven't been down there in a long time. There are lots of cheap trips this time of year. It'll be fun!" he finished enthusiastically.

"Count me in," said Lucy.

"That's a great idea!" Millie joined in. "Let's all *go!*"

They all looked at her. "Well, Sleeping Beauty finally woke up," Gerald teased. "Haven't heard from you in a while. How have you been?" he inquired elaborately.

James cleared his throat into the general hilarity that greeted this riposte. "I can't," he said mournfully, drawing out the long British *a*. He glanced at Peter Goldsworth, then looked at each of the others in turn. "I can go, all right. By myself, with fifty dignitaries. They'll line up Mickey and Minnie in formation, and they'll close the park for the day, and I can watch all the rides go round and round," he finished miserably. "But it's a fine idea. You all go."

They all looked at him sympathetically, realizing he was right. "In that case, I think I'll stay in town, too," Millie ventured casually, then blushed, as they all chuckled.

James put his arm around her and kissed her lightly on the cheek. "I think it's time we took this little girl home."

They collected their things and moved toward the front of the restaurant. They waited while Peter Goldsworth settled the bill. Lucy turned to James. "How long will you be in town, sir?"

Her deft return to the proper address now that they were no longer secluded did not escape the Prince. He smiled at her appreciatively. "A fortnight, all told."

"Thank you so much for dinner," Lucy said. "We've enjoyed ourselves so much. It was lovely meeting you." Her smile included Peter Goldsworth, who had rejoined them. Gerald added his words of thanks. Millie was still struck dumb, but it didn't seem to matter. Her friends were covering for her.

"The pleasure was entirely mine, I assure you," Prince James responded warmly. "I haven't laughed so much in a long time." He flattened his vowel sounds and raised the pitch of his voice and continued. "I feel real distinguished by such a distinguishing honor and the y'know, the distinguished company . . ." The result was an uncannily accurate portrayal of George Gilhooley.

Laughing, they walked out of the restaurant. "How do you *do* that?" Gerald asked enviously.

"It runs in the family. We can all do it. My aunt is really top-notch. She can talk to someone for five minutes and—" He broke off. "What the bloody hell!" he exploded.

They all followed his glance. The gleaming silver-gray Rolls Royce, flying its telltale standards, was parked directly in front of the restaurant. A uniformed chauffeur sat, facing front, in the right-hand driver's seat, nearest the curb. When he heard the Prince's voice, he leapt out, opened the passenger door and stood behind it at attention.

"Has that thing been sitting out there all evening? What in bleeding hell are you trying to do to me? Why don't you just send up signal flares!" Despite his white-faced fury, the Prince's voice was pitched low, controlled.

"But, sir—" Goldsworth began.

"But, sir, my arse! You're sabotaging me, Goldsworth!" James turned his back on his equerry and spoke, calmly, politely, to the chauffeur. "Please take Miss Rogers and Mr. Rubin to their homes."

He stepped out into the street and, with a shrill, two-fingered whistle, stopped a cruising yellow cab. Quickly, he opened the door and assisted Millie in. MacCrae made a leap for the front seat. "Sixty-eighth and West End," James said, giving Millie's address with perfect aplomb. James put his arm around Millie and hugged her, exuberantly. "How'd you like that?" he asked with a triumphant grin. "I've always wanted to whistle up a cabbie that way. They do it so nicely in all the movies."

Millie leaned back into his arms and found her voice. "And I've always wanted to ride in a Rolls Royce."

He looked down at her. "And so you shall, my dear. I promise."

Chapter IV

James prevented the detective from accompanying them into the building with a wordless, steely look. When they reached the door to Millie's apartment, however, his assurance deserted him, and he faltered. "May I . . . would you . . . Shall I come in?"

"I think you'd better," Millie said, taking command.

The room was filled with shadows, the darkness broken only by the curtain of pendant lights outside the large windows. Millie turned to face the Prince. James took her in his arms and held her. They were silent for a long moment. "I think you've been thinking and . . . worrying about this," he said.

She rested her chin on his chest, looking up into his face, illuminated by the spill of ambient light. She could feel the rough softness of his blazer and the smoother texture of his white cotton shirt. His eyes reflected soft gleams in the shadows. "I think we've *both* been thinking too much," she said slowly. "Let's go to bed."

He burst out laughing and hugged her to him with delight. She took him by the hand and led the way, down the length of the darkened room, turning into the small bedroom area.

He sat on the bed, facing her. She stood between his knees, slipping off her white jacket. He reached his hands behind her neck, and in a single, sliding motion undid the zipper of her dress in a long, even glide. The silk fell away, revealing her slender body, with its small, shapely, rounded breasts.

He sucked in his breath with a sharp, distinct sound, and leaned forward, resting his forehead in the shallow between her breasts. She cradled his head in her hands, leaning her cheek on his soft hair. Then he helped her step out of her dress and her scrap of panties and her strappy sandals.

Slowly, deliberately, she reached for his tie and loosened it. He pulled it over his head and tossed it on the floor. It landed next to her crumpled dress. Deliberately, one button at a time, she undid his shirt and ran her hands under it, over his chest and back, feeling the smoothness of his skin and his muscles tense.

Millie leaned forward and kissed the base of his throat, feeling the pulse leaping. Her tongue followed her hands over his chest, licking tiny licks, lighting for a millisecond first on one nipple, then the other. He groaned and fell back on the bed, taking her with him, supporting her so that she landed easily, stretched full-length on his body. His hands ran lightly over her, touching, exploring.

He grasped her buttocks in both his hands and squeezed, hurting her. She squeaked her distress. "Sorry," he whispered, his mouth close to her ear, and found the place on her neck where the pulse throbbed. He kissed it, his lips a soft, demanding pressure.

When he entered her, she was more than ready. "I feel I've come home," he whispered.

He began, with long, slow, lavish strokes, to move. Millie stared at his collarbone, frozen. I feel I've come home. His words echoed in her mind, mocking her.

"What's the matter, Millie," the Prince asked softly. He waited, poised above her, his eyes searching her face. "Shall I stop?"

Millie didn't answer. He started to withdraw, and she clutched at him. "No, don't!"

He thrust once, sharply, shoving his penis all the way inside her, so that it touched the secret, electric place, and her back arched, and she moaned. He clasped her face between his hands, his thumbs bracing her chin, his fingers tangling in her curls, and covered her mouth with his. His tongue, questing and gentling and arousing all at the same time, matched the strokes of his body, and he knew that she was with him again.

She followed him on the striving uphill climb, and, when she heard her own shuddering cries, she was ashamed and tried to suppress them. "No, don't!" he commanded. And then a plea. "Please don't."

And she yielded, joyfully, overcome by a profound, chiming sense of rightness, to the sweeping, primitive, onrushing tide, clinging to him with her hands, her legs and her mouth, till something inside her exploded, shattering into separate, exquisite, piercing convulsions.

"Thank you," he whispered, when she had done, and his smile held something of victory and something of pride. He began the swift, sure strokes that soon brought him, quivering, to pour himself into her. Millie held him, feeling the hard muscles of his hips working under her hands, and, when he climaxed, the involuntary, answering contractions of the muscles of her vagina, draining him, so that he groaned, helplessly, grinding himself into her.

Millie lay next to him, her head resting on his shoulder, treasuring all the dampnesses of her body. She turned on her side and looked at the Prince. His face, in sleep, was defenseless, unguarded, with none of the strict composure she had come, very quickly, to expect. His chest rose and fell in a deep even rhythm, and his eyelashes threw crescent-shaped shadows on his cheekbones. Carefully, fearful of disturbing his sleep, Millie dropped a light, hummingbird kiss on the crest of his cheekbone and felt his sweet, warm breath against her face. She wondered how many people had seen him this way, utterly unprotected. Perhaps not many, she admitted, reluctant to encourage useless flights of fancy. Perhaps it is a greater intimacy than sex, to be able to rest, and know that one is safe.

She reached down and touched his penis, feeling the vulnerable, moist softness. "Mmmmmm," he murmured, and she knew that he had awakened. "What time is it?" James asked lazily.

Millie squinted at the luminous dial of the clock radio. "Two-thirty."

"What do you suppose all those people are doing up so late?" Outside, one or two lights still glowed against the night sky. "Have you ever considered getting binoculars?"

Millie laughed. "I got some when I first moved in here. Everyone does when they first get an apartment like this. Then after a few nights you get bored. I'm hungry," she added. Millie shaded his eyes with her hand, then snapped on the light. He covered his hand with hers for a second or two, then, as his eyes got used to the light, moved her hand down to his mouth and kissed her palm. "I'll be right back," she said, and kissed his mouth. Millie got out of bed and started toward the kitchen.

"Aren't you going to close the curtains?" he asked.

"Sure, if you want. I generally don't bother. I figure that anyone who's that bad off that he wants to peek in at my naked body is welcome, as long as he doesn't get any bright ideas about joining me. And, with all these apartments, it's impossible to figure out which is which."

"That makes sense," James laughed. "It's just that I've had too much experience with telephoto lenses."

Millie drew the drapes and walked, naked, to the small kitchen off the little foyer. "What would you like?" she called.

"Why, I don't know. Anything you've got," he called back.

Millie generally didn't keep goodies in the house, knowing that when she was in the mood she could cut a swath through a Sara Lee cake that left it looking like it was Georgia and she was General Sherman. The freezer yielded up a container of ice cream and the fridge a chilled bowl of lichee nuts.

The night was warm and the coverlet they had thrown aside lay on the floor, crumpled and forgotten. Millie blithely stepped over it and sat cross-legged, tailor-fashion, on the bed, facing the Prince.

James lounged against the headboard, arms clasped behind his neck. Millie looked at him, at his muscular arms, the skin of the underside paler than the rest, at his hair, normally parted and combed with precision, now tousling in waves over his forehead. Why, his hair's curly, she thought in surprise, loving it, loving all of him, down the little tufts of light brown hair in his armpits. She leaned over and buried her face in his underarm, exulting in the tangy, masculine scent of fresh sweat. He dropped his fingers to the nape of her neck, and caressed it.

"The Häagen-Dazs has to wait for a while. It's only good when it's melted," she informed him with a professorial tone and a wicked smile. The Prince accepted this intelligence with equanimity. "So I brought us some lichee nuts while we're waiting."

At least here he was on familiar ground. "They're delicious, aren't they."

Millie hid her smile, enjoying teasing him, and carefully, one hand under the spoon to catch the drips, fed the Prince one of the silky round perfumed fruits. He savored the succulent taste and the satiny texture in his mouth. "That's the sexiest food I know," he laughed. Then his face lit with inspiration. "Lie down, Millie."

"What for?" she asked around a mouthful of lichee nut.

"Just do what I tell you," he said peremptorily.

Millie shrugged, elaborately, and, with the kindly air of one humoring an engaging, if moderately deranged person, did as she was commanded. She lay on her back in the center of the bed.

"No. Not that way. This way." James lifted and turned her so that she lay across the bed, legs dangling over the side.

"Did you suffer from a lack of Play-Doh as a child?" she inquired. The Prince, absorbed in his labors, ignored her. He clasped her ankles and lifted her feet to the bed. "That's right," he murmured, pleased with his arrangements. He knelt on the floor between her legs, then made a minor adjustment to their position. He nodded with satisfaction.

Millie felt a shock of smooth cold in her vagina, then his warm mouth, sucking, and then another long whish of coolness. "What—" she began, and then dissolved in giggles as the Prince lifted his head from between her thighs. His face was bright with gypsy laughter, and he was chewing on a lichee nut.

"That's the most delicious thing in the world," he told her. "You must taste it." He leaned over her, kissing her mouth, transferring a bit of the tender fruit from his mouth to hers.

Millie choked, laughing and swallowing and trying to talk all at the same time. He sat her up and pounded her on the back, none too gently.

"The trick, my dear Millie," he informed her loftily, "is to swallow *before* you speak. And not to laugh at all."

Millie collapsed on the bed, flooded with helpless mirth. "I can't help it," she gasped, when she could catch the breath to speak.

"Are you all better?" he asked solicitously. Millie giggled. "Good," he said briskly. He resumed his kneeling position between her thighs. He leaned his arms negligently on her bent knees and looked into her face with a distinctly pensive air. "I was reared with much devotion," he reflected. "Considerable time and careful attention was paid to my education. Steadfast adherence to those hallowed virtues, which form the bedrock of our society, was instilled in me from my earliest days. *Honor, duty, chivalry*, were words familiar to my ears before I myself could speak."

"What are you talking about, James?" Millie asked politely.

He overrode her. "—Such a person, once having committed himself, heart and mind, to the execution of a task, would never, ever leave it half-finished." With a fluid, practiced motion, he buried his head between her thighs, his mouth clamped unerringly on the tiny apricot fold of tissue.

Millie giggled uncontrollably, swept away by gales of laughter, which soon turned, under his expert, insistent tongue, to cries of a very different sort.

When her juices flowed, he licked at them with the avidity of a child sucking on a forbidden sweet. "That's scrumptious," he said finally, when he lifted his head.

* * *

"That's scrumptious, too," said the Prince, as Millie fed them each alternate bites of superbly melted ice cream.

"Chocolate chocolate-chip. The best," she grinned at him. "What's the thing you like best to eat in the middle of the night?"

"Why, I don't suppose I'm used to eating at all, late at night. Perhaps it's a practice I should institute," he added, reaching for another spoonful.

"Don't you ever get hungry? When you're working late, maybe?"

"I expect it's all a question of what one's been trained to. I haven't been used to expect food, except at mealtimes. I suppose, if I thought of it, I could have something laid on for me, but I never think to ask. I have a small fridge in the bar, but that holds tonic and soda water and things like that."

Millie looked at him with pity. Her modern, eighties, fashionable self knew it was better to be lean and hungry. Her primitive, mothering self felt sorry for someone who considered midnight raids on the fridge a rare treat. "I have to tell you," she said, shaking her head, "it sounds just awful. Like being on location all the time, living at Holiday Inns."

"My flat is really quite comfortable," he defended.

"Nah, you're right." She waved her hand dismissingly. "It's just my Jewish mother's heart thinks that, if you don't have enough food on hand to feed the Yugoslavian army, you're about to die of malnutrition."

"Well, perhaps I would like another life better, but this is the only one I know," he said somberly. "What does it mean to be a Jewish mother?" he asked, after the smallest of pauses.

"What are you asking me, James? Are you asking me what it means to be Jewish?"

"I guess I am. What it means to you."

"It's hard to put in words. It's a school of thought, a way of life. It means knowing what you are, what you belong to. I know that I'm Jewish the way you know . . . what you are. Can you possibly imagine being something else?"

The Prince shook his head slowly. "None of us can imagine that."

"That's how Gerald and I first became friends, by the way. He's Jewish, and he doesn't know the first thing about it. He would come to me with all these questions that no one around him had been able to answer. 'Why do Jews not ride on the Sabbath? Why do they keep kosher?' "

"Why *do* they keep kosher?"

"First of all, it has nothing to do with health or trichinosis or anything like that. That's patent nonsense. The reason for keeping kosher," Millie said, thinking that there are things about every religion that it's hard to explain to an outsider, "is to . . . as a form of separation between the Jew and the other nations. It's a mark of difference. And there's another reason. It says in the Torah that, if a calf is born that is perfectly, one-hundred-percent red-haired, without a single hair of brown or black or white, that cow is not to be used for any normal purpose, but to be set aside and sacrificed to the Lord. So you ask yourself," Millie grinned, "what does God want with a red cow? What does he need it for? What's he gonna do with it? And the answer is, 'Because I said so.' It's a lesson in discipline, and in unquestioning faith."

She scooped out a spoonful of ice cream and fed it to the Prince. "How's that? Jewish philosophy and ice cream all at the same time."

"It's wonderful," James said, swallowing the ice cream.

Millie laughed suddenly.

"What's funny?" asked the Prince carefully.

"I was just thinking, there's an old tradition that, on the day a child first begins to study Torah, his parents would feed him raisins and honey so that the holy words would always be sweet in his mouth."

"That's lovely! Did your parents do that for you?"

"No. No, they didn't. My parents have a tremendous aptitude for squeezing the joy out of everything. They perform every mitzvah, every commandment, very carefully, and they miss the whole meaning behind it."

Millie dug a spoonful of ice cream out of the container and licked it thoughtfully. James watched her and waited, sensing there was more. "It's very important to me," she said after a while. "I don't practice my religion now, but I see that as sort of a hiatus, a recess."

"Will you practice again?"

"Yes. When I have children. I won't be the one to break the chain."

Prince James nodded once, sharply, understanding. "And you will give them sweetness along with their studies . . . You're an awfully good person, you know," he said abruptly. "I like the way you do things."

"You're just bucking for another spoon of ice cream," she laughed and followed her words with action. "This is going to look very good on my thighs. Did you know that my thighs have been declared a disaster area by the Federal Government? That's right," she nodded sagely at him.

"I love your thighs," he laughed and kissed them. "I wonder who the ponce was who first decided that women have to look like adolescent boys. I'd like to find that bloke and have a word or two with him. Do you know that a reporter once wrote that I have big ears?"

"You *do* have sort of big ears. But they're very *pretty* big ears," Millie said, kissing each of the presumptively offending items. "It must be dreadful having your worst faults come out in print. At least if I've got fat thighs, *Time Magazine* hasn't found out about it yet. It must drive you nuts."

"It doesn't anymore. It used to upset me frightfully. I used to sick up when awful things were printed about me. When I was a schoolboy, while I was away at public school, my Form went on an excursion on our yacht. She was a sweet ship . . ."

"The *school* had a yacht?"

"Uh huh." He smiled at her and, taking her hand, toyed with her fingers. "And we ran a Coast Guard station, too." It beats James Madison High School, Millie thought. "Anyway," the Prince continued, "we put into port on the Isle of Lewis." Millie looked at him blankly. "In the Outer Hebrides," he explained. This didn't help a whole lot. Millie wasn't even sure where the Inner Hebrides were. "I went ashore with all my fellows. We were wandering about this small town, on the edge of nowhere, and there were some tourists, who unfortunately recognized me. I'll be damned if I know how. We all looked so alike in those uniforms. My detective had gone off somewhere, thinking it was all quite safe, and these people were sort of . . . after me. And I'm afraid I . . . panicked. I ducked into the first door I saw and turned and found myself in a bar."

"How old were you?"

"About fourteen. Well, if you're in a bar, you must needs order something to drink." Millie nodded. "So I ordered the only thing I could think of. A cherry brandy. Which I had often seen the grownups drinking before a day's hunting, when the weather was raw. I'd tasted it once or twice, and it was the best I could come up with on the spur of the moment."

"What happened?" Millie knew from his face that this youthful misdemeanor had not gone unnoticed.

"This god-damned bastard!—" He looked his apology at her. "This journalist walked in and saw me, sipping away at this bleeding cherry brandy. It was all over the newspapers. PRINCE JAMES IN CHERRY BRANDY AFFAIR. To this day, I can't abide the stuff," he finished glumly.

Millie laughed. He smiled at her. "At the time, I didn't think it was funny. The Palace issued a denial and then retracted when I confessed. I told them it was true. I *had* been nipping at the hard stuff. At the time, when the story broke, I thought it was the end of the world. I was all ready to pack my bags for Siberia or somewhere."

"How did your parents take it? Were they mad?"

"No. They're all right about things like that. My father thought it was funny. For months after that, whenever I was home he would ask me if I fancied a spot of cherry brandy."

Millie laughed. "He sounds wonderful."

"He's an alright chap. Once, when I was really small, about six or seven, I would say . . ." James shoved two pillows behind his back and leaned against them, his face alight with amusement at the memory. "I made this whole pile of snowballs. Can't remember where it was—Sandringham, maybe—and, having made them, I needed to pitch them."

"Naturally," Millie smiled.

"Well, there was this absolutely heaven-sent target. The sentry standing at attention outside. No, it couldn't have been Sandringham, must have been somewhere else. No guards at Sandringham . . . Anyway, there I was, having a right gay old time pitching snowballs at this poor bastard. I only hit him about ten percent of the time," he recalled. "And Father walked out and spotted what was going on."

"What did he do?"

"He burst out laughing and shouted at the guard, 'Don't just stand there like an imbecile, man, throw some back at him!'"

"That's lovely." Millie looked down into the rapidly emptying container of ice cream and licked at the spoon, thoughtfully. "You've got a really nice family. You're lucky. I was thinking that, when you mentioned your aunt, just before you had your little tantrum." She looked at James severely.

"Yes, well," he said, abashed. "I don't ordinarily behave that way. I'm very careful not to, as a matter of fact, but—" He broke off and looked at her, reaching over to brush a lock of her dark hair back from her forehead. "You've got such pretty hair, you know that? It looks almost black but it isn't. It's a very, very dark brown. In this light it has red glints in it.

"I'm dead scared that people . . . that the press will find out about you," he continued after a pause. "If they do— Well, they shan't. I'm bound that they won't. Not until— What have you got on for tomorrow," he asked, abruptly changing the subject.

"I have a seven o'clock call out at the pier. Bob Jones, whom you know and love, is directing. That should be fun."

"Nasty piece of work, that one. I wasn't enthralled when he screamed at you, but I'd had my eye on him before that. I saw him browbeating one of those trainees— 'P.A.'s,' you call them?"

Millie nodded. "Production assistants."

"He was really tearing into this fellow for something. I never did hear exactly what. It sounded bloody trivial if you ask me. And, of course, this chap just stood there and took it. There wasn't much else he could do. I thought of intervening. Then I realized that there are other Bob Joneses about, and that kid will run across them, and he's got to learn to stand up to them sometime. It really burns my arse, though."

"I know. He's a creep. Let's forget about him." She put down the ice cream and stretched out next to James.

"Right. Let's talk about tomorrow evening, instead. I've been thinking about it. I won't be free until quite late. Would . . . would you be willing to meet me, after, at my hotel?" James looked distressed. "I don't want you to feel that I . . . I know it's an imposition, but you see, I'm determined to see you every day."

Millie covered his mouth with her fingers. "Sssshhhh. Don't worry. I'm used to people working till all hours. And I'm not booked Friday, so there's no problem."

"Good," James said briskly, relieved. "That's all right then."

Millie turned on her side, facing away from him. What she had said was true. There was no reason why she shouldn't give the Prince the same leeway she gave her other friends, and had given previous lovers. All production people knew that appointments and dates were always contingent upon work being completed as scheduled. There was no way you walked off a set that was still shooting, explaining that you had a dinner date. That didn't bother her.

What did was the echo of his voice. "I'm determined to see you every day"—for as long as I'm here—he had been too polite to add.

James turned so that his body cupped hers, spoon fashion. "What would you like to do this weekend?" he asked, hitting the word "weekend" on the second syllable, in the British manner. "What would you like most to do?"

"Get out of the city," Millie returned promptly.

"Where does one go to get out of the city?"

"The Hamptons, Fire Island, Connecticut, lots of places." She sensed him taking mental notes. Without changing their positions, he reached across her and switched off the lamp on the end table. He groped around on the floor, found the coverlet, and drew it over them.

"Good night, love, let's get some sleep," he said, tucking the sheet under her pillow, cradling her body in his.

Millie giggled. "What's funny?" he asked.

"The alarm's set for five-thirty."

He rubbed his face against her hair. "Want to hear something funnier?"

"What?"

"I've never spent the entire night in someone's—in a woman's flat before."

Millie thought about that one for a few moments. "Then how do you . . ."

He hesitated, and Millie thought he was a little sorry he had brought the whole thing up. "I, and the person in question, usually form one of a large house party at my friends' homes, or at a resort like Gstaad or St. Moritz."

"But that's just weekends and vacations."

"Yes. In London, I just go home. It's too complicated otherwise. To leave late at night is one thing, but to leave the next morning is another. There's always the chance that I might be recognized." His bright laughter rang out. "I got into trouble once when my *car* was parked outside a friend's house all night, and it wasn't even me. I hadn't driven it that night."

"I don't think that's funny at all," Millie said softly.

* * *

"Bore da," said the Prince, lazily stretching his arms over his head.

"What's that?"

"That, my darling, is 'good morning' in Welsh." He leaned over and kissed her.

"Oh." She smiled up at him. *"Boker Tov."*

"What's that?"

"That, my darling, is 'good morning' in Hebrew."

James laughed, delighted. "Just for that," he kissed the tip of her nose, "you can have the first shower."

"Not a chance, Your Royal Highness. *You* take the first shower, and *I* get ten minutes more sleep."

"Right you are."

Millie rolled out of bed and walked two steps to the tiny linen closet. "Here. And here." She handed him a large bath towel and a washcloth. "And here." A plastic disposable razor.

He looked at the razor dubiously. "This'll kill me," he said cheerfully.

"Let the water run, and it'll get hot," she instructed, making a dive for the bed.

"Never touch the stuff."

Millie looked at him, feigning shock. "You're going to take a *cold* shower?!"

"I used to run three miles and *then* take a cold shower. *Before* breakfast. I'm made of tough stuff, I am, I am."

"Sick," she moaned and burrowed back under the pillows.

He came out of the bathroom barefoot, clad only in his trousers. Millie stood in the foyer, naked, a freshly folded *New York Times* in hand. "There's a guy outside. Loitering. It's not MacCrae," she told him.

"Of course not!" the Prince responded, buttoning his pants. "Do you think I work my people day and night? What do you think I am? It's whomever MacCrae got to replace him. Let's have a look." He opened the door a crack and peeked out. Millie stood behind him, craning her neck to peer over his shoulder. "Where?" he whispered theatrically. "I don't see the little bugger."

"There. Across the hall," she whispered back. "Behind the door." The top half of the door leading to the largely unused staircase was made of glass lined with hexagons of wire. The form of a man could indeed be glimpsed, standing a foot or two back from the door.

"Nevins," said the Prince, satisfied. "Go have your shower."

Millie kissed his bare back between the shoulder blades and turned away. She glanced down at the paper in her hand. "Oh, my God! Look." She handed the paper to James.

"What is it? My bloody face again?" he complained. "Can't we have someone else for a change?" He looked at the paper she handed him.

On the bottom of the page, below the fold, was a four-column shot of the Prince and Denise. Denise was in the act of raising the slice of cake towards his mouth. Her body was turned towards the Prince, but her triumphant smile was entirely for the camera. He, too, was smiling, and there was something intimate about the photograph. Pictures do indeed lie.

The caption said: "PRINCE JAMES CLEARLY LOVES NEW YORK," a reference to the ongoing "I Love New York" ad campaign. "That's super!" James said, eyeing the photograph. "I hope they all go after Denise. Go shower!" He looked at her sternly. "I don't want to have to speak with you about this again," he said, in the tone of a schoolmaster admonishing a laggard pupil.

"I'm going, I'm going," she laughed. And went.

When she came out, dressed in jeans and a T-shirt, she smelled the savory odors of something good frying. She heard the Prince singing, "For it's good old reliable Nathan, Nathan, Nathan, Nathan Detroit. It's the oldest established permanent floating crap game in New York!" He had caught not only the American accent, but the flamboyant New Yorkese of Damon Runyan. Laughing, Millie went to investigate.

James looked up from the stove when she entered the kitchen. "Smoked salmon—I mean lox—and eggs. My favorite," he said happily.

"What do you drink in the morning?" she asked, kissing him. "Tea?"

"No, milk."

Millie offered up a short prayer. Milk, as far as she was concerned, was a condiment for coffee, not a beverage, and she often ran out. She was in luck—an almost full container. She looked at James, carefully scrambling the eggs. "You're going to make someone an absolutely marvelous wife," she teased.

He turned to her, his face serious. "As will you," he said, his eyes holding hers.

Millie stood still, the container of milk forgotten in her hand. She had suddenly remembered who the half-naked man standing in her kitchen was.

He saw the frozen look on her face and turned off the gas under the skillet. He crossed to her and pulled her against him, gripping her elbows in his hands. "Hey." He shook her gently. "Don't do that. Please? It's just me, remember?"

"I remember."

"Excellent. See that you don't forget it," he warned, turning back to the stove. "Now get out of here and make yourself useful. Go set the table or something."

"Yes, sir." Millie saluted.

"That's right," he approved. "A little respect is always in order."

"How are you getting to work?" he asked, as they collected the breakfast dishes and carried them into the kitchen.

"Just stack them. Let's not bother washing them," Millie said.

"Nonsense. It'll take two minutes. Besides," he looked at her mischievously. "You don't know when you'll be coming back. You don't want the washing up staring you in the face. So? How are you? Getting to work, I mean."

"Subway, I guess. What time is it?"

He looked at his watch, careful not to drip soapsuds on it. "Six-forty."

"Cab," she amended, staccato.

"We'll drop you."

"Don't be silly. It's all the way to hell and gone. Down by the docks."

"All the more reason."

Millie marveled that he, for whom all the small difficulties of life simply did not exist, was so aware of them and how they impinged on others.

"Whenever you're done working, just nip over to the Sherry-Netherland. Shall I send a car to collect you?"

"No. Don't do that!" She had visions of a uniformed chauffeur waiting for her on the set.

"All right. When you get to the hotel, ask for Jimmy Chester." He grinned at her. "Well, I'm Jimmy, and I'm the Earl of Chester, aren't I? I don't think it's working, though," he confided, in the tone of one sharing a heretofore undisclosed secret. "I think . . . I'm pretty sure they've penetrated my cover. I've been blown, as they say in all the best spy movies. P'raps you'd better ask for Suite 2200 instead."

The detecitve joined them as they stepped out into the corridor. "Good morning, Your Royal Highness," he said, bowing slightly. "Good morning," he added to Millie. Unlike MacCrae, this one looked her over, avidly, curiously. Perhaps for that reason, James did not introduce them.

"Good morning, Nevins," he said evenly. "Oh, ta!" he added, as Nevins handed him his tweed cap. He jammed it on his head and winked at Millie.

The world glittered, skittered and gleamed with that fresh, early-morning sparkle that comes after a night with no sleep. Millie sat next to the Prince in the back seat of the Buick, looking out at the streets whizzing by, feeling the adrenalin buzz in her veins. "I feel as if I'll never need to sleep again," she said exultantly.

He grinned at her. "Where in God's name are we?" he asked, looking out at the warehouses and industrial blocks, their harsh contours softened by the early morning sun.

"It's called Chelsea."

"How original of them."

The car turned into the dead-end street leading toward the pier. "See you later, ducks," James said, giving her a parting hug. He slunk down on the seat and covered his face with his cap, whether to conceal his identity or to take a short nap, Millie couldn't tell.

She watched the car make a swift U-turn and head back uptown. Then she stepped from the concrete of the sidewalk onto the wooden slats of the pier.

The sun sparkled off the water, and Millie drew a deep breath, trying to damp down the exhilaration that sang through her. She forced herself to assume a businesslike air and joined the group gathered around the folding table, where chrome urns of coffee and the traditional complementary breakfast had been set up. Unexpectedly, instead of greasy crullers and drippy donuts, Millie saw a tempting array of fresh fruit, oranges, bananas, melons, even small baskets of strawberries; cheeses, Jarlsburg, Meunster and cream; crisp fresh pumpernickle, rye and wheat breads.

She looked up in surprise and met the twinkling eyes of Phil Tovman. "I should have known," she laughed.

The tall producer smiled down at her. He wore a plaid cotton shirt, jeans, boots, and a Texas-sized cowboy hat. The effect, however, was expensive rather than trendy. He had dressed that way before the advent of the urban cowboy and would continue to do so, if it pleased him, after its demise.

"What's the shoot?" Millie asked, balancing her large book on the railing.

"Here." Tovman handed her a storyboard. Millie scanned the xeroxed sheets of paper that outlined, cartoon fashion, the action for the shoot. Two men would walk the length of the pier, earnestly discussing the virtues of the new potato chip they were munching. It, in an absolutely mind-boggling advance, was neither flat nor ridged, but wavy.

While they walked, they would be so engrossed in this revolutionary potato chip that they would fail to notice a bright-red race car pass behind them at ninety miles an hour and dive right off the end of the pier. They would continue their discussion, oblivious, while the car was lifted out of the drink. Camera would pan to the driver, who, giving the traditional thumbs-up signal, would remark, "Yes, but could I have a Wavie."

"Brilliant," Millie muttered, as she transferred information to her book.

Tovman smiled. "It pays the rent, Millie. It pays the rent."

The entire day, Millie noted, would be devoted to shooting footage that would comprise the background of the eventual screen image. Since expensive race cars that can only take one dive off a pier are at a premium and all it needed to blow the shot was for one of the actors to stumble or fluff a line or drop the bag of potato chips, the foreground action, with the actors' dialogue, would be shot against a blank backdrop in the studio. When the two images were joined, the foreground and background would merge seamlessly, giving the impression that they had been shot simultaneously on the pier.

"Five cameras! I wonder how long it'll take Jones to set it up," Millie commented.

"An eternity," Tovman laughed. "I'll send him out to pick the particular bag of Wavies he feels is the most photogenic, and Harry and I"—he referred to the cameraman—"will set it up. By the time he gets back, it'll be all done, and he'll think he did it."

"Why'd you hire him?" Millie hazarded.

"Why'd I hire him?" Phil looked at her, aghast. "Millie, you wound me! Give me *some* credit! The agency has the hots for him. Don't ask me why. Just for that, Millie, I'm going to leave you."

She followed his glance and saw what had attracted his attention, a group of stagehands standing in a knot, looking down at a tangle of equipment, shaking their heads in consternation. Phil's long legs carried him swiftly over to them, and in a moment they dispersed, each with an assigned task.

The day passed slowly. Millie immersed herself purposefully in her work, ignoring the little jolts of excitement that leapt up in her when, occasionally, the word "James" would flash in her brain.

She took a sandwich and an apple from the lunch table and wandered off by herself to the end of the pier. She felt uncharacteristically reluctant to join in the friendly conversations and teasing banter, yet she was too unquiet to simply relax and enjoy the sun. So she checked her timings and double-checked her notes. Since there was no dialogue, she was hard put to stretch the task out to a full hour, but she did her best. Thoughts of James, if she were to allow them, would overwhelm her and destroy her concentration.

Just after four in the afternoon, they were ready to make the big shot, the bright-red race car driving at high speed off the pier. Phil, Harry the cameraman and the stuntman stood to one side in a huddle. Millie joined them, since she, too, would have to know how the shot would work.

They were computing the rate of undercranking, a technique that films the action at a slower speed in real life, and makes it appear faster on the screen, thus allowing a greater margin of safety for the stunt driver, since it is clearly more desirable to hit the water at forty miles an hour, rather than eighty or a hundred-twenty.

Millie glanced at the stuntman, Stan—swarthy, medium-build, muscular. It never ceased to amaze her that they approached these acts of derring-do with all the apparent apprehension she felt when confronting a grilled cheese sandwich. She had seen stuntmen fall off roofs, horses, vehicles of every description, burning buildings, planes and boats; and only the elation they unfailingly displayed at the end of the stunt betrayed any misgivings they may have had.

Still, there was a heightened degree of tension on a set just before a difficult stunt. Stuntmen and women have, despite precautions, been maimed and even killed. She knew that Tovman would not allow any undue risks, even if the stuntman were willing.

Bob Jones wandered up to them and caught the drift of the highly technical conversation. "I don't want to undercrank," he complained.

"I want reality." The stuntman shot him a quick, contemptuous glance, and turned his back. Phil and Harry, the portly cameraman, exchanged glances. "Go check the angles," Phil suggested. "It's all set up, waiting for your approval." Bob wandered off and peered through each of the five viewfinders, a happy man.

The cameras had been set up, two on each side of the pier and one to catch the action from the rear. Millie took up her post between the two cameras on the right side of the pier. The assistant director's voice came over the loud-hailer. "Everybody pick a spot and STAY THERE! DO NOT MOVE! Until you hear 'cut.'

"When Stan reaches this point," he walked to a place about twenty feet in from the end of the pier, "we are committed to the shot. He will not be able to brake, and the car goes into the water, whether we get the shot or not." Millie listened to his familiar spiel, while she worked on her book. "So PLEASE," the A.D.'s voice half-pleaded, half-threatened, "from this moment on, NOBODY MOVES!"

Millie exchanged smiles and winks with the grip who stood between her and the camera operator, who was fine-tuning his camera's focus. "No matter what happens," the A.D. went on, "even if you think Stan is in trouble, DON'T HELP HIM!"

"Stan's beyond help!" someone yelled. The A.D. ignored the laughter from the crew and continued his warnings. Millie looked all the way down to the beginning of the pier, where the sleek race car was being wheeled into position. Stan, goggled and silver-suited, was in the driver's seat. Prop men sprayed the crimson body and shiny chrome with special chemicals that deepen the color and bring out the shine, which is why one's own car never looks quite as glossy as the ones in television commercials.

"Okay, here we go," the A.D. said distinctly into the loud-hailer. "Roll 'em. Very, very quiet now everybody. Aaaaaannnd . . ." Nothing. He looked across at Bob Jones, who took up a position next to Millie. In the formalized, hierarchical world of film production, the next word should have come from the director.

After a beat, Jones was recalled to his task. "Action!" he said. Millie clicked her stop watch on the word. There was a brief pause while the car's motor revved up. Then it started down the pier.

Stopwatch in hand, eyes riveted to the action, waiting for the 'cut,' Millie sensed Jones, on her left, shuffling about. He took two steps to *his* left, away from her and, in doing so, bumped into a hi-boy. The tall metal stanchion held a large, framed, silk square about five feet above their heads to diffuse the light that hit the subject.

The whole thing started to fall, its trajectory taking it in *front* of the camera on Millie's right. She had a glimpse of the grip standing next to the camera, mouth open in bemusement, watching it fall.

Millie turned, reflexively, dropping her book and her watch. She caught and held the metal rod, keeping both it and the silk square *above* the camera's lens. Just as she did, she turned her head and saw Jones trip over a cable and fall, passing in front of the camera to her left.

She was dimly aware of a shiny red blur and then the mighty splash and the A.D.'s yell, "CUT!"

"Someone pushed me!" Bob Jones screeched to no one in particular over the clatter of the crane, moving rapidly into position, seeking and finding the hidden harness on the car.

Stan's face appeared, grinning from ear to ear, over the edge of the pier, then his torso, sopping wet, as he was helped up by grasping hands.

"She made me fall!" Jones screamed. Millie realized she was still clutching the stanchion. Someone took it out of her hands.

Phil Tovman strode the length of the pier, his face grim. All eyes, overtly or covertly, were locked on him. He shook hands with Stan, who was wrapped in a blanket, toweling his hair. "Nice work," Tovman congratulated.

He turned and walked over to Jones, who opened his mouth and drew in a breath. Tovman spoke first. "Do I have to tell you you're fired? You're fired."

"I'll tell the Director's Guild," Jones sputtered.

"You *do* that," Tovman encouraged. "Tell them to give me a call." He turned to Millie. "I saw what happened. Thank you."

Tovman strode off, into a huddle with the agency people. "Fifteen minutes," the A.D. yelled over the loud-hailer.

The double excitement of the successful stunt and the extra added attraction of a director's on-set firing, occupied everyone's

conversation. Several people came over to congratulate Millie, telling
her they had seen the whole thing, admiring her quick thinking.
Nobody seems to have been watching the action, she thought to
herself, amused. She dug a Tab out of the ice-filled metal tub and
turned to see Phil coming to her.

"Let's talk," he said, taking her elbow. He drew her to one side.
"Look, here's the situation. We have a couple of pickup shots to do,
nothing fancy. I'll be goddamned if I let Jones get the credit for this
job. I'm not allowed to do it, and neither is the A.D." Millie knew
that the Director's Guild did not allow any member to replace another
on a given job. "So I want to put you down as director of record,"
Tovman said. Millie looked up at him, surprised. "I'll really finish up
the day, but you'll get the credit."

"What about the cameraman?"

"Don't push your luck." Tovman smiled at her. "Harry doesn't
need this. You've been wanting to direct for a long time, haven't
you?" Millie nodded, wordlessly. "Look, I've got a quick-and-dirty
shoot coming up week after next. It's all yours."

"You mean . . . to direct?" she asked idiotically.

Tovman grinned at her, understanding. "Only if you're interested, of course," he said, his eyes twinkling.

Millie restrained herself from throwing her arms around his neck.
She knew that curious eyes were watching them. "What about the
agency?" she asked, knowing that they had to approve and did not
look with favor on first-time directors.

Tovman threw his head back and laughed. "It's the same agency
as this one. They picked one director, and I think they'll let me
choose the next. How about it?"

"Thanks," she said simply.

"*De nada,*" he answered, tipping his cowboy hat. "I owe you
one."

Millie's mind was on fire all the way home. She glanced through
the file folder Phil had given her, but was too excited to absorb its
contents. She turned instead to the *New York Post*, which featured on
its widely touted gossip page essentially the same photo as the *Times*,
taken from a slightly different angle: Denise about to feed the Prince

a slice of cake. The caption, however, was far less restrained. In large letters it read: "JAMES IN LOVE? AMERICAN GIRL TAKES THE CAKE FOR PRINCE."

Millie quickly skimmed the article. Denise had been quoted as saying, with pleasing dignity, that she couldn't possibly reveal what the Prince had said to her privately. "If I did, he might never confide in me anymore." Millie cracked up and ripped it out to show James.

She showered quickly and packed an overnight bag with cosmetics and a change of clothing. Then the impropriety of arriving at the Prince's hotel with anything resembling a suitcase struck her. She dumped the whole thing out on the bed and repacked it in a tote bag.

Millie looked out at the soft spring twilight as the cab meandered through the winding Seventy-second Street drive to the East Side. The technical production term for this hour was uncharacteristically tender in an industry that favored harsh acronyms and flippant slang. It was called "the Magic Hour." And so it was. The lights of the city, suspended against the darkling sky, glowed with that special brilliance reserved for the fleeting interval on the cusp between daylight and darkness.

Millie thought over the events of the past few days, running them through her mind like film through a movieola. The word "director" loomed in front of her, it's aura challenging, and a bit frightening. She tested the word "James," throwing it up on the screen. There was no sense of strangeness, of the newness that haloed the word "director." James seemed like an integral part of her, as if the final, maddening piece of the puzzle had been found, and she was stunningly, elegantly, and for all time, whole.

The clerk behind the front desk ignored Millie in favor of two business-suited gentlemen, who appeared more prepossessing than the slender, gamin-faced Millie. When she asked for Suite 2200, however, he snapped to alert attention and respectfully inquired as to her name.

"Miss Millie Myerson is here," he said unctuously into the house phone. "Yes, sir. Right away." He nodded to Millie and snapped his fingers for a bellman. "Please conduct Miss Myerson to Suite 2200," he said importantly.

Ian MacCrae opened the door. He nodded dismissingly at the bellman and greeted Millie warmly. "Nice to see you again, miss, I'm sure."

Millie found herself in a large, formal salon, with dark antique furnishings and several roccoco sofas. It was a kind of decor Millie hated, finding it at once uncomfortable and visually displeasing. Two large journeyman office desks had been moved in, and the spindly chairs behind them looked awkward and out of place.

She heard James's voice coming from one of the several rooms that opened off the main salon. "I keep hearing what a splendid idea this is. None of you can tell me why it hasn't been done yet." His voice was firm, cool, without heat.

"The Prince is in conference," MacCrae said. "He asked that you wait for him in here." He ushered her into a smaller room to her left. Millie thought it looked a lot more comfortable, with its two solid, white Haitian-cotton-covered sofas placed at right angles to each other. Bright pillows were strewn about, lending a touch of color, and the far wall was entirely glass, leading to a wide wraparound terrace. She dumped her stuff on one of the sofas, determined not to be influenced by the reverent hush she sensed in these formal apartments. "Thanks." She smiled at MacCrae.

"I'll inform the Prince that you've arrived, miss," he said, and left.

Millie stepped out on the terrace, glorying in the sight before her, one of the truly spectacular vistas on the face of the earth. The terrace faced East and South, and the entire city lay before her, a magic carpet of lights, purple shadows and brilliant sunset sky. The bridges, outlined with fairy lights, twinkled in the distance.

She turned to see MacCrae stepping out onto the terrace. "I could look at this forever," she said to him.

"It's very beautiful," he said simply. He omitted to add his habitual 'miss,' and Millie was pleased. Some things transcend convention and allow human beings to talk to each other as equals.

He handed her a folded note, just two words, "Hello, darling," and an exuberant exclamation point. Its firm, slanting scrawl brought James into the room with her, and it seemed an eon since she had seen him.

Millie realized she'd been looking down at the note, an imbecilic smile on her face, for several moments. She glanced at MacCrae. He was watching her, a small, answering smile on his face. Then he, too, collected himself. "If you would like a something to drink, miss, there's a bar inside, all set up." With a slight bow, he left her alone.

Millie went back inside and fished out the file folder Tovman had given her. She walked back out onto the terrace, reading, and dropped into one of the wrought-iron chairs, heedless now of the glorious panorama. She smiled to herself as she read realizing that Tovman's gesture had not been in any way quixotic. The spot was almost ridiculously easy.

In each of three separate sequences, a man, a woman and a child would be showering when, to his or her utter amazement and delight, the soap would speak, extolling its own virtues. The "soap's" dialogue would be prerecorded and would be the same for all three sequences. All the talent had to do was shower and react. There was no synch sound. The angles would be simple, and the spot would be shot on location in someone's bathroom, rented for the day.

Peter Goldsworth entered the sitting room. Through the open doors Millie caught a snatch of James's conversation. ". . . can convince you to build the factory in Wales, gentlemen, I can assure you that—" His voice was cut off as Goldsworth closed the door carefully. "Good evening, Miss Myerson."

"Millie! Remember? Please don't go all formal on me now," she pleaded.

The equerry's somber countenance warmed. "Millie," he agreed. "The Prince wishes me to convey his compliments—" She was sure James had never said that. "—and to tell you that he will be free within the hour. He wishes to inquire if you would like something to eat now, or would rather wait and dine with him. He begs to be forgiven if he sounds like . . . er . . ." The intrepid Goldsworth faltered. ". . . a Jewish mother."

Millie repressed the giggle that bubbled up inside her. "I'll wait," she said. "Thank you." The sandwich at lunch seemed a long way away, but, given her choices, there was no contest.

"And there's a telephone call for you," he added. "Shall I bring the phone out here?" Millie nodded, and he disappeared, to return in an instant with a phone, which he placed, carefully, in the dead center of the round, glass-topped table. With a nod, he turned back inside. In an unconscious commentary on Goldsworth's stiff correctness, Millie pulled over a chair and stretched her feet out on it. She picked up the phone, gingerly, knowing that no one in the world knew where she was at the moment. "Hello?" she said carefully.

"Hiya, light-of-my-life," Gerald said airily.

"How did you know I was here?" she asked without preamble.

"Piece of cake, cupcake. Listen, I gotta job for you. Next Friday."

"Next Friday?" she repeated slowly.

"One week from tomorrow," he explained patiently. "You see they got this rotation system. They didn't have enough names to go round, so each day could have it's own little—"

Millie cut him off. "I think I'll pass."

"You booked, or what?"

"No, I'm not booked, but . . . I think I'll pass." The voluble Gerald fell silent. "Hey!" she yelled. "You don't know what else happened to me. I'm a director!" Millie shouted over the rooftops of New York City. She filled him in, rapidly, stumbling over her words in excitement. "You're the first to know! I haven't told anybody else yet," she finished.

"Not even Princie?"

"I haven't had a chance," she admitted. "I haven't seen him yet."

"Oh. That's not why you're turning down script work, is it, shit-for-brains? I mean this is a break, but it could be a long way till your next one."

"No. That's not why."

"Oh," he said again. "Listen, you gonna be around this weekend, or what?"

"No. I'm going away. With James," she added needlessly.

"Might one inquire where?" Gerald asked with elaborate politeness. Millie, distracted, didn't reply. Through the glass doors, she saw the Prince, followed by four or five dark-suited men, enter the sitting room. His eyes, searching, found her and lighted.

"I don't *know* where," she replied, smiling at the Prince, striding swiftly toward her.

"Terrific," Gerald said sourly. "You're going away with a guy who you don't even know for a week, and you don't know where."

Millie arched her back, luxuriating, as the Prince kissed the nape of her neck. "Listen, Gerald, I've got to go."

"Is that Gerald? Ask him if he wants to come along. And Pretty Lucy as well."

"I heard that," Gerald said in her ear. "Yeah, I'll come. Somebody has to keep an eye on you."

"Marine Air Terminal. Four o'clock," the Prince instructed. "And bring sailing clothes."

Millie swiveled in her seat, turning to the Prince in surprise. "Marine Air Terminal! Are we flying somewhere? Where are we going?"

James grinned at her. He clasped his arms in front of his chest and winked at her, underscoring his nonreply.

"That's for small planes," Gerald said. "Can't be too far. Probably the Hamptons or Montauk or something. Okay, toots, I'll catch you later."

Millie hung up and rising, slid into the Prince's arms. "How are you my love?" he whispered, hugging her to him.

"Better, *now*," she laughed up at him and watched his face glow in response.

"I've done with meetings, but I've got lots and lots of paperwork to do. Let's . . . er . . . lose all these people, as Lucy says, and have some dinner first. How does that suit you?"

"Sounds good to me" she replied breezily.

"That'll do for today, Gentlemen," the Prince said, leading her by the hand into the room. "Take the rest of the evening off—and do put it to good use, won't you? You too, MacCrae. I shan't be going out again, tonight." He pronounced "again" so that it rhymed with "swain."

MacCrae looked at him stolidly. "I'll be on call in case I'm required, sir," he said, knowing whom he had in charge.

"I shall be as well," Goldsworth said.

"Nonsense!" The Prince retorted to his equerry. "Why don't you ring up that nice Lucy Rogers and see what she's doing for dinner? I think she liked you. Hmmm? Why don't you?"

Goldsworth flushed purple. "Why, thank you, sir. I think . . . I don't . . ." he stammered.

"Why don't you just tell me to get stuffed, I wonder?" James inquired genially. "Well, suit yourself. Just organize us some dinner before you go. I'll see you all in the morning."

Each of the men bobbed his head and said, "Good evening, Your Royal Highness," and they were gone.

"You *are* a Jewish mother," Millie teased. "No doubt about it." The Prince looked at her blankly. "Matchmaking," she explained.

"Oh," he laughed. "I step over the line with him sometimes, and I shouldn't. He's very good at his job. But I'll tell you what . . ." James kissed her, very thoroughly. "Let's forget about Goldsworth."

Over dinner, James listened intently, while Millie excitedly told him what had happened that day. "What does this mean, exactly," he asked, when she finished.

"It means—it's a whole new world. It means I have the beginning of my sample reel, that I can show around. All thirty seconds of it," she laughed. "All it takes is the first job. Then you become a member of the Directors Guild, and you can go out and hustle work. Directing isn't one of those things you can do by yourself. Not like painting or sculpting or music. It's more like . . . conducting an orchestra. Someone has to hand you the baton. Who knows?" she said, her eyes sparkling. "Maybe in a year or two I can get to direct a feature. God knows, I don't want to do commercials the rest of my life." She burst out laughing. "I haven't even done my first spot yet, and here I am thinking about a feature film!"

"That's the way!" James enthused. "See! I've brought you luck." He jumped up from his chair and rushed around the table to Millie, his steak forgotten. He knelt by her chair, hugging her. "I'm most awfully proud of you," he said ardently.

"This Tovman sounds like a gent who knows what he's about," James continued, more conversationally, resuming his seat. "He wouldn't have done this if he weren't dead certain you could handle it. You've *earned* it, Millie. It's lucky, but it isn't, really."

Millie smiled at him, pleased by his wholehearted response. It had never crossed her mind that James might be the type of man who is threatened by a woman's career. Then she remembered his mother's job, and realized why not.

Peter Goldsworth entered, hesitantly, just as they were finishing dinner. He stood in the doorway, holding three large red-leather cases. "The boxes, sir," he said, clearing his throat.

"Yes. Quite ready," James answered cheerfully. The waiter, who had evidently been hovering outside, quickly cleared the table and rolled the serving cart out of the room.

The two men waited until the door closed behind him. Goldsworth set the cases down on the table, while James dug into his trouser pocket, coming up with a tiny gold key. Goldsworth glanced over at Millie. James grinned at him. "She's all right. You won't peek, will you, Millie?"

Millie walked over to the couch and ostentatiously picked up a newspaper. James opened the top case and riffled through it. Absentmindedly, he hooked a chair with his foot, drew it to him and sat down, lifting papers out one by one. He scanned them quickly, gold pen in hand. When he finished reading one, he scrawled a rapid initial on the bottom and placed it, blank side up, on a rapidly growing pile.

Millie remembered that the British monarch received, once each day, dispatches of secret papers—cables, documents, and the like, the inner workings of the government, for Her Majesty's eyes only. She recalled reading that Prince James had, some time ago, become the only other person who saw the contents of the boxes, in preparation for the day when they would once again be seen by one person's eyes only.

They sat in companionable silence. Once the Prince muttered under his breath, "What on earth can they mean by this?" Peter Goldsworth, sitting across from him, hands clasped on a pile of file folders in front of him, waited patiently.

"What's a four-letter word for 'diluted spirits'?" Millie wondered, half-aloud.

"Grog," the Prince replied, without looking up. "The Queen does those. Right fanatic she is about them, too."

An hour and a half later James locked the third box and replaced the key in his pocket. "That's done. Let's have the news, shall we?"

Goldsworth switched on the large color television set. "Next up," the announcer said, "more on Prince James's visit to New York City." The screen was filled with shots of James, visiting the World Trade Center, the Statue of Liberty, Fraunces Tavern, and finally, a children's hospital.

Through it all, the Prince wore what Millie had come to think of as his "stage face." He was graceful, affable and controlled, combining friendliness with distance in a neatly judged measure. He seemed like a different person from the one who sat across from her, shirtcuffs negligently turned back, one foot jiggling on the other knee.

The piece ended with a clip from the Magna Carta program, with many jocular expressions of regret that the entire program would be seen "on another network." "Let's get a copy of that and send it back home. Show them I'm working," James quipped. "Now then, Peter, what's next?"

Millie stepped out on the terrace, the low-voiced murmur of the two men's conversation a backdrop to the vista before her. "Robert Stokes has just completed his first year at Oxford," Peter Goldsworth was saying. "He was the 1977 recipient of the Prince of Wales Trust Scholarship," he added pedantically.

"Jolly good!" the Prince approved. "Let's write him a letter." Then, after a beat. "How'd he do? Better than me?" Millie heard his light laugh. "Oh, well, I had the investiture to worry about that year."

Millie walked back in and stood behind James, gently rubbing his neck and shoulders. He leaned back against her. "That's wonderful," he said. Then, "Here, have a look at this." He held up a sheet of paper so Millie could read it.

Jam (Gooseberry): two jars
Walnuts: one pound
Biscuits: two packets
Wine (port): one bottle
Cheese (Stilton): one round
Dried fruits (mixed): one sack
Tea (Earl Grey): one-pound tin

Millie ran her eyes rapidly down the list. "What is it?"

"It's the Christmas box that will be given out to certain residents of the Duchy of Cornwall, retired people, pensioners, grace-and-favour recipients, people of small means who've been of service to the country."

"Why don't you give them a subscription to a magazine or a newspaper as well?" Millie asked. "I remember when I was dirt broke that was something that really killed me." Two pairs of eyes stared at

her. "Not being able to afford all the magazines I wanted, I mean
. . ." she added weakly. "Well, it was just an idea!"

James jumped up from his seat, kicking the chair aside. "A
bloody brilliant idea!" he crowed. "An absolutely bloomin' marvelous
idea!" He lifted her off the floor and whirled her around exuberantly.
"Why didn't any of us think of that?" the Prince demanded of Peter
Goldsworth over Millie's shoulder. "She's got a knack for the job, she
does!!"

"Very nice, miss," Goldsworth said. He nodded at her. His
glasses, reflecting the light, veiled his eyes.

"Anything else on your mind, Peter?" the Prince asked meaningfully, his arms around Millie.

"No, sir," Goldsworth answered. "I'll be taking my leave now."
He dipped his head. "Good night, Your Royal Highness."

"Good night, Peter," the Prince responded warmly. His face,
shining, included his equerry in its radiance.

"Good night, Miss Myerson."

"Millie! Please! Good night, Peter."

Chapter V

Peter Goldsworth entered the small bedroom assigned to him, off the main reception room of the suite. He turned on the bedside lamp and sat motionless, staring unseeingly at the polished toe of his shoe, eyes fixed in concentration.

Then he picked up the phone. "Please ring 556-0203. In Newport, Rhode Island." He spoke decisively, with no trace of hesitation. "No, I don't know the area code."

He waited patiently.

"Good evening, My Lord," he said, after a while. "I'm sorry to disturb you at this hour. There are matters here that require your attention."

He spoke for several minutes, then listened for several more. "No one is more familiar with His Royal Highness's . . . escapades, than I, My Lord. But it is possible that this is something more than the usual . . . caprice. Prince James just told me—quite off-handedly, I must say—that the young woman in question . . . he said she would make a good— He said she had 'a gift for the job.' Perhaps it meant nothing. I thought, however, that I should let you know. . . . Yes, I knew you *would* see. This wasn't an easy thing for me to do," he said unemotionally. "Thank you. I'll hear from you in the morning, shall I? Yes. Goodnight, My Lord."

Chapter VI

CLICK. Millie awoke. Coming instantly out of a deep sleep, with the New Yorker's instinctive alertness, she knew, with certainty, that someone was in the room. She was lying on her back, Prince James on his side, facing her. His outflung arm lay across her body.

She heard a second click, followed by muffled footsteps crossing the deep carpet. Involuntarily she let out a squeak. The Prince sleepily covered her mouth with his hand. "Ssssshhh," he whispered, his mouth close to her ear. His body shook with his silent laughter.

"Good morning, Your Royal Highness." A white-haired man, immaculately attired in a black morning coat with a silver and black striped vest, set down the large silver tray he was carrying on a table at the far end of the room. "It's a lovely morning, if I may say so," he continued. The personage crossed to the windows, stately, unhurried, and opened the drapes with a single swift tug at the cord. Then he was gone, the door closing softly behind him.

"Does he always walk in like that? Without knocking? What if we were . . ."

James smiled. "It's amazing how one doesn't see what . . . would be awkward if one did see it. Speaking of which . . ." he added, sliding over on to her. She laughed her eagerness, looking up at him and, receiving him, folded him into her arms.

Millie stepped out on the terrace. It was a banners-flying, trumpet-blaring, heart-stoppingly beautiful day, even more so twenty-two stories up in the air. Sunlight danced on the river, and gray and white pigeons wheeled against the piercing blue of the sky. It was a day for singing and a day for flying.

James, however, was buried in a newspaper that he had propped against a crystal water pitcher. Millie brushed her lips against the back of his neck in passing and sat down opposite him, lifting the cover off a platter as she did so. "Zweiback?" she asked, incredulous. "You eat zweiback for breakfast?"

"Rusks," James said, laughing at her expression. "When do you eat them?"

"I *don't!* We feed them to babies when they're teething." She poured herself a cup of coffee from the heavy silver coffeepot and eyed James thoughtfully. "Why're you all dressed up?"

James was, in fact, formally attired. His light blue shirt intensified the darker blue of his eyes. His tie was precisely knotted, and his suit jacket lay, neatly folded, on a nearby chair. "My working clothes. I've got one appearance this morning—at the Cloisters—and then I'll pick you up at your flat, and off we go, all right? Oh, and that reminds me, we're having a reception for the Queen's birthday. Next Tuesday. Will you come?"

"Sure!" Millie said cheerfully, spreading black currant jam on a croissant.

"Good. That's settled then." James returned his attention to his newspaper.

Not a morning person, this morning, Millie thought. She riffled through a stack of newspapers piled on a chair and chose a copy of *Figaro*, a Paris daily. On page three she spotted a photo of Prince James over the caption "LE PRINCE DE GALLES S'EPOUSERA." Quickly she skimmed the article. "It says here you're getting married to a Belgian princess," she informed him.

"Really?" James returned, drawing out the syllables. He searched for a word, and found it. *"Mazel tov,"* said the Prince of Wales.

The Prince strode briskly through the front doors of the hotel, with a flash of a smile for the doorman, and halted, cocking a quizzical eye at the Cadillac sedan waiting at the curb. "What's the matter, don't I rate the Rolls anymore?" he asked jauntily.

Peter Goldsworth faltered briefly. "It was thought we could do with a little less show, sir," he said, recovering. The Prince shot him an acute glance. Goldsworth opened the door to the front passenger seat and stood aside, waiting for the Prince to enter. "Besides, I thought you'd gone off the Rolls, sir."

"Clever," said the Prince under his breath and, walking swiftly past his equerry, opened the rear door and slid into the back seat.

Goldsworth nodded his head in acceptance and, closing the door, moved around to the driver's seat.

"How long till we get there?" the Prince asked as the car pulled into traffic.

"About twenty-five minutes, sir. We're scheduled to stay for three-quarters of an hour. You'll make a brief tour, say a few words. There'll be a photo opportunity, and Bob's your uncle."

The Prince made no response to this pleasantry. He opened his attaché case and busied himself with his papers, spreading them around him on the car seat. The equerry glanced back at him in the rearview mirror. The Prince's demeanor did not encourage further conversation. They drove on in silence.

A sudden crash, the unmistakable sound of glass shattering, penetrated the sealed, silent hush of the air-conditioned car. The Prince looked up, startled. He swiveled in his seat, turning to look out the rear window.

Four men, their impromptu card game interrupted, waved their arms menacingly at the bottle-thrower, who, from the safety of his vantage point on the roof of the three-story building, returned their promises of future grievous bodily harm and slighting references to his ancestry in kind.

The Prince snapped his attaché case shut and settled himself in his seat, looking out the window, intrigued. "Where are we?" he asked.

"I believe it's called the Bronx, sir," the equerry answered.

The neighborhood, while not yet a slum, was what is euphemistically called "in transition." Once a sleepy, heterogenously middle-class enclave, it now bore the stigmata of its varied residents like the layered strata of an architectural dig. A *bodega* nestled between a kosher butcher shop and Paddy's Bar, to which, a neon sign proclaimed, "Ladies" were invited. A restaurant advertised *comidas criollas*, while another called itself Star of Haiti.

A red fire hydrant had been, contrary to city ordinances, opened, and half-naked children ran in and out of the fine spray, screeching. Their wiry brown bodies glistened with droplets of bootleg water, and the word "motherfucker" was prominent in every shouted sentence. As the Prince watched, a chasid passed, hands clasped behind his back, lost in thoughts of a more sacred place and a holier time. His incongruously red beard and dangling *peyes* made a vibrant splash of color against his unrelievedly black attire. His two small sons, miniature copies of their father, followed him, darting furtive glances at the uninhibited street urchins. Their hair was cut so short as to be merely a layer of reddish fuzz on their black-skullcapped heads, and their ginger *peyes* dangled as they walked.

The Cadillac overtook and passed a pimpmobile, a shockingly fuscia Lincoln Continental limousine, equipped with every option known to Detroit, plus a few that are not.

A young Puerto Rican blood, his approach heralded for blocks around by the blare of disco coming from the oversized cassette player he carried, gave the Cadillac a cursory, contemptuous once-over and danced away, keeping time to the beat of the music from his "box."

The car stopped for a light in front of a small, concrete-block, one-story building, proclaiming itself, via the sign over the entrance, to be "Jehovah's Church of the Blood of the Precious Lamb." Two black men sat on the ground out front, their legs spread-eagled, sharing a bottle of encouragement concealed in a brown paper bag.

One of them got up and stumbled, shakily, to the side of the building. There, only partly sheltered by the wall, he unzipped his fly and urinated copiously. He shook the last drops away and, with a smile of relief and accomplishment, resumed his position outside the church.

The Prince watched, fascinated, and a little repelled.

The car turned the corner and moved down a street that was somewhat neater and a little less seedy, lined with brownstones. Here and there, a woebegone, stunted tree added a touch of much-needed cheer. The Cadillac traveled down the street, slowly, then pulled over and stopped in front of a particular house, in the middle of the block. "Why are we—" James began and stopped, as Peter Goldsworth, with a lift of his chin, directed the Prince's attention to a couple sitting on the narrow stoop of the brownstone.

The man sat nodding over the heavy, brown-covered tome resting on his lap. He was a small man, shriveled almost, an impression intensified by the fact that his clothes appeared to have been purchased for someone quite a bit larger. His nylon short-sleeved shirt was tinged with yellow, and the sleeves flapped loosely around his thin arms. As the Prince watched, he extracted a wooden toothpick from his shirt pocket and used it, absentmindedly, to probe between his teeth.

The woman wore a checked housedress and, over it, an apron, none too clean, the strings of which ran over her shoulders and around her thick waist. Her face was coarsened with habitual discontent, and her pinched mouth had a mean quality.

Her hair, home-cut, escaped in untidy wisps from under her flowered headscarf. It was graying now, but it bore the remnants of a glossy brown so dark as to appear almost black, and in the golden sunshine it had vagrant glints of red.

She looked up. Her dark-brown eyes, which may once have sparkled with gaiety and anticipation, were sullen and dulled. They traveled listlessly over the Cadillac.

The Prince shrank back, forgetting for the moment the tinted windows that shielded him from view.

The woman dropped her gaze, disinterested. She put aside the bowl of apples she was paring and pulled up her sagging stocking, rolling it to just below the knee. She retied the knot that held it in place, exposing in the process the sagging, lumpy flesh of her thigh. Then she sighed and resumed her labors, adding a long, twisting peel to the growing pile on the newspaper spread at her feet.

"Mr. and Mrs. Myerson," the equerry said, his voice toneless, uninflected.

"How did you—" The Prince bit off the needless question. He sat motionless for a few seconds, then he nodded, sharply. He brushed a hand across his eyes once and then again. "Let's get going," he said. And stared, stone-faced, out the window as the car pulled away.

When the doorbell rang, Millie was packed and ready. She sped joyously to the door and threw it open. She stopped, cold, on the point of flinging herself into the Prince's arms.

James looked at her, his face a fortress, impenetrable. "Hello, Millie," he said politely. "Are you ready?"

She reached out her hand and drew him into the apartment. He unslung the battered leather bag from his shoulder and stood in the foyer, toying with his signet ring, sliding it up and down on his little finger. She reached up and kissed his cheek. He returned her kiss woodenly.

She looked into his eyes and saw, with a sinking heart, that they were vigilant, withdrawn. Something's happened, she thought. He got the shit kicked out of him. She stepped back a little and, wondering how to reach him, examined with careful attention, the emblem emblazoned on the faded blue sweat shirt he wore.

The insignia was a larger version of the crest she had seen twice before, on his stationery and on Peter Goldsworth's lighter: three graceful, symmetrical plumes rising out of a crown, with a motto in gothic letters on either side. "*Ich Dien* . . . I serve," she translated triumphantly.

"Do you read German?" the Prince asked in surprise.

"No, but I speak Yiddish. A little from here and a little from there, and I get by."

The Prince threw his head back and laughed. The sound pealed out, joyously, and with it the immobility drained from his features. He lifted her off her feet in a giant bear hug and kissed her, wholeheartedly.

Millie kissed him back, pleased. She had no idea how she'd done it, but she knew that the drawbridge had been lowered, and he was hers again.

"All this for a little German?" she teased, her arms around his neck.

"No. For being you. And for reminding me," he answered, setting her down on the floor.

She leaned back contentedly in the circle of his arms, her hands resting on his chest. "Do you think it's ever been on a sweat shirt before?" she asked, contemplating the venerable device.

"I *know* it hasn't!" James laughed. "It's the three feathers of the Prince of Wales. It goes where I go."

The intercom buzzed, and Millie, grimacing, went to answer it. "Listen, I'm glad you're home. The kids have to go to the bathroom. We're on our way up." Tact was not her sister's watchword.

"Brace yourself," Millie warned and opened the apartment door. Shrill voices heralded the arrival of the four mini-cyclones that converged on Millie. They jumped on her, fighting for handholds on her body, nearly knocking her to the floor.

"We rode in the elevator!"

"And *I* pushed the button!"

"You pushed the wrong one! You're stupid!"

"I did not! I pushed the right one. You're stupid!"

Millie disentangled herself and intercepted a foot outstretched to kick, preventing it from landing on its intended target. As one, four small bodies raced to the window.

"Look how high up we are!"

"This is higher than the Empire State Building!"

"No, it's not, stupid. This is the tenth floor. The Empire State Building is a trillion floors!"

"Knock it off," Millie yelled amiably and, retrieving a yarmulke thrown to the floor in the melee, went to greet her sister and brother-in-law, whose entrance was, at once, slower and less imperative.

Gladys came heavily through the door, followed by Sam. Gladys was two years older than Millie, three inches taller and forty pounds heavier. She wore a polyester print dress and clutched a large black vinyl purse. Sam's Dacron suit, an improbable shade of olive green, was stretched nearly to bursting over his paterfamilias paunch. He had rust-colored hair that waved back from his rapidly spreading forehead and a pompous dignity. "We took the kids to the zoo," he announced.

Millie kissed her sister, smiled at Sam and turned to James, who stood in front of the couch, waiting. "I'd like you to meet . . . James," Millie introduced, taking refuge in first names only, rapidly uttered. "James, this is my sister Gladys and her husband Sam." Something flickered, briefly, in the Prince's eyes. Millie wondered uncomfortably if it was because she'd done the introduction backward.

"Didn't I see him on TV?" Gladys asked in a loud whisper. "What is he, a movie star?"

Millie glanced at James. He was shaking hands with Sam, his face perfectly serene. "Come here, kids," she called. "James, this is, in order of age, Sarah—"

"I'm eight," Sarah interjected.

"—Joshua, Simon and Danny."

"How do you do," James said gravely, shaking hands with each of the children in turn. Danny gazed up at him with interest.

"I'm five," he informed James, craning up to look at him. "I go to kindergarten. My whole name is Daniel Joseph Frankel. I can write it," he added, completing his curriculum vitae. "What's your whole name?"

Millie's eyes met James's, hers exasperated, his amused. "James is really all there is. I'm afraid the rest gets rather complicated," he answered, according a reasonable question the dignity of an honest answer.

"You talk funny," Simon put in, feeling his brother had held center stage for too long. "Why do you talk funny?"

"That's because he's from Scotland," Josh explained, giving his brother the benefit of his seven years of experience. "He talks like James Bond."

"I don't know where they get these things from," Gladys sighed.

"James Bond is English," Sam corrected his small son, inaccurately.

"Joshie is right," Millie objected. "James Bond is Scottish."

"And Sean Connery is as well," James added, zeroing in on the probable source of Josh's information.

The conversation had gone on for too long on matters of no interest to Danny. "Are you Millie's boyfriend?" he inquired.

"Millie has *lots* of boyfriends," Josh said, loyally defending his heroine.

"But she should have just one, like Lois Lane. Mommy said so," Sarah added, citing her source. Millie looked at her, quietly contemplating child murder.

"Well, are you?" Danny of the one-track-mind persisted.

"I rather hope I am," James said simply.

Six-year-old Simon's imagination had fixated on one point. "Do you wear a skirt?" he wanted to know.

"It's called a kilt," James answered, unperturbed. He dug into his canvas bag and pulled out a handsome leather tablet. When he opened it, revealing two framed photographs, a "compliments of" card fell out, which he retrieved. Millie realized that this was a hostess gift and would have bet her next two paychecks that he was the only one of the four of them thus prepared. He showed Simon the picture.

Millie leaned over to look. The photograph was an exceptionally handsome informal portrait of the royal family. They were ranged against a low stone wall, all kilted and all smiling as if they shared a happy secret. On the left was the Duke, exuding a gay virility and

Viking good looks. Next to him stood the Queen, looking up at her blond husband. Then the younger children, the three Princesses: Helena, two years younger than James, married, matronly; Victoria, in her early twenties; and the youngest, Sarah, newly a teenager, smiling rather shyly, leaning against her big brother's arm. James, at the far right, smiled at Sarah, his stance an unconscious echo of his father's. The two men on either side were turned slightly inward, a shield and a protection for the family.

"I didn't know women wore kilts," Millie said to James.

"They do. That's the Balmoral Tartan, reserved for the royal family."

"You wear alot of things nobody else does don't you," Millie observed tartly, eyeing his sweat shirt. Then she dropped her eyes, ashamed. James let it pass, understanding, perhaps, that in the presence of her family Millie's nerves were scraped raw.

"Here, Sarah, this is for you." James drew the child to him, displaying the second picture. She leaned contentedly against his knee.

The photograph had been taken some years ago and had, with good reason, clearly become a favorite. The photographer had caught James, shirt-sleeves rolled up, arms outflung against a backdrop of a Scottish heath, turning to scoop up a small blonde child, his youngest sister. Her hands stretched up to him, her face shining with that blinding, immaculate happiness of childhood, at exactly the same angle that his looked down at her from his towering adult height. His kilt swirled with his movement, and his face mirrored her joy. It was a poignant moment of shared emotion, caught by an artist's eye.

"Her name is Sarah, too," James said. Sarah looked up at him, ecstatic. Children blossom with attention, and Millie noted that James had found something to say to each of them.

"She's younger than me," Sarah pointed out, seizing every advantage.

"Well, she was when this picture was taken. Now she's very grown up. She's a young lady. But do you know what?"

"What?" Sarah asked breathlessly, pink with pleasure.

"She's every bit as delicious as you will be when you're grown up." He smoothed back her bangs and brushed a light kiss on her forehead.

Millie felt the hot tears rise, stinging her eyes. She bit down, hard, on the inside of her mouth, forcing them back, filled with a wild, uncontrollable longing. She wanted James for her brother, her father, her son and her lover. She felt, watching him, the abyssmal, yearning loneliness of her childhood.

"I want to talk to you," Gladys hissed. She grabbed Millie's elbow, hustling her into the kitchen. "Who is he?" she demanded.

Millie leaned back against the sink. "He's Prince James. The Prince of Wales. From England."

"*I* know that," Gladys said, irritated. "Any fool can see he's from England. Isn't he dead?" she asked, without missing a beat.

Millie was wise in the thought processes of her family. "You're thinking of the Duke of Windsor. He was also the Prince of Wales."

"Oh. Why do they use the same name twice?" Then Gladys reverted to more serious matters. "Is he Jewish?"

"That's my business."

"You'll kill your mother and father," Gladys warned.

Millie drew in a breath. "Look," she said coldly, "I've said this before, and I'll say it again. I have my life to live, and they have theirs, and if they threaten to drop dead every time I do something they don't like, that's their fucking problem."

Gladys winced at the swear word. "Mommy and Daddy will sit shiva," she said, referring to the seven-day, ritual mourning period for one's nearest relatives. "None of us will ever talk to you again."

That might be the best thing that could happen to me, Millie thought bitterly. Except for the kids. I'd miss the kids. She turned her back on her sister. "It's always wise, when you threaten, to have something to threaten with," she advised.

"Huh?"

"I'm Jewish, and James is not, and that's a problem. It's not a problem," she corrected fiercely. He's only here for two weeks. That's it! There's no problem. He'll be gone in *one week!* She turned back to her sister. Gladys was munching a cookie she had abstracted from her bulging purse.

"Well, I didn't mean to hurt your feelings . . ." Gladys said placidly.

Millie raised her hand to her mouth and licked the bloody half-moon her nail had etched in her palm. "You never do. None of you ever do."

"I hope you're not eating anything that isn't kosher," Gladys said.

Millie smiled. She had long since accepted the difference between ritual performance and a sense of identity. She ushered her sister back into the living room. To her horror, she found Sam filling in the Prince, in glorious detail, on the current political situation in his shul. James was listening with every expression of interest on his face.

"Let's go kids," Gladys called. "Did you all make a pish?"

Millie winced. The children answered in the affirmative, and they all trooped to the door, each of them hugging Millie en route.

"It was nice meeting you," Gladys called to James. "I hope you enjoy America," she added politely.

Danny, last in line, hesitated for a moment. Then he made his decision. He marched back to Prince James. "I like you," he said earnestly. "Here." He rummaged in his corduroy pocket and pulled out a live frog, which he handed to the Prince with great ceremony.

"That's a super frog," James said, holding it up to the light, the better to admire it. "Wherever did you find him?"

"His name is Kelev," Danny disclosed.

"Sweetheart," Millie objected, *"kelev* in Hebrew means *dog."*

Danny looked at her with disdain. *"I* know that," he said and turned back to James, who didn't clutter up his world with irrelevancies.

"You know what, though," James said thoughtfully. He looked worried. "I don't really have room for a frog in my luggage." He brightened as a possible solution struck him. "Perhaps you'd be good enough to keep him for me?" he inquired of Danny solemnly.

"Then you'll *have* to come visit him," Danny exclaimed, his small face alight, secure in the powers of his pet to attract.

"Danny! Come *on!"* Gladys yelled from the corridor. James handed him the frog, and Danny raced out, his small body hurtling towards the door, certain he had the best of the bargain.

"You were wonderful," Millie said, walking into James's arms. "How could you touch that thing?"

"Frogs are super," he laughed. "It's very clear to me," he added, unbuttoning her blouse, "that you were never a little boy."

"I'm sorry about Sam," she said, looking worriedly into his face.

"You should have a chat with *my* brother-in-law, sometime." James nuzzled her neck. He took a deep breath, inhaling her fragrance. "Drive you bonkers, it would."

"And I'm sorry I got . . . cranky there for a minute," Millie continued, not finished unburdening herself.

"You came all over funny. 'Appens to the best of us," he said in a broad Cockney accent. "Don't give it a thought," he added, unzipping her jeans.

"They're all waiting for us!"

"That's one of the advantages." The Prince sank down to the floor, drawing Millie with him. "The party doesn't start until I get there."

"James! I'm too old to make love on the floor."

"Rubbish," said the Prince. And proceeded to prove it.

He followed her through the revolving door into the bright afternoon. A low-slung yellow convertible, buffed to a high gloss, waited, top down, in front of her building. In the back seat sat Ian MacCrae, his stocky body filling the tiny space. Millie stopped in her tracks and turned to James. "It would be nice to go someplace, sometime, without a chaperone," she said mildly.

"Yes, wouldn't it, though. Just stash your things in the boot," the Prince instructed, opening the trunk of the car. "And count your blessings. They wanted to give me an escort, complete with sirens and going through red lights and all that rot. Can you imagine? All those people going about their business, and they get bollixed up because of one person. My father says that's a good way to put paid to the monarchy, tieing people up in traffic jams for no reason."

James crammed his tweed cap down on his head and turned the key. The engine caught, instantly, and Millie guessed it had been tuned to within an inch of its life.

"We're off," he said, smiling at her happily.

"Where are we going?"

"Mind yer own business. It's a surprise."

The Prince headed east, finding his way unerringly through the complicated Central Park drives. They turned on to the Fifty-ninth Street bridge. Millie's heart lifted with the sight of the river, sunlight bouncing off the water, with the humming of the little car, with the exhilaration that comes with weekend escape, and with something more.

She turned to James and found his face a reflection of her own. She slouched in her bucket seat and lifted her sneakered feet, resting them on the dashboard. "Oooooooklahoma! Where the wind comes sweeping down the plain," she sang lustily, finding release in the upward slide of the musical line.

"Do you ride?" James asked, apparently picking up the image of cowboys and cowgirls.

"Carousels," Millie said, grinning happily.

"Now if we can just find the BQE," he muttered. "Ah, here we are." The little car shot onto the highway. The Prince held the wheel easily as he zipped in and out of traffic, switching lanes at high speed. Millie opened her mouth to protest, then closed it without speaking.

"That's right," James approved. "No nattering."

They drove in silence, comfortable, enjoying the spectacular day, each with his own thoughts.

James arched his back, holding the steering wheel steady against his stomach for an instant, as he stretched both arms above his head, in his now familiar gesture of contentment. "How're you doing back there, MacCrae?" he asked, grinning mischievously.

"Just fine, sir," MacCrae answered stolidly, ignoring James's shenanigan.

"James!" Millie protested. He reached his arm across and hugged her close. "Both hands on the wheel!" she ordered.

"Best save your breath to cool your porridge, miss," MacCrae advised bleakly.

"What have you brought along to read?" James asked.

"A Travis McGee—"

"He's fun."

"—and Bettleheim's book on fairy tales."

"That man is great! First rate! Have you read his others?"

Millie nodded. "What did you think of *Children of the Dream?*" she asked, curious to know his reaction to an analysis of child-rearing on an Israeli kibbutz.

"Interesting. But I think the contrast is greater for some than for others. All that stuff about the kids nurturing and helping each other in the children's houses—I went away to school at an early age and lived with other boys, and, while there isn't the unifying passion and idealism of the kibbutz, it isn't as *different* as it appears to someone who grew up in a nuclear family and saw his parents every day and slept alone in a room. I never had a room all to myself till I got aboard ship in the Navy. A cabin, about seven-foot by seven-foot, and a bloody joy it was, too, I can tell you."

James started to switch lanes. Unfortunately, seeing his maneuver, a battered, dusty, chrome encrusted '58 Chevy decided to occupy that eminently desirable space at the same moment. James turned the steering wheel hard, swerving back into his own lane narrowly averting a collision.

"James!" Millie yelled. "For God's sakes."

"Do put a sock in it, darling," he said cheerfully. "I've been driving since I was twelve."

"How could you drive when you're twelve?"

"Private estates," he answered tersely.

The Chevy passed them at high speed, its passengers bellowing in celebration of their victory and derision of the vanquished. One of them tossed an empty beer can at the MG. "And a bloody rude bugger, you are, too," James said mildly.

Millie glanced back at Ian MacCrae. He sat quietly, unmoved by their narrow escape. "What did they call you in the Navy?" she asked, turning back to the Prince.

"Lieutenant, the Prince of Wales." He pronounced it "Leftenant." "As in 'Will Lieutenant the Prince of Wales bring his royal arse up to the bridge.' My mates called me 'Prince James.' Aboard ship, I called my superior officers 'sir,' and, when we went ashore, they called *me* 'sir.' It was fun."

"Sounds schizy to me," Millie observed.

"My whole *life* is schizy," he said with a grin, enjoying the new word. He leaned back in his seat and, for no particular reason, began to sing, full-throated, hearty. "We sail the ocean blue . . ."

"Our bonny ship's a beauty," Millie joined in.

"Saucy," James corrected.

"What?"

"Saucy. Our *saucy* ship's a beauty."

"Bonny," Millie insisted.

"Care to make a little wager?"

"Sure. What do you want to bet?"

James leaned over and, pulling her close to him, whispered in her ear. She looked up at him, eyes sparkling. "That's no bet," she said. "Either way, I win."

James threw back his head and laughed. Then, as if unable to contain his joy, he sang loudly. His rich, accurate baritone rang out:

> *When I was a lad I served a term*
> *As office boy to an Attorney's firm.*
> *I cleaned the windows and I swept the floor*
> *And I polished up the handle of the big front door.*

Millie joined in:

> *I polished up that handle so carefullee*
> *That now I am the Ruler of the Queen's Navee!*

James continued:

> *As office boy I made such a mark*
> *That they gave me the post of a junior clerk.*
> *I served the writs with a smile so bland*
> *And I copied all the letters in a big round hand . . .*

Millie joined him:

> *I copied all the letters in a hand so free*
> *That now I am the Ruler of the Queen's Navee!*

"I only know one more," James said. And, slowing the tempo dramatically, he sang:

> *Now landsmen all, wherever you might be,*
> *If you want to rise to the top of the tree,*
> *If your soul isn't fettered to an office stool,*
> *Be careful to be guided by this Golden Rule*
> *Stick close to your desks and never go to sea . . .*
> *And you all may be Rulers of the Queen's Navee.*

Millie finished the song: "And you all may be Rulers of the Queen's Naveeeeee!"

As Millie's sweet voice faded, drawing out the last note, they looked at each other. It was a moment of pure, transcendent, overpowering bliss. The Prince, unable to contain his euphoria, tore the cap off his head and, waving it in the slipstream, yelled exuberantly. Millie, hearing him, laughed joyously, understanding.

Trained from birth not to betray overwhelming emotion directly, wary, perhaps, of precipitous speech, he took refuge in an oblique expression of his feelings. "I'M THE HEIR TO THE BLEEDIN' THRONE!" he yelled, stating the basic truth of his life.

The Prince pulled up and parked, illegally, in front of the Marine Air Terminal at La Guardia. "Spiffy car," he commented to the embassy functionary who materialized out of nowhere to take custody of the little MG.

They crossed directly through the small terminal and out the back doors. Through some prodigious feat of teleportation, Millie's suitcase had beaten them to it, and, along with the Prince's leather cases set with a tiny gold crest above the lock, was being lifted into a bright-red, twin-engine Cessna.

Gerald, Lucy and Peter waited next to the plane, seated on their luggage. Gerald wore a T-shirt inscribed with a production joke: "Where's the coffee? What time is lunch? When's the wrap?"— reputedly the three most asked questions on the set.

The equerry had traded in his formal suit for a beige turtleneck and slacks. Lucy, looking cool and elegant in her white linen culottes, was, for some unfathomable reason, teaching him to play jacks.

Peter stood up as James approached. "How was your journey, sir?" he asked, looking from the Prince to the radiant Millie. "Uneventful. I hope."

James regarded him steadily. The equerry lowered his gaze and, strangely, blushed. "My journey was enlightening," the Prince answered obscurely. "Even . . . confirming, one might say. Come along, Millie," he said curtly and stalked toward the plane. Millie returned Lucy's questioning shrug with one of incomprehension and followed the Prince up the metal ladder. Why do I get the feeling he just threw something in Goldsworth's teeth, she thought.

Although she had flown a lot commercially, Millie had never been in a private plane before. The passengers sat directly behind the pilot and copilot in the cramped cabin. It felt, Millie thought, rather like the crowded screening rooms in which rushes were screened.

James managed, with difficulty, to contain himself during take-off, but they hadn't been aloft ten minutes before he unbuckled his seat belt and, with a radiant, parting smile to Millie, tapped the pilot on the shoulder. "Off you go, mate."

The pilot hesitated. "You'd best let him," MacCrae called. The pilot wordlessly handed the Prince the headphones, unbuckled himself and left his seat. James took over the controls. He handled the plane expertly, routinely, with the ease born of many hours of practice. The copilot eyed him warily for a few minutes and then relaxed.

Millie watched him, sensing the joy with which he abandoned himself to his task. No wonder he loves it, she thought. It's . . . objective. It's either/or. Either you can fly the plane or you can't. If you can't, being a prince won't help you, and, if you can, nobody can take it away from you.

She looked across the aisle at MacCrae, engrossed in a game of solitaire. He felt her eyes on him and looked up. "I spend many hours waiting," he said with a smile. "It helps to pass the time."

"Does he always do this?" Millie asked, with a gesture at the back of the Prince's head.

MacCrae nodded. "I'm afraid so, miss. So does his father. The Prince is probably more expert than any commercial pilot," he consoled, mistaking the reason for her question. Millie had no fears for her safety. She was simply indulging her compulsion to talk *about* James when she wasn't talking *with* him. "He's qualified in every conceivable kind of aircraft from supersonic fighters to helicopters. He'll be off to bloody outer space, next," MacCrae predicted morosely. "He's got this sort of . . . friendly competition with his father. About who logs more time in the air. But, lately, I don't think Prince James has been claiming all of his hours." He glanced at Millie, his face betraying a glimmer of pride. "He moves about so much, you see. And he doesn't have . . . the killer instinct."

Millie smiled at him. "No, he doesn't," she agreed.

"He's a good lad," MacCrae added somberly.

"So! Madame Director! Tell me about the shoot," Lucy said, dropping into the empty seat next to Millie.

"Did you have any trouble getting out of work early?" Millie asked.

"No, and I swear, I'm so pissed off there that, if they gave me any kind of a hard time, I would have just walked out." Millie accepted this, as it was meant, routinely. Bitching and moaning was a habitual pastime in the industry. "So when's the shoot?"

"Prep next Thursday, location scout, and then the shoot's the following Monday. That's two days after James leaves," Millie said, counting by her new calendar.

"Better that way," Lucy countered. "When you're on the set, there's no way on earth you'll be able to think about anything else." The concentration required of a director on a shooting day compared favorably with that of a test pilot.

"But the day always ends," Millie said, disconsolate. "How about you?" she asked, deliberately putting away thoughts of her future. "Would you ever like to direct?"

"Who, me? No, I'd hate it. I think that's the worst. You can't sleep, you can't eat, and you can't even take the time to pee!" Lucy enumerated. "Not for me, kiddo. No, what I'd really like to do is—"

"Millie!" James called imperatively.

"Gotta go," Millie said with a smile and stood up, resting one hand on her friend's shoulder for leverage. She walked to the Prince and stood behind him, her hands resting on his shoulders. James pushed back the headset, letting the earphones dangle negligently under his chin. "Want to fly her, Millie?"

"Are you crazy? I can't even drive a stick shift!"

"It's not half so difficult as that," he coaxed, wanting to share his other love with her. "This thing is a proper joy to fly." He looked at the copilot. "Go get yourself some coffee, mate." The copilot, thankfully, remained seated.

"James," Millie said crisply. "I do not want to fly this plane. I do not want to land us all in the Atlantic. I do not want to go swimming. At least not this minute," she amended.

James leaned his head back against her chest. "All right, darling, another time, then." He reached up and, with his hands on either side of her face, pulled her to him and kissed her thoroughly, upside down.

"Hey, Millie!" Gerald yelled from the back of the plane. "Leave the pilot alone. 'Do not talk with driver while vehicle is in motion,'" he quoted from the placard, largely ignored, that appeared on every New York City bus.

James turned in his seat. "How about you, Gerald? Care to take the controls for a while?" he offered, with all the friendly swagger of a small boy allowing his buddy a ride on his shiny new birthday bike.

Gerald stared at the Prince with flagrant animosity. "No, thanks. I'm on a diet," he called surlily.

The Prince held his gaze expressionlessly. "Suit yourself."

"Jesus, Gerald!" Millie exploded. "When did you become so touchy. He only meant to—"

"That will do, Millie," the Prince cut her off sharply and turned back to the controls.

James brought the plane down smoothly, for a perfect landing. "Mind your heads," he called, unbuckling his seat belt. He stood up in a half crouch and beamed with delight as Gerald smacked his head against the ceiling with an audible crack. "Nobody ever listens to me," the Prince complained, swallowing his grin before it became an out-and-out smirk.

Millie rubbed the top of Gerald's head, laughing as she recalled his merciless teasing about her pint-size. She was the only one of them who could, just, stand upright in the low-ceilinged craft.

The door was lifted away, and a small metal flight of stairs was wheeled into position. "Where the hell are we?" Millie asked, blinking in the bright sunlight as she followed James down the ladder.

"Newport, Rhode Island," said the Prince, over his shoulder.

Chapter VII

A car horn tooted to attract their attention. Parked across the field was a mint condition "woody" station wagon. A girl got out, slamming the door, and moved rapidly across the tarmac toward them.

She wore white shorts and a sleeveless blouse knotted under her breasts, revealing a slender waist and a fetching expanse of tanned skin. Her auburn mane bounced as she walked.

Millie was suddenly conscious of the lipstick she had forgotten to reapply after James had kissed her. "Her thighs don't even know what a jiggle is," she whispered bitterly to Lucy.

"Relax. Barbie Doll lives. Besides, I don't think James goes for that type."

"I do," Gerald remarked brightly.

"With luck, you'll grow out of it," Lucy informed him tartly.

The girl reached James, dropping him a quick, graceful curtsey. "It's good to see you again, sir," she said with an intimate smile, leaning up to kiss his cheek.

"Thanks for having us." The Prince turned to the others. "This is Lady Dorothea Marling," he introduced, adding with a grin, "everybody calls her 'Dolly.'"

Lucy shot Millie a glance filled with pure triumph and smiled benignly at Lady Dolly, acknowledging the introduction. Lady Dolly looked from Lucy to Millie and back again, her eyes speculative, appraising.

"And Peter, of course you know," continued the Prince. Lady Dolly favored Peter with a sultry, coquettish smile and hooked her arm through James's for the short walk across the field to the car.

Lady Dolly opened the door to the front passenger seat and, with a graceful wave of her hand, gestured the Prince inside. James reached behind him in a swift, tugging movement, and the unsuspecting Peter Goldsworth found himself ensconced in the seat of honor.

Dolly, having no choice, moved to the driver's seat. "Are you sure you'll have enough room, Your Royal Highness," she inquired.

"Definitely not," James responded. "We'll just have to make do, won't we?" He grasped Millie around the waist and slid deftly past her into the back seat. He pulled her down into his lap and grinned at her, pleased with his maneuver.

Lady Dolly watched in the rearview mirror, her eyes burning with curiosity. "Now, then, what's holding us up?" the Prince inquired ingenuously. Dolly put the car in gear and drove off.

Millie sat sideways on James's lap, her arm round his neck, her feet dangling perilously close to MacCrae's knees. The detective did not appear to mind. Judging from his serene countenance, he had seen nothing untoward. As long as his charge was hale and hearty and in the *back* seat of a car, he was a happy man.

Millie felt James harden against her thigh and looked at him, her eyes mirroring her surprise. He smiled at her and shrugged, half rueful and half proud. "It's not me. It's him," he confided with an infinitesimal gesture toward his cock. Millie smiled into his eyes, letting him see her own desire, rising in response to his.

"Now, how am I going to get out of the car?" he asked plaintively.

"Here," Millie said. She reached down into the tote bafl8on the floor and pulled out a baby-pink angora sweater. "Carry this over your arm. Nobody'll suspect a thing."

James eyed the fluffy bit of wool meditatively. "I'm trying to decide which I'd rather have my future subjects suspect," he mused. Their laughter range out, joyously. Millie buried her face in his neck, trying to muffle her hilarity. "That took care of it," James said presently, hugging her.

The car pulled up to a massive set of wrought-iron gates. Lady Dolly pressed a button on the outside of the guardhouse, and they swung slowly open.

They drove along the winding gravel drive. As they neared the house, Millie saw an enormous Union Jack on a staff, snapping proudly in the breeze. Above it flew a larger version of the rectangular banner she had seen on the Rolls Royce: three gold lions against crimson in the upper left and lower right; a crimson lion rampant against gold in the upper right and in the remaining quadrant, a harp against a field of royal blue. In the center was a shield and a coronet and across the top a bar of white.

"What *is* that?" she whispered in James's ear. "I see it all over."

"It's the standard of the Prince of Wales. It's to tell you I'm here," he added whimsically, relishing the joke.

The car slowed to a stop in the dead center of a circular driveway, in front of a massive, prerevolutionary graystone house, properly ivy-covered.

A man ran lightly down the stone steps and opened the door for James. His eyes widened slightly in surprise, as Millie, of necessity preceded the Prince out of the car. He recovered immediately, however, and extended his hand to James, his face alight with affection. "Welcome, Your Royal Highness," he said, inclining his head. Then he threw his arm around James's shoulder and hugged him. "How are you, James?"

"Better than you know," James responded, with a hint of challenge in his eyes.

"I'm glad to hear that," the man answered simply.

"David, I'd like you to meet my friends," James said and introduced them. His British accent sounded stronger now that it had company. His quick ear had been unconsciously flattening his vowel sounds in imitation of the Americans he had heard around him.

Lord Marling had a genial smile for Gerald and an appreciative twinkle for Millie and Lucy. If his gaze lingered on Millie a trifle appraisingly, it was barely noticeable.

Lord David Marling, Earl of Rossbourne, was a tall, vital man in his early sixties. His face was craggy rather than handsome, his bearing military, his manner authoritative, and he exuded a lively virility. A man who likes women, Millie thought, following him up the broad stone steps.

She found herself in an immense drawing room, its vaulted cathedral ceiling arching two stories above them. The marble floors were scattered here and there with priceless rugs, each of which would have overflowed Millie's apartment. A full-size grand piano stood across from the vast fireplace, and early-American antiques mingled in happy congruity with Victorian pieces.

A burnished oak staircase, agleam with many polishings, divided into two branches, leading to the upper story. Old masters hung on the walls, each with its individually placed spotlight, interspersed here and there with Picassos and Klees in a breathtakingly impetuous concession to modernity.

An enormous portrait of a woman presided over the mantelpiece, and, under it, its subject waited for them. The Countess curtsied to James, greeted Peter warmly and the rest with dispatch. Evidently unpedigreed colonials were not milady's dish of tea.

Hester, Lady Marling, was tall, and very British, with sharp, pointed features and the delicate pink-and-white complexion for which her countrywomen are justly famed. Her brown hair curled smartly back from her face in even, controlled waves, and her back was ramrod straight. "You'll all want to spend a penny," she said euphemistically. Already she was setting Millie's teeth on edge.

Lady Hester led the way up the lefthanded branch of the majestic staircase, which was lined with portraits of ancestors long departed, and, in solitary splendor, a formal study of the Queen, elaborately gowned, jeweled, sashed, her dark hair waving softly under a diamond tiara, Orders gleaming on her breast.

Millie paused before it, searching out, in the regally impenetrable face, resemblances to her James. "Let's not dawdle now," Lady Hester called, and Millie turned, suppressing the sinking feeling in her stomach, the glittering image of James's mother, alien, remote, still before her eyes.

Lady Marling paused at a door at the head of the staircase and flung it open, affording them all a glimpse of the magnificent chamber within. The prince's room was at the corner of the house with two right-angled window walls, one facing down to the sea, and the other to the extensive, beautifully manicured gardens. A third wall was lined with books, forming a frame for the massive fireplace. In the center of the fourth, taking pride of place, stood a majestic four-poster brass bed, elaborately canopied and covered with an authentic early-American quilt.

The procession moved on, minus one member. Peter and Gerald were dropped, like sacks of mail in the Old West, at rooms midway. MacCrae had disappeared, no doubt to a domicile appropriate to his station.

Lady Hester marched Millie and Lucy down the length of the corridor to a room at the far end. "Drinks in the library at seven," she said sweetly. "I do hope you won't mind sharing. We've got rather a full house this week*end*."

Millie closed the door behind her hostess and eyed the twin beds mournfully. "What am I going to do now?"

"Relax, hon. They won't put anyone in with *him*," Lucy laughed.

A tap on the door, and Gerald entered. "Everybody naked I hope?" He settled himself on the bed. "I think I shot here once," he cracked. Although the most unlikely people rented their houses out as movie locations, Lord and Lady Marling were definitely not of their number.

Another light tap. "All settled then, are we?" James inquired. "Good," he said, answering his own question. "Come along, Millie, I've got something to show you." He clamped a hand over her wrist and drew her imperatively out of the room.

He neatly avoided a collision with Lady Hester and, maintaining his firm grasp on Millie's wrist, favored her with an imperious, heedless nod. Millie glanced back over her shoulder and saw Lady Hester looking after them, her eyes censorious.

James, oblivious to the uniformed maid who was diligently unpacking his suitcase, dragged Millie through his bedroom and around a corner into the bathroom. "Have a look at this!" he said, displaying his discovery.

The bathroom was larger than the bedroom to which Millie and Lucy had been assigned, and its decor matched the opulence of the Prince's bedchamber. It was done in an exotic shade of aquamarine, with royal blue accents and a lavish use of mirrors. All of which was lost on James. What had compelled his attention, however, was the tub.

The sunken bathtub was as much a work of art as the Old Masters that adorned the drawing room. It was about six feet square and three feet deep, set with the same aqua tiles as the walls. A built-in ledge invited underwater lounging, and gleaming brass fixtures shaped like elongated seashells arched over the top. An array of blue bath salts stood at the ready, and fluffy, rug-sized, royal-blue bath towels warmed on the heated brass stand.

Millie's eyes brimmed with laughter as she registered the immediate use to which James intended to put it. James shushed her and peeked around the door. "She's gone," he reported.

"Every two hours, James?" Millie complained, as she enthusiastically ran water in the tub. "I'm getting sore."

"A warm bath is just what you need," counseled the Prince, watching the bath salts foam as he poured with a liberal hand. "Fix you right up."

"I'm sure you know best, sir," Millie said demurely. She stripped off her clothes and plunked herself into the tub. The water came up to her neck. "What's taking you so long?"

The Prince shucked off his sweat shirt and slacks and landed next to her with a splash. He glanced around the tub, weighing its possibilities. "You sit on my lap. I don't think there's any other way in this bloody thing."

He hoisted himself onto the underwater ledge and, with his hands around her waist, lifted Millie onto his lap, lowering her carefully onto his rigid cock. Millie twined her arms around his neck. With the first upward thrust of his hips, his feet lost their purchase on the slippery tile floor. James and Millie tumbled into the tub, splashing water over the sides. Millie, considering that the job was half-done, planted her hands on James's shoulders and pushed, dunking him under the water, squealing with triumphant glee.

He came up, sputtering bubbles and bathwater and laughter. "What are you trying to do, for God's sakes. My sister Helena will never forgive you!"

"Helena?" Millie asked, puzzled.

"She's next, if anything happens to me," he laughed.

"Oh."

James looked at her stricken face and took his revenge. He put his arms tenderly around her and, with one mighty shove, ducked her into the bath, cascading water all over the floor.

Millie wrestled with him, shrieking and splashing. "James! My hair!"

"And very pretty hair it is, too," he said blandly. "I've always admired it."

She climbed on top of him, attempting, without success now that he was forewarned, to repeat her ducking.

James froze suddenly, and Millie, listening, heard the bedroom door open and the sound of muffled footsteps crossing its expanse.

James looked at her, the laughter wiped off his face. "Did you lock the bedroom door, Millie?"

"Who, me? Why didn't you?"

They looked at each other in dismay, listening to the busy footsteps. "Jesus," James whispered. "This is a fix. I hope whoever it is, is female."

"Your Royal Highness?" the maid called tentatively.

James put the palms of his hands together in a prayerful attitude. "Thank you, Lord," he murmured. "Is there anything I can do for you? I'm having a bath," he called in his most authoritative drawl.

Millie giggled. "That's the broadest *a* I ever heard, even out of your mouth."

He clamped his hand over her mouth, shushing her, intent on the drama being played out in the next room.

"Oh, no, Your Royal Highness," the maid stammered. "I was just— I came in to . . ."

"Perhaps we can discuss this further a little later. And would you be good enough to close the door on your way out," he suggested politely.

He listened for the slam of the bedroom door and, with a sigh of relief, released Millie. "Now, then. Back to our problem." He reached out and snared three fluffy bathtowels off the rack.

Millie watched him as, eyes intent, he deftly knotted the towels together. He has an . . . immaculateness, she thought, as if every inch of him had been burnished. She stared at his hands, transfixed, watching the adroit, capable, quick fingers with their blunt-tipped, white-edged nails. She captured his left hand and slid back the signet ring, exposing the pale, untanned strip of skin underneath, loving its naked vulnerability. It occurred to her suddenly that this was perhaps the one single, tiny bit of his body that no one else had ever seen since the day of his investiture.

She sensed that he was waiting and looked up at him. His eyes, glittering with amusement, were riveted on her face. "Done admiring, have we? Good." He tested the rope he had made with a swift, hard tug. "This'll do."

"James, this is dumb. Here we are, sliding around like porpoises . . . porpoisi? Porpoi? And we have that great, big, *dry* bed in there."

"We'll do that, too. But first I mean to get the better of this bloomin' tub."

He reached behind him and looped the terry-cloth rope around the marble column supporting the sink. When he turned back to Millie, he pulled the towel/rope taut behind him, so that he sat between the legs of a vee. "Come on, Millie," he urged.

Millie climbed on to his lap. He handed her, with great ceremony, the two ends of the towel. "Take one in each hand. Pull your weight against them instead of me, and we won't slide off."

Millie tried it. "It works!" she said incredulously.

"Of course, it works. I'm a very ingenious bloke. What I don't know is what we're going to do about *that*."

Millie followed his gaze. His cock curled, sweetly pink and soft, drifting against his brown thigh in the water. He grinned at her. "Got any ideas, little girl?"

He hoisted himself up to the upper ledge of the tub. Millie kneeled between his knees, the water coming just to the top of her breasts. She took him in her mouth and instantly he rose, stiff and engorged with blood. She smiled up at him impudently. "Magic."

"Sometimes I rather think it is," James said.

She looked down at his cock rising proudly from a nest of curly brown hair. "I think that's the prettiest one in the world."

James chuckled. "Millie the expert."

She circled the base of his penis with her hand. She could, just, enclose it in her grasp. She bent her head and licked at it, avidly, her tongue hungrily sucking up the pearly white droplets of moisture at its tip. She slid her mouth all the way down, engulfing him, and then slowly, teasingly up again.

He groaned and gripped the sides of the tub for balance. Millie looked at his face. His head was thrown back, and the tendons of his neck stood out, taut and straining. His eyes were closed in concentration and the muscles of his arms were rigid with his desire.

This is power, Millie thought, and took him in her mouth again.

* * *

Dinner was served in the formal dining room, attended by a butler, several uniformed footmen and two maids. David Marling and his lady reigned at either end of the polished, gleaming mahogany table. The Prince was seated to Lady Marling's right, with Lady Dolly next to him, and Gerald contentedly next to her. Millie, at Lord Marling's right, cater-corner to the Prince, had Peter on her right. Lucy next to him, completed the table.

The china was Wedgwood, the crystal, Waterford, and the silver, heavy and monogrammed. Conversation, expertly guided by Lady Hester, was smooth, if uninspired, a replica of a thousand previous dinner parties.

Millie recalled the hilarity and easy companionship of the dinner the five of them had shared at Des Artistes and was saddened. With a shock, she realized that it had only been two nights ago. It seemed like an event out of her distant past.

Lord Marling broke into her reverie. "What do you do, Miss Myerson? Do you hold down a job?" he inquired genially.

Millie looked at him in surprise. "Of course. As a matter of fact, I'm about to direct my first commercial."

"A commercial? An advert, do you mean?" Lady Hester pronounced the word as if it meant "snake." "For what, may one ask?"

"For soap," Millie responded, with as much assurance as she could muster.

Peter Goldsworth cleared his throat. "I understand that it's quite a big step up," he volunteered. "I don't believe there are many women directors."

"On feature films probably less than five," Lucy said. "And two of those who come readily to mind, Anne Bancroft and Lee Grant, are big stars."

"Which sure as hell couldn't hurt," Gerald put in.

"I know it's considered the fashion these days for young girls to follow a smart career," Lady Hester pronounced, "but I find that it makes them somewhat . . . hard-looking. I prefer young women to remain unspoiled."

"It's called earning a living," Millie said quietly.

"Something," the Prince observed, "which a good proportion of the citizenry is required to do. So I've been given to understand," he finished drily.

Lord Marling fielded the ball. "I'm told that you are currently a script supervisor. I've heard the term, but I can't say I'm familiar with the work itself."

In explaining exactly what her job entailed, Millie related an event that had occurred recently to another member of her union. The script supervisor had been mugged in the vestibule of her apartment building. When interviewed by the police, she had, with enormous attention to detail and complete accuracy, related the "action" down to such fine points as the left-handedness of one of the muggers and the half-healed scratch on the cheek of the other—and had been disbelieved. The NYPD, broad though their experience was with victims of violent crime, had not been led to expect, or to appreciate, such acuteness. "How do you know that?" they asked repeatedly.

"Because I *do!* I can't help it," the script supervisor had responded.

Millie, calling on her considerable gifts as a raconteur, honed in late-night production meetings in coffee shops around the country, told the story with wit and éclat and was rewarded when she finished with hearty laughter from around the table, not the least of which was Lord Marling's.

She glanced over at James. His face, for a fleeting moment, was naked, suffused with pride. Then it was wiped clean, devoid of emotion, save for his normal expression of thoughtful, courteous interest.

But Millie, seeing it, felt welcomed. The sense of being a stranger in a strange land fell away. Her muscles unclenched and, under the table, she wiggled her toes in celebration.

From the specific, the conversation moved to the general, a discussion of the Equal Rights Amendment. Lady Marling was concerned about the possibility of shared lavatories ("That *can't* be sanitary") and Dolly about the draft, with its ensuant loss of femininity. Peter Goldsworth tried, vainly, to divert the conversation, which had become heated, while Lord Marling, with evident enjoyment, fanned the flames. James held his silence, toying with his wineglass, listening intently.

"We don't have an Equal Rights Amendment in England," Lady Hester observed, clearly under the impression that she had delivered the coup de grace, "and we seemed to have muddled through quite well. But then again, we didn't require a civil war to free *our* slaves."

"The sociology in England is different," James said, addressing the subject for the first time. "And the American Civil War had less to do with the abolition of slavery than with other factors."

"And we've certainly had our civil wars," Lord Marling observed.

"You miss the point," Lady Marling told her husband acidly. "An Equal Rights Amendment isn't necessary. Women *are* equal. In all the most important things. The things that really matter."

James set his glass down a trifle too forcefully, so that a little wine sloshed over the rim. "I find it hard to fathom," he began slowly, "that an amendment guaranteeing equal rights to a majority of the citizenry, whether needed or not, would meet with resistance. I've read the amendment—what is it? thirty? thirty-five words?—and it seems quite simple and straightforward to me. And by the way," he added deliberately, turning to Lady Hester, "you are aware, I am sure, that all my sisters, when of age, serve in the armed forces of our country. I can't see," he finished mildly, "that it's diminished their femininity in any way."

Millie, Lucy and Gerald exchanged surreptitious grins. "Why don't you announce that you support it," Millie asked, carried away. "That would be a tremendous help."

"I can't!" The Prince's voice, pained, drew out the long *a*.

"Nothing like putting your money where your mouth is," Gerald murmured.

The Prince ignored him. He looked at Millie across the long table. "Darling, I can't get involved in the internal politics of my own country, let alone those of a foreign one!" Millie glanced around the table and saw that neither the exchange nor the endearment had gone unnoticed. The Prince returned his attention to the wineglass he twirled between his fingers. "That's one of the disadvantages," he said softly.

James looked up, and his eyes met Millie's. She smiled at him, remembering what one of the advantages of his position was. His face brightened, whether because he shared the same association or because of the encouragement he read in her face, she couldn't say. Lord Marling looked from Millie to Prince James and back again, missing nothing.

Lady Marling, her voice clearly calling the company to attention, reverted to a subject less likely to call down the Prince's displeasure on her head. She inquired after the health of James's sisters, the three Princesses. This, unfortunately, turned the conversation to the latest cause célèbre.

The youngest Princess, thirteen-year-old Sarah, had recently been caught by a trespassing photographer in a most unflattering pose. She had been eating an ice-cream cone, which she had inadvertently allowed to drip down the front of her blouse. In an instinct left over from childhood, she had pinched the fabric of her blouse with her thumb and forefinger and, drawing it away from her body, had attempted to lick up the ice cream.

While the photo had a certain innocent charm and had been taken while the Princess was off guard, in the privacy of her own gardens, it had evidently raised questions as to the manners and general deportment of the younger members of the royal family.

"It's not fair," Gerald protested. "She's just a kid."

"She'll get used to it," James said brusquely.

Millie, unphotogenic herself, felt for the young girl. We all have awkward moments, she thought, but at least they don't come back to haunt us with our breakfast cereal. "They'd have a field day with me," she mused. "I photograph just like Lady Bird Johnson."

Silence. Every British eye bored into her. Millie had spoken the tail end of her thought, actually a commiseration with the faraway teenage Princess, aloud. She had meant exactly nothing by it. Her dinner companions, however, had taken it to mean that she, too, had expectations of the press taking an interest in her—in the very near future.

She glanced around the table. No help. Gerald stared off into space, while Lucy busied herself with the careful alignment of her knife and fork on her plate. Peter Goldsworth examined his place mat minutely, while Lady Dolly stared at her with interest.

She looked at James. He leaned decorously back in his chair, his face a mask of saintly composure, while his eyes gleamed with unholy glee. Let's see you get out of this one, ducks. She could hear his unspoken thought as clearly as if he had actually said it.

Lady Marling stepped into the breech. "Let's all have coffee in the library, shall we? I know you young people would like to spend some time together," she added with a meaningful look at her daughter.

The "young people," however, were not destined to enjoy each other's company undisturbed. After dinner they were joined by what seemed to Millie to be the whole of a flourishing British colony on the shores of New England. Mr. and Mrs. Carlton-French, Lord and Lady Bannisford, Professor and Mrs. So-and-So. Millie lost track after a while.

She sat, quietly, cognac in hand, in the corner of one of the leather sofas watching James, in politician's parlance, work the room. He moved about, speaking to each person individually, gracious, confident, at ease. They had come for one reason only, to see the Heir Apparent, and he knew it and fulfilled their wish. Occasionally, he threw back his head, in his characteristic gesture, and laughed. But more often he smiled.

Millie watched him accept, routinely, the acts of fealty, a bow or a light curtsy made by each new arrival, and found it hard to reconcile this with James, her James, whose bed she had gotten out of that morning, and whose predinner bath she had, joyously, shared.

He seems . . . different, Millie thought, watching him. Then she corrected herself. It wasn't *he* who was different; the people reacting to him were different. It was even more evident when they spoke *about* him than *to* him. When they addressed him directly, they called him "sir." When they referred to him in conversation, they called him "His Royal Highness," running the words all together, as if he were the possessor of an unusually long first name. "Hisroyalhighness looks well," she heard someone say.

One of a group of people gathered around James, encouraged by the pleasant demeanor and easy informality of the young Prince, referred, apparently with undue familiarity, to "your mother." James did not appear to hear. The man repeated his comment. After a beat, in which it appeared to be touch-and-go as to whether James would acknowledge the remark, he replied icily, "The Queen does not agree with that position."

Millie realized for the first time that he had given her and her friends an unaccustomed degree of leeway, whether because of the rollicking good time they were having, or because he didn't expect Americans to know the drill, she couldn't say.

Gerald had the frosty Lady Dolly off in a corner and was talking animatedly. Probably regaling her with old production stories, Millie thought. And evidently with some small success, for Lady Dolly unbent enough to laugh out loud.

Lucy circulated almost as much as the Prince. Millie watched her moving easily from group to group, admiring her cool poise, her grace and her ease. She's the one who'd make a good queen, she thought, loving her. She'd look good on a stamp.

Lord Marling, handsome in his pin-striped suit, stood in front of Millie. "May I?" he inquired, gesturing to the seat next to her. "Or shall I get you another brandy first?"

Millie smilingly covered her glass with her fingertips, declining the brandy, and invited him to sit.

"Tell me about yourself, my dear," he invited, settling himself on the couch.

Millie looked into his eyes. "What would you like to know?"

"The beginning's a good place to start," he smiled at her.

She looked at his ruddy face, framed by his thick, neatly combed silvery hair, responding to his easy charm, his evident interest. "I've lived in New York City all my life. Except for college. I went away to Wellesley, on a scholarship. I graduated cum laude and came back to New York, determined to have a glittering, exciting, demanding, stupendous career." She smiled in deprecation of her youthful enthusiasms. "And here I am."

"And do you plan on continuing with your career," he asked intently.

"Of course. What else?"

"Certainly. Certainly." Lord Marling replied. Millie sensed that her answer had somehow gratified him. "You seem like a sensible girl. And I like that. For I'm the same way myself. If one approach doesn't work, I try another." Despite his laudatory smile, the chilling sense of unease returned, sweeping over Millie so that she repressed a shiver. She glanced at Lord Marling from under lowered lids. His eyes were on the Prince, attracted by the sound of his infectious laughter. "He is our bright hope," Lord Marling said somberly. "We must care for him. We must see that nothing . . . untoward happens to him."

"What are you talking about?" Millie asked bluntly.

"Hallo!" the Prince interrupted. He held out his hands to Millie, and, smiling up at him, she put both her hands in his. With the departure of the die-hard Lord and Lady Bannisford, they were left just "family," and James resumed his off-duty effervescence.

Lord Marling stood up to relinquish his seat. James restrained him with a gesture. "I insist," Lord Marling laughed. "You young people don't need an old war-horse like me to come between you."

James thanked him with a smile and, loosening his tie, sat down next to Millie. "How are you, love?"

"Better, now," she responded.

James leaned back, resting his arm along the back of the couch, not touching her, but sheltering just the same. Millie let the talk swirl around her, not listening. She'd had enough of watchfulness and let James, one foot resting on the other knee, jiggling with his boundless energy, stand guard for both of them.

"Tired, darling?" he whispered after she had not spoken for a long while.

"No. Just quiet," she smiled at him. "Maybe just a little."

"It's time we put you to bed, then."

"Will you make love to me?" she asked, with the directness and the sweet simplicity of a child.

James's eyes gleamed. "With all my heart," he whispered. He got to his feet with a graceful, unhurried gesture. "Well, that's it for me," he said aloud.

This appeared to be a signal to the entire company. They were all suddenly recalled to the lateness of the hour and stood up, collecting scarves, eyeglasses, books and other requisite belongings.

James followed her up the grand staircase, his right hand sliding along the bannister, his left casually trailing along the wall, so that, without touching her, he held Millie in an almost embrace.

She glanced back over her shoulder and spotted Peter and Lucy headed for the door that led to the lawns and thence to the sea. "What do you suppose that's all about, hmmmmm?" James asked, following her glance. "Curiouser and curiouser."

"Who knows? Could be something, could be nothing."

Peter, as if feeling the Prince's eyes on him, turned and walked back across the large salon. He stood at the bottom of the staircase. "Good night, Your Royal Highness," Goldsworth called, inclining his head.

James stopped, looking over the bannister at his equerry. He waited just a tiny, measuring beat before answering. "Good night, Peter," he said evenly.

Outside her door, he hugged her briefly. "Come quickly," he said. She watched his tall figure move swiftly down the corridor to his room and opened the door to hers.

Millie lay, luxuriating, while the Prince lingeringly fulfilled his promise. She cradled him between her legs, her hands tangling in his soft hair, and watched the luminous three-quarter moon play hide and seek with the clouds.

Later, the ravening hunger that clamored between them quiescent for the moment, they lay, silently, listening to the thunder rumble in the distance.

"I had the strangest conversation with Lord Marling," Millie said suddenly, as her lassitude faded. "He said you—"

"Don't you worry about Lord Marling," James said, his voice unwontedly harsh. "Leave David to me." His tone closed the door on that subject once and for all time.

"Okay." Millie turned over, leaning on her side, looking into the Prince's face. "Is something wrong between you and Peter?"

"I don't know," the Prince answered thoughtfully. "I don't want to get an idea fixed in my head until I'm sure." His laughter rang out suddenly. "I think he may rather have done me a favour," he said jubilantly.

"How come you don't look at him like he's done you a favor?" The Prince didn't answer. He kissed the top of her head by way of response. "You know who looks at you funny?" Millie persisted. "Gerald. What do you suppose got into him?" She sat up, propelled by indignation. "I've never seen him act that way."

James laughed. "It's very simple—"

"He thought you were trying to show him up. He's jealous of you."

"No, my darling. He is, but not in the way you mean. I don't think that Gerald envies me one thing that I have, except— He loves you."

"And I love *him*," Millie returned promptly.

"Not like that. Gerald *really* loves you. I see it in his eyes."

"Don't be silly. We've known each other for ages, and it's never been that way between us."

"Nevertheless," the Prince said, reaching up to her. "And now, madam, would you mind coming back down here and—"

He broke off. Someone had tapped on the Prince's door, lightly. Millie and James froze, waiting. It came again. Three light, deliberate knocks. Millie looked at James questioningly. He shrugged, miming his incomprehension.

"James? Sir? Are you awake?" Lady Dolly's whisper, sibilant, hushed.

"What the hell—" James muttered under his breath. He slipped his arm out from Millie's shoulders and, shoving a pillow behind him, sat up. "What is it, Dolly," he asked firmly.

"I can't sleep," she called through the door, low-voiced. "I thought you might like a few minutes . . . chat."

Millie buried her face in the Prince's bare chest, stifling her giggles. He toyed with her hair, absentmindedly, thinking. "Try some warm milk," he advised kindly. "That always fixes me right up when I can't sleep."

They waited, breathless, listening. Silence. Lady Dolly had apparently adjourned to her own boudoir.

Millie sat up, leaning against the headboard next to the Prince. "Warm milk makes me nauseous," she confided.

"It does me too," the Prince agreed, convulsing her.

"I don't believe it!" Millie expostulated, when their laughter had died down. "I honestly don't believe it. I wish I had that kind of guts."

"Yes. Well." James cleared his throat, a touch embarrassed.

"How does it feel to be the world's foremost sex symbol?" Millie teased.

"Well, as . . . was it Marilyn Monroe who said that if you've got to be a symbol, sex is a great thing to be a symbol of? I met her once," he added, clearly intending to divert the conversation. "When I was a kid. At a command performance. I don't remember quite how she got there. I think she was making a film in London."

"Probably *The Prince and the Showgirl*."

"With Olivier. You're right! I remember it very well. Because she was so nice to me. Here I was, this chubby kid—"

"You were not!"

"Yes, I *was*. And painfully shy. I think I was about nine or ten.

And she was so nice. She didn't talk down to me, and she didn't . . . coo, the way the grown-ups often did. She spoke to me just as if I were her equal. I thought she was the most beautiful creature . . ."

Millie watched his mobile face, tender, lost in recollection. A flash of lightning streaked across the heavens and was gone, leaving the darkness intensified, followed almost instantly by a crash of thunder so close the stone mansion seemed to vibrate.

The skies opened, and rain sheeted down in torrents.

"Oh, good!" Millie said, jumping out of bed. " A storm. Let's watch."

They flung open the casement windows and sat on the window seat, side by side, elbows resting on the windowsills, absorbed in the driving power and the majesty of the storm, breathing the air fresh with rain and the sea and the scent of wet grass.

"But you're right, you know," James said, after a while, turning to her. Half his face was shadowed, and half illuminated by the play of clouds and light and sheeting rain. "It really is a symbolic thing. It has nothing to do with me at all—Lady Dolly, I mean."

"Doesn't it bother her? Hasn't she figured out that we're . . . together?"

"That's exactly the point. She has, and she hasn't. People don't think of me in quite the same way they do others. Often they see me as someone who is somehow . . . reserved for them . . . sexually. I'm more of a symbol, an institution to them than a man. I haven't quite got a handle on it, but I can see it operating. I can see it working. People . . . women think that, if they make love with me, some of the magic they think I've got will somehow rub off, transfer to them."

"You've thought about this a lot, haven't you?" Millie asked quietly when he paused.

"What else have I got to think about," he answered wryly. "That's one of the reasons I read anthropology at University. I wanted to try and understand how I fit into things. And how others before me had. I'm a link in a very long chain. Do you remember Fraser's *Golden Bough?*"

"Vaguely."

He stared out across the lawns to the sea, hidden from their view by the torrents of rain. His face was austere, remote. Millie waited, listening to the drumming of the rain on the slate roof, the brushing of the foliage in the garden beneath their window, the distant rushing of the surf.

"In ancient times," he began finally, his voice very low, his words measured. "In ancient times, the King was thought to be the source of many things that were essential to the people's lives. He had it in his power to regulate the natural order, giving, or withholding, sunlight, rain in its season, winds, earthquake, literally the things that mean the difference between life and death. He could send either calamity or blessings down upon them. He was a bridge between the divine and the mortal, and he himself was neither. He was . . . between.

"So the question became . . . It's a short step from there, to—how do you control the King? How do you ensure that his power would be used only for good, that he would bestow the blessings in his gift, in the right way at the right time? And one way was sexual union. The King, by joining sexually with a woman chosen by the populace, would somehow convey to *her*, and thus to them, some of his magical powers.

"And, by expending his sexuality, his life force, solely in a ritual manner, at a time and place and with a partner of their choosing, they could, in turn, leash this power, contain it, make it . . . manageable."

Lightning cracked above them, spilling a white glare over the Prince's face, lending a fleeting, eerie quality to its stern, controlled severity. "In ancient Cambodia," he continued, "and in Japan as well, the ruler was kept in absolute solitude from the moment he began his reign—till the end of his life. He was given extraordinary privileges, he led a life of incalculable luxury, but he never saw a human face."

He fell silent. The storm had passed, and in its place the clouds, windswept, scudded over the face of the waxing moon, unfolding a drama no less theatrical, no less mysterious, no less compelling.

Millie framed her question delicately. "Does . . . anyone else see this the way you do?"

James smiled at her indirection. "No, she doesn't. At least, I don't think so. I've never spoken with anyone about this quite so . . . personally." He turned to face her, returning from his solitary exile. "Anyway, the point is," his voice was pitched at a more conversational level, its customary resonance and gaiety returned, "what happened with Lady Dolly, and with . . . others, has virtually nothing to do with me. With who I am. Inside. Despite my staggering good looks and devastating charm." He drew Millie to him and hugged her. "What did you read at University?"

"Literature and French. Do you know I'm the first person in my family ever to graduate from college?"

"I am too," the Prince responded.

"Want to hear the best thing I ever learned?" James nodded and, releasing her, looked out at the changeling sky. Millie recited, the musical French syllables rising and falling in the quiet room,

> *Les sanglots longs*
> *Des violons*
> *De l'automne*
> *Blessent mon coeur*
> *D'une langueur*
> *Monotone.*

> *Tout suffocant*
> *Et blême, quand*
> *Sonne l'heure,*
> *Je me souviens*
> *Des jours anciens*
> *Et je pleure;*

> *Et je m'en vais*
> *Au vent mauvais*
> *Qui m'emporte*
> *Deçà, delà,*
> *Pareil à la*
> *Feuille morte.*

James remained motionless for a moment after she finished. Then he turned to her. "Thank you," he said simply. His eyes glistened, whether with moonlight or the sheen of tears, Millie wasn't sure.

"Isn't it lovely?" she said softly. James nodded. "I'm not sure who wrote it. I think Paul Verlaine. We had this one professor, Michel Mendelsohn, his name was, who made us learn tons and tons of poetry by heart. That's not usual in this country, but he was European and didn't care. We all hated it then. But now I carry it with me all the time."

He drew her to him then and kissed her forehead and then her mouth, deeply. "The Verlaine was beautiful," he whispered. "You're beautiful. Come. Let's go to bed."

We give each other gifts, Millie thought, drifting off to sleep.

She heard him say, softly, "I wonder how many women would be banging on my bedroom door if my name were James Smith."

"I would," she answered.

"And I, yours," he responded. And they slept.

Chapter VIII

Millie awoke to find the sun streaming through the casement windows. The other side of the bed was empty. She pulled her robe over her naked body, smiling to herself, wondering if James owned a pair of pajamas, wondering if he wondered the same thing about her. She opened the door, carefully, and peeked down the corridor. Empty. Millie sped to her room. She dressed quickly, pulling on shorts and a top over her bathing suit.

She stepped out on the landing and leaned over the balustrade. She could see into the sunny, plant-filled breakfast room that faced out over the sea. It was, she realized, directly under James's bedroom.

Everyone got there before me, she thought. James, absentmindedly crunching a piece of toast, was concentrating on a newspaper, as were Lord David, Peter and Lucy. Lady Dolly stared out to sea, Gerald stared at Lady Dolly, and Lady Hester watched Gerald, very carefully.

James glanced up from his newspaper and saw her. He started to raise his hand to beckon to her, then changed his mind. He scraped his chair back from the table, crossed the large salon with rapid steps and stood at the bottom of the stairs, waiting, looking up at her, his face joyous with his welcoming smile.

Millie started down the stairs, slowly, deliberately. James folded his arms across his chest, ostentatiously, allowing her to take her own sweet time. When she was halfway down, she halted, retieing the lace of her sneaker with elaborate attention. And then, all patience expended, ran headlong down the rest of the steps. He caught her around the waist when she was still four or five steps above him and, lifting her off her feet, whirled her around and down into his embrace. "Good morning, darling," he said in her ear. "You were sleeping so soundly, I didn't have the heart to wake you. Not that I didn't want to," he added, grinning broadly.

She looked up at him, her heart in her eyes, and hand in hand they walked into the breakfast room. "Good morning," Millie said, smiling her happiness out to them all. She took the empty seat next to James.

"I'm an early riser, myself," Lady Hester announced starchily. "It pays to get a good start on the day, I've always said."

"That depends on what kind of a night you've had, doesn't it," the Prince said smoothly, putting finis to that subject.

Lucy choked over her coffee, Gerald coughed into his napkin, and even the staid Peter Goldsworth found it necessary to bury himself deeper into his paper. Lord Marling shot the Prince a glance filled with amusement and a sort of masculine approbation. James accepted the older man's wordless salute calmly, buttering another slice of toast.

"Thank you, that's fine." Millie smiled up at the uniformed maid, helping herself liberally from a large silver dish of scrambled eggs and sausage. "No, just a second," she corrected, stabbing an additional sausage. And immediately regretted it. If anybody makes any cracks about my appetite, I'll scream, she thought.

"I never saw you eat breakfast before, Millie," remarked Gerald, possessed of the devil. "She usually just drinks gallons and gallons of coffee," he informed the world, giving them the benefit of his experience.

Millie glared at him and transferred her eyes to her plate, concentrating on her food. James, thankfully, had kept his mouth shut, she thought, missing the solemn twinkle he exchanged with Lucy.

"What will you all do this morning?" Lady Hester inquired, unchastened.

"Let's all have a ride, shall we?" Lady Dolly suggested. "There are some lovely trails around here. I think we can mount you all."

"Splendid idea!" James enthused.

"Capital," Peter Goldsworth endorsed.

"That's terrific!" Gerald smiled at Lady Dolly.

"Let's do it," Lucy said. "I haven't ridden in ages."

"I think I'll just hit the beach," Millie said, when the enthusiasm had died down. "Well, there's only one sport I'm really good at," she defended. "And that's lying on a beach in a bikini with a glass in my hand. I don't *do* horses. They don't like me."

"I think I'll have a go at the beach myself," James said, grinning innocently at the surprised assemblage.

"That sounds very relaxing. I think I'll join you," Peter Goldsworth put in.

"I could do with a nice sunbath as well," Lady Dolly said.

"Count me in," Gerald followed quickly.

"Well, I'm not going riding by myself," Lucy said, amused.

Millie looked at each of them in turn, flabbergasted. This was the first time she could ever recall an entire group of people opting for an activity in subjugation to her whim. Not mine, she corrected. His.

"I've got an idea!" James exclaimed. "Let's take the *Dorothea* out!" He cocked an interrogative eyebrow at Millie. "How about it? D'you fancy a sail?"

"Fabulous," said Millie.

"Have a care," the Prince warned, steadying the motor launch against the side of the yacht as best he could in the rough waters of the bay. "Move along, now." In a break with their by now routine practice, he ushered everyone up the ladder before him. MacCrae, looking somehow out of place, despite his black bathing suit and gray sweatshirt, demurred, giving in only to his boss's repeated urgings.

Lady Dolly, her generous figure contained, just, by a violet flowered bikini, accepted Gerald's bracing arm and helpful boost and smiled her thanks—at the Prince. Millie, watching her, involuntarily glanced down at her modest cleavage, outlined by the thin nylon of her yellow maillot, and shrugged ruefully. Lucy, catching her, burst out in laughter.

The Prince bounded lightly up the ladder. "I hope none of you gets seasick!" he teased. James moved unerringly to a specially designed concealed cabinet, and pulled out a set of rolled charts held together with rubber bands. "Don't do that!" he called sharply, adding a heartfelt "Please!" and arresting Peter Goldsworth in the act of raising the rectangular crimson, gold and blue pennant that advised of the presence of the Prince of Wales. "We'll have those bleeding photographers all over us," he muttered. "Check the engine instead, why don't you. We'll head out of the bay under power. MacCrae, see to the lines. Make sure they're not tangled. Dolly, get us a weather report. The radio should be tuned to the marine channel, but if it isn't, find it!" He barked his orders, then grinned, abashed, as it dawned on him, belatedly, that he was not in fact aboard the HMS *Clarington*, and these were not his junior officers. "Make sure we've got enough life vests, would you, Lucy?" he asked, more conversationally.

"Aye, aye, sir," Lucy returned, with an elaborate salute. James acknowledged her parody with a small smile.

"Just turn the goddamn key and get the mother going," Gerald stared at the Prince. "This is a pleasure cruise, not a naval maneuver, remember, fuckhead."

Lady Dolly sucked in a horrified breath. "Well, I never—"

The Prince quelled her with a look. "Quite right," he said unperturbed. "I get carried away sometimes," and transferred his attention to the charts, as they all dispersed to their assigned tasks.

"And me? How about me? What should I do?" Millie confronted the Prince, indignant at being overlooked.

"Keep me company while I chart us a course," he replied, with the flash of an intimate just-for-her smile.

"I'm not an ornament, I'm a human being. And a capable one, too!" Millie glared at him, outraged. "Concubines belong in harems," she added icily, by way of scholarly exposition of her position.

"Sorry. Beastly of me," James apologized contritely. "It's just that I so much . . . want you near me all the time. I'm sorry," he repeated, crestfallen. "Help with the canvas, will you."

Finally they were under sail. The *Dorothea* rode easily in the water, making short work of the choppy seas. Millie wandered away by herself, stretching out in the narrow space between the cabin wall and the metal guardrails that rimmed the ship. She lay on her stomach, her head pillowed on her folded arms, and gave herself up to the sun, which baked into her skin with that special intensity it has only at sea.

She lay, trancelike, her every muscle relaxed, flowing with the motion of the ship, listening to the slap of the waves, the creaking of the sails, the breeze a cooling caress on her heated body, the sun a golden aura behind her closed eyes.

Millie roused to a cool hand on the small of her back. "Turn over, darling, you'll get roasted." She flipped over on her back and shaded her eyes. James kneeled by her side, bending over her, outlined against the brilliant azure sky. "You're not still miffed, are you? I don't like it when we row. It . . . frightens me," said the daredevil Prince.

"No." She smiled at him. "You came all over funny. 'Appens to the best of us," she quoted. He grinned at her, schoolboyish, relieved.

Millie pulled down the strap of her bathing suit, craning her neck over her shoulder to peek at her blossoming tan. "You're getting golden," James said.

"Yes." She turned back, meeting his eyes.

Eroticism, fanned by the sun and the salt air and the motion of the ship, crackled between them. James glanced around, checking to see just how secluded they were. Not enough. Even given the fact that no one was likely to intrude upon them.

Millie turned on her side, resting her back against the cabin wall. James stretched out alongside her in the narrow space where there was barely room for one, bracing his back against the guardrail, his face close to hers. They lay, basking in the hot sun, their eyes locked, each feeding upon the other, listening in the silence to the elemental melody that between them never went unheard, hearing it rise in pitch and intensity till it sang with clarion sweetness, as it played from one to the other.

Millie, looking her challenge into his eyes, ran her hand lightly over his chest, down to the edge of his blue-and-white-striped bathing suit, and then up again, feeling the soft hairs rustle under her palm.

His eyes, accepting the challenge, held hers fixedly. His face was drawn with his concentration, and his breathing quickened. He brushed her hair off her forehead and with the palm of his hand traced the delicate curve from her temple, alongside her face, down to her throat. He clasped her shoulder, hot from the sun, his fingers gripping, feeling her begin to tremble. He strengthened his grip, his fingers digging into her skin, counterpointing, and intensifying, the convulsive clutch in her pelvis.

Millie drew in a breath and held it, letting it out slowly. With a smile of pure impudence, she upped the stakes. She slipped her hand between his legs, cradling him.

His face, schooled with a discipline instilled in the nursery, betrayed nothing. But his eyes glowed, and his body quivered imperceptibly.

The game, however, was becoming more than Millie could bear. Her own desire blazed, soaring higher and higher, so that she contained it but with difficulty.

"Millie—" James began. His voice caught in his throat, husky. He started again. "Millie, I—" He stopped, unable, for the moment to continue.

"Excuse me, Your Royal Highness," Peter Goldsworth stood on the deck below, shading his eyes as he called up to them. "We're all going to have a bit of lunch now, if you'd like to join us." He glanced uncomfortably at Lady Dolly, the clear instigator of this lèse majesté.

"Thank you. We'll be right with you," the Prince called, sitting up. "And God rot your bones in everlasting hell!" he added under his breath, to Millie's delight.

Resigned, he got to his feet and helped Millie climb down to the deck. She sensed that he hadn't followed her and turned in time to see him, standing on the guardrail, execute a high, arcing dive into the ice-blue Atlantic. A moment later another body hurtled into the water, following suit.

Millie watched them both surface, spitting water, grinning from ear to ear, and wondered, smiling to herself, if the voluptuous Lady Dolly had inspired in Gerald the need for the same emergency measures to which the Prince had found himself compelled to resort.

Late in the afternoon, showered and changed, skin tingling with the newly minted suntan, Millie wandered across the lawns to join the house party, lounging on wicker chairs, enjoying the magnificent sunset.

James, oblivious to the splendor behind him, was engrossed in the contents of the boxes; reading, and then initialing, at a rapid pace.

Millie helped herself to a gin and tonic from the waiting tray table and settled in a chair, knees bent, feet resting on the edge of the seat.

Conversation was desultory, idle. The sailors were pleasantly tired from the day at sea, and the resplendent sunset, shading the sky and in turn the bay with indigo, magenta and gold, commanded attention. Lucy and Lord Marling conversed in low tones, while Lady Dolly sat apart, sulkily tracing designs with her lacquered forefinger on her frosty glass. Peter Goldsworth sat across from the Prince at the round table, at the ready.

Gerald came out of the house, and Millie watched his long, loping stride carry him across the expanse of lawn. "So what's goin' on?" he asked cheerily.

"Pull up a chair," Millie invited.

"What's *he* doing?" Gerald wanted to know.

"Paperwork," sighed the Prince, glancing up. "I drown in it. It never stops."

Gerald shrugged. "Well, that's show biz." He took his seat, impaled by several shocked, stony glances. The only exception to this censure was Prince James, who calmly transferred his attention to the papers on his makeshift desk.

The sound of a door slamming, shockingly loud in the silence, drew their attention from Gerald to the house. A uniformed maid trod heavily down the steps at the side of the house, moving toward them as fast as her dumpy body would allow.

Lady Marling frowned at this further erosion of seemly behavior. "She's not one of our regulars. Extra help. I just got her yesterday."

No one responded. Even from a distance they could see that she was quivering with excitement. James put his pen down, and they all watched her approach.

"Your Royal Highness," she began, while she was still ten feet away. Her voice had the musical lilt of the islands. The maid reached them and paused, catching her breath. They waited, knowing instinctively that it was futile to rush her. "Your Royal Highness," she repeated. Millie saw the beads of sweat on her café-au-lait skin, and a tremor of disquiet ran through her.

"Yes? What is it?" James asked calmly, his voice low. "What is it?" he repeated, a shade too quickly.

"It's . . . there's a telephone call for you . . . Your Royal Highness," she stammered, "from Buckingham Palace! They say it's important," she finished breathlessly.

The maid's trepidation communicated itself to them all. The same ominous thought came, unbidden, to each of them simultaneously. All eyes turned to the Prince, as if controlled by a string wielded by an unseen puppeteer.

James turned, visibly, several shades paler under his tan. He sat very, very still.

Lord Marling stood up. "I'll take it, sir." He strode across the lawn, covering the ground very quickly, his body leaning forward, head bent. The maid, with one last, awed look at the Prince, trailed after him.

No one looked directly at the man who was a woman's heartbeat away from the throne of England. He sat, rock still, hands resting on his knees, staring at nothing, waiting. A small muscle in his temple, pulsing, belied the iron impassivity of his face.

Millie rose and crossed to the Prince's side. She sat down next to him, wordlessly. She hesitated, fearing to jar his crystalline composure, then covered his hand with hers. He did not turn his head, nor did he look at her, but he turned his hand, palm upward, and gripped hers tightly. His hand was dry, and a little cold.

Lord Marling emerged from the house, waving his arm above his head in an "all-clear." "It's all right," he called, when he got within earshot. He walked directly over to James and, strangely, dipped his head, making the formal obeisance with which he greeted and took leave of his Prince each day. "Your sister, Princess Sarah, would like to speak with you, sir."

Everybody breathed, seemingly for the first time in minutes. James stood up, stumbling just a little. "What in blazes was wrong with that wretched woman?" he asked grimly.

"Nothing," Lord Marling replied, with a wry shrug. "Just one of your loyal subjects who never dreamed she'd have the honour of speaking face to face with her future sovereign."

"Jesus," Gerald exclaimed involuntarily. The Prince shot him a quick, noncommittal look and started toward the house.

James returned, smiling. Resuming his seat, he announced with a fair assumption of his normal jocularity, "My sister, it appears, has succeeded in falling off her horse and in love at one and the same time. The young gent in question has apparently won both the race and Sarah's heart. A masterstroke," he added enviously. He picked up his pen and unscrewed the top. "She wanted my advice as to whether it was proper for a woman to ask a man out for the first date."

"What did you tell her, sir?" Lucy asked, amid the general laughter.

"I told her she'd pretty much *have* to. If this bloke has the guts to ring her up at Windsor Castle and ask her to a matinee at the local cinema, he's a better man than I am." He picked up a file folder and turned his attention from affairs of the heart to affairs of state, more pressing perhaps, but no more important.

Millie watched him intently, oblivious to the carefully inconsequential conversations going on around her, not one word of which touched upon the event uppermost in all their minds.

James looked, to a less discerning eye than hers, refreshingly normal. His color was mostly restored, and his hand was steady as it scrawled his hasty, flowing initial J. But to Millie, the vestiges of strain were abundantly clear. He was still somewhat paler than usual, and his concentration appeared a trifle studied. She watched him read a document, finish it and, with a grimace of disgust, start over again at the top of the page. He glanced up and met Millie's watchful, appraising gaze. His blue eyes were dark with leftover shock.

I can't let him be like this, Millie thought. She stood up purposefully. "C'mon," she said gently. "Let's go for a walk."

He looked up into her face, wordlessly debating this breech of self-discipline, then nodded, conceding. He swiftly replaced the papers in the red boxes, locked them, and restored the little gold key to the pocket of his slacks. Peter, ever alert, took custody of the leather cases.

Millie took him by the hand and drew the Prince to his feet. She led him down to the narrow strip of beach, and he followed passively, all authority fallen away.

They walked along the water's edge, following the curve of the bay, the curling wavelets teasing at their ankles. They walked in silence, the Prince availing himself of the rare luxury of not having to speak. Occasionally he would reach down, pick up a pebble and toss it out to sea, watching attentively to see where it fell. The sun hung redly on the rim of the horizon, its glory reflected in the glassy pools left by the outgoing tide. A flock of sandpipers landed on the wet sand, each of them a doubled image, mirrored in the shallow pools.

After a while, Millie began to talk. She kept up a stream of bright inconsequential chatter, carefully avoiding questions, which might require James to answer. She picked up seashells, speculating on their prior tenants, pointed out a seagull, unerringly swooping down on his dinner, laughed as the hem of her flowing cotton dress was soaked by a careless wave. And, finally, directed his attention to the first star, which appeared, shining, in the sapphire sky.

Slowly, with enormous delicacy, with infinite care, she brought him back to himself.

"Sun's going down," he said suddenly, recovering his powers of speech. "Let's turn back." She looked into his eyes and, satisfied, nodded. He threw his arm around her shoulders, and they walked, the lingering brightness at their backs, into the gathering twilight. But their silence now had no quality of strain, and Millie forgot her watchful alertness.

When they had retraced almost the entire distance and the stone mansion appeared around the curve of the bay, Millie began to speak. "There's a story—I don't know whether it's in the Talmud or the Mishna or just a legend—about a man who was visited with all kinds of tribulations. His youngest child died, swept away by a virulent plague, and then his wife. His business failed, leaving his remaining children with no means of support. And he cried out to God. 'Why do you give me such burdens. They are more than I can bear.' And God said, 'If that is so, I will help you.' He took the man to a field dotted with *pekelach*, with bundles, each of them a burden. Some were very small and some were very large.

"And God said to him, 'Choose that burden which you feel you can bear.' The man searched through the field carefully. He disregarded those burdens which were too small, and those which were too large. He chose a burden of a medium size, not the smallest, but one of the smaller ones. He said, 'This, Oh Lord, I think I can bear.' And God said to him, 'That, my friend, is the burden you bore in the first place.'"

The Prince halted. He turned to look into her face. "Millie—" he began, and his voice broke. He turned away and waded ankle deep into the foaming surf.

Millie waited, tranquil, at peace.

When he spoke, finally, his tone was casual, his voice nonchalant. "Millie," James said, looking out to sea. "You know I love you, don't you." There was no trace of a question in his voice.

The world blurred before Millie's eyes, spinning giddily. Then it focused, with incandescent clarity. She stood, her toes digging into the wet sand, unable to speak for the drumming of the blood in her ears.

Millie looked out at the bay. Its opalescent surface shimmered with the lingering glory of the reflected sunset. She recognized, with a shock of familiarity, the landscape of her dream exactly one week ago.

James turned to her, his smile teasing, affectionate. "Well, say something, can't you?" He crossed the small space between them and clasped his hands around her waist. He looked down at her, his face radiating his joy and his release. "What's the matter? Cat got my Millie's tongue?"

Millie looked into his face. She saw the sea change in his eyes as clearly as one can see, deep in the ocean, the swift darkening as one current replaces another. Something fevered appeared in his eyes, something volatile, consuming, and barely under control.

"Let's go home," he said and scooped her into the curve of his arm. They walked back to the house, skirting the edge of the incoming tide.

The lawn was deserted, the wicker chairs empty and the darkness complete. James opened the door for Millie, and they blinked against the sudden bright light of the drawing room.

"Where *were* you?" Lady Hester snapped. "We've been waiting dinner for you."

The Prince raised a single, silent eyebrow, and she faltered. "Thank you very much, Hester, but I'm afraid we can't." With his hand at the small of Millie's back he propelled her through the room and up the grand staircase. At the top, he turned and looked down at the astonished Marling family. "Please excuse us. We don't feel well. Or something." He turned away and resumed his swift march down the corridor, sweeping Millie along before him. "Christ, that was rude," he muttered. "But right now I don't care."

He threw open the door to his room and pushed Millie inside. She stood, her back to him, in front of the fire. Although the month was June, the night sea air had a chill, and Millie welcomed the warm crackling and the pungent scent of burning applewood. She stretched her hands out to the fire and waited.

"Millie!" the Prince snapped. For the first time, his voice sent a little shiver of fear up her spine. "Turn around."

She waited as long as she dared, then turned, slowly, to face him. The Prince stood in front of the closed door, arms crossed over his chest, his feet planted firmly apart, watching her. His face was gaunt with a violence repressed, a turbulence he held in check with a formidable effort of will, a violence that threatened at any moment to erupt and sweep him away.

"James," she said. Her voice came out in a whisper through lips that were strangely dry. She licked her lips to moisten them and saw the answering current electrify the Prince's body.

He covered the few steps between them with long, swift strides. He put his hands to the throat of her sundress and ripped it to the hem in one savage movement. The soft material fell to the floor, a puddle of gaily striped cotton around her ankles. "James!" Millie heard the whimper in her voice and was ashamed.

"I'll buy you a new one!" he said hotly. He curled his fingers in the lace of her panties, and, with one strong twist of his hand, they followed the dress on to the floor. She stood before him in the firelight, shivering just a little and trying mightily not to show it.

He stepped back a pace and confronted her, fully dressed. Deliberately, his eyes surveyed her body, accentuating her nakedness and his ownership. His gaze fastened on her small, rounded breasts, and, as he watched, the nipples peaked and stiffened. His eyes gleamed with reflected firelight and with the hunger that was in him.

He put his arm around her shoulders, and she relaxed a little, leaning against him. He bent down and, with his other arm around her knees, knocked her off balance so that she fell. He caught her in his arms and lowered her gently to the floor. It was his last gentle act of the night.

When he had stripped off his clothes, Millie didn't know, for all at once he was on top of her, thrusting his penis into her dry vagina. "James, I'm not ready! It hurts!"

"I can't . . . I can't help it! I'm sorry." He touched his fingers to his mouth, moistening them, and then shoved them inside her, roughly. Millie winced and then cried out, as his penis, in one sharp thrust, entered her body.

He tore at her, with his hands, with his mouth and with his cock, as if he were trying to leave his mark on her so that she would carry it for all time. Or to join them, irrevocably and finally, so that they would never part.

And with his wild desperation, he carried her, so that the pulsing, insistent drumming suddenly coalesced into an exquisite sensuality on the knife edge between pain and a rapture unmatched by anything Millie had ever known. When she screamed, never knowing whether it was with her orgasm or with anguish, he climaxed, his body shuddering with great, heaving gasps.

She lay under him, cradling his head on her breast, soaked with his sweat and hers, with his saliva, with his semen and her juices, panting, unable to catch her breath. In the moment she felt him slip out of her, she realized he was crying. She touched his damp, matted hair and curled her arms and legs around his long body, feeling the sticky wetness of his cock against her stomach, smelling the eucalyptus smell of his sperm that rose from their heated bodies.

She shifted her hips under him, and he misunderstood her movement. "Don't!" he said, his voice muffled against her breast. "Don't ever leave me!"

"I won't," she promised. "I won't, my darling James."

Suddenly he was hard again. He raised his head to look into her eyes. His own were liquid and shining and blue. And, with courage derived from the resurgence of the most elemental of passions, he smiled at her.

She reached down her hand to guide him into her. He stopped her, clamping his hand over her wrist. "No!"

He looked at the swelling curve at the top of her breast and ran a light finger over the raised welts. "I *bit* you!" Millie laughed at the astonishment in his voice. "I don't think I've ever done anything like that in my life." He placed his mouth over the mark left by his teeth and sucked on it, nursing at it. Then he dropped his mouth to her nipple, taking the small tender mound against his teeth, licking tiny searing circles until Millie's back arched and her hips quivered and she began to moan, soft wordless moans.

The Prince sat up suddenly. Millie opened her eyes and looked at him in surprise. "What—" she began. He stopped her with a forefinger against her lips.

He took her hand and drew it gently down between her legs, cupping it over the curving mound. "Show me."

Millie pulled her hand away, embarrassed. "I can't."

The Prince captured her hand and held it. His eyes bored into hers. His voice, used to command, resonated with certainty, "You will." He forced her reluctant hand down, keeping his own over it, preventing her from drawing away. "I must know all about you."

"I can't, James. I've never done that in front of anyone."

The Prince's eyes gleamed the color of lapis lazuli in the firelight. With his hand over hers, he parted her lips and moved her fingers till, with his sure knowledge, he found the silky core.

Millie looked down and saw her own coral-tipped fingers covered by his strong brown hand. The three-feathered signet ring glowed, burning as if it, and not the fire, were the source of the light. She sucked in her breath and closed her eyes. The Prince's insistent hand guided her own. She moved, slowly at first, shyly, and then faster, until she was lost in an abandon approaching delirium and never knew when he took his hand away.

She spasmed and pressed down harder and spasmed again and again, knowing he was watching, her excitement sharpened by his unseen presence.

When she lay, spent, and dared to open her eyes, she found him leaning over her, his eyes blue and intent. He kissed her mouth voluptuously. "You're beautiful," he whispered. "You are so unbelievably beautiful."

* * *

Millie awoke and knew instantly, from the special, hushed quality of the silence, that the house was deserted. I feel like he's still with me, she thought, savoring the delicious languor, the tender abrasions of delicate tissues, the sense of having journeyed to the extreme, perilous edge and returned, enriched.

She dressed quickly and ran down the stairs, looking for a sign of life. "In here, Madame Director," Lucy yelled from the sun porch.

Millie dropped down next to her friend who lay, stretched out on the pillowed settee, in an obvious state of relaxation. "Where is everybody."

"Church." Lucy sat up, her eyes glinting with amusement. "You should have seen it. It was like something out of a novel. They all set off in this gorgeous antique Daimler, the squire, his lady and the guest of honor in the back seat, the servants following in the station wagon. I waited for them to wave to the gathered serfs, but they didn't," she said regretfully.

"How come you didn't go?"

"Didn't feel like it. Gerald went though." Lucy smiled, enjoying the irony. "He said he'd never been to church before and he wanted to see what it was like. I *know* what it's like, so I gave myself the morning off."

"How do you get a cup of coffee in this place?"

"I think there's a vending machine in the basement," Lucy joked. "No, it's all laid out in the breakfast room."

"Want some?"

"Yup. I was just too lazy to get up and get it."

Millie returned, her attention riveted to the two brimming Spode china cups she was carrying, balancing them cautiously. Lucy reached up and relieved her of one of them. "Jesus," Millie said, "if you break a dish in this place it's a major disaster."

She settled herself next to her friend on the settee. "Lucy— Lucy, I'm so happy," she bubbled. "I'm just so happy!"

"*And* articulate," Lucy observed with a smile.

"Anything going on between you and Peter?" Millie asked with the bluntness that comes with long intimacy.

Lucy waved her hand in a *"comme ci, comme ça"* gesture. "I don't know. I think we're too much alike in all the wrong ways. There's just no *ta'am*." She used the Hebrew word for spice, flavor, piquancy. Millie smiled her appreciation of this linguistic tour de force. "I like him a lot though," Lucy continued. "He's very bright."

"I think there's something funny going on between him and James. I can't put my finger on it, but every now and then I catch James giving him this *look*. He can be very chilling."

"What does James say?" Lucy asked carefully.

"I asked him, and all he would say was that Peter may have done him a favor. He wouldn't say anything else. I think Peter knows it, though. Did he say anything to you?"

"I'm sure if there is anything," Lucy said, after a small pause, "they'll work it out. Anyway, it can't have anything to do with you." Millie caught her hesitation, wondering. "Not in any way that means anything," Lucy added, then abruptly changed the subject. "Do you know what else Peter told me?"

"What do you mean, 'what *else*'?"

"He told me that he almost wet his pants yesterday when that whole thing with the telephone call happened."

"I'll bet that's not *exactly* how he phrased it," Millie said gleefully, picturing the staid equerry.

Lucy chuckled, then continued, her cool voice thoughtful. "It never occurred to me, but can you imagine what it would be like for Peter if James suddenly ascended the throne? I mean, being sort of an . . . executive assistant to the Prince of Wales is one thing. And they're both used to that. Between them they've got that whole operation working like a charm." Millie nodded. She had seen even more of its clocklike precision than Lucy. "But King of England— that's something else."

"It's hard for me to believe that it's James we're talking about," Millie said wistfully. "When we're on our own, it doesn't seem so strange. So people bow or curtsy to him. And they call him 'sir.' You get used to that very fast. It just feels natural, and after a while you forget about it. But the minute we're out in public, forget it. It's a whole other ball game."

"I don't think James forgets for a minute."

"I guess not."

"Do you know what else. Prince James never travels without a complete set of mourning clothes. Just in case."

"You're kidding."

"Nope. But what's really amazing is that he carries a special box of black-bordered stationery, so that if anything does happen he can still send out thank-you notes before he goes home to face . . .whatever he has to face."

"That's awful!"

"No, it isn't. It's stagecraft. It's always being prepared to do the right thing. It certainly is no more awful than a lot of the things we do in production. And we're just making movies. At least what James does is real. It's illusion in *service* of something."

"Do you think it's real?"

"Of course, it's real. It's just as real as any other intangible— patriotism, honor, idealism. People *die* for intangibles," Lucy said dispassionately. "Maybe you have to live in London like I did for a year, to really understand it. Almost every day there's a photograph in the newspaper of someone in the royal family doing *something*. Generally useful, or inspiring, or maybe just plain nice. They're role models. They don't tell you how to live, they show you, by example."

"Like that business with the princesses serving in the armed forces."

"Exactly. And they do it with a lot of flair. When they show you the royal children going someplace, the opera maybe, with the Queen Mother and smiling and having a great time, they're making a statement, indirectly, about youth and old age, for example. It's really an art form in a way."

Millie stared into her coffee cup, listening intently. "And perhaps," Lucy continued, "perhaps that's why the monarchy still exists in England. Because it works. Who was it who said that in the future there will be only five kings left in the world: hearts, spades, clubs, diamonds and England."

"King Farouk. What am I gonna do?" Millie moaned.

"What are you gonna do? You'll do what you've always done," Lucy said brusquely.

"It's not the same. I've had affairs before, and God *knows* I've been all kinds of worked up about them, but not like this! This is different. And don't tell me it's not!" she warned furiously.

"I wasn't about to," Lucy said calmly. "I must say, I never expected things to turn out this way. You and James just came together, THUNK!" She clapped her hands together forcefully. "Like two powerful magnets."

"It's strange. We're so different."

"You keep *saying* that," Lucy laughed. "Now that I've seen the two of you together, I think you're exactly alike."

"Are you crazy? He's—"

"I know, I know. You miss the point," Lucy chided. "I think you and James have identical . . . natures. Temperaments. You both feel things very deeply—too deeply if you ask me. Neither one of you has the smallest sense of proportion, of distance. And it gives you both a lot of grief. And you both cover it with an awful lot of bravado. Most people think you're tough, and I think most people think James is easygoing. He's not, and you're not. All that other shit has no meaning at all . . ." Millie looked at her.

". . . unless," she added thoughtfully, "it happens to get in your way. In which case, you two will just have to unthunk yourselves," she finished briskly.

"How can you *say* that! My stomach ties in knots just thinking about it!"

"I guess I'm just not the passionate type," Lucy replied. "So my advice to you, young lady, is just don't think about it. Enjoy what you have while you have it."

"I'm having such a good time," said Millie wistfully. "And I haven't been thinking at all. All I think about is the next hour and my shoot."

"Things are probably just happening too fast for you," Lucy said sympathetically.

"No. The other way around. I feel like things are happening very, very slowly. It feels like . . . a lifetime," she said a trifle tremulously. "It's hard to believe that last Sunday at this time I didn't even know him.

"I wonder sometimes," Millie continued after a pause. "I feel like I know James down to his . . . *depths*. And then sometimes I wonder, am I crazy? I mean, have I finally gone off the deep end, or what? How can this be? It worries me. And then James walks into the room, and it's all over. I *know* again."

Millie bent her head over the needlepoint pillow, examining it minutely, as if she were about to attempt the construction of one very like it and needed to flush out its secrets. "Did James look like he *wanted* to go to Church? Or was he just . . . going?"

"I wondered the same thing myself, having little tolerance for organized religion. And it's hard to tell what James is thinking most of the time. But I imagine he did. It would be awfully hard to be Defender of the Faith and not care about that faith. I think that, for your own sanity, you'd make very sure that you did care."

Millie picked up the pillow, placed it gently on the couch between them, and punched it, hard. "God *damn* Henry the Eighth!" she said.

"Who's that swearing at my ancestors?" James wanted to know. He strode briskly into the room, overflowing with vitality, as he entered all the rooms of his life.

"You look pretty," Millie said, admiring his navy, gold-buttoned blazer and crisp pin-striped Turnbull and Asser shirt. "And you, too!" she said to Gerald, surprised. Gerald was generally persuaded only with difficulty to climb into his single, dark-blue suit. He claimed he had tried it once, at his bar mitzvah, and determined then, once and for all time, that he didn't like it. Millie detected Lucy's fine hand in the mere fact that he had brought a suit with him on a summer weekend.

Now, reminded, Gerald loosened his tie and pulled it, still knotted, over his head. "That's enough of that!" he declared, unbuttoning his shirt collar and rolling up his sleeves. He dropped onto the settee between Lucy and Millie and threw an arm impartially around each. "So? How're my girls?"

"Ready for luncheon, I hope," James interjected. "I'm famished!"

They all stood up, amid a chorus of "Me, too's." Gerald grabbed Millie's elbow, preventing her from leaving with the others. "How'd you like shul?" she asked him, unable to resist.

"Well, I'll tell you. There's a lot less sitting-down-and-standing-up than we do. But the rest of it is just about the same. You sing, you read some stuff, and a guy makes a speech." Thus ended Gerald's foray into comparative religion. "Listen, shit-for-brains, I gotta tell you something."

"I know. You and Lady Dolly are eloping. You're going to get her a union card, and she's going to become a grip," Millie laughed up at him.

Gerald, uncharacteristically, didn't even award this a disparaging smile. "Listen, buttercup. About James? He's not for you, you know."

"Are you trying to tell me I'm out of his league?" she asked defiantly.

"No, dumbbell, I'm trying to tell you *he's* out of *yours*. You got a hundred more times on the ball than he does. Please! That guy's a lightweight! God help him if he ever had to go out in the real world and hustle. He's never even peeled his own carrots—"

"Is that all you wanted to tell me?" Millie asked him murderously.

"No. I don't really *want* to tell you anything, but I gotta or they'll take my Eagle Scout badge away from me," he said with a fair assumption of his normal breeziness. "I had a talk with—"

"Millie?! Where did you get to?" Millie turned, happily, at the sound of James's voice. He stuck his head in the room. "Millie? Oh, sorry, I didn't mean to intrude."

"You didn't," she informed him, walking away from Gerald. "We were all finished anyway."

Luncheon, despite its being the Sabbath, was an informal affair. Millie, sitting across from James, watched him devour everything that was put before him and greet with delight the dessert, specially prepared. "My favourite," he crowed, eyeing the elaborate peach melba with, as he enthusiastically noted, "lashings and lashings of whipped cream."

He's precious, Millie thought. He's precious to me. He had for her an aura, a charged luster that, like a pointillist painting, hit her with even greater force across the width of the table than when she was in his arms, as if her sense of sight, undistracted by the scent and touch of him, was sharpened. His lean body, lounging negligently back in his chair, seemed to her to be composed of angles, planes and electricity.

Her eyes were drawn to him, inexorably, and, whenever they were, she found his on her.

Unable to bear even the few feet of distance between them, Millie slipped off her sandal, and, sliding down in her seat just a little, she stretched her bare foot onto the Prince's lap. He looked up, eyes widening in surprise, a spoonful of peach ice cream halted midway between his plate and his mouth, to be greeted with a look of angelical innocence.

He grinned broadly then bent his head over his plate, to hide his pleasure and his response. He dropped one hand into his lap casually and caressed her foot, running a finger along the curving arch, circling her ankle and finally simply cupping it in his hand, telegraphing his love, clandestinely, maintaining all the while a look of supreme equanimity.

"May I suggest to all of you that the south terrace is a superb place for a sunbath. Or even a little nap." Lord Marling, with an urbane smile, scraped his chair back from the table. Everyone agreed that this was a delightful idea and stood up, prepared to follow his recommendation.

Lord Marling stopped the Prince, with a diffident hand on his elbow. "Perhaps I could have a few words with you, sir. In my study. If you've got the time, that is." Millie thought the Prince's face hardened, fleetingly. He hesitated, then with a flippant wink at Millie, followed His Lordship.

Millie, in turn, followed the others out to the sunny, stone-flagged terrace. She stretched out full-length on a canvas-covered chaise, cradling her head on her folded arms. Do *not* think about this.

This has nothing to do with you. They have tons of stuff to talk about. A whole country to run, for God's sakes. You're turning into an insufferable, egotistical prig, and I don't like it.

"What are you all talking about?" James asked jauntily, stepping out on to the terrace. They all looked up, hard put to answer, since no one had said a word for the past fifteen minutes.

That was quick, whatever it was, Millie thought, searching the Prince's face. It was perfectly, innocuously bland. See! she told herself.

James settled on the chaise at Millie's feet, only to spring up in an instant. He sat first in one chair, then another, unable to settle down. He peered through the standing telescope, favoring them with a crisp reportage of the various styles, virtues and deficiencies of the boats out in the bay. Tiring of that, he finally simply paced, moving from one end of the terrace to the other. "I say, why didn't I think of that before!" He pivoted on his heel, turning to face them. "I've got an absolutely stupendous idea! We'll all go waterskiing." His enthusiasm was infectious, and James was munificently congratulated on his ordering of the afternoon's agenda.

"I want to get up on one ski this time. I've never done that," Lucy enthused.

"It's not hard," Peter Goldsworth assured her in his quiet manner. "I'll help you."

Ian MacCrae, sitting unobtrusively off to one side, cleared his throat into the general glee. "I don't want to put a damper on the occasion," he said with only the briefest of salutes to his own pun, "and I can't speak for the others, sir, but I'm afraid that I have to advise against it. The sea is entirely too rough."

They all, as one, looked out at the bay. Whitecaps, kicked up by the stiff breeze, frisked on the blue surface. "I'm afraid it's out of the question," the detective continued.

"He's right," Peter affirmed quickly.

"It was a good idea, though," Lucy consoled.

The Prince turned, confronting his detective across the length of the terrace. "What do you mean, out of the question?" he asked evenly. "I've skied worse than this. It's not all that bad, actually, just gives you a good ride."

"I know you have. I've seen you," Lady Dolly put in. "Remember? When we were in Greece that time? It was far worse than this."

James turned to her, his low-pitched voice sharp with intensity. "Don't remind me! Don't bloody remind me!"

"What the holy fuck is wrong with that broad," Lucy whispered to Millie.

"I don't know, but I sure wish she'd shut up," Millie said, her eyes on James.

He stood, feet apart, hands clasped behind his back, staring at MacCrae. "I'm going," he said quietly. "There's no reason not to. If I thought there was any danger— Well, there isn't. The worst that can happen is that I get a little wet."

"Your Royal Highness—" the detective began, with only the lightest of emphases on the title.

"I'm tired of being mollycoddled! I've had enough!" James snapped, coming as close to shouting as Millie had ever seen him.

"None of us is a good enough swimmer to help you if you get into trouble," the Scotsman said diplomatically. Millie knew that Lucy had been a competitive swimmer in college and held every life-saving badge the Red Cross had to offer. She also knew that Lucy would keep her mouth shut.

"Well, I'll just have to stay out of trouble then, won't I? Now. Who's going to have first crack at steering the motor boat?" he asked, turning to the group at large. No takers.

"Is it really not safe?" Millie asked Lucy, worried. "I don't water ski."

"Well, it's not good. I should have realized it myself, but James has a way of sweeping you along with him, you know?" Millie nodded.

"I beg you to reconsider, sir," MacCrae said firmly, without an ounce of entreaty. "Accidents can happen very fast in waters like these."

"Rot!" said the high-spirited Prince, his steel-blue gaze crossing swords with the Scotsman. "There are other people skiing out there, and they look like they're having a right gay old time of it, too."

"They are not . . . who you are," MacCrae said gently. "You can't afford to take the chance."

The Prince turned away from him. "Who's going to pilot the boat?" he asked again. His face was grim, determined.

"I will," Lady Dolly offered into the silence.

"Right. And I'll take turn and turn about with you," the Prince responded handsomely.

"He's a very strong swimmer," Millie told Lucy, her voice pleading.

"I know that, hon, but if he falls and gets conked on the head with his ski . . ."

"Oh, Lord," Millie moaned. She looked at James. He leaned against the terrace wall, elbows resting on the top, his pose one of negligent ease. But his face, staring out to sea, was stormy.

Millie walked over and rested one hand, lightly, on his rigid arm, feeling the tension of his locked muscles. He didn't acknowledge her, and she waited, wondering if he was aware that she was standing next to him.

"They pulled me out of helicopter training just when I was getting good at it," he said levelly. "Every bloke in my course qualified without a mishap, and I didn't. All that bloody effort shot to hell. For no reason. And that's not all of it. Not by half, it isn't."

He's . . . caged, Millie thought. In a funny way he's caged. She looked into his face, her eyes mirroring her sympathy. "James, I don't ever want you to not do the things you want to, just because I'm afraid for you. But I am. If anything happened to you . . . I couldn't bear it." She looked at him candidly, not attempting to hide her vulnerability, her dread, her fears.

"Nothing's going to happen to me," he chided gently, looking down into her worried face.

"*I* know that! I *know* that. It's just . . . I'd feel better if you didn't . . ." She broke off, realizing she had just contradicted herself.

His face softened, the anger and frustration evaporating as swiftly and completely as if someone had wiped them away. "You spoil all my fun," James whispered, brushing a kiss across her brow. "Well, not all of it," he amended in the interests of accuracy, and laughed, all the thunderclouds gone.

"Thank you," she whispered, stretching up to plant a chaste kiss on his cheek. He put his arm around her waist, and they turned, rejoining the others.

Lord David Marling stood, leaning against the doorjamb, arms folded, watching. Millie wondered how long he'd been there, then decided she didn't care.

"I'll tell you what!" James announced, his need for action

undiminished. "There must be a town hereabouts. Let's go have a look at it, shall we? See what it's like?"

"There are lots of historic places around here," Lucy told him. "Let's go. It'll be fun."

"Please! No monuments! If there's anything I don't want to see, it's another buggering monument. Let's just wander about and sightsee." MacCrae cleared his throat. James glanced at him warily.

"I think that's a jolly good idea," Lord Marling interjected. "You'll all have yourselves a fine time." From his vantage point in the doorway, he glanced at MacCrae and nodded, imperceptibly. The reins had just been, of necessity, loosened a little.

"Right, then," James said. "It's all settled. I'll just go change and be right with you." A chore, which they suddenly realized, was incumbent on all the church goers.

"I'll tell you, I felt sorry for the guy." Gerald, on his way into the house, paused briefly in front of Millie and Lucy. "Everybody has the right to do something stupid now and then." Immediately catching his mistake, he delivered before they could get the chance what would most assuredly have been their next line. "And I should know," he agreed, nodding vigorously, and walked into the house.

Amid the general stir, MacCrae came up to Millie. "You've been a big help, miss," he said to her in his broad Scots. "It's not too much to say you've done a service to the realm, this day. Not to mention, to Her Majesty personally. She dotes on that lad," he finished, with a trace of his deadpan humor. He bowed slightly and followed his charge into the house.

"Well!" Lucy said. "Maybe they'll give you an OBE or something. Then you'll be Dame Millie!"

Millie turned and found Lord Marling's eyes on her, regarding her steadily, without expression. She looked back at him, with mingled challenge and amusement. "They should only know," she told Lucy, "how little I care for their precious succession. I just didn't want James to break his goddamn royal neck!"

* * *

"Good God, it's gorgeous," Millie breathed, stopping at the head of the wide stone steps, the better to absorb the full majesty of the gleaming black Daimler that awaited them in the precise center of the graveled driveway. It's immaculate canvas top was rolled back, secured with leather straps. It's shiny finish reflected the rippling treetops overhead, and, much to the Prince's chagrin, there was room and to spare for all of them in the spacious interior. MacCrae sat up front next to the chauffeur, while his boss slouched in his by now customary place in the right rear passenger seat, tweed cap pulled down over his eyes, one arm draped negligently around Millie at his side.

They parked on a quiet corner and, leaving the chauffeur to stand guard over his treasure, wandered through the narrow, tree-shaded streets, exploring, mingling with the other casually dressed tourists who crowded the resort town.

James and Millie wandered hand in hand, forgetting for the moment the keen, watchful eyes of Ian MacCrae. Gerald swiftly claimed the attention of the auburn-tressed Lady Dolly. James nudged Millie, as Dolly burst out in a peal of unaffected, lusty laughter. "Good for him!" the Prince applauded. "I think all Dolly needs is a good fu— some of what Gerald has to offer," he finished lamely. Millie nodded sternly, approving his hasty substitution.

They looked in shop windows, admiring the wide variety of items offered for sale, a melange of antiques, both real and dubious, elegant clothing, sporting goods and touristy kitsch. "Everything around here is either 'Pilgrim' or 'Mayflower,'" James remarked. "I'm beginning to think you people don't want to change your minds." He paused, irresistibly drawn by Ye Olde Ice Cream Parlour, studying the menu posted in the glass window with careful attention.

"You can't *possibly*," Lucy told him as the others caught up with them. "You just ate a *ton* of ice cream."

"Research," he told her sagely. "I'm just trying to figure out what a 'Puritan's Delight,' could be. Hmmmm, Millie? What do you think?"

"I think it's time to move on," she said, tugging at the arm of the inveterate nosher. He tussled with her playfully, forgetting for the moment his decorum.

"Over there! Across the street! In front of the ice cream parlor!" A piercing shriek, shrill, imperative, cut through the lazy afternoon hush. They all pivoted, turning instinctively to the source of the screech. A young woman in a denim skirt with a golf hat on her head pointed directly at the Prince. All the sightseers, following her outstretched hand, stared, searching for the cause of the commotion.

James melted back against the store window while the others formed a ragged semicircle around him, trying to shield him from view, while at the same time to appear eminently nonchalant.

A small girl, about seven years old, darted across the street and retrieved her bright red and blue ball from the curb in front of them. "And don't bounce it in the street if you're going to lose it," her mother yelled, adding a resounding slap as a mnemonic.

"False alarm," Gerald laughed, and they continued on their way.

"Look at that!" James exclaimed, his attention caught by a store window across the street. The sign atop the store said: "Compton and Sons, Shipwrights Since 1732." The window display featured a scale model of a nineteenth-century whaling ship, perfect in every tiny detail, sails, lines, ladders, down to the miniature gaffs. Etched in the wood, in the smallest of letters was the name: SS *Bridgeport*.

The Prince stood before it, lost in admiration, pointing out its diminutive marvels to the others. "Wouldn't you have liked to have sailed the tall ships?" he asked Millie wistfully. "You could steal away and pass as a cabin boy and have all kinds of adventures."

"I think you've read too many novels," Millie told him and slowly became aware of a third party watching them intently, eyes narrowed in concentration.

"You are, aren't you," the plump, bermuda-shorted man told him.

The Prince turned to face his inquisitor. "That all depends," he said charily.

James's British accent was all the confirmation the man required. "You see, Agnes! I told you he was! Come here, kids, take a good look. You might never get another chance." Three solemn faced children and Agnes stood in a row, staring at James.

MacCrae and Peter moved swiftly into position, one at either side, looking not at James, but out at the street, eyes alert. In seconds a crowd, alerted to the presence of celebrity in their midst, had gathered ten deep, pushing and shoving each other for a better view.

"Hiya, Jimmy!" a man yelled from the back of the crowd, exuberantly. "Watcha doin' in Newport?"

"On holiday, just like you," the Prince called genially.

This response was greeted with great favor. "Well put 'er there," the man said, thrusting his way through the crowd. James shook his outstretched hand and then, the crowd having gotten the idea, as many others as he could reach, avoiding as best he could the grabbers and the pinchers.

"I touched him! I touched him!"

"Let me look! I can't see! Get outta my way!"

"He's cute! He's much skinnier than he looks on TV."

"No he isn't," the girl's companion objected. "It's his hair. It's lighter than it is on television."

"They talk about him as if he's deaf," Millie, amused, told Lucy. "Or really, what it is, is that they don't believe he's real. They think that somehow he's still on television, and they're free to say anything they want. You can't hurt a television screen's feelings."

"Hey, Prince!" a woman called. "Can I have your autograph?"

"I'm sorry, I don't give autographs," James said with a friendly smile.

"Then can I take your picture?" she persisted, brandishing her Instamatic excitedly.

"I can't bloody stop you, can I," James muttered under his breath. The idea caught on, signaling a general reaching and digging into pockets and purses and the retrieval of cameras of every size and description. The crowd clicked away, capturing for posterity and their family albums the genial, smiling image of the Prince of Wales.

"Can I take a picture *with* you?" a woman, emboldened, called out. "Quick! Melvin! Take my picture." She thrust her camera into her husband's hands and, pushing her way through the crowd, arrived, smiling hesitantly, at the side of the Prince. James turned toward her and smiled, directly into Melvin's camera. The woman beamed, as her husband captured her image alongside a superstar.

"What's everybody looking at? I can't see anything," a small boy's plaintive wail, lost in the crush of the crowd.

James searched the crowd and, finding the boy, extricated him. "There, now, is that better?"

"Who are you?" the boy inquired, looking up at James.

"My name is James. What's yours?"

"Richie."

James kneeled down to the boy's eye level. "Hello, Richie," he extended his hand.

The boy dutifully shook the Prince's hand. "Why is everybody looking at you?" he asked, encouraged by James's smile. While James attempted to frame a suitable answer to this, Richie turned on his heel and rejoined his family. "It's nobody," he informed them loudly, to the Prince's delight.

"What does it feel like to be a Prince?" someone called.

"I can't answer that," James called back. "I've got nothing to compare it to. What does it feel like to be an accountant?"

This sally was greeted with approving laughter. The crowd was growing by the minute, and a fair-sized traffic jam was developing as motorists parked their cars wherever and joined in the fun.

"Look at me! Look at me!" a new arrival shrilled. The people at the back turned to her and, understanding, laughingly hoisted her on to a man's willing shoulders.

"Oh, my God," James moaned. "Millie, it's finally happened!" The girl wore, over brief denim cutoffs, a bright orange T-shirt emblazoned on the front with a large, full-color headshot of the Prince of Wales. "Nice T-shirt," he called eyeing the pneumatic brunette. "Where'd you get it?"

"Times Square. In New York City," she called back, waving her arms excitedly. "It cost $8.95," she told him proudly.

"Cheap at half the price," James retorted.

"Do you like it? I'll give it to you," she offered, yelling over the heads of the crowd.

"No, no," James returned hastily, as she started to pull the T-shirt out of her shorts. "It looks much better on you, anyway."

"Can I give you a kiss instead?" she asked, jumping lightly down. The people made way for her, and she swiftly planted a kiss on the surprised Prince's cheek, then darted back into the anonymous safety of the crowd. The crowd awarded her a handsome round of applause, saluting her daring maneuver. "Thank you, that was delicious," James called after her. This set off a barrage of attempted kisses, most of which James, with the aid of Peter and MacCrae, managed to deflect.

"What I don't understand is, why not me?" Gerald asked. "I'm cute!"

A wide-billed baseball cap was passed hand over hand through the crowd to the Prince. "What's the 'B' for?" he asked.

"Boston Red Sox!" came the shouted answer.

"What are Boston Red Sox?" James wanted to know, examining the incongruously blue cap.

"The best goddamn baseball team in the country!" The roar

came from several throats simultaneously.

"In that case . . ." The Prince swept off his own cap and replaced it with the blue one. The crowd, enchanted, whistled it's approval, highlighted with a fresh round of yells and picture-taking.

"Hey Jimmy! This is for you!" A sailor in the back of the crowd, inspired, whipped off his round white uniform cap and tossed it over the heads of the crowd to the Prince.

James caught it handily and started to raise it toward his head. He arrested the motion, however, and, reversing it, tossed the cap back to it's owner. "Keep it, mate," he called good-humoredly. "The brass don't like it when you're out of uniform," thus, Millie realized, stopping himself just short of being photographed in the military garb of a foreign country. You have to be so careful, she thought. You have to watch every little thing.

"I never thought I'd see you," someone yelled from the other side.

"Same here," James retorted puckishly.

The crowd was growing progressively wilder and more feverish, jostling and shoving with increasing turbulence. An out-thrust arm grabbed at the Prince, closing on a fistful of his shirt, ripping it. MacCrae's hand came down swiftly, gently separating the grabber from the Prince.

Millie spotted a professional camera and realized that the ruckus had, logically enough, attracted the local reporters. James saw it at the same moment. "I'm in trouble now, I am," he murmured.

Millie wondered why and then forgot it, as someone shoved against her, knocking her off balance, so that she fell against Lady Dolly. "Animal!" Lady Dolly hissed at the perpetrator, a protective arm around Millie.

James shot her a warning glance. "Back to the car!" MacCrae ordered. Slowly, Peter, Gerald and MacCrae in the vanguard, they made their way through the heaving crowd.

"Ohhhhhhh, you're going?"

"Sorry, I've got to," James called over his shoulder.

"Nice meeting you!" a woman yelled.

"Same here, I'm sure," the Prince returned gallantly.

Quickly they covered the few short blocks to the car, followed by the ever-increasing mob. The chauffeur, anticipating, had flung all the doors open and waited with the motor running.

"Get up so we can see you!" a voice yelled as the car started away. James obligingly hoisted himself onto the back of the open car. The crowd cheered this display of easygoing noblesse oblige, and cameras clicked ever more furiously. The car moved at a crawl, inching through the mass of cheering, waving people.

A young blonde woman following the car reached up and handed the Prince a full-blown red rose. He accepted it with a smile and inhaled its fragrance. "Lovely," he said and, with a graceful, courtly gesture, reached down and handed it back to her. "Keep it," he smiled into the blushing girl's eyes. "And think of me."

With a final, meltingly sweet smile, he turned back to his friends. "Come sit up here with me," he begged. "I feel like an ass up here all by myself." Millie, Lucy, Dolly and Gerald hoisted themselves up and perched on the back and sides of the car, laughing and joking with the crowd. The equerry, despite all their blandishments, remained seated, all by himself.

Gerald waved expansively at the crowd. "Thanks for coming to see me," he yelled. And the crowd, enjoying his chutzpa, applauded him wildly.

"You got some pretty ladies there," a masculine voice complimented.

"Aren't I lucky?" James agreed, laughing.

With a final, parting wave from the Prince, the Daimler sped off. "Well, that's that," James said, sliding down into his seat.

"You do that very well," Millie told him.

"Practice," he said impudently. "The first time I had to meet a crowd of people all by myself, my equerry had to kick me off the plane. Which is a story he will be pleased to tell you, should you ever run across him," the Prince added wryly. "But it's true. I was about seventeen and shaking in my boots. But when I finally got up the nerve to go over to them, I found it was easy. They're just people, and they want to like you and they want you to like them. The girls, though," he added in an afterthought, "that came as a surprise. Not an unpleasant one, I must say."

"I noticed," Millie observed, and was rewarded with a quick, reassuring hug.

"But you see, it's important," James continued, sobering. "In the Commonwealth, for example, for most of the people it's the only chance they'll have to see, up close, someone to whom they'll owe their allegiance. And they have a right. And I always must remember the trouble they've gone to. In Africa, once, more than a million people turned out, lining the route from the airport to the capital city. Bloody astonished I was, too. But, you see, I can't disappoint them if they've been up all night, perhaps, or traveled from God knows where. They at least rate a peek, don't they?" he grinned at Millie.

"Don't you ever feel that you're . . . on display?"

"Don't be bloody stupid, darling," he said tartly. "I am on display!"

"I hope I have the pleasure of seeing you again, Millie," Lord Marling said, shaking her hand warmly.

Millie looked into his eyes. They held nothing but the courtesy of a gracious host bidding farewell to a welcome guest. "I hope so too," she replied. "I've enjoyed meeting you very much." Why does he make me so nervous, she wondered, running lightly up the steps to the plane.

Inside she turned and watched Lord Marling incline his head to the Prince, then throw his arms around him affectionately. He said something that made the Prince throw back his head, in his characteristic, lighthearted gesture, and laugh. Millie, watching, felt suddenly bereft. She leaned her head back against the seat rest and looked out at the small airport, its beacon flashing against the darkness.

James, with his inexhaustible energy, took the controls all the way back to La Guardia, while the rest, including the pilot, napped.

"Too windy for you, darling?" James asked.

"No. I love driving at night. It's my favorite thing in the whole world." Millie snuggled deeper into her heavy sweater. The little MG buzzed along the highway, the heat coming up from the floor enveloping them in a cocoon of warmth, despite the wind that whipped against their faces. Lights, haloed by mist, sped by, streaking against the night.

James hugged her to him, oblivious of MacCrae in the back seat. "This is the very best," he said contentedly, steering easily with one hand, the accelerator pressed to the floor. "What's the best thing you ever did?" he asked after a while.

"Leaving home," she returned promptly. "What's the best thing *you* ever did?"

"The best thing I ever did, the single most wonderful, absolutely the most super thing I ever did, was when I was stationed at a naval base in Scotland. I convinced the company clerk—he wasn't the real one, he was acting clerk, the real one was having his tonsils out or some damn thing—anyway, I convinced this chap, and it wasn't easy, mind you, I convinced him to announce over the public address that the bootmaker who had furnished all the officers' boots had found a fault in the left heel." James chortled, anticipating what was to come. "So he was respectfully requesting that all officers turn in their boots at 1600 hours, which was about ten minutes away, so that they could be repaired.

"All these officers queued up pulling off their left boots, piling them up very neatly, this being the Navy, and trotted away, one shoe on and one shoe off, the most marvelous collection of April Fools you ever saw!" His laughter rang out, spirited, free, reveling in the memory of a most neatly turned prank.

"That's terrific," Millie said enviously. "I never did anything that great."

"Wasn't that super?" He basked unashamedly in her admiration. "I never quite reached those heights again. I think it was some sort of an epiphany," he said regretfully. "What time is it?"

Millie turned her watch so she could catch the light from a passing lamp. "Nine-thirty. Why?"

"Good," he nodded with satisfaction. "We'll just make it."

"Make what?"

"Where do you want to stay tonight?" he asked.

"Your place or mine," they finished in concert, laughing.

"My place, I think, if it's all right with you," Millie said. "It just seems more comfortable."

"No argument there. I'm not crazy about hotels either."

"It's not the hotel. It's all those people in the next room. Breathing."

He laughed. "I know what you mean."

"What will we just make?" Millie asked doggedly.

"Mind yer own business, Chit."

"Speaking of minding my own business, what happened in Greece?"

"Pardon?"

"What Lady Dolly was talking about."

"Oh. Oh, that. I was waterskiing, and these four photographers pitched in and hired a launch."

"What did they do? Sneak up on you?"

"Worse," he said with a trace of embarrassment. "They crisscrossed my path so that I got dumped time and again, and they had lots of lovely pictures of me falling off my skies. Made me out to be a proper clod, they did." The graceless photos clearly rankled the sportive Prince more than the repeated dunkings.

"That's not fair! Making you look like you can't do something you can do very well."

"Fair has nothing to do with it. Not the littlest, foggiest thing."

"I'm sorry," Millie said gently.

"It can't be helped. I'm a long-suffering bastard, I am," he added buoyantly.

He glanced at her, feeling her eyes on him. The hell with it, Millie thought, and curled up next to him, her head in his lap, knees bent, her small body just fitting in the confined space. She felt the smooth cotton of his trousers against her cheek and watched his hands on the wheel, the three-feathered signet ring throwing off tiny glints in the green glow of the instrument panel.

He dropped his hand to his lap, caressing, tracing aimless patterns on her face, twirling his fingers in her hair. She captured his hand, cupping it against her mouth, and kissed his palm. He placed his thumb between her lips and, with a gentle pressure, parted them slightly. He ran his finger along the inside of her mouth, limning the shape, feeling the sensitive, moist silkiness and the shudder that ran through Millie's body.

She felt, underneath her cheek, the separate, answering tugs, as he rose in response. "Damn MacCrae!" she whispered.

"The things I do for England!" he said, rue mingling with mirth in his voice.

* * *

"Just dump your stuff," Millie instructed, as they entered her apartment. "I'll make some room in the closet." She busily shifted hangers, ripping clothes off and piling them unceremoniously on the closet floor.

"Millie!" James said imperatively.

"What?" she called from the depths of the closet.

"Millie! Front and center!"

Millie stood in front of him, arms at her sides, back rigid, the effect of her strict military comportment somewhat diminished by her giggles. "Yes, sir."

He enfolded her in his arms. "That's better." James kissed her, deeply and thoroughly. "Forget the buggering clothes, why don't you."

"I never was a very good housekeeper," Millie said, slowly undoing the buttons of his shirt.

He caught her hands in his. "Wait. We're going to be interrupted."

The doorbell rang. Millie looked at him, eyes wide with astonishment. "Well, answer it, why don't you?"

Millie unhooked the chain and opened the door a crack. MacCrae tipped his hat to her. "Good evening, miss," he said politely, handing her a large Zabars shopping bag. "Made it just in time."

Millie unpacked a connoisseur's selection of salads, cheeses, a cold roast chicken, bagels, lox and the pièce de résistance, a pint of chocolate chocolate-chip Häagen-Dazs. "I'm a quick study," James crowed, swaggering with the success of his exploit. "Doesn't take *me* long to find out what's what!"

"No, it doesn't. In bed or on the couch?" she inquired, holding the laden tray.

James gave that question the short shrift it deserved. With a disparaging look that spoke volumes about senseless inquiries, he stripped off his clothes, leaving a trail across the parquet floor.

"It's a good thing you have a valet," she called after him.

"Yes isn't it," he agreed amiably, stretching out on the bed. "What's taking you so long?"

Millie set the loaded tray down on the end table and crawled in next to him. She greedily uncapped each of the containers, inspecting their contents.

"How hungry are you?" James wanted to know.

"That depends," she answered, judiciously weighing her options.

And shortly found that she wasn't that hungry after all.

"Do we have any more poppyseed?" the Prince inquired lazily.

Millie examined the plate of bagels. "For a guy who ate his first bagel of any kind five days ago, you sure got picky in a hell of a hurry. One left!" she said triumphantly. "Split it with you?"

James nodded. "Can it really be just five days? It feels like a whole . . . history."

Millie watched him covertly, as she cream-cheeseaf32a bagel, pleased. She had wondered if James was living through the same time-warpy sensation she was, but had hesitated to ask for fear that . . . well, she just didn't want to ask.

The phone rang, startling in the quiet room. Millie looked at James. "Well, you won't know until you answer it, will you?" he said reasonably.

"Hello?" Millie said into the phone. Then, swallowing hard, "Just a moment, please." She covered the phone with her hand. "It's for you. How . . . how did they know?"

"My darling," he said, taking the phone from her, his eyes glinting with amusement. "There's never an hour in the day when someone, somewhere, doesn't know exactly where I am. Prince James," he said crisply into the phone. Then, warmly, "Hallo, darling."

Millie looked at him, startled. "I'm fine. And how are *you*, Mummy?" James impishly mimicked a greeting left behind in the nursery. Millie blinked and instinctively drew the sheet higher over her breasts.

"I've had a marvelous weekend," the Prince continued. "The Marlings were super. Or *he* was, I should say. Hester was her usual sweet self. I never pay her the slightest mind." He shoved a pillow behind his back and settled himself comfortably against the headboard. "I'll *bet* she knows it," he laughed, heartily. "I haven't forgiven her yet for tattling on me when I lost my dog lead that time . . . Has David been on to you?" he asked, with an infinitesimal hesitation. "No reason, I just wondered . . . No, we sailed and generally lay about the beach . . . I took some friends up with me. Sarah rang me . . . yes . . . yes . . . Well, she had to discover boys sometime," he chuckled. "What's he like? Her new beau, I mean . . . I *do?*" he asked, surprised. "Oh, him! He's nothing but an upper class twit. With spots!" His merry laughter rang out. "I beg to differ with you. I always had exemplary taste . . ." There was a silence, while the Prince was evidently recalled to certain youthful passions. "Well, mother, I *could* point out that she had certain . . . attributes, whose appeal is perhaps not readily apparent to you. Two of them, I might add . . . Yes, that *was* crude," he agreed sunnily. "But I will grant you that it takes some time to refine one's taste." James stretched out his arm and, finding Millie, drew her close to him. He planted an absentminded kiss on her forehead.

"How's everybody else? Uh huh . . . uh huh . . ." He listened for a time, evidently receiving a detailed accounting of the doings of a numerous extended family. "What again? Got one in the oven, has she? Well, at least they can't name this one after me," he said gleefully. "Country is being overrun with bleeding Jameses."

He reached for the container of ice cream and, his eyes distant, preoccupied, rummaged about for a spoon. Millie handed him one, which he accepted without really noticing where it came from. "And Granny?" he asked around a spoonful of the rich chocolate dessert. "Tell her I send my love," he said earnestly. "How's Robert Redford?" Millie looked at him in surprise.

"Tell him I said keeping it in his pants is also an option." Evidently the party on the other end declined to convey this particular message, for the Prince said, rather grimly, "All right, I will. I *will* tell him myself . . . New York is wonderful," he exulted. "I'm *so* glad I did this. Listen, darling, when I get home we've got to have a talk . . . What do you mean, what kind of a talk? A talk. An ordin'ry chat . . . No, it'll keep. Love to all. Bye, darling."

He hung up, his face reflecting leftover happiness and amusement. "Did she . . . ask you anything?" Millie ventured. "About where you— about who answered the—"

"No. No, she didn't. Neither of them *does* that. I'll bet she wanted to though," he added, roaring with laughter.

"Who's Robert Redford?"

"My cousin Randolph. Randy Randy, we call him. Eighteen, and popping in and out of girl's beds faster than you can count. At his age, I thought it was just to pee with," he said reminiscently and a touch wistfully.

A thought struck Millie. "How come you didn't wish your mother a happy birthday?"

"Because it isn't her birthday," he said quizzically, his eyes twinkling.

"I thought you said—" Millie accused.

James laughed at her expression. "And so I did. It's her *official* birthday. Her real birthday's in January, but the official celebration, with the flags flying and the Trooping the Color, is held in June."

"Sure. That makes sense."

"Because of the beastly weather. It wouldn't do to have all those soldiers riding up and down in full dress uniform presenting colors and all that in a sleet storm, would it? And the Queen riding sidesaddle. Now," he said energetically, tossing the sheet aside. "Let's clear up this mess." He started collecting containers, cutlery and other debris of their midnight supper.

"Leave it. I'll do it tomorrow."

"Not a chance!" the Prince glared at her and started toward the kitchen.

Millie made a face at his naked back. "Well, they won't walk away."

"Let's get ourselves organized," James said, busily running water in the sink. "You're not working tomorrow, are you?"

"No. Just Wednesday and Thursday. Wednesday I finish up Tovman's shoot, and Thursday, Millie Myerson, Girl Director, preps her own shoot."

"Good. I've got a meeting in the morning. Want to meet me for lunch? About noon?" He glanced questioningly at Millie leaning against the doorjamb.

"Why are you so neat?" she complained.

"I don't know. Maybe the Navy. Although I never could stand clutter. Will you? Meet me for lunch?"

Millie pretended to waver, considering the matter. Then, seeing his face, she gave up the pretense and the joke. "Of course," she said, wielding her power with the greatest of benevolence.

"That's settled then." James concentrated on the dishes. Millie smiled to herself, watching Queen Victoria's great, great, great grandson do her dishes. James turned the water off with a deft movement of his wrist. "Needs a new washer," he commented, looking at the dripping tap with displeasure. Millie pulled the dish towel off the side of the fridge where it hung and tossed it to him. "Or better still," he ventured, "why not bring your things along and plan on staying. If you'd like to, that is."

"I'd like to," Millie said softly.

"It's better with just the two of us," she said later, snuggling close to him. "Isn't it?"

The Prince didn't reply. Perhaps he was asleep.

Millie awoke abruptly, from a heavy laden sleep. She glanced at the blue light of the digital clock. Four-thirty. She looked at James, trying to figure out what had awakened her. He lay, turned away from her, his head buried under a pillow, fast asleep. She ran an experimental hand along his side. His body was hot, and damp with fever. "James? Are you all right?" she whispered cautiously. The Prince grunted sleepily and, without awakening, reached behind him and drew Millie close. She tucked herself around his long body and pulled the sheet over them both.

"What do you mean, I've got a cold!" the Prince challenged grumpily, wadding up his fourth tissue. "I don't get colds. Can't remember the last time I had one."

"Well, you have one now," Millie answered cheerfully.

"Rubbish!" he said and stood up, throwing the sheet aside. His nose was red, his eyes teary and his voice thick and nasal. "A cold shower'll fix me right up."

"Don't you dare! That's all you need is a cold shower! What you're getting is a hot bath, and if you're very good I'll put some bubble bath in. It's all ready, just climb in," she coaxed.

"Don't tell me what to do," he said peevishly and slid meekly into the tub.

"Here." Millie handed him a glass of orange juice and a handful of pills.

"What's that?"

"Orange juice," she answered innocently. "And aspirin and Contac," she clarified under his baleful stare.

He eyed the colorful pill warily. "What's Contac?"

"Antihistamine. Come on, swallow it down."

"I don't take pills," he informed her loftily.

She swallowed her smile before it could reflect on her face. He sounded uncommonly like her nephew Joshie, who, when spending the night at Millie's house, had labored manfully to convince her that he never went to bed before eleven o'clock. "Now you do. Let's go! There, that wasn't so bad, was it?" she inquired in the mindlessly cheerful tone of a particularly irritating night nurse. And escaped, laughing, as he pitched a damp towel at her.

"I shouldn't kiss you," the Prince said, taking her in his arms in the small foyer of her apartment. He looked a bit fresher in his crisp suit and tie, but still very coldy.

Millie leaned up and deliberately kissed his mouth. "I held you in my arms all night. Did you know that?"

"I knew," he nodded. "God, I feel rotten."

"Can you cancel your meetings?"

"Not on your Nellie!" And with a flash of a smile, and the brush of a kiss, he was gone.

Millie stood for a moment in the sunny room, listening to the silence. It feels strange to be alone, she thought.

She ran a hot tub and sank into it, luxuriating. The phone rang. Shit!

"Hi, there, petunia. Hold on a minute." Millie waited, naked, dripping and cursing. "Sorry," he clicked back in. "This place is a zoo here today."

"Gerald, I can't talk now. I'm in a rush. Can I call you back?"

"No. Let's have lunch. Come to the studio, and I'll share my brown bag with you."

"I can't. I'm meeting James in—"

"You have to," Gerald said.

"What's the big panic? Can't we do it next week?"

"No. No next week. Today. I'll buy," he added, as an inducement.

"Jesus, you sure pick your moments."

"Thanks a lot, Miss Myerson," he shot back. "Look, don't argue with me, just meet me for lunch."

"But I still don't see—"

"That's the trouble," he said pointedly. "Where are you meeting His Majesty?"

"His Royal Highness," she corrected automatically. "Sorry."

"Terrific. So where are you meeting fuckhead— I mean, Princie," he amended sourly.

"At the Sherry. At twelve. And, if all you want to do is make smart remarks—"

"No. I promise. No smart remarks. Okay. Meet me at The Salad Bar. That won't take you out of your way. Eleven-thirty."

"Flaming assholes!" Gerald began without preamble, setting his lanky form down in the bentwood cane chair across from Millie. He shot a murderous look at the hanging green plant suspended an inch above his left eyebrow.

"You're in a good mood," Millie laughed.

Gerald eyed her intently. "What's that for?" He gestured at her suitcase.

"I'm just taking a few things over to the Sherry." Millie wondered why she felt uncomfortable.

Gerald shoved at the plant, annoyed, and, of course, it swung back in front of his face. "Not my day," he said.

"What's on your mind?" Millie asked bluntly.

Gerald toyed with his salad. "We got this shoot. In Nassau. One of those things where a lady wanders along the beach in her underwear and a fur coat, with the sun coming up behind her, you know?" Millie nodded. She knew. "So they prep on Friday, and the unit manager tells the crew, 'Pack everything in this corner.' And he splits. He's got a half-share in a house in Fire Island," Gerald said bitterly, "and he wants to beat the traffic.

"So they pack all this shit and crate it carefully, 'cause they're going to put it on a plane at this end and hand-carry it off at the other. They're real careful. They pack it all, lights, prop box, grip equipment, audio shit, and twenty-two sand bags. Filled!"

Millie burst out laughing. Sandbags, filled, were part of the standard equipment taken to location to anchor lights, poles and other equipment, but carefully shipping, at enormous expense, sandbags that were to be used on a beach famed for its white expanses of same was too ludicrous for words. Millie knew instantly that this story would become part of the annals.

"And that's not all," Gerald continued. "They pack all this crap, but they forget the raw stock. It was in the fridge, not in that corner of the studio. So nobody shipped it. And the nearest place to get raw stock is Miami. But the director won't use Kodak. He wants Fuji." The two film stocks, with the exception of the finest of differences, were identical.

"I bet you didn't take that too well."

"Are you kidding? I told the fucker straight out. I told him he was shooting a goddamn brassiere commercial, not *Birth of a Nation.*"

"Sounds like fun. Sorry I'm not on it," Millie said facetiously. "Is that why you were so hot to have lunch? Are you going down to Nassau?"

"No. No, I am not going to Nassau. Gilhooley does not want me to go to location." His voice took on the deliberate cadences of someone reading, laboriously, from a Dick and Jane primer. "Gilhooley thinks the Nassau shoot is doing just fine. Gilhooley is playing with himself. Gilhooley signs my paychecks. Gilhooley is right," he concluded, his head bobbing up and down with the rectitude of Gilhooley's position.

"So what was the big—"

"You're really nuts about him, aren't you?" Gerald stirred his coffee with immense concentration.

"Yes, I am," Millie said simply.

Gerald lifted his eyes to hers. "What I don't understand," he said forlornly, "is why not me?"

"Because it just . . . happens that way sometimes," Millie said as gently as she could. "I'm sorry."

Gerald shifted in his chair. "I gotta tell you something. I had a talk with James. Yesterday. On the way home from church."

"About what!"

"What do you think about what? About you. And him."

Millie felt her face flush with fury, and with shame. "You have a *hell* of a nerve. Who the hell gave you permission to—"

"Nobody. But I did anyway."

Millie opened her mouth to speak and closed it again. "What did you say?" she asked finally.

"I told him," he began lightly, "that, since you really don't have any family except for us, that it was up to me to find out . . . to see that he didn't . . . that he wasn't just fooling around," he finished lamely. "I told him that I'd held your hand through all kinds of shit, and that I didn't want anybody fucking with your head. And that I love you a little bit." He swallowed the words, embarrassed. "And that I didn't want anything rotten to happen to you."

"What did he say?" Millie asked, despite herself.

"He said that he knew that. And that you loved me, too."

"You had no right!" Millie stood up, furious.

"I had a right," Gerald said softly. "I had to."

Millie picked up her purse and her suitcase and, with a final angry glare at Gerald, stalked out of the restaurant.

"But he didn't answer my question," Gerald said to her retreating, stiffly rigid back.

Millie didn't hear. Just forget this whole thing, she instructed, hailing a cab. "Sherry-Netherland," she ordered crisply.

Chapter IX

Millie paused for a moment outside the hotel, craning up to look at the dazzling sky and the flags flying from the top of the building. Now she recognized the rectangular standard that flew alongside the Union Jack: lions of crimson and gold, the square of royal blue and flash of white. Her heart lifted with the sight. That's for me, she thought. That's for me!

The Prince opened the door to the suite himself, looking somehow the more elegant for his rolled shirt cuffs and loosened tie. "I'm in the soup," he greeted her. "It's a right balls-up. I'm in total disgrace."

Millie followed him into the crowded living room. The phones rang steadily, and there was an atmosphere of controlled chaos, not unlike a well-run production office. "What *happened?*"

"Let me introduce you to all these people," James said, his arm at her elbow. All these people turned out to be a press secretary and his assistant, a private secretary and his *two* assistants, another equerry, evidently junior to Peter Goldsworth, and one or two others whose names and positions Millie didn't quite catch.

Against one wall stood an enormous calendar, about four feet by four feet, for the month of June. Next to it was another for the month of July. Each of them was overlayed with several sheets of clear plastic inscribed with vari-colored inks. Both calendars were so heavily overwritten as to resemble a particularly intricate tapestry.

"Sir, what time do you want to leave for Palm Springs on Wednesday?" an aide, standing in front of the calendar, queried.

The Prince looked at him blankly. "Pardon?"

"Your polo game, sir," he explained patiently to his suddenly dull-witted boss.

"Cancel it. I'm not going," James said gaily and grinned at the astonished looks on the faces of his staff.

"That's a first," the aide muttered under his breath.

"God help us," a man murmured.

"Very nice, Tony," the Prince approved. "A proper sentiment, I'm sure."

"Sir," one of the aides said imperatively, ushering a tall, imposing man toward the Prince. "The doctor is here."

"Why on earth send for a doctor?" the Prince asked mildly. "All I've got is a cold."

"That's not for you to say, Your Royal Highness," the doctor harrumphed.

"Sir, this is Dr. Tobias Foxworth, from the embassy," the aide introduced.

"A pleasure to meet you," James said cordially, shaking hands. "I don't need a doctor, but you're welcome to a bit of breakfast," he told him, with a rogueish nod toward the coffee and sweet rolls arrayed on a side table.

"There are others to think of besides yourself," the doctor pronounced. He peered down his long nose at the recalcitrant Prince in a way that was rapidly setting Millie's and, she guessed, the Prince's teeth on edge.

"Oh, well, if I must, I must." James gave in, generously, betraying not the slightest irritation. "Have some coffee or something, Millie. I'll be back in two seconds," he added, much to the doctor's displeasure. James disappeared into the bedroom, followed at a far more stately pace by the doctor.

This is his big chance, Millie thought, pouring herself a cup of coffee from the massive silver pot. He's not going to miss a single, blessed, self-important minute of it.

"Hello, Millie," Peter Goldsworth greeted her. "I'm sure Prince James has told you we've got a bit of a flap here this morning."

"What's going on?" she asked bluntly. She had no patience for British indirection at the moment.

Peter smiled his small half-smile. He picked up a sheaf of newspaper clippings from the desk and handed them to her. Millie flipped through them rapidly.

They were all basically the same, featuring a large photograph with varying captions and stories of differing lengths. The Prince, perched on top of the Daimler, arm curved above his head, waving to an unseen crowd, his face lit with his infectious smile.

On his left were Lucy and Dolly. Lucy, every blonde hair in place, secured by her sunglasses worn as a headband, looking coolly elegant. Lady Dolly, her auburn mane waving attractively, smiled fetchingly.

On the Prince's right, mercifully turning her head away from the camera, was Millie. "Thank God, I'm blurry," she said, under her breath. She smiled at Peter. "Lucy looks lovely."

"She always does," he agreed.

"It's a nice picture. So what's the matter?"

"This went out over the wire services." Millie looked at him blankly. "The press corps that travels with the Prince is very upset. They're *paid* to deliver charming little photographs and stories like this."

"Are you serious? Is it really a big thing?"

Peter nodded gravely. "Their papers have been telephoning from all over—this country, and Britain and Europe as well, wanting to know . . ." his voice took on the sarcastic tone of the inquiries, ". . . how the reporters spent the weekend. And just why they thought they were being paid those exorbitant salaries."

"Jesus," Millie breathed.

"Prince James is probably *the* most photographed man in the world. Everything he does is news. It doesn't even have to be anything special. Just arriving someplace or leaving some place is enough. He calls it the 'James-watch.' It sells papers," he added tonelessly. "In any case, the papers have been putting the pressure on their reporters, and they in turn on us."

"At least they can't give me the sack," said James jauntily, retieing his tie.

"So what are you laughing about, if it's so serious?" Millie wanted to know.

"Darling," he said softly, after a quick, checking glance to see who was in earshot. Then, in a more conversational tone, "If I didn't see the funny side of things, they would have put me in an institution a long time ago!"

The doctor reentered, snapping his black bag shut. He took center stage in the room and waited till he had everyone's attention.

"His Royal Highness is suffering from an acute upper-respiratory tract viral infection with associated rhinitis, mylagia and arthralgia," he announced importantly. And was greeted with blank looks of incomprehension. "A cold. With a runny nose," he translated. "And muscle aches," he added, defeated.

James's eyes met Millie's with barely suppressed hilarity.

"They're all here, sir," the press secretary informed the Prince.

"Lions all assembled, are they? All right, Matthews, tell them their dinner is ready. We've laid on a press conference, to try and soothe the raging beasts," he explained to Millie.

"I'll go first," Matthews offered deadpan. "To take the edge off their appetites." He crossed the large room and opened a door on the far side.

James waited a few seconds, then, taking Millie by the hand, threaded his way through the room and opened the door, silently, just a crack. He raised a warning finger to his lips and peered through the crack into the conference room. Thirty or forty people were seated on metal folding chairs. Some of them had pads and pencils at the ready, while others appeared to have settled somnolently for a short nap.

"Why was the doctor here?" a voice called.

"The Prince has a cold. An upper respiratory tract viral infection," Matthews quoted. He stood at a wood lectern, leaning his elbows on it informally. "That's not as bad as it sounds," he added jocularly. "It's just an ordinary cold."

"Is he going to cancel his schedule?" another voice queried.

"No, he will not. And we will not be issuing hourly bulletins, either."

"Got me on my ruddy death bed," James whispered cheerily in Millie's ear.

"If it's just a cold, why was the doctor here?"

"A woman after my own heart," James commended.

"I suggest we drop this line of inquiry," Matthews advised. "It's fruitless, I assure you. I'd like to say a few words about our little fuss over the weekend."

This characterization met with hoots of outrage, which the intrepid Matthews stared down. "As you all know, the Prince's visit to New York City was planned more than two years ago. Originally he was supposed to spend no more than one week here. But, as you may recall, one of his other engagements fell away . . ." Millie thought he was purposely going into rather boring detail as a device to lower the temperature ". . . and the Prince may have *helped* one or two others out of his calendar—off the record," he said quickly, smiling, "so that he could clear the time to spend a second week here on semi-holiday. He'd never been to New York for any length of time, and, as it is one of the great metropolises of our time . . ." He trailed off, finding the rest self-explanatory.

"How's he liking it," a voice called.

"You may quote the Prince as saying that New York is definitely one of the most vibrant, exciting and challenging cities in the world," Matthews dictated. "You may also say that he's pleased by the warm response he's received and glad to have had the opportunity of experiencing this great city firsthand."

"Never mind that bilge," a voice called. "What happened in Newport?"

"Yes. Well, as we told you, the Prince spent the weekend privately at the home of Lord and Lady Marling. Old friends of the royal family."

"You promised he wouldn't *do* anything!" an aggrieved voice challenged.

"So I did. And he didn't. His Royal Highness, on a sightseeing expedition, inadvertently allowed himself—was inadvertently photographed, and the photograph was printed. And that's it. We did not intentionally mislead you. We had no way of knowing it was going to happen."

"Tell that to my publisher!" a voice yelled.

"I'll give you all signed notes to the headmaster, excusing you," Matthews said drily. "Look, those are the breaks. It happens. It wasn't intended, we didn't plan it or generate it in any way. You're all big boys and girls now, and that's enough of that."

"Can we have the Prince?"

"Yes, you can. In just a few moments. But first I'll give you a couple of routine announcements of his—" He looked out at them meaningfully. "Of his abbreviated schedule. The man's on holiday. Let's keep that in mind, shall we."

"Right. I'll tell my publisher to shut down," a voice called genially. Matthews ignored it.

Millie looked up at James. He ran a hand over his hair, then licked his lips, nervously. He straightened his absolutely straight tie and, finding no further adjustments to make, toyed with his signet ring, pushing it back and forth over his little finger. He glanced down and caught Millie watching him. "Have some," he said, digging into his pocket.

"Some what?" she whispered.

He reached out an offering hand. "Barley sugar. Good for butterflies in the tummy," he explained, a trifle apologetically, unwrapping a piece of candy. His eyes lit up as he got an idea. "Can you look like a reporter?" Millie nodded, catching on. "Just go out that door," he gestured toward the main entrance to the suite, "and there's another just to your left, that leads into the conference room. There's an empty seat, right there, in the back row. See it?"

Millie nodded conspiratorially. "Okay," she whispered. She grabbed a steno pad off the desk to use as a prop and swiftly moved to the adjoining room. She tiptoed to her seat just as Matthews, his voice routine, uninflected, said, "His Royal Highness, the Prince of Wales."

James stepped into the room, confident, at ease, without a trace of nervousness or apprehension. He moved briskly to the lectern vacated by Matthews and smiled out at the congregation. "Good afternoon," he said, and was greeted by a perfunctory chorus of answers.

Several voices called out questions simultaneously, drowning each other out. The Prince held up his hand in a restraining gesture. "First let me say that no one is more aware than I that this is your livelihood, and all of you have editors back home who are, each and every one, fearsome creatures whose idea of an afternoon well spent is to kick the crutches out from under Tiny Tim." He smiled, acknowledging the laughter.

"So while I'm sure that this will in no way make up for any displeasure you may have incurred on my account, I would like to invite you all to be my guests at a private luncheon, tomorrow, before the reception. Off duty," he added to appreciative murmurs. "I know it rather smacks of a sop to Cerberus," he said with a disarming smile, "but it's all I've got at the moment."

His eyes twinkled as questioning whispers spread through the room. The reporters, not all of whom had had the benefit of a classical education, queried each other as to the meaning of the Prince's scholarly allusion.

He scanned the room while the reporters digested this cordial invitation. He's counting the house, Millie thought, amused. Sure enough, the Prince asked after a moment. "Where's Mary Hunter?"

"At her hotel, Sir. She's got tourist's tummy," one of the reporters called out.

"Damn shame. I *told* her not to drink the water," the Prince quipped.

"How's your cold, sir. Have you got a fever?"

"Do stow it," the Prince pleaded. "Haven't we had enough of that?"

Someone obligingly changed the subject. "Sir, any talk of marriage between you and Lady Dorothea?"

"We're friends. We've known each other since we were children," James replied in the bored voice of one reciting a lesson long since learned by rote. "And I don't have to remind you of Lord Marling's long and distinguished career in service of his country."

"No, you don't," someone muttered. And was frozen with a look quite sufficient to congeal the blood in his veins.

"Sir!" a hand waved urgently, "who are the other two girls? The blonde's dishy," the questioner observed.

"Friends," the Prince said succinctly.

"But who *are* they? We don't recognize them," someone complained bitterly.

"Pity," said the Prince, grinning broadly.

"Any romance there, sir?"

"Friends. Something you lot might not have had much experience with."

"Well, we did," a burly reporter told him, "until we got this bleeding marvelous job chasing around after you at ninety miles an hour. Sir. I lost ten pounds when you toured Asia," he confided plaintively.

"You're looking very fit, Jackie. I've been meaning to tell you." Prince James leaned one elbow on the lectern informally, relaxed. "Anybody want to discuss my article on the need to preserve indigenous Eskimo folklore and art forms? Hmmmmm?" This proposal met with a palpable lack of enthusiasm. "How about my speech on conservation?" the Prince persisted.

No takers. "What's the name of the dark-haired one? In the photo? She's turned her head away," a reporter said indignantly. Millie bent her head industriously over the steno pad.

The Prince waited just a beat, to make it clear he wasn't going to answer. "Can't we get back to my cold?" he asked brightly.

Amid the laughter, Matthews stepped forward. "I think we've about covered the ground. That'll be all, ladies and gentlemen. Thank you very much."

The Prince nodded once, sharply, and turned on his heel. A man at the back of the room stood up. "Who is Miss Myerhoff, sir?" he called sharply.

The Prince turned, his hand arrested on the doorknob. "I don't believe I know a Miss Myerhoff," he said studiously. His face was a paradigm of benign interest. "Is she pretty?" And, with a smile of utter serenity, he stepped through the door.

The name Myerhoff ricocheted around the room. "Jewish?" she heard someone ask. Some of our best queens are Jewish, Millie thought, and darted back into the Prince's suite.

The aides buzzed around James, clamoring for his attention. "Not now!" he said brusquely. His face, in marked contrast to the offhand nonchalance he had displayed a moment ago, was drawn and tense. He looked tired and somehow older.

A pertinacious secretary brandished a phone message in his face. "But, sir, the Palace requires an immediate answer as to—"

"I said not now!" the Prince snapped. Then, disciplining his voice, in a quieter tone, "Where's Millie? Oh, there you are." With a hand clamped on her shoulder, he drew her to the adjoining sitting room. "Matthews!" he barked over his shoulder, and the press secretary joined them.

"What do you say, Matthews!" James asked, closing the door behind them. "Are they on to Millie?"

"Oh, I don't think so, sir. I think that Miss Myerhoff's name," he smiled at Millie, "just floated to the surface as a result of the er . . . coffee incident. It was just a shot in the dark, I'm quite sure. They hoped you'd be caught off-guard and say something printable—or unprintable, if they'd got lucky."

"Thank you, Matthews." The Prince's tone was a dismissal. "But I can't take that chance," he murmured as Matthews left the room.

"Why are you so upset?" Millie asked.

The Prince paced, head bent, tracing and retracing a small circle in front of the glass doors leading to the terrace. "I'm not upset! Oh, hell, yes, I am."

"I know they gave you a hard time, but—"

"It's not that. I don't mind that. It's been this way since I hit puberty."

He stopped pacing and stared out the glass door, apparently lost in contemplation of the skyline and the pigeons that frolicked on the terrace. Suddenly he wheeled around, his eyes searching. He spotted a half-eaten roll abandoned next to an empty coffee cup and, crumbling it, slid the door open and tossed it out to the birds. Millie suppressed a smile.

"Promise me something," he said. He turned to Millie and, taking both her hands in his, looked earnestly into her face. "Promise me that if they *do* get on to you, even after I've left, you'll let me know. I have layers to protect me, and you don't. There are things I can do to help." He took a small diary out of his pocket and scrawled something on a page. "Here. Don't lose it," he said sharply.

"What is it?"

"My private telephone number. They can patch you through to me anywhere in the world."

"I'll memorize it and chew it up and swallow it," Millie promised. And was rewarded with the darkest of dark looks. "Look, I'm not made of glass. It's not as if I've led a sheltered life. I work in a high-pressure business. I've been around stars and celebrities. I've had my dinners interrupted by autograph seekers—"

"It's not the same!" James shook his head in exasperation and resumed his pacing. "You simply don't understand. The stakes are higher here. They'll scratch through your background, they'll—"

"So what? I haven't done anything so terrible. I haven't robbed any banks lately. The worst thing I ever did was, I got a ticket for jaywalking. Yes!" She nodded at him. "I was crossing Sixth and—"

The Prince shook his head, undiverted by her clowning. "You don't understand! They'll dig up your old boyfriends, and you'll be reading interviews congratulating me on how good you are in bed.

'And you'll be . . . compromised."

"Compromised! James, that's an awfully Victorian word."

"Nevertheless. I know it. It's happened to me before. And when it did I had to give up the pers—the friendship. They'll track down your sisters and your parents . . ." He fell silent, concentrating on his pacing. "I simply cannot let this happen," he said after a while, more to himself than to Millie. "I simply cannot let this happen."

He's afraid, Millie thought. I've never seen James afraid before. "Nothing's happened yet, James. Maybe it'll all blow over."

"And maybe it won't!" The Prince clipped the words off tersely.

Millie stood up and walked into his arms. "I still think you're upset over nothing."

"Oh, you do, do you? Jolly good!" He kissed her warmly. And sneezed violently. "I've got a terrific sense of timing, haven't I?" he laughed. "I really know how to do up a romantic moment." He clasped her face between his hands and looked into her eyes. "I'm most awfully sorry about this. I had wanted to take you out to a really posh restaurant. Although what possessed me to think I could, I don't know," he said wistfully. Then his face brightened. "I *do* know! I know what!" He snatched up the phone. "Get me Lady Cecilia Worthington, please, Tony. Right away!"

"What—" Millie began. And stopped as the Prince, oblivious, resumed his pacing.

In a moment the phone buzzed. James leapt for it and picked it up swiftly. "Cilly?" he asked eagerly. His laughter rang out, lightheartedly. "What do you mean, what in bloody hell do I want? You always did have frightful manners . . . New York is wonderful. That's what I'm calling about. What have you got on for the rest of the week? . . . Cancel it. Get on a Concorde and join me," he coaxed. "You can be here in just a few hours . . . Don't say 'not a chance,' Cilly. I'm not just joking about. I need you." He listened in silence for a few minutes. "If you don't I'll have to get nasty. I'll tell who *really* dropped that ice cube down the back of the Archbishop's wife's dress . . . How can you say such a thing?" the Prince asked, affronted. "My conduct has always been exemplary . . . Of course, I have a reason. Don't you know me by now? I'll tell you when you get here." He listened for a moment, then said simply, "Please, Cilly?"

The party on the other end evidently capitulated, for the Prince's smile mingled relief and satisfaction. "Ring my office. Tell them to send a car to take you to Heathrow. I'll have a helicopter waiting at this end. And Cilly? Thanks. I won't forget this," he promised. And hung up.

James turned to Millie. "What shall you do this afternoon? I've got that meeting that we put off from this morning—and a speech to deliver tomorrow that I haven't written yet."

"What was that all about?"

James grinned at her. "I just took care of our problem."

"How?"

"What are you going to do this afternoon?"

Millie gave up. "I don't know. Go to the library. Hit Bloomingdale's maybe."

The Prince looked at her somberly. "Perhaps you'd better not. You're here, you're inside and safe. It would be foolish to risk another coming and going. I'm sorry."

"Where can I stay?" she asked him sadly. "I'll be in the way, and I hate to hang around when people are working. And those people out there—" she gestured toward the main room, which held the Prince's staff, "they're always *looking* at me."

"I'll *bet* they are," said the Prince sympathetically. "How about right here? It's private. There's a TV and the terrace . . ."

She glanced around the room. Protective custody, Millie thought. "Do you have anything to read?"

"Lots." He kissed her gently, without heat. "Poor Millie. You're learning. I'm sorry."

Millie sat at one end of the couch, leaning against the arm, her feet stretched along it's length. The Prince sat at the other end, facing her, his legs alongside hers. Millie attempted, with little success, to work out the shot list for her shoot. How can you be innovative about a close-up of somebody showering? she wondered.

She looked at James. He scribbled on a yellow pad, covering page after page with his slanting scrawl. At intervals he would scoop up a large handful of peanuts from the dish on the coffee table and eat them, absently, one by one. Millie glanced at the large glass doors. The night sky turned them into mirrors, and she saw herself and the Prince and the shaded glow from the twin lamps at either end of the couch. She stretched, clasping her hands together and arching them over her head, savoring her contentment, listening to the swirling, plashing notes of Handel's "Water Music" coming from the radio. Like an old married couple, she thought. All we need is an elderly tabby cat purring on the hearth and the knowledge of sleeping children dreaming sweetly in the nursery.

James slashed a big *x* across the page. "I hate writing speeches. It's always a major sweat."

"Can't you get someone to write them for you?"

"Of course. But then what's the point of my delivering them?" He stared glumly into space for a few seconds, and then, with a muttered "Screw it!" tossed the yellow pad onto the coffee table, oblivious to the pile of papers he knocked to the floor. He slid down on the couch, so that his head rested on the arm and, tucking one hand under Millie's legs, closed his eyes.

Millie picked up the black, hard-covered passport that had fallen to the floor and leafed through it curiously. "Name: James Nicholas Andrew George." Four first names and no last, she thought wryly. "Hair: Brown. Eyes: Blue. Height: 6'. Occupation: Prince of Great Britain and Northern Ireland; Prince of Wales." In the oval cutout space on the front, large enough to accommodate the customary nine or ten digits, was the single number 1.

"How come yours is number one?"

"What?" He opened his eyes, peered at Millie, and then closed them again. "She hasn't got a passport."

"Why not?"

"Because they're issued in her name, idiot. It would be bloody stupid if she gave herself a passport, wouldn't it?"

The door opened. A dashing young woman ran into the room. She paused in front of James, sketching him the briefest of curtsies, then hurled herself on his body, covering his face with teeny, boisterous kisses.

"Get off me, you lunatic!" James stood up, catching her as she rolled off his lap. "Well, it certainly took you long enough to get here, didn't it?" He grinned at her brashly. "We waited dinner for you."

"How *nice* of you!" She threw her arms around his neck. "How are you, Dilly?"

"I'm super. How about you? Are you still seeing that twerp?"

"Which twerp?"

"You know very well which twerp. Misty."

"Roger," she corrected.

"Misty. Because he's gray, damp and sneaks up on you." James laughed so hard he could barely get the words out. Cilly punched him in the ribs, hard. He doubled over, groaning histrionically. "Watch it, Cilly. I'm not a well man."

"You're bleeding right, you're not a well man. I've been telling you that for years."

"Just for that—" he scooped her up in his arms, "you're going right over the side! Off the terrace! Twenty-two stories."

"Ouch! Stop it, James! Put me down!" she shrieked.

The Prince carried her a few feet, staggering dramatically under her weight. "You're getting right chubby. Better watch those sweets," he advised, through his laughter. He set her down on her feet.

"I'm not getting fat, sir. You're getting *old*."

Millie watched them, enchanted. They had all the rambunctious charm of twin puppies, newly littered.

The Prince took his friend by the hand. "Come, Cilly," he said, suddenly grave. "There's someone I want you to meet." He led her over to Millie on the couch. "Cecilia Worthington, Millie Myerson."

Lady Cecilia regarded Millie steadily. "Call me Celia. Everybody does but Prince James."

"I call her Cilly because she *is*," James said severely.

"And I call him Dilly, because *he* is," Lady Cecilia said simply.

Millie laughed at their practiced routine. "I'm very glad to meet you, Celia."

"And I think I'm very glad to meet *you*," Lady Cecilia told her frankly. She was a slender, medium-height woman with shoulder length, very fair hair, which she wore severely straight, parted on one side and caught in a tortoise shell barette at the other. She had mischievous gray eyes and an impudent, tip-tilted nose. Her smartly tailored linen dress and high-heeled pumps contrasted sharply with her extraverted vivacity. The entire effect was elegantly contrived, and she radiated panache.

"What do you do, Millie?" Celia asked as they seated themselves around the table. She made no attempt to conceal her very evident interest.

"I work in film production." She loves James, Millie thought. She's . . . careful for him. "And I'm about to direct my first commercial."

"Super!" Celia looked at her with genuine warmth. "Are you nervous?"

"Not at all," Millie said, with an airy wave of her hand. "Just scared shitless."

Celia laughed. "Well, that's an honest answer. Will it be harder for you because you're a woman? It *is* a command position, isn't it? Some men find it hard to take orders from a woman."

"And she's so very . . . slight," James said softly.

"And I've got to control all the gorillas," Millie put in. James laughed, getting the image instantly. "But it has nothing to do with size," Millie continued. "It's in the way you shake hands, in the way you say hello. It's a distance you keep in your head. Except for old friends, like Morty Aronson. You know him, James. He was the gaffer on the Magna Carta shoot."

"Nice chap," James winked at Cilly. "He's got quite a collection of risque stories."

"He's a dear," Millie said warmly. "He's been around since the year one, and he's seen it all. But the point is that you keep a psychological barrier in your head that is quite effective, you know?"

"I know," the Prince said. Then, wistfully, "I wish I could come watch you. Do people ever . . . do friends ever just come and hang about and watch?"

"All the time," Millie told him gently. The fact that his inability to be present at Millie's directorial debut had nothing to do with either protocol or security was something neither of them cared to mention.

Millie turned to Lady Celia. "What do you do?" she asked, hoping that this was not another idle Lady Dolly.

"She's a marine biologist," James supplied.

"But, actually, I just do that to support my real passion. I race sports cars," said Lady Cilly.

"Do you really!" Millie asked, impressed.

"And very good at it she is, too." James said, his voice tinged with envy.

"It's great fun. And besides, I look so adorable in my little helmet." Millie laughed, liking her.

James stood up abruptly. "It's time for the news." He snapped on the TV and stood in front of it, hands thrust into his trouser pockets, waiting.

"And now, on a lighter note," the blonde, ravishingly good-looking anchorman proclaimed, "Prince James, one of the world's most eligible bachelors, appears to have lost his heart to New York City. Or *in* New York City, I should say."

"James, are you in disgrace again?" Celia demanded. "Is that why I'm here?" James shushed her, intent on the newscast.

"The lucky lady is . . ." the announcer paused dramatically, ". . . unknown to us at the moment. But, whoever she is, the lovelorn Prince spirited her away for a romantic weekend rendezvous at a private seaside estate in Newport, Rhode Island! So that narrows the field."

The announcer's face was replaced with a grainy black-and-white close-up of Lady Dolly. Celia accorded her a loud, inelegant raspberry. Even in private, James smothered his grin, while Millie fell in love with Lady Cilly on the spot.

"Pretty, isn't she," the anchorman remarked. "Lady Dorothea Marling, well-born, rich, beautiful. Absolutely top-drawer, as are all the dashing Prince's ladies. *And* her family is very, very close to the Queen and the Duke. Sounds perfect, doesn't it?"

The camera pulled back to show the rest of the picture: Millie, the Prince, Lucy and Dolly perched on the back of the Daimler. Then it closed in on Lucy. "There's nothing wrong with this blonde stunner, either, wouldn't you say?" The announcer continued. "But we do have one very important clue. The mystery lady who has succeeded in running away with the catch of the decade is . . . a brunette!" As the camera zoomed in, a white circle appeared outlining Millie's blurred face. "At least, we have reports that a raven-tressed beauty has been seen going in and out of the Prince's hotel room."

"Shit!" the Prince muttered. And followed it with a string of curses he could only have acquired in the Navy.

The photograph on the screen was replaced by another: James, his eyes brimming with laughter, the sailor's cap he had tossed back to it's owner frozen in mid-flight. His outstretched arms obscured Millie, who stood behind him and a little to one side. "There she is again," the announcer said. "Shy little thing, isn't she. So, if you know this girl, be very nice to her. You may be looking at the next Queen of England!"

"Bloody bastards!" James snapped off the set with a grimace and resumed his seat.

"Are you at it again?" Lady Cilly teased raffishly. "Can't you manage these things without getting the press in an uproar?"

"I don't believe it," Millie said, still stunned.

". . . or perhaps you could just cool down a bit," Celia continued. "It wouldn't hurt, you know, now that you're getting on. It's always difficult," she informed Millie with a diabolical twinkle, "when we have a Prince of Wales who's hot-blooded."

"That'll be enough out of you, Cilly," James laughed.

"I'm just putting the situation into its historical context," she told him demurely.

"Watch it! Or I'll have you sent to the bloody Tower. I can you know," he assured Millie. "It's quite within my power."

"Tower, my arse!" Celia retorted. "You fall in love like I change shoes." She turned to Millie and shot her a wicked wink. "He can't help himself," she said with a compassionate shake of her head. "He's got a very romantic nature. Dilly's got . . . dozens of darlings," she cracked.

"And hundreds of honeys," the Prince returned.

"And a plethora of paramours," Millie supplied.

Cilly's turn: "And millions of mistresses."

James topped them neatly. "And a googol of girls. Don't listen to a word she says," he warned Millie. "Why do you think I call her 'Silly?'"

"Wretch!" Cilly dipped two perfectly manicured fingers into her water glass and flicked the droplets at the Prince.

James laughingly dodged the shower. "That's high treason, wouldn't you say, Millie?"

"You two have a vaudeville act going," Millie laughed.

"Well, we've had enough time to develop it," Celia told her. "When I stayed out all night for the first time, and my parents were tearing their hair out—"

"Only seventeen she was, the tart!" James interjected.

"—Prince James told them it was with him. And suddenly it didn't seem such a bad idea," Celia said drily.

James and Celia grinned at each other, their faces glowing with remembered triumph. "And when he tipped this entire boatload of photographers into the drink—"

"I never did! Anyway, you helped! You tipped that boat over as much as I did."

"Did not! I was just an innocent bystander."

"Well," James conceded, "maybe it was before I grew up and got decorous. Anyway," he turned to Millie, "Cilly took the blame for it, and she stuck to her guns—"

"So there wasn't much of a story, and the whole thing died down. And it was *your* idea to start with," she informed James.

"Was not!" He returned promptly.

"Was too!"

"Stop it!" Millie pleaded, clutching at her cheeks. "My smile hurts from laughing so much. Cilly, you're just—" She broke off in dismay. "I'm sorry. That was clumsy and intrusive. Forgive me."

Lady Cecilia regarded her thoughtfully. "That's all right. I think you can be the second person to call me Cilly."

All three looked at each other happily, warmed by the fellowship. James was the first to speak. Oddly, it was he who said, "Thank you, Cilly."

There was a light tap at the door. Peter Goldsworth stuck his head around it. "I hope I'm not disturbing you, sir. I just got in, and I wondered if . . . I was out for the evening and . . ."

"With a pretty lady, I hope," said the Prince genially, lounging back in his chair.

"With Miss Rogers," the equerry admitted.

"Good for you! No, there's nothing I need— Oh, yes there is. There's a first draft of my speech on the couch over there. Have it typed first thing in the morning, will you? The first draft will have to be the last," he told Millie morosely.

Goldsworth stepped into the room. "Lady Cecilia! I didn't know— I mean, I didn't know you were here," he finished lamely.

"Well, now you do," she said calmly, taking out a cigarette.

"Good to see you," Peter said.

"And you, Peter." Celia offered the pack of cigarettes to Millie. "Never did like him," she commented, as Goldsworth, speech in hand, left the room. "He's a prig."

"No, he's not," James defended. "And, even if he is, he's got a job to do, and he does it."

"Still," Cilly told him, as she lit Millie's cigarette, "he's a cold fish."

"That's all right, so's Lucy," Millie blurted. She broke off, aghast. "Lucy Rogers," she explained to Cilly somewhat embarrassed. "She's a dear friend of mine."

"That's all I need," James complained. "Now I've got two of you blowing smoke in my face."

"Go fuck yourself," Cilly said politely.

James's blue eyes darkened and turned to ice. "There are very few people who can get away with that," he remarked matter-of-factly.

Cilly dropped her eyes and concentrated fixedly on her cigarette. She had crossed an invisible line, and she knew it.

"Gerald did," Millie said, wanting to help Lady Cilly. "Gerald called you a—"

"Gerald doesn't matter," James interrupted, his eyes on Lady Cecilia.

Millie suddenly remembered. "Why didn't you tell me that Gerald spoke to you?" she accused.

The Prince transferred his gaze to Millie. "Because it wasn't important."

"Not important? It's embarrassing! It's none of his business. I'll never talk to him again. He had no right to come at you like some mid-Victorian poppa."

"Who is this flaming Gerald?" Cilly asked, recovering.

"A friend of Millie's. Everybody wants to get into the act," James said philosophically. "Some of mine and some of hers."

"But why didn't you *tell* me?" Millie persisted.

"Because Gerald is not a factor. He doesn't count. I don't mean that his sensibilities don't matter. They do. But he's got no power. You certainly ask a lot of questions."

"And I never get any answers."

"All in due time, my girl." James grinned at her. "All in due time. You can't expect a man to show his hand too soon, can you?"

Cilly watched the Prince, her eyes alert. "Who's been interfering from *your* side?"

"Never mind that. You know what I want you to do, don't you, Cilly?" Cilly nodded, her face aglow with amusement. "Good." The Prince leaned contentedly back in his chair.

Millie looked from one to the other. "*What* do you want her to do?"

The two conspirators exchanged mischievous glances. "You'll see," the Prince promised.

"Sometimes you sound like you're playing a game," Millie said bitterly. "Are you playing a game?"

James cocked a considering eyebrow at her. "I rather think I am," he said sardonically. He tilted his chair back and stared thoughtfully at a point just over Millie's head. Then he smiled, an inward, secret smile, as if he alone were privy to a joke so fiendishly delicious that he found it too delectable to share. "I rather think I am."

The Prince stood up decisively. "Good night, Cilly," he said, bending to kiss her on the cheek. "And thank you. If you like," he offered nobly, "I'll even be nice to Roger."

"Misty," she corrected impishly. "Good night, sir."

Millie looked around the Prince's dressing room. It, and the adjoining bathroom, was lined with ponderously gold-veined black marble and decorated with a profusion of swans, crystal, brass, onyx and gold, depending on their location. "I wonder how many birds gave their lives so that this place might live," she mused.

Prince James choked over his toothbrush. "Don't *do* that to me," he laughed, spitting toothpaste into the sink.

Millie watched him towel off, rubbing his face briskly. "Do you think about going home?" she asked suddenly.

James stopped drying himself and looked at her over the towel. "Yes, I do," he said candidly. He resumed his vigorous toweling. "I'm always thinking. Don't you know that yet?"

She followed him into the bedroom. He pulled the coverlet off the massive bed. "They keep *doing* that!" He picked up the pajamas laying in readiness on the pillow and tossed them onto a chair. "I never wear them. I often wonder if it's the same pair all the time, or do they launder them or what?"

Millie watched him climb into bed. She wandered around the room aimlessly, picking up first one object then another. She kneeled in front of a long, rectangular table, examining the stacks of books, neatly piled, that covered its surface. Alexander Solzhenitsyn, E. F. Schumacher, Barbara Tuchman, Oriana Fallaci. She picked up a copy of Emily Dickinson's collected poems and riffled through it.

"Millie," the Prince called firmly, "now is not the time for reading. Now is the time to turn one's attention to other things." He patted the empty side of the bed encouragingly.

Millie stayed where she was. "Lady Cilly is wonderful, isn't she."

"The best!"

"Did you ever . . . have anything with her?"

"Well, we did, actually. Years ago. I think we were each the second person the other slept with." His laughter rang out. "As soon as we figured out how it's done, we tried it with each other. But it wasn't—there wasn't any spark. Is that what's bothering you?"

Millie shook her head. "No."

"Because there's no reason to—"

"No. I knew how it was between you right away." She walked over to the bed, but instead of getting in, sat cross-legged, facing him. "Do you mind that I forget to call you 'sir' half the time?"

"I wasn't aware of it," the Prince said slowly, "but, yes, I do mind. When there are others present, I do. Not for me," he explained quickly, "but for what I represent." He kissed her forehead, fearing she was hurt. "I'm never just me, you know."

"I'll try to remember," Millie promised. She twisted the edge of the sheet around her finger and having completed the task, untwisted it and started again.

"What else?" James asked gently.

She raised her eyes to his. "What's it like where you live?"

"My own suite you mean?" Millie nodded. "Well, it's sort of blue . . . with a little brown," he said vaguely. "There's a sitting room and a study and a bedroom and a bath. All the modern conveniences." He smiled at her.

"Where do the . . . others live?"

"The Queen and the du— My parents live two floors up in another wing, and each of the girls has a suite. Sarah and Victoria share a sitting room. Helena is married, but she still keeps a flat in Buckingham Palace."

"But where *you* live, what's it like?"

"Well, there're lots of leather sofas and glass tables, and paintings on the walls. Mostly contemporary—I think it's important to encourage artists. I have framed cartoons hung in the bathroom. Mostly political or about me or my family. If I see one I like, I call the artist and get the original. And I collect primitive sculpture, so I have that stuff displayed on glass etageres. At night it's lighted, and it looks quite nice. And lots and lots of books and tons of records. I have a terrific stereo, a beauty. I built it myself. And there's a TV and a video recorder so I can catch the programs I didn't have time to see."

He touched an explorative finger to her cheek. "What's the matter, Millie?"

"Nothing. Tell me more."

"Come next to me, first."

"In a minute. Tell me more."

"Well, I have a suite at Windsor Castle, where we spend most weekends. In late summer we go to Balmoral. In Scotland. It's beautiful there. All woods and heaths and rivers. And secluded. Totally private. It's never open to the public."

"You mean the others are!?"

James smiled. "Buckingham Palace is . . . official. It's offices. People work there. We live above the shop." He grinned at her. "And Windsor is . . . a monument."

"It's so strange," Millie said, disconsolate. "How do you ever remember where your things are? How do you find your blue sweater or your sneakers?"

"You get used to it. And I travel so much. The whole family does. We have printed schedules so we can keep track of each other. We're almost never all home at the same time. Except at Christmas. Then we're all together at Sandringham."

"*Another* place!"

"Norfolk," he said gently. "The shooting there is the best! Grouse and—"

"It's all so strange," Millie interrupted dejectedly.

"Millie, look at me." He tilted her chin up with his forefinger and waited until she raised her eyes to his. "I thought you'd done with that . . . this rot about how different I am."

Millie dropped her eyes under his clear gaze. "Is it true what Cilly said? About all your girls?"

"I thought that was something else we'd done with!" The Prince's voice was sharp with exasperation. "Millie, make some sense. As far as the world is concerned, I've got two women in my suite right now!"

"I never thought of that."

"I can see that," he said with a grin. "If I slept with half the girls they put me in bed with, I'd be a dead man. A very *happy* dead man, perhaps. A very *contented* dead man, but dead nonetheless." Millie smiled. "That's better," James said. "Millie, don't ever believe anything you may read about me in the papers. About sixty percent of what they print is false, and the other forty percent is exaggerated. Remember all that stuff we talked about, about the need to see a ruler as a sexual power?"

"Yes."

"Well, there you are. Unless you hear something directly from me, or from someone close to me, someone who *knows*, don't believe it. The thing that does burn me up sometimes is that I can't answer back. I can't give my side of the story or set the record straight."

"Why not?"

"Because it just isn't done," he replied with peculiarly British logic.

Millie, lost in thought, toyed abstractedly with the hairs on his chest, twining them around her fingers. "Ouch!" James jumped as she accidently pulled one out. "Leave them alone." They're *supposed* to be there." He took her hand away and raised it to his lips. "What else?" he murmured, dropping a kiss into her palm.

"Did you see *Rebecca*? On TV?"

"Part of it. Too soppy. I like Monty Python though. Do you get that here?" Millie nodded. "I have a tremendous affinity for juvenile comedy."

"Absurdist," Millie corrected. "It's because everything in your life is . . . has such import."

"You may be right. My life is certainly complex, I grant you. But perhaps it's just that I have a prepubescent sense of humor." He laughed, with that ironic sense of self-parody that came so easily to him.

"Did you see that thing on the Duke of Windsor? 'Edward and Mrs. Simpson'?" Millie hazarded.

"Yes. Don't let's talk about that now."

"Can I ask you something?"

"Well, you never have before," he teased. "It might make a nice change." Then, seeing her unwontedly serious face, "What, darling? What is it? Tell me what's bothering you, and I'll kill it," said the dragon slayer, fiercely.

Millie smiled and brushed her hand over his bare shoulder. "When we were at the Marlings . . . in Newport," she explained unnecessarily and then trailed off.

"Yes?" the Prince encouraged. "What about the Marlings?"

"You were . . . different."

"How, different?"

"You were . . . open about us. You didn't seem to care who caught on. Sometimes I thought that it was even . . . deliberate. That you were doing it on purpose."

The Prince smiled. "Clever little thing, aren't you," he murmured. "Well, there were two reasons. One is, I have very few friends outside the family. But those that I do have are rock solid. Trustworthy. David has been like a second father to me all my life. He's one of the few people who understands, fully, what I'm up against. I've always been able to go to him for advice. And I've always found him worth listening to. Any more questions? No? Good. Come to bed."

Millie snuggled down next to him. The Prince reached over and snapped off the light. "Are you ever lonely?" Millie asked.

James burst out laughing. "Millie, I love you!" He buried his face against her breast. Still laughing, he kissed first one nipple and then the other and looked at the twin peaks, stiffened, despite her preoccupation, by the touch of his tongue. "That's nice," he murmured.

Millie folded her arms around him, feeling the softness of his skin and the hardness of his muscled back under her hands. "But are you?" she persisted.

He rested his chin against her chest and looked up at her. "Sometimes. Late at night. When I've done working and I'm listening to music and there's no one in particular I feel like calling. And it's too late, in any case. It can get frightfully quiet," he said softly. "Resoundingly quiet."

Millie rubbed the back of his neck gently. "What do you do."

He grinned at her impudently. "Turn the record over. What do you do?"

"Just bear it. Go for a walk."

"That's something I can't do. I'd give six people coronaries," he said gaily, adding, "I can see this situation calls for emergency measures." He slid down on the bed and buried his face between her thighs.

Millie instinctively raised her legs and bent her knees, allowing his tongue to find the place that very soon sent the shudders of release through her body.

"What was the second reason?" she asked, much later, into the darkness. "About the Marlings?"

"I'm asleep," James said. "Mind yer own business."

The Prince's face split with his winsome grin. "Hallo, darling," he said.

The camera pulled back, and Millie saw that he was juggling. He kept the brightly colored balls in the air; red, blue, green, purple, orange, yellow. "How's that, Millie?" He tossed them up in the air and caught them in perfect rhythm. "It doesn't take me long to learn what's what," he crowed. "I'm good at games."

He dropped a ball, and it fell to the floor, out of frame, and shattered. The Prince glanced down at it. "Oops. Lost one." His smile gleamed with mischief. "I guess I'm not as good as I thought."

As Millie watched, the colorful balls he juggled in the air turned, eerily, into spheres of green glass, the kind that coca-cola bottles used to be made of. And, in a whistling uprush of horror, she slid sickeningly down into a bottomless abyss lined with green glass. She flailed about, desperately searching for a handhold, and could find none.

"Darling! Millie, wake up! You're having a nightmare." The Prince shook her gently, whispering in her ear.

She clung to him, trembling. "Thank God. I thought it was real. James, it was awful!"

"Never mind, sweetheart. It's all right. I'm right here, and it's all right."

Chapter X

The Prince coughed, raspingly, into his handkerchief. "You look perfectly ghastly," Cilly told him.

"I've just got a cold," he said hoarsely. "And besides, Millie here—" he dropped his voice as an aide passed within earshot, "kept me up all night asking questions. She thinks I'm a ruddy encyclopedia." He raised his hand to his lips, casually, and touched it to Millie's. And was seized again with a fit of coughing.

"Why don't you have the doctor?" Cilly asked him.

"Not you too! I *had* the doctor. He told me in six different kinds of Latin that I had a cold." James deepened his voice and took on the cultured, precise cadences of Dr. Foxworth. "Your Royal Highness must learn to take care of your royal self. One cannot take one's health for granted. One must get enough sleep and eat one's vegetables." He finished up with the rude noise that takes its name from Millie's home borough, the Bronx.

The Prince's audience of two giggled appreciatively. "I still don't know how you *do* that," Millie said admiringly.

"It's in their genes, I think," Cilly supplied tartly. "Princess Sarah does all her teachers—"

"And half the diplomatic corps," James put in with a wicked grin.

Matthews came out of the conference room and closed the door carefully behind him, shielding the group from the eyes within. "Ready when you are, sir."

"Quite ready," James said firmly. "Cilly?"

"Might as well," she laughed. "And a one and a two and—"

Matthews flung the door open and, on the beat, they stepped into the conference room, Cilly a pace behind the Prince, both flashing the brightest of smiles.

Millie and the press secretary followed, eclipsed by the blinding glamor of the pair in front.

The metal chairs had been removed and the room transformed into an intimate dining room. A buffet luncheon, complete with bar, lined two walls. Little tables scattered around the room afforded seats to the guests.

"Lady Cecilia!" someone called. "We didn't know you were here."

"Do you mind?" she retorted impudently. "I only crash the best parties, you know."

"When did you get here?"

She smiled demurely. "Just last night."

"How long will you stay?"

"She's going home with me," the Prince answered crisply.

The press corps smelled blood. They gathered around the happy couple, throwing questions at them faster than they could answer.

"Here we've gone to all this trouble, done up a delightful luncheon for you, and you're not even eating," the Prince chided.

"Who's that?" a man inquired, with a blunt gesture toward Millie.

Millie found herself, for the first time in her life, in the situation which had been James's lot from the day of his birth. An entire roomful of strangers focused on her unwaveringly, to the exclusion of everyone else.

Millie smiled out at the reporters. To her great surprise, she found that she wasn't flustered at all. As a matter of fact, she realized, and her smile broadened with the thought, she was actually having a good time. James turned to her, warily, and opened his mouth to speak. Millie winked at him, and he closed it again.

Lady Cilly reached behind her and caught Millie's hand. "I'd like you all to meet one of my dearest friends. This is Millie Myerson."

"That's the one who was in Newport!" a woman called excitedly.

"How's your upset tummy, Mary?" Lady Cilly asked sweetly, having done her homework, "all better?"

"Yes, thanks," Mary Hunter said, somewhat mollified. But

apparently not enough. "What was she doing in Newport?"

Lady Cilly linked her arm possessively through Prince James's. "I asked Millie to take good care of His Royal Highness for me," she said, with angelically downcast eyes.

Prince James smiled down at Cilly and tweaked her nose affectionately.

Flashbulbs popped.

"Sir, can we have that again? I missed it."

"No, you can't, Nigel," the Prince said. "I'm not a bl— I'm not a film star."

"How long have you and Lady Cecilia known each other, Miss Myerson?" a man, gifted with a suspicious nature, asked pointedly.

Lady Cilly turned around and casually lifted a glass off the table behind her. "Were you ever in Europe?" she whispered to Millie.

"France. June to October. Seventy-four," Millie whispered back.

Lady Cilly completed her turn, sipping decorously at her wine. "Let's see . . ." She tapped a contemplative finger against her pursed mouth. "I think it was about, oh . . . nineteen seventy-three or seventy-four. Millie was spending a few months in France . . ." Her voice took on a reminiscent note. "She was so excited. It was her first trip to Europe, and—"

"I had a *wonderful* time," Millie interjected, finding her sea legs.

"And so did I, that summer. One of the reasons for my trip here . . ." Cilly lowered her eyes shyly, "was to see something of Millie."

Amusement bubbled up in Millie, glossing her smile. She hasn't said one thing that isn't true, she thought gleefully. And neither has James.

"Est-ce que vous parlez Français?" a French-accented reporter challenged.

"Bien sûr, monsieur. Et j'espère que vous vous bien amuser à New York," Millie answered politely, her accent flawlessly Parisian.

The Frenchman's eyes lit with delight. *"Merci, Mademoiselle. Et si vous permettez, il faut dire que vous êtes très charmante."*

Whether the Prince could follow the rapid-fire French or not, Millie didn't know, but he broke in, cutting off both the exchange and the budding flirtation. "Why don't you all settle yourselves down and have something to eat," he suggested cordially. "And you too," he whispered aside, to Millie. "Let's not push this thing too far. Matthews, you go with her."

The press secretary ushered Millie to a table near the entrance, while the Prince moved from table to table, exchanging a moment's banter at each.

Lady Cilly made the circuit with him. She behaved with properly becoming decorum, except for those moments when, overcome by passion, she gazed lovingly into the Prince's eyes. And he, forgetful of his surroundings, gazed dreamily into hers.

Millie watched, admiring the skill with which they played their charade. The press secretary followed them with his eyes, noncommittally.

"Well, that's that," James said, drawing out a chair for Lady Cilly. He glanced around the room. The reporters, finally, devoted themselves to their food. But not without keeping an attentive eye on the Prince's coterie. "What do you think, Cilly? Are they buying it?"

"I don't see why not. You just might have to make an honest woman of me one of these days."

James put one arm around her shoulders for the benefit of his audience and, with his free hand, pinched her forearm, hard.

"Ouch! Stop it, you lunatic. That hurt!" Cilly slapped his hand away and smiled adoringly up into his eyes.

"You couldn't take it, you know, Cilly," James said conversationally.

"Damn right! I wouldn't have that job and that life for anything in the world. You never draw a free breath. I'd rather marry the dustman."

"Thanks a lot!" James leaned over to kiss her on the cheek.

"Don't overdo it. There's a limit you know. But while we're on the subject . . . I *am* getting married, James."

The Prince's face lit with genuine pleasure. "You're not! To whom? Not—"

"No," she laughed. "Not Roger. Rupert Gallagher."

"You can't marry a man named Rupert," James objected. "It sounds like something out of Rudyard Kipling."

"Well, I am. Are you happy for me, sir?"

"Very," he said and kissed her, much to the press corps's delight, on the mouth.

"I never thought I would do it," Lady Celia told Millie. "I could never see tying oneself down like that. And, all of a sudden, I could see it."

"I'm glad for you," Millie said. And she was. They don't come any better than Cilly, she thought.

"But who *is* this chap?" Prince James wanted to know.

"He's an executive with Thames Television."

"Well, if he's nice . . . if he's *very* nice," James teased, "I'll stand godfather to your first child."

Cilly looked at him gratefully. "Thank you, James," she said quietly.

Millie realized that what he had offered was no small thing. Having the King of England as your godfather wouldn't ensure a smooth path in life, but it sure as hell couldn't hurt. Cilly's eldest son will be called James, she realized with a shock and a surge of envy.

"When are you going to announce it?" Matthews asked carefully.

"Yes, when?" James echoed.

Cilly laughed. "I guess not just yet."

Peter Goldsworth suddenly appeared at their table. "Sir?" he said, with a meaningful glance at his watch.

"Yes. Thank you, Peter." The Prince stood up. There was a great scraping of chairs as the press corps followed suit. "No, don't." The Prince held up a cautionary hand. "Go on with your meals. I'd love to stay and play with you a while longer, but . . ."

"When can we expect an announcement, sir?" a man called.

"This is not for attribution," the Prince warned, thus ensuring a barrage of stories that would begin: "Sources close to Buckingham Palace say . . ." He paused, waiting just a beat until every eye was on him. "Lady Cecilia and I—" he took Cilly's hand, "intend to remain the same good friends we always were." And, hiding a triumphant grin, he turned to leave the room.

Mary Hunter's voice cut through the rueful laughter. "Can we have your thoughts on the Princess Helena episode, sir?"

The Prince blinked. His startled eyes met those of his press secretary. Matthews returned his gaze and, with a slight lift of his shoulders, signaled his incomprehension.

"What episode?" the Prince inquired cautiously.

"My editor just told me." She stood up, enjoying her temporary position as the cynosure of all eyes. "The Prin*cess* was out riding, and the reporters were following her—just doing their job," she commented sourly. "Suddenly, for no reason at all, she turned on them. Although it seems things had got a bit out of hand. The Princess's horse shied at all the fuss and almost bolted away with her."

"So what *happened?*" an impatient voice prompted.

"The Princess inquired," the woman read from her notes, sweetly, "'Don't you people have anything constructive to do instead of following me about all day?'"

James winced, visibly. "I have no comment at all," he said flatly. His tone brooked no appeal.

The reporters, trained to his nuances, accepted it and wrote busily in their notebooks. Although what they could be writing except "no comment" is a mystery to me, Millie thought.

* * *

James stood when Millie entered the sitting room. "That's a smart outfit you've got on, my girl."

Millie smiled to herself, glancing down at her aubergine stock-tie silk blouse and just-off-white linen suit with satisfaction. James never seemed conscious of his attire and probably just pulled on whatever his valet chose for him, yet he always seemed to notice what she had on. "I had no idea what to wear to the Queen's reception," she said, dropping down on the couch next to him. "They didn't teach me that in the Bronx."

"I wish you'd drop that," James said, helping himself to a sandwich from the heaping plate on the coffee table. "It's nothing but an affectation. You have nothing to do with your . . . background. Have a sandwich?"

"No, thanks. I ate at the luncheon. Didn't you?"

The Prince shook his head and swallowed a huge mouthful. "I never do. I find that, when I try to eat with five hundred people staring at me, I lose my appetite."

"Where's Cilly?"

"Taking a nap. She said something about being tired. I can't imagine why." He grinned at her. "I don't get jet lag myself. Don't believe in it." He put down his half-eaten sandwich and searched Millie's face inquiringly. "How about you? Caught my cold yet? Sneezing? Scratchy throat? I can't see why I should have to go through this by myself."

"Not a one," she said proudly.

"There's no justice in this world," the Prince lamented.

Millie laughed, marveling at his flair for nonsense, his ability to relax, completely, in a very short space of time. He doesn't *worry*, she thought enviously. "What was all that about Princess Helena?" she asked suddenly.

"Her Royal Highness, the Princess Helena Alexandra Marguerite," he proclaimed in the stentorian tones of a BBC announcer, "is an ass," he finished, around a mouthful of sandwich.

"Maybe it wasn't so polite, but it didn't sound all that terrible to me."

"The minute she made that crack about finding something constructive to do, she was a cooked goose—which might very well be what I'm eating." The Prince cocked an explorative eye at the filling of his sandwich. "What do you suppose this is, Millie? Hmmmm?"

"But *why?*" Millie persisted.

"Because there are a lot of people who don't think the monarchy does anything constructive either," he said patiently.

"Oh." Millie digested this for a moment. "They don't let you get away with much, do they? You have to watch yourself every minute."

"You get used to it." James reached into his pocket for his handkerchief and blew his nose vigorously. "If this thing has any meaning at all, it means the subjugation of one's own . . . whim to one's duty. Or it should," he added, with a baleful glare for the absent Princess. "That's why it helps to be born into it. You know what to expect." The Prince, finding this line of thought displeasing, truncated it and fell silent.

"Is that why you don't give autographs?"

"It's not so much the autograph as what you might be signing without knowing it. It could turn up, even ten years later, to haunt you. Could be anything. A petition to overthrow the government—Heaven forfend," said the Prince piously. And then grinned at her wickedly. "Or to legalize marijuana—"

"Which might not be altogether a bad thing," Lady Cilly said cheerily, coming into the room. "Don't you look nice," she told Millie.

"And you, too," Millie said. In fact, Lady Cecilia's teal blue crepe dress set off her fair beauty admirably. "Come sit."

Lady Cilly promptly kicked off her high-heeled sandals and dropped into a chair across from them. "And how is His Royal Highness faring? Got your speech ready, chum?"

"Nope. I'll just have to wing it, won't I?" said her chum, glumly.

A light, warning tap on the door, and Peter Goldsworth stuck his head in. "His Royal Highness is on the telephone for you, sir."

"Who's *that!*" Millie asked in surprise.

"Well, there's only one other," James said gaily. He reached out and punched the flashing button on the telephone. "Hello, Papa." He stressed the last syllable, so that, to Millie's ear, it sounded almost French. He grinned into his handkerchief, listening, and blew his nose loudly. "Well, I was also under the impression that you had raised three reasonably civilized adults. Perhaps Sarah will do better." Then he caught on. "Just a minute. What's Vicky done? . . . Was she hurt?" he asked quickly, and was evidently reassured. "Did she damage the car? . . . You tell her," he instructed, "that, if she ever takes my car out again, I'll break both her hands for her. Let her smash up her own cars."

Lady Cilly burst out laughing. "She always *does* that," she told Millie gleefully. "Prince James has this absolutely super Aston Martin DB6. He won't let anybody else drive it, but every now and then Princess Victoria sneaks it out. And every time she does, she puts a dent in it," said the race-car driver with satisfaction.

"Cecilia Worthington is here," James said into the phone. "I suddenly found I couldn't survive without her another moment. We're madly in love, and an announcement is imminent." He laughed. "I believe the expression you're groping for, Papa, is 'Tell it to the Marines' . . . Has David Marling been on to you?" The Prince's voice sharpened with interest. "How did I know? I'm psychic." His eyes shone with an antic glee. "The Masters told me . . . "

Peter Goldsworth opened the door. He caught the Prince's eye and held up ten fingers, then another five, and closed the door behind him.

"Got to dash," James said into the phone. "I've just time to take a piss before the reception," he added earthily to his father. Then he laughed. "Bye, now. See you next weekend."

Another tap on the door. "All *right*, Peter!" James called irritably.

The door swung open. Lord Marling, smiling and dapper in a charcoal gray double-breasted suit, stood in the doorway.

James jumped up, his face lighting with affection. "David! I didn't know you were coming!"

Lord Marling inclined his head to the Prince. "That makes us even, Sir. I didn't know Lady Cecilia was here. How are you, my dear?"

"I'm very fine, thank you. And, in case you're wondering, Prince James found that he couldn't go on without the help and support of the woman he loves—" James jerked his head up in surprise. "So he sent for me, and here I am," Lady Cilly concluded blithely.

Lord Marling greeted this explanation with the same skeptical tablespoonful of salt that His Royal Highness the Duke had shown. "Well, you're most welcome," he said smoothly. "Now that I'm here, may I have the pleasure of escorting these two lovely ladies to the reception?"

He extended two gallant elbows. Both lovely ladies obediently stood up.

The Prince placed a restraining hand on Millie's arm. "One lovely lady. Millie stays with me."

Lord Marling nodded. "Lady Cecilia?" Cilly gracefully took his arm, and they walked out of the room.

James waited until the door had closed behind them. Then he punched the intercom button on the telephone. "Goldsworth, please," he said crisply.

Goldsworth opened the door almost before the Prince had hung up. "Yes, sir?"

"Peter, take Millie down to the reception." Goldsworth opened his mouth to demur. "Don't worry, the other lot will baby-sit me. See that you take good care of her. But not too good, mind you." He brushed a kiss on Millie's lips. "I'm a sick man. I can't do with any competition."

"Yes, sir," Goldsworth said expressionlessly.

Millie swallowed her laughter for his sake. He doesn't tease easily, she thought, feeling sorry for him, considering his boss's penchant for relentless, ongoing badinage.

"Bye, darling," she said. She reached up to kiss the Prince. Her movement was awkward and uncoordinated, and, instead of his mouth, she hit the bottom of his chin.

Peter cleared his throat. Millie realized he was waiting for her. She smiled brightly at him and walked to the door. She turned back with a final smile for the Prince, but he was already striding toward his bedroom, his mind occupied, as always, with the immediate task ahead. She followed Peter out of the room.

"Each year, on the Queen's birthday, every British embassy and consulate in the world holds a reception for all British subjects in the area," Goldsworth explained. He was clearly making polite conversation, and Millie turned her attention to him, realizing that woolgathering was contraindicated. "This year," he continued, "since there will be a member of the royal family in attendance, not to mention its being the Prince of Wales . . ." he chuckled. That's as close as he comes to a joke, Millie thought. " . . . it was decided to shift it to a reception room in the hotel. We expect quite a crush. By the way," he added diffidently, "should you happen to run across the ambassador, the correct address is 'Mr. Ambassador.'"

"Thank you," Millie said warmly. "That was sweet of you," she added, seeing his relief. It was, she thought. By his lights, he stuck his neck out for me. She suddenly remembered that he had been out with Lucy last night. Well, if they fell madly, crazily, fizzily in love, he shows no signs of it, she thought flippantly. But, then again, he's not the fizzy type. And Lucy isn't . . . passionate either, she thought, saddened at the insight.

The elevator doors opened directly onto the reception room, all dark paneling, gilt and gleaming mirrors. A military band, resplendent in spit and polish uniforms, strolled the room. Millie, with a surge of suppressed hilarity, realized that they were playing "Everybody's Talkin' at Me," the theme from *Midnight Cowboy*. There's something peculiar about that, she thought. It's either very right or very wrong.

The room was, as Peter had predicted, crowded. The subdued hum of genteel chatter was broken occasionally by a hearty laugh, quickly hushed. There was an anticipatory buzz in the room, an air of expectation just bordering on tension, which Millie sensed as soon as she stepped off the elevator.

"Shall I get you a drink?" Peter offered.

"Some white wine would be nice," Millie replied and looked around, interested, as Peter disappeared in the direction of the buffet. Everybody's dressed up, she thought.

The men were formally business-suited and vested, while the women wore floaty summery prints and gauzy voiles. Each and every woman, without exception, wore a hat. They ranged from fashionable straws to elaborate confections in which flowers, berries and leaves figured prominently.

The hatless Millie looked down at her sleek suit and decided she liked it better. I'd look dumb in cabbage roses, not to mention that I'd feel like I was wearing my drapes. And *he* likes it, she thought, delivering the coup de grace.

"It won't do to plant strawb'ries anymore," a woman proclaimed in elegantly plummy tones. "It's far too late. I'm afraid that, if one hasn't already, one's missed the bus."

"We spent last week*end* at Windsor," a stout man disclosed. "We've just arrived in the States, actually. We had the jolliest day's shooting. The Duke is the best shot in England, you know. And *that*," he confided in an intimate whisper, "means in the world."

"And we played charades," the wife put in. "The Queen was as keen as ever."

Millie turned and saw Lord Marling deep in conversation with Lady Cecilia. Lord Marling bent his head to catch something Cilly was saying and then spoke, forcefully and at some length. She's welcome to him, Millie thought. He gives *me* the creeps.

And turning away, she moved on.

"I'm a socialist myself," she heard someone say. "I don't hold with all the royal trappings. Nor did my pa before me." Millie watched the speaker, a florid man in an ill-fitting suit. His wife, next to him, nodded her agreement. The cherries on her hat bobbed with her movement. Her half-rimmed glasses evidently pinched her nose, for she took them off and, resting them on the capacious shelf of her bosom, rubbed the two red dents on either side of her pointed nose.

"I wouldn't have come myself," she concurred twangily, "but 'Arry, 'ere, 'e wanted to."

"Well, I always did like a bit of show," 'Arry admitted. "And the royals, they do put on a good one."

Millie spotted Peter Goldsworth searching the room for her, holding two brimming glasses. She waved to him, and he started toward her.

The band broke off in the middle of a sprightly, if somewhat incongruous, rendition of "Raindrops Keep Falling on My Head" and began, without the apparent exchange of the smallest signal, what was clearly an anthem.

"That's 'God Bless the Prince of Wales' . . . what they're playing, I mean," Goldsworth volunteered. He handed Millie a glass of wine. She smiled her thanks and looked up at his stoic face. Oh, dear, she thought, I don't need him to chaperone me around, but

James told him to, and that's that. Millie opened her mouth to reassure him and stopped, as the heavy, wooden double doors at the far end of the room swung open.

A frisson swept through the crowd. Conversations were halted in midsentence, forgotten, as attention triangulated on the man whose sweating, feverish body Millie had embraced through the night.

The Prince stood, poised on the threshold, for a timeless moment, hands clasped behind his back, ramrod straight, his eyes sweeping the room.

He wore a formal dress uniform, scarlet and gold and black, dazzling the eye. "Colonel-in-chief of the Royal Regiment of Wales," Peter Goldsworth whispered. Millie nodded, staring at the Prince, mesmerized.

Gold braid edged the black velvet standup collar clasped under his lifted chin and rimmed the edges of his flaring, waist-length scarlet jacket, forming an inverted vee over his chest. Tiny gold emblems, the three-feathered device of the Prince of Wales, winked from either side of his collar. A thin, red-satin stripe on the outsides of his black trousers ran from his waist to the top of his burnished black boots.

Three orders gleamed on his breast: the eight-pointed star of the Garter, the Order of the Thistle and, at the top and perhaps most prized by this stalwart Prince, the wings denoting a parachutist. Gold braid looped from his epauletted right shoulder, sweeping in graceful curves, the ends dangling free across his chest, motionless now, as the Prince was motionless.

Millie raised her eyes to his face, severe, ascetic, without a hint of his ready laughter. His full, sweet mouth was set firmly, in a straight, uncompromising line. "Good afternoon," he said quietly, his voice resonant.

His words were a signal for the assemblage to resume breathing. A wave of motion swept the room. The women curtsied, and the men inclined their heads.

Millie alone stood upright, self-conscious, unable to follow suit.

Prince James nodded his acknowledgement then smiled, brilliantly. He strode into the room, to an apparently prearranged point just in front of the large windows. There he was joined by a tall, portly, bald-headed man, dignified in a dark, vested suit, complete with a gold watch chain across his ample waist.

James's presence changed the chemistry of the room. Although the band started up again, and conversation picked up, presumably where it had left off, all attention was focused, however surreptitiously, on one figure.

The Prince's aides, augmented for the occasion by consulate personnel, herded separate groups of twos, threes and fours out of the crowd with practiced ease. They accompanied them to the Prince, insuring each of those present his private moment of conversation with his future monarch.

Millie watched, fascinated. This was a side of James she had not as yet seen, different from the affable, easygoing public personage, or from the superstar, handling the informally gathered crowds with aplomb, different from the playful, gallant companion who remonstrated with her for leaving dirty dishes around. And far, far different from the lover who knew with certainty, sometimes before she did, when she lagged behind, and returned, joyously, to bring her back with him.

The people who were brought to him were, almost without exception, reduced to babbling incoherence. Direct face-to-face contact with royalty had, it seemed, the strangest effect on heretofore reasonably competent human beings. They stuttered and stumbled. Flustered, trying to recover, they simply dug themselves in deeper. James helped them, his manner easy, confident, putting them at ease.

He exchanged a few words with each, appearing to remember, at least long enough to use it once in conversation, each of the names whispered into his ear by the aide stationed to his left and a little behind him.

He shook masculine hands that trembled and helped shaky women, unused to curtsies, to rise gracefully. Now and then he rocked back on his heels to ease cramping muscles. Occasionally, bringing a clutch of amused affection to Millie's heart, he would try forgetfully to put his hands in his pockets and, finding that he hadn't any, would clasp his hands behind his back.

Millie was vastly amused to see 'Arry, the self-proclaimed socialist ostensibly immune to the effects of royalty, unable for the moment to recall, in response to James's genial question, just what it was he did for a living. 'Arry looked at the Prince blankly and summoning his scattered wits, replied, "Beastly weather we're 'avin' isn't it?" while facing the window, looking straight out at the gloriously sunlit street.

Prince James nodded, unfazed. He listened to a whispered sentence from his aide and responded, "I do hope these high interest rates aren't having an adverse effect on your real estate business." And 'Arry, dignity intact, was handed over to the ambassador, in favor of his no-less-flustered wife.

"How are your children liking school in America?" James inquired amiably, after an informative whisper from his aide. "I hope they're having better luck with their maths than I did."

"That's a nice tie you have on," the woman replied, idiotically fixated on the middle of the Prince's uniformed chest.

James glanced down, covertly, as if to confirm that in fact his uniform didn't include one. "The Welsh Guards is my regiment. I'm pleased you like it," he answered gently, if obliquely. And Mrs. 'Arry, too, was passed down the line.

"What you again?" James shook hands with the hapless Dr. Foxworth. "I thought I'd done with you."

"I hope your Royal Highness is feeling better," the doctor said pompously. "A viral infection is not to be taken lightly."

Millie realized that not once since he had entered the room, had James sneezed, coughed, sniffled, blown his nose or otherwise displayed any symptoms of his debilitating cold. Even his voice betrayed no sign of hoarseness. All good actors have that knack, she thought. They could be shaking with fever, dripping, hacking, and coughing blood, for God's sakes, and, the minute they get on stage, it's all gone.

The next couple in line was more familiar with the court, and their conversation, conducted in lower and more intimate tones, was not audible to Millie. But in them, too, she was aware of something unnatural, of a lack of spontaneity, a careful control of their words and their demeanor, an internal pressure to make the most of their brief intercourse with the heir to the throne.

She felt a sudden need to move and made a circuit of the room, sipping her wine. She, too, found after a while that she couldn't stay away. Drawn by the same magnetic force that held the others in thrall, she moved to the Prince's other side, to the area where people gathered after their moment in the sun. She stood unobtrusively to one side and listened.

A grizzled, aged man was next in line. "'Appy to shake your 'and, sir. My missus would'a been 'ere too, but she's laid up. With

arthyritus. 'Ere.'' Unexpectedly he thrust a creased, much-folded
document into the Prince's hand.

"What's this?'' James asked gently.

"My discharge papers, sir. Signed by your great-grandfather,
meaning no disrespect, sir. In 1919, it was, after the Great War.''

Prince James unfolded the tattered document with care. He
scanned it intently, oblivious to the bottleneck he was creating in the
receiving line. He looked into the man's eyes. "I'm glad you showed
me this. P'raps you'd better have it back.'' Unconsciously he had
picked up the man's Cockney accent. "To show you've done your
duty,'' he added gravely.

The man accepted the return of his treasure happily, a broad
smile creasing his weathered face. "Ever so glad to 'ave met you, sir,''
he said, beaming affectionately at his Prince.

"Same here.'' With a tender smile, James handed the aged
veteran on. "And my best to your wife,'' the Prince added, not
forgetting.

The old man took out a rumpled handkerchief and blew his nose
stentoriously. "The toff's a smasher!'' the man said to no one in
particular. "You could put a suit of armor on that lad and send him out
to Agincourt.'' Solemnly, unashamed, he wiped his eyes.

"We hit the jackpot this time.'' A woman standing near him
agreed. "Bloomin' lucky, I calls it.''

"Luck 'ad nothing to do with it,'' 'Arry retorted. "It's a bloody
miracle, is what it is, if you ask me.''

"Reminds me of our Dickie,'' another man said, "our son. We
lost him at Dunkirk. He was as like that boy as two peas in a pod.''

His wife, standing next to him, nodded agreement. "He's a fine
lad,'' she said simply.

Millie, listening, was moved almost to tears, watching the
subjects of the newest, and perhaps most beloved, guardian of an
ancient heritage—the bond, fragile yet tensile, woven over centuries,
that bound a leader to his people, everlastingly.

It was both a mystique and a mystery, in the Catholic sense of the
word. Millie could feel its power intuitively rather than rationally. It
had to do with worship, with belief and with faith, with transcendence
and triumph over despair, over pain and loss. The woman who had
sacrificed her son for his country over thirty years ago, saw him reborn
in the person of the young Prince and was comforted.

Now I understand why the touch of kings was once thought to have the power to heal, Millie thought. Because it does. People are transformed, changed somehow, by contact with him. It touches a chord in them, something primitive, visceral—and effective. It gives them hope.

That's why they endure. Why they persevere. At Balaklava, in the forests of the Argonne, and at Normandy. People need something to look up to. A focus for the best that's in them, a symbol of sanity in an insane and shifting and unstable world. They need somewhere to put their hungers, their feelings of pride, of loyalty, of aspiration and of love. That's why they call him "sir," she thought. It's to underscore the difference for *them*, not for him.

It was a relationship that was, at its core, symbiotic. Waves of emotion swelled from the gathered people to the young Prince, who, rejoicing, radiated an allure, a magnetism, that held its recipients in thrall and brushed them, however transitorially, with magic. And the result was a kind of passion, an exultation—unspoken, unexpressed, and yet very real.

Now I understand what consecration means, Millie thought, a shiver running up her spine. He *is* their heir.

"Would you care to meet His Royal Highness, Miss Myerson?" Peter Goldsworth materialized at her elbow.

"What!" Millie looked up at his deadpan face. He was absolutely serious.

"Prince James specifically requested . . . inquired . . . if you would be so kind," he fumbled.

Millie's eyes sparkled with the fun of it. "Sure," she agreed and was conducted therewith, Goldsworth's guiding hand at her elbow, to a place in line.

"Miss Millie Myerson, Your Royal Highness," the aide, clearly having been coached, introduced. "Miss Myerson, His Royal Highness, the Prince of Wales."

"A pleasure," Millie said, smiling decorously.

"A very *great* pleasure," the Prince returned, gravely shaking her hand. "What is it you do exactly, Miss Myerson? How interesting," he murmured, as she opened her mouth to reply. "See that door over there?" His left shoulder raised imperceptibly, gesturing. His hand, ostensibly in an unusually prolonged greeting, still held hers.

"Got it," Millie said.

"Delighted to have met you, Miss Myerson," he said, louder. The Prince handed her on to His Excellency, Her Majesty's Ambassador to the United States, who informed Millie that she was a charming girl and patted her hand.

Millie, after a short detour to the buffet table for a refill, opened the door James had indicated, its outlines almost invisible in the wood-paneling. She found herself in a small, apparently empty, sitting room.

"Be right with you," James called cheerily, over the unmistakable sound of a man pissing. "As King George the Fifth was reported to have advised his sons," he said, coming into the room from the adjacent bathroom, "never miss a chance to take the weight off your feet or to empty your bladder."

Millie looked at him, confounded, unable to assimilate the ease with which James switched gears. She found it hard to reconcile the twin horses James rode in easy tandem, the venerated and the ordinary, the public and the private.

"What's the matter?" he asked, seeing her face.

"It all seems a little . . . overwhelming."

"That's only because it *is* overwhelming," he replied, very gently. "Have a biscuit," he offered with a raised plate and a deliberate return to the mundane. "They're good."

Millie shook her head. "I've never seen anything like what went on in there. People falling all over themselves, coming apart at the seams . . ."

"They're not, really. They're just nervous and a bit overcome, some of them. One has to watch for it and help them. Else they'll feel just rotten afterward. Although," he laughed, "they do say the most imbecilic things sometimes. The hardest part is just keeping a straight face. But I'm used to it. All in a day's work."

"'Another day, another penny,' Lucy says."

"Quite right she is, too," James concurred. "Did you see that old codger? Wasn't he super?"

"Do you know what he said? He said that they could send you out to Agincourt and the people would follow."

"Did he really!" James's smile started in his eyes and spread over his face. "Did he really?" he asked again, earnestly. He took a swig from his glass of milk, then, raising it heavenward, declaimed:

We few, we happy few, we band of brothers;
For he today that sheds his blood with me
Shall be my brother; be he ne'er so vile,
This day shall gentle his condition.
And gentlemen in England, now a-bed,
Shall think themselves accurs'd they were not here,
And hold their manhoods cheap whiles any speaks
That fought with us upon St. Crispin's Day!

"Good old 'Enry," he finished in a milder tone. "Did he *really* say that?"

Millie smiled. "Yes."

"Perceptive old gent, isn't he," James said flippantly, covering his very real emotion. He swallowed the rest of his milk in one lengthy draught and, setting the glass down, gathered Millie into his arms. "Do you know how long it's been since we made love?" He glanced at his watch. "Exactly nine hours and twenty minutes."

"Want to try for a record?" Millie offered graciously.

"No!" the Prince said firmly. Then, as the door opened, without glancing away, "Blast you, Peter!" He covered Millie's lips with his own. "You taste good," he said, unashamedly feeding on her mouth. With a final, light kiss, he was gone, called back to duty.

As soon as Millie stepped into the reception room, she realized, suddenly and imperatively, that she needed to follow King George V's precept. She turned back to the anteroom and tried the door. Locked.

She turned and spotted Peter Goldsworth in the crowd. "Where's the—" she began, walking up to him.

"Through that archway on your left." Evidently his ability to read the Prince's mind had extended itself to Millie.

Millie saluted her flushed, jubilant face in the bathroom mirror and quickly availed herself of the facilities, hurrying so she could get back in time for James's speech.

She was halfway out of the stall when the door to the lounge opened. Millie recognized the aristocratically pinched tones of the Countess of Rossbourne, Lady Hester Marling. "—and so we had to take a commercial flight. Most uncomfortable. I can't imagine how people manage."

Millie instinctively moved back into the stall and carefully shut the door. Shit! I had enough of her to last me the rest of my life, she thought.

"How tiresome," a woman said, her voice tinged with envy.

"How perfectly awful," a third woman echoed.

"Just so," Lady Marling acknowledged. "But one must make sacrifices when one entertains royalty, mustn't one."

We took their plane! Millie thought, with a rising bubble of laughter. She lowered the toilet seat noiselessly and sat down, prepared to wait them out.

"Oh, I wouldn't, Margo!" Lady Marling called sharply. "After all, one can't be sure who's sat there before one, can one?"

Margo heeded her Ladyship's advice, and the three women settled themselves in front of the long mirror to make minor adjustments to their coiffures and major ones to the reputations of their acquaintanceship.

Millie listened with half an ear to the vacuous chatter. They really trash their friends, she thought, amused. Does James remember I'm working tomorrow? That means we should stay at my place tonight. She stood up, prepared to confront the dragon lady. I better remind him in case he needs to bring any—

Her hand froze on the doorknob as she caught a sudden, hushed confidentiality in the third woman's voice. "What do you think? Are we to have a wedding in Westminster Abbey at long last?"

"I rather doubt it, Alice," Margo said. "He's been dancing around Lady Cecilia for years, and nothing's ever come of it."

"He's got to settle down sometime," Alice argued. "We can't have the heir to the throne forever running around like some—" She bit off her words just short of serious indiscretion. "It's his duty. It's that simple. Besides, if he waits any longer, there's likely to be no one left," she giggled. "The Duke told Prince James so himself. I know that for a fact, because my Reginald was there and heard him. And Reggie captains the Prince's polo team, you know." Alice snapped her compact shut with a triumphant click.

Apparently she had succeeded in imbuing Margo with a reverence for her access to Royal Family secrets. "Do *you* think he'll marry Lady Cecilia?"

"I know it for a fact," Alice returned smugly. "I had it straight from Phyllis Crumbley. That's why he brought her over here. They've definitely decided. The wedding's to be at Christmas."

That's what *you* think, Millie told her silently, enjoying herself.

Lady Marling's laugh trilled plummily, as if in response to Millie's wit. "I'm *so* sorry to have to disagree with you, Alice," she said sweetly. "Prince James is *not* going to marry Cecilia Worthington. He's no more in love with her than he is with . . . with . . ." She groped for a metaphor caustic enough to convey her feelings and came up with, " . . . the man in the moon."

"You never can tell," said Margo, the peacemaker. "People change. His Royal Highness may have discovered that he's in love with Lady Cecilia after all."

Lady Marling hooted, most unbecomingly.

"Or perhaps he's just ready to settle down," Margo tried.

This earned her a scornful laugh from Alice. Millie was beginning to feel downright sorry for poor Margo.

"Settle *down?*" Alice said, when she had finally managed to contain her mirth. "That one? You can't be serious. Prince James is after anything in a ski—"

Lady Marling's voice cracked like a whip, cutting her off. "What of it? Certainly no one in this day and age expects the Prince of Wales to . . . restrain himself. He's entitled to his larks. As long as he's not married. I have no fears about Prince James. When he does marry, he'll choose someone who'll make a splendid Queen. You won't find him foisting one of his . . . trifles off on us. And it won't be Lady Cecilia!"

"Perhaps, Hester, it will be your Dorothea." Alice sank the knife in, then twisted it neatly. "At least—or is it at most?—she doesn't putter about with those filthy engines." With that Alice swept out of the room, leaving her opponent, bloodied, on the tile floor of the lounge.

"Alice Parker never did know what she was about," Lady Marling said sourly. "His Royal Highness has no intention of marrying Cecilia Worthington, I assure you."

"You seem to know all about it," Margo invited delicately.

This was too much for Lady Marling. "I do know we've had quite a close call lately."

"Close call?" Margo prompted cautiously.

Lady Marling hesitated. "You mustn't tell a soul."

"Of course not!"

"It seems . . ." Lady Marling lowered her voice and scraped her chair even closer to her confidante. "It seems that Prince James was very . . . taken with a young woman. American apparently," she said with almost no sneer.

"Unsuitable?" Margo asked breathlessly.

"My dear! Unsuitable is not the word! I had her up to the house for the weekend, so I'm not just speaking through my hat. I had a houseful of the most appallingly vulgar people. The most rag-mannered young man and—"

Margot had no patience for digression. "But what about . . . *her?*"

"A nice enough girl, I suppose," Lady Marling conceded, with a salutary display of fair-mindedness. "But just a touch common. Not our kind."

"But, surely, Prince James has had his romantic interludes in the past. And they've always . . . melted away."

"But *this* time—" Lady Marling's voice sank to a whisper, "this time, Prince James was entertaining thoughts of the young woman with an eye to . . . the future!"

"No!"

"Yes! We had it straight from Peter Goldsworth."

Lucy knew! Millie thought with the utmost certainty, and a stab of pain.

"He's the Prince's chief equerry, you know. As was his father before him and his grandfather before that. Going back a hundred years."

Margo recalled her to the subject under discussion. "But what did he *say* exactly?"

"He rang us up late one night, last Thursday, I think it was. He told David that Prince James had told him that this girl—" she pronounced it somewhere between "gurl" and "gel," "was fit to be Queen! What do you think of *that*, Margo?"

"I'm speechless," Margo lied. "Has His Royal Highness gone daft?"

"Not at all. But I have to admit that Prince James was quite besotted with her," Lady Marling continued. "And our little Miss Myer— our little arriviste was just as cool as she could be. She went 'round smiling all weekend, behaving as if it were nothing out of the ordinary. I'm sure she's already having herself fitted with the robes in which to be installed as a Knight of the Garter."

"But what if she's right? If the Prince is as besotted as you say, we might have a repetition of—"

Lady Marling laughed complacently. "Not likely. David took care of it. Nipped it in the bud, you might say."

"How?" Margo breathed.

Yes, how? Millie echoed silently.

"Very simply," Lady Marling retorted triumphantly. "David arranged a little . . . tour for the Prince. A sight-seeing expedition, one might call it." She chuckled. "Prince James was introduced to his future in-laws."

Who are they talking about? Millie wondered, as her denial mechanism clicked faultlessly into place.

"An elderly couple," Lady Marling recounted. "From Czechoslovakia or somewhere. Without the slightest address. Quite ill-bred. Shopkeepers. And Jewish!" She finished triumphantly.

Millie crossed her legs, primly, at the ankles. She folded her hands in her lap. "That's enough. No more," she whispered.

"How did the— What about Prince *James?*"

Lady Marling's light, silvery laugh bounced off the tiled walls. "His Royal Highness was completely disenchanted. He's very fastidious, you know. He found the whole thing a trifle . . . distasteful. After all, Margo, can you just picture it? The opening of Parliament, and the Queen and the Duke and Prince James, in their velvet robes, all scarlet and ermine. They look up, and there, in the Family Gallery are . . . are . . . " The Countess, overtaken by mirth, found herself temporarily unable to continue. "Why, even if one dressed them up and cleaned them up and taught them some deportment, you can't make a silk purse out of a sow's ear," she said wisely. "And the acorn never falls far from the oak. You know what they say. If you want to see what a girl will be like in twenty years time, have a look at her mother today."

"So it's all over then?"

"Quite," Lady Marling said crisply. "Although I must admit I was surprised when the Prince brought her up for the weekend. But David wasn't. He likes to see young people enjoy themselves. 'There's nothing wrong with having a bit of jam on your bread if you've got a sweet tooth,' David told him. As one man of the world to another," Lady Hester tittered. "In the end, Prince James realized David was right."

"But how do you *know?* Did he tell you?"

"Well, not exactly. But it's been my experience, and His Royal Highness all but grew up in my house, you know, that Prince James is very cautious about revealing himself. He's almost . . . secretive," she said with some displeasure. "I've found that the more something means to him the less likely he is to talk about it. Oh, he'll talk about anything under the sun, quite cheerfully. But not about the things he really cares about. He plays his cards very close to the vest."

"But—"

"That proves it, Margo! Prince James simply flaunted this girl all weekend. Hardly took his eyes off her. She never entered the room but he jumped up and ran over to her."

That was the second reason, Millie thought. To show his friends . . .

"So perhaps it's not over?"

Lady Marling laughed. "You mistake my meaning. Of course it's over. Prince James *is* sensible. He himself told David that he'd learned a lot from the encounter. The Prince thanked David most sincerely for his forethought in saving him from making a mesalliance. It did take a bit of talking, of course, but in the end, His Royal Highness agreed that David had done him a favor."

The world slid sideways, sickeningly. *"I think he's rather done me a favour,"* James *whispered into her hair in the moonlit darkness heavy with the scent of the approaching storm.*

Millie braced herself with her outstretched arms against the trembling tile walls of the stall. Why are they shaking? she wondered.

Then the fringe darkness spread, filling her vision, and time stopped.

* * *

It seemed like a long time later when Millie came back to herself. She had no idea how much time had passed, but she knew that she was alone. Carefully, she unlocked the door to the stall and walked out.

She found herself on the curb, looking up into the cheerful Irish face of the Sherry-Netherland doorman. "Cab, lady?" he asked, apparently for the second time. She must have nodded, for soon she was in a cab heading West.

The cabbie, undaunted by her lack of response, kept up a steady, garrulous stream of conversation, while Millie concentrated on keeping down the concentric waves of nausea that swept over her.

She thrust a handful of bills at the driver, and must have given him a handsome tip, for he disengaged himself from the taxi and opened the car door for her. Millie slid out, carefully, and almost tripped as she pushed the revolving door to the building too hard.

"Hey, Millie! Not so fast!" She turned, bewildered, and found a large cream-colored envelope in her hand.

"Thank you, Victor," she said to the doorman, and smiled nicely.

This doesn't hurt. There's nothing to hurt. This doesn't hurt. There's nothing to hurt. She repeated the litany all the way up in the elevator, pulling at her silk blouse, trying to loosen the hot wire that burned around her chest.

Millie opened the door of the apartment and moved swiftly to the bathroom. "This doesn't hurt," she said and retched, great, heaving, empty, wracking spasms. She kneeled on the floor, holding onto the sides of the toilet, while the room spun around her.

She leaned her head against the cool porcelain of the sink. The migrainous throbbing in her temples, instead of easing, intensified. I've got vertigo. Alfred–Hitchcock-Vertigo. Kim Novak. Barbara Bel Geddes. And who? One more. Stewart. Something Stewart. I *know* it. Dammit! I know it! Her brain stubbornly refused to yield up the missing name.

She got up, rinsed her mouth, and was immediately seized again. Resume the position, she thought. And she did, heaving vast emptinesses.

The answering machine clicked into life. She jumped, startled. A country mile. I've jumped a country mile, Millie thought disjointedly. She listened to James's voice.

"Millie? Are you there? . . . I guess not," he said to himself. He hung up. Click. Clickety clack clickety clack clickety clack. The mindless rhythm set up in Millie's brain. The little engine that could, that could, that could.

SHUT UP! she shrieked voicelessly. "What you need is a drink."

She walked unsteadily to the kitchen and poured herself a whopping dose of scotch. I don't drink scotch, she thought, and drank the whole glass down. I drink oblivion.

The large envelope lay on the parquet floor in the foyer where she had dropped it. Millie ripped at it, tearing it open.

HIS EXCELLENCY, SIR IVOR ST. JOHN
HER MAJESTY'S AMBASSADOR TO THE UNITED STATES
REQUESTS THE PLEASURE OF YOUR COMPANY
AT A FAREWELL BALL

IN HONOUR OF H.R.H., THE PRINCE OF WALES
FRIDAY EVENING, NINE O'CLOCK
GRAND BALLROOM SHERRY-NETHERLAND HOTEL

"Keep it," James's voice said in her head, "and think of me."
Millie ripped at the heavy vellum, tearing the invitation into shreds. "Fuck 'em if they can't take a joke," she said, and threw the tiny pieces of parchment up in the air.

* * *

It's dark out, she thought, looking at the lights outside her windows. When did it get dark? She was lying, fully dressed, flat on her back in bed. Her mouth was very dry. Her head throbbed in a relentless, driving rhythm.

"Millie?" James's voice said. "Are you there? Ring me whenever you get in. No matter how late."

"*I'm sorry to have gotten you up so early, and I thank you for coming,*" James's voice played in her head.

"*That's okay, Prince. We get paid for it.*" Now the raucous laughter played back in the brain, grotesque, carnivallike, bizzare.

"*They could use a nice Jewish girl in Buckingham Palace,*" Morty Aronson smiled down at her.

"*Common. Common. Not our kind,*" Lady Marling taunted.

"That's enough!" Millie yelled.

"*Quite right,*" the Prince said briskly. "*I said I was going to call and so I have I'd like it very much if you would call me James do stop thinking of me as a creature from outer space my father calls Buckingham Palace a tied house lose the job lose the house I want very much to hear it and your mother? sweet and funny and brave or you get hurt don't leave me don't ever leave me I didn't think I was different early on tonight, Ian, I don't think! I'm only a link in a chain would you sleep with me if I were not who I am?*"

James's voice faded, blessedly. Only to be replaced by Lucy. She smiled at Millie. "*What's wrong with some nice juicy no-strings-attached sex? I don't think the world is ready for Queen Millie the First.*"

"*Is our Miss Millie ready to play with the jest set?*" Gerald asked.

That's *jet* set, Millie corrected. You were right, Gerald, she moaned. You were right! Princes are for fairy tales.

"*I always thought Charming was a bloody stupid name don't give it a thought ducks.*" James's voice started up again in her brain. "*They'll line up Mickey and Minnie in formation and I can watch the rides go round and round and round and round and round I feel I've come home,"* James whispered, his voice filled with longing. "Bore da," he said, stretching his arms over his head. *"It's the three feathers of the Prince of Wales. It goes where I go."*

"Terrific," Gerald said sourly.

"You came all over funny," the Prince told him. *"'Appens to the best of us. And now I am the Ruler of Queen's Navee."*

"Tell me about yourself," Lord Marling smiled menacingly. *"For I'm the same way. If one approach doesn't work I try another and it works it works it works."*

"With all my heart," James said. *"I think he may rather have done me a favour."* Millie's insides lurched. *"I hope none of you gets seasick."* James laughed uproariously, enjoying the joke.

"She can't help it," Cilly told him. *"She's got a romantic nature."*

"Millie?" James said in her ear. He waited silently. "I'm at the Sherry-Netherland," he said idiotically. And then the tape ran out.

"Goody goody gumdrops," she told him. "Go find yourself another playmate."

She rolled over on to her stomach and the room spun, dizzyingly. I think I'll go to sleep now.

The hot tears came and, with them, the clenching agony. "I hurt," Millie cried. "I hurt." The hot wire was back, coiling itself around her chest, making it hard to breathe. It's white, she thought, detached. The pain is white.

She heard a high, keening wail, anguished, distraught, the voice of a little girl. "Mommy, Mommy, Mommy, Mommy." The word held no comfort for her, and she cried, wordlessly, burying her face in the pillow. Please, no more, she begged, and felt, with complete kinesthetic clarity, James's body curled around hers. She smelled his scent, felt the texture of his skin, the whisper of his breath against her cheek and for a moment, forgetting, was comforted.

She leapt out of bed, stripping off her clothes, dropping them where they fell. Finding her way by reflected light from the street, she paced the darkened apartment trying, in an infantile instinct, to walk away the pain.

Endure, she thought. Endure. Hugging the word like a talisman, she got back into bed.

* * *

Finally, mercifully, the alarm went off.

Millie rolled out of bed, groggy, uncoordinated, and moved to the shower. She soaped herself automatically, concentrating. "Wavies. Two—no, three talent," she repeated, like a charm against evil.

The phone rang while she was putting on her makeup. Unthinkingly, Millie picked it up before the answering machine. And immediately regretted it.

"Hello, Millie? Did I wake you?" her mother asked considerately.

"No. I was just on my way out to work."

"That's all I ever hear from you, is work, work, work." Millie sat down on the bed, passively accepting her just due. "Hello? Are you there?"

"I'm here, Ma," Millie said, fighting against the bitter taste in her throat.

"There's a picture of you in the paper. You tried to hide your face, but I recognized you. Miss High-and-Mighty. You always did want to be a big shot. City College wasn't good enough for you. You had to go to Wel-les-ley." Her mother gave each syllable its individual dollop of scorn.

"Ma, I had a scholarship!" Millie, trapped by habit, slipped into the old patterns, the old defenses.

"Now you're running around with a shaigetz. And a shaigetz from England! What's the matter, we don't have enough goyim in this country? You had to go import one?"

"That's funny, Ma," Millie said softly.

"Funny? Your father has a heart murmur!"

"Take him to a cardiologist," Millie retorted, knowing they wouldn't. Her father's heart murmur, which she had heard about since childhood, was about as substantial as his long-lost yeshivas.

"You never cared about anybody but yourself. You're selfish. Selfish, selfish, selfish." Her mother repeated, in case the message wasn't getting through.

"Bye, Ma." Millie said and, blinking hard, went to the bathroom to repair her smeared eye makeup.

She gathered up her purse, her keys and her book and started toward the door. Just as she reached it, the phone rang. She waited while the answering machine picked up.

"Millie, it's James." His voice was cool, remote. "If it's that you don't want to see me anymore, please tell me." He waited silently till the tape ran out.

He's up early, Millie thought. She fought back the rise of tears, threatening her newly repaired eye makeup. Here we go again, she thought. Cut it out! What are you? The sole support of Estée Lauder? She turned and swept determinedly out the door.

* * *

Kantor-Yorty Studios was known familiarly as Kiwi and even more familiarly, and rather salaciously, as KY.

"So how are you?" Phil Tovman greeted cheerily. "Nervous about tomorrow?"

"A little," Millie said cautiously. One didn't normally admit to insecurity in this business.

"Good. *I'd* be nervous if you weren't. They're polaroiding today, and we'll look at the pictures this afternoon. We'll make the final selection tomorrow on the scout. We have to find the bathroom of the soap company's dreams. None of which you'll see on camera, except for two tiled walls and a shower head."

Millie laughed. The piercing agony inside her settled down to a dull ache, just at the threshold of bearability.

Phil took a file folder out of the canvas bag he wore slung over his shoulder. "Tell me what you think." He read off a list of crew for her approval.

Given the case of a first-time director and a powerful producer, Millie would, in fact, have little say in the matter. The luck was that Tovman had gotten her the best, old pros, with that something extra that used to be called heart. "Okay with you?" he finished gallantly.

"Better than okay."

* * *

Tovman laughed. "Not too many people know the difference. Maybe I'm making a mistake, Millie. Today may be one of your last days as a script supervisor. It's a shame to lose you. Maybe I should reconsider."

"It'll be a long time before I can make my living as a director."

"Hustle, Millie, hustle. That's the secret. The day after your shoot, call every production company in New York and tell them you're the hot new director."

"Who, me?"

Tovman grinned at her. "What do they know? They'll believe you. But do it *now*. Before it becomes old news. If you were planning two weeks at Club Med, cancel it."

"I'm not going anywhere," Millie said dully, "I'll be right here."

"Good. If you really push this, you just might have yourself a career."

Three harsh, rasping buzzes sounded, indicating readiness for a take, and Tovman turned away. Millie settled into her chair and picked up her book.

The two actors who strongly resembled, and not by accident, Laurel and Hardy began their walk down the length of the studio, extolling the virtues of Wavies. On the monitors, the grime-gray walls gave way to the bright sky and cobalt sea of the pier.

"I'm tired of flat chips," Laurel said.

"Me, too," Hardy agreed. "And chips with ridges are just . . . ridgy."

"What we need is a chip that isn't flat . . ."

" . . . And isn't ridgy!"

The actors started their walk, time and again, and most often were halted midway. Either they walked out of frame or stumbled over their lines or their line readings did not please the agency people.

"Hit it harder on 'ridgy'!" One called. "More warmth."

"No! Less warmth on 'ridgy.' Save it till you get to 'Wavies.'"
The conflicting instructions came, and somehow were followed.

Finally they started, for the umpteenth time, on their long trek down the stage/pier. Millie knew, with the gut feeling that comes with experience, that this was *the* take. The money. The actors' timing was precise, the agency people seemed pleased with the degree of warmth, and the technical aspects were jelling perfectly.

An irate scream cut through the action. "Get that—that motherfucker is in the shot!"

"Cut!" Phil Tovman's voice cracked a millisecond later.

Sure enough, at the far end of the studio, at the end of the "pier," a P.A., a boy of about eighteen stood, frozen, like a fawn caught in the headlights of a speeding car. He stared at the ground, mortified, while abuse, in plentiful portions, was heaped on his head.

"That's enough!" Tovman called authoritatively. "We'll take it from the top. Robbie, find yourself another place to stand."

Robbie skulked away.

The shot they got was not, according to the agency people, the conceptual masterpiece that the other, spoiled, shot would have been, but acceptable nonetheless. Millie spotted Robbie standing off to one side, his adolescent ears still burning with shame. She walked over to him and tapped him on the shoulder. He turned, bracing himself for another wisecrack.

"Everybody does it once," Millie told him.

"Did you?" His fingers worried at a button on his shirt.

"Sure. Only I didn't do it on a lousy Wavies commercial. I did it on a feature. To George Segal."

A glimmer of a smile appeared in the boy's eyes. "You're kidding!"

"Nope. I was an apprentice then, and had no business being where I was. I was just caught by the bells, you know?"

"I feel like an idiot," Robbie disclosed mournfully.

"Of course you do. What else? But I'll bet you anything that half those people carrying on out there have walked into a shot or two in their time. When you get a chance, ask Phil Tovman if he ever did."

"Phil *Tovman!*" Robbie said incredulously. "Phil Tovman never walked into a shot in his life!"

"Maybe yes and maybe no. But if he did, he'll tell you." Millie smiled at him and turned back to her seat.

"Hey, Millie," he called after her. "Thanks."

"Don't worry about it," she called over her shoulder. "When you're a big movie mogul, just remember. And pass it on."

Florence Nightingale Myerson, she thought, smiling to herself. Patch them up and send them out to fight another day.

Tovman's secretary, a large, heavy-boned, efficient woman, walked rapidly up to Millie and dropped a slip of paper in her lap. "Hi, Millie. Bye, Millie," she said, U-turning away.

"Bye, Jeannie." Millie picked up the paper. "Mr. Jimmy Chester called," the preprinted telephone-message slip said. Under it were a selection of boxes to be checked denoting various standard messages. Jeannie's bright-green pen had checked both "Please Return Call" and "Will Call Again."

Millie stared at the innocuous pink slip, wondering at its power to send an electric shock of anguish through her. How did he find me? I never told him where I was shooting today. I can't take anymore of this.

She ripped a ruled page out of her notebook and carefully and precisely, with unusual attention to her normally slapdash handwriting, wrote:

James,
The best news! I got a job offer. A feature film—in the Bahamas! It's only scripting, but still, who can turn down a free trip to an island paradise.

I'm terribly sorry to cut our little fling short, but *c'est la vie*, as they say in all the best novels.

Anyway, it certainly has been fun, and it's been a thrill knowing you. I certainly hope the weather is as nice as the travelogues claim. So it's off to LaGuardia and sun and fun on the white sands of the Caribbean!

All the best to you. Have a safe trip home.

Millie Myerson

"And God bless you," she whispered. She dropped it off, on her lunch hour, at the Prince's hotel.

Chapter XI

With the words "It's a wrap," the sick dread returned, blanketing Millie in a fog of bleakness. It's better than . . . the other, she thought, with an inward wince of recollection. Numb, I can handle. Numb is just fine.

"Seven-thirty tomorrow morning, Millie." Phil Tovman waved from the doorway. "In front of my office."

Millie waved back. "See you then," she called brightly. She gathered up her book, her purse and her sweater and headed for home. At least nobody noticed anything funny, she thought. I pulled it off. Yyyyaaayy, Millie!

Millie snapped on the light in the foyer of her apartment. I've got to eat something. When was the last time I ate, she wondered, and veered away from the memory of the cooked goose sandwiches and the loving, laughing phone call from Buckingham Palace.

She skimmed the contents of her cupboard and, finding nothing else she thought she could swallow, opened a can of tomato soup. She examined, with fixed concentration, the geometric pattern of the wallpaper while she waited for the soup to heat.

I'm fine, she thought, carrying the bowl, and her body, precariously into the living room, as if one or the other might splinter apart at any moment.

She ran the tape of her answering machine, listening to the breezy messages of her friends, some of which bordered perilously on what Ma Bell would classify as obscene.

The last message on the tape was Lady Cilly's. "If there's

something wrong, Millie, perhaps I can help. I'd like us to be friends no matter what happens between you and Prince James. When you ring me, ask for extension 2264, and it'll go directly into my room. You won't have to speak with anyone else. Bye, Millie. Do ring me."

I can't just yet, Millie thought. Maybe tomorrow when I'm all better. She turned on the TV set, seeking distraction, any distraction. Shit! The news! She reached out to turn it off and then couldn't. She sat on the couch, slowly spooning up her soup, watching.

"Prince James today visited Gracie Mansion and had lunch with the mayor," the announcer voice-overed. The video showed the Prince and the tall, ebullient, stoop-shouldered mayor of New York City standing together on the steps of Gracie Mansion, presumably postprandially. They faced a phalanx of print and television reporters.

"How'm I doin'?" the mayor called. "Huh? How'm I doin'?"

"Ask him!" someone yelled.

The mayor turned to Prince James. "How'm I doin'?" he asked impishly.

James looked, as he always did in public, poised, assured, serenely at ease. He displayed, at one and the same time, an affable interest and a cool reserve, marred only by the eldritch, fleeting glint of humor in his eyes. "Well, I'm pretty sure we hit a pothole on the way over here," he said judiciously.

The mayor took a notebook out of his pocket. "Where?" he asked with an impeccably straight face.

James shoved his hands in his trouser pockets. Then he caught himself and clasped them quickly behind his back to remove temptation. "Park and 73rd," he said solemnly.

The mayor scribbled in his notebook. "I'll take care of it." He put his notebook away with a satisfied smile. The two men looked at each other, enjoying the joke, and shook hands with an unfeigned camaraderie.

James looks rested, Millie thought. He looks like he got a good night's sleep.

The anchorman, every shining blonde hair irritatingly in place, came on the screen. "Two nice men," he commented. "We can't tell what they talked about over lunch, since they wouldn't let us join them, but we can tell you this. If Prince James chose to confide in our mayor about his love life, he's got a lot to tell. Still, if the ladies don't flock around you if your rich, handsome, debonair and a prince, then I guess something's wrong. And if you have to have complications in your love life . . ."

The announcer disappeared, to be replaced with a color photograph of Lady Cilly, smiling raffishly up from the driver's seat of a sleek, low-slung, emerald-green race car. She wore a silver metallic crash suit and an emerald-green helmet with the name "Lady Cecilia Worthington," emblazoned in silver letters across the front.

"How's this for a sweet complication?" the announcer laughed. "Lady Cecilia Worthington, known to Fleet Street as 'Smashing Cecilia,' is an old flame of Prince James's. And he, as we told you in our exclusive story yesterday, has fallen madly in love with a raven-tressed American beauty. Are you surprised to hear that the blue-blooded Lady Cecilia packed herself up and grabbed the first plane to New York? My wife assures me she would have done the same thing," the announcer chuckled.

The screen split, Lady Cilly's picture taking up the left half, while the right was filled with a black-and-white shot of Prince James, likewise helmeted, reaching down from his polo pony, mallet in hand, his eyes concentrated on the unseen ball. "Don't they look nice together?" the announcer queried. "Sources close to the Prince say an announcement can be expected at any moment. The Prince himself is mum on the subject."

The blurred, grainy photograph of Millie and James perched atop the Daimler appeared on the screen. "But we are sticking by our original story. Our mystery lady has disappeared from view. Rumor has it that she's left the country. And we can confirm that. A reliable source tells us that Prince James has sent her home to London to buy a trousseau and, incidentally, to meet his folks!"

Millie's laugh sounded harsh to her own ears. She fought down the rise of hysteria and sneezed, violently, several times. He left me a souvenir, she thought. I have a royal cold. She went into the bathroom and looked in the mirror. Her face, strained, haggard and drawn with lack of sleep looked back at her. You look like shit she told herself.

The phone rang. And rang and rang. Shit, I forgot to reset the machine. Millie listened to it ring. I can't live like this she thought and, disgusted with herself, picked it up on the seventh ring.

"What took you so long?" Lucy demanded. "You only have about three feet to walk from any point in your apartment."

The familiar, cheery voice broke down Millie's reserve. "Lucy," she moaned. "Lucy!"

"What's up, hon? What's the matter? The sun go behind the clouds again?"

Then Millie remembered. "Why didn't you tell me what Peter did?"

Lucy didn't bother to pretend she didn't know what Millie was talking about. "Because I knew you'd get yourself all worked up over nothing."

"Over nothing! That was a betrayal! I would have told *you!*"

"Betrayal, my grandmother's ass. I was right, wasn't I? Millie, for God's sakes, stop carrying on over every little thing. You always knew this thing wasn't going anywhere. Prince James is not about to run off to Tahiti with you or something. What do you care what he thinks about your parents. What difference does it make? He's not fucking them, he's fucking you!"

Her words pierced Millie's brain like needles. She felt her skin burn under the onslaught. She clutched at the phone, feeling it slip under her sweaty hand. "Obviously it did make a difference," she said, surprised at the calmness of her voice. "Or they wouldn't have bothered, would they."

Lucy was silent for a moment. "Well, I still think you take everything too seriously."

"And you know what? You don't take anything seriously enough," Millie said softly. And hung up.

I'm alone, she thought. Alone like a stone.

She awoke suddenly in the middle of the night, jolted from sleep to wakefulness without transition. Grief blanketed her like a pall, palpable, distinct. This is familiar, she thought. The sense of loss, immutable, irrevocable and too deep for tears, swung open a door in her mind that was always closed. She had felt this way once before, when her beloved brother had died, at the age of thirteen, and she had waited through the night for his funeral.

Millie waited for the dawn, and she mourned.

As always, the agency people approached the location scout with all the barely suppressed hilarity of schoolchildren on an outing. They got to wear their designer sweat suits and Addidas instead of natty suits and skinny ties, and a day driving around Westchester county poking about in other people's houses sure beat eight hours in a color-coordinated cubicle on Third Avenue. As an added bonus, they got to play "insider." People who didn't know one end of an Arri from another threw around movie jargon with glamorously negligent ease, well aware of the effect they had on bystanders.

Phil introduced Millie, and his offhand acceptance of her as director had a lot to do with the cordiality of the agency people's smiles. Still, they eyed her speculatively, wondering how she had managed the treacherous leap from below to above the line.

Millie smiled back confidently, blessing her foresight in wearing a skirt and heels. It pays to dress the part, she thought, and the extra three inches couldn't hurt.

She sat next to Phil in the front seat of the car on the ride up, as befit her new status. Phil drove in silence, ignoring the chitchat in which the names Grenouille and Le Cirque were prominent.

The location scout leaned his arms on the back of the front seat. "Hey, Phil. Wait till you see the Holloway place. It's fourth on our list, and it's double-dynamite. The minute I saw it I knew that was the one. You're gonna love it."

Millie glanced at Phil to see how he was taking the intelligence that the first three stops of the day were apparently designed to give him a tour of a series of second-best bathrooms. Apparently exercises in futility were not new to him, for he drove on in silence.

They spent the morning and part of the afternoon solemnly inspecting strange bathrooms. Why people rented their homes out as locations was always a mystery to Millie, despite the fact that they were handsomely paid. Whatever residual glamor it held for them couldn't possibly compensate for the early morning arrival of a catering truck, thirty huge-bellied gorillas and a shitload of equipment.

The minute she stepped into the Holloway bathroom, Millie knew she was in trouble. It was, as advertised, double-dynamite.

Three glass walls looked out into a garden, lush with springtime greenery. The high-tech decor, chrome, glass and gray felt, contrasted dramatically with the verdant backdrop. The polished steel tub was supplemented by a bubbling Jacuzzi a few feet away. The futuristic black lacquer toilet looked like it had been designed by Henry Moore after a few drinks. Three chrome spotlights overhead were angled so that their beams centered on it, lending it, to Millie's eye, a rather menacing ebony gloss.

The agency people crawled all over it in transports of delight. "This is it!" they burbled, and "Divine!" and "Such flair!"

Millie exchanged glances with Phil. She wondered when he would put a stop to the ecstatic fugue and realized with a jolt that he was waiting for her to do it.

Now or never, she thought. She waited for a lull and then spoke, putting all the authority she possessed into her voice. "This is a spectacular bathroom. It's a shame we can't use it."

Doleful agency eyes fixed on the person who had had the temerity to announce that there was in fact, no tooth fairy. "Why not? It's adorable?"

"Because you can't light it," Millie explained calmly. "You'll get too many reflections. Every one of our lights will be reflected in the glass. All you'll see are little circles of light. Also, you're at the mercy of every passing cloud. If the light outside changes, we can't match the shots. If it's raining, we're dead."

Location Scout gave her a "show's how much you know" look. He turned and pressed a button on the console near the toilet. Gray felt shot along hidden tracks and covered the glass walls. The result then bore a strong resemblance to a freight elevator in which someone had whimsically placed a john. Apparently it was too much for Phil. "If I wanted to shoot against a felt drop, I'd shoot it in the studio. Let's go."

At the end of the day, as they piled back into the station wagon, having selected the lucky Mr. and Mrs. Marmelstein's mint-green extravaganza, Phil took Millie aside. "You don't look so hot," he told her uncomfortably. "Is anything the matter?"

"No. I just have this miserable cold." Millie blew her nose to prove it.

"Chicken soup," Tovman advised with a laugh. "Just be sure you're okay by Tuesday."

"Right, chief. Will do," Millie said, and they joined the others in the car.

The agency producer, a woman who labored under the unfortunate name of Polly Bangs, shoved a copy of *Newsday* in Millie's face.

"Did you see this? Didn't you once date him or something?"

Millie looked at the paper. Under a charming photo of Prince James, his arm intimately linked through a radiant Cilly's, the caption read, "ARE THEY OR AREN'T THEY?"

Millie found her voice. "I had dinner with him once—and a lot of other people," she said with as much poise as she could muster.

"You lucky thing!" Polly told her. "Is he as cute as he looks?"

"Cuter," Millie said and turned away to face the front of the car.

Millie opened the door to her apartment, fearful, for the first time in her life, of its emptiness. What will I do? she thought despairingly. What I'll do is, I'll clean up the place. I'll make it nice and neat for the cleaning lady.

She checked the answering machine. No messages. That's that, she thought, and turned it off. She changed into the cutoffs and ragged T-shirt reserved for such operations and threw herself into a mindless blitz of housecleaning, scrubbing, polishing and waxing, absorbed in the rhythm, shrinking her world to the size of the next tile on the kitchen floor. She moved from there to the bathroom, and, when she finished, its pristine sterility rivaled that of an operating room.

Don't stop, she thought, and stripped the linens off the bed with a frenzied, violent motion—and saw, in the narrow space between the bed and the window, a crumpled, faded blue sweat shirt.

Don't she told herself, and picked it up. More than the three-feathered crest, and the motto *"Ich Dien,"* the scent of him, permeating the fabric, shattered the embryonic shell she was carefully, painstakingly, nurturing. She buried her face in the sweat shirt, sobbing uncontrollably.

The phone rang. She let it ring several times, while she fought for control.

"Hi there, morning glory! You still miff— pissed at me?"

"Gerald," Millie whispered. And then again, a rising, agonized moan of pain. "Gerald!" She sobbed bitterly, gasping for breath, clutching at her stomach.

"Hey! Hey, take it easy. What's happened to my passion flower?" Concern darkened Gerald's bright, breezy voice.

"Gerald, you were right! You tried to tell me! I should have listened to you. It's my fault. I never listen to anybody. I think I know it all. I deserve this!" The words tumbled over each other.

"What happened? Tell me, sweetheart."

"He . . . he . . ." The pain tore at her with separate, jagged knives.

"Is it James? Did that creep do something to hurt you?" Millie nodded voicelessly. "Are you there? Speak to me, petunia."

The floodgates broke. "It was all my fault. I took him seriously. He *made* me take him seriously. All the time he was— he was laughing at me. He was playing. I believed him. I believed him." The words spewed out in a virulent, incoherent stream.

"How do you know all this?" Gerald asked carefully.

"I know," she said dully. "He has a sweet tooth, and I'm barley sugar." Millie laughed and found she couldn't stop the upward, rising curve of hysteria.

"Okay, okay, sweetheart," Gerald murmured. "How do you know all this?" he asked again.

"I didn't want to fall in love with him. I tried not to. But he's so— he just sweeps you along with him. And don't say I told you so, please!"

"I won't. I'm not. How do you know all this?" he asked for the third time.

"Lady Hester."

"That cunt! Hester told you all this?"

"No, she told this woman all about it."

"Who?"

Millie fished gingerly in her memory for the name. "Margo."

"Margo who?"

"What do you care, Margo who," Millie said fiercely. "You don't know her anyway."

"Quite— You're right. Never mind. Go on. What did Hester say, exactly?"

"She said . . . she said . . ." Millie stopped, gasping. "Oh, Gerald, it hurts me. It hurts me," she wept.

"I know, sweetheart, I know. Tell me. What did Hester say?"

"She said that Peter Goldsworth told them that—"

"Peter?" he asked sharply.

"He told them that James and I were— and they took him to see my parents . . ." she flushed, hot with shame, "and it worked. He was *disgusted*. But he didn't tell me or anything. He *could* have. He could've said, 'Look, you're a real nice person and all that, but you come from a drecky family, and they're beneath me, and I don't want to get my aristocratic little hands dirty, so if I never see you again, have a nice life.' But he didn't. He said he loved me, and I believed him." A searing stab of pain shot through Millie. "And that was *after!* When he knew! He didn't have to do that, Gerald. And Lucy knew, too, and she didn't warn me. Only you did."

"How did Lucy know?"

"Peter."

"Of course."

The telephone beeped in her ear, signaling another call on the line. "Hold it, Gerald. My call-waiting's going." Millie depressed the receiver once, transferring to the second call. "Hello?"

"Hi, Millie. You sound funny. You sleeping or anything?"

"Who *is* this?" she asked, stunned.

"How fast they forget," he laughed.

"Gerald," she whispered.

"The same."

Millie knew, with certainty, who was on the other line. "I can't talk now, Gerald. I'll call you tomorrow." She clicked back to the first call. "James," she said with finality. Silence. And then again, "James."

"You wouldn't talk to me," the Prince said helplessly. "I didn't know what else to do."

Millie hung up.

It seemed like seconds later when her doorbell rang, insistently, continuously. She stood in the middle of the room, frozen with indecision.

"Millie! Open the goddamn door!" James yelled.

"Go fuck yourself, Your Royal Highness," she called elegantly.

James pounded his fist against the door steadily. "Millie, open up, or, I promise you, I'll break the sodding door down!" he yelled.

"Miss Millie!" MacCrae called through the door. He pitched his voice just loud enough to carry over the sound of the doorbell and the unremitting banging. "Miss Millie! Please!" The Prince of Wales was causing a riot in the corridor of a luxury building in a foreign city. "Please!"

Millie walked slowly to the door and opened it a crack. The Prince slammed it open violently.

"How did you get here so fast?" she asked idiotically.

He stared at her. "*I* drove!" Without taking his eyes off her, he closed the door, deliberately, and locked it.

Millie stared back at him. His vaunted sangfroid had utterly vanished. He trembled, visibly, and his blue eyes burned with cobalt fire. "What do you want?" she asked coolly. She clasped her hands behind her back to hide their tremor.

"You twit! You stupid twit!" His voice rose until he was shouting, out of control. "How the holy fuck could you be so stupid!"

"It's not easy. I'm just not good at games. I don't waterski, and I don't hunt. I *hate* horses. About all I do is bike ride and that's not a very challenging sport for an upper-class sportsman like yourself."

"Millie, what are you ranting about? I haven't understood one word you've said," he thundered. "Of *course*, I ride bikes!"

"Stop yelling!" she yelled back.

"I'm not yelling!" he roared. "Millie, I warn you, don't trifle with me!"

"I wouldn't *dream* of trifling with you. Trifle," she repeated with an insane giggle, "isn't that a dessert?"

"What was all that rot you were telling Gerald about my having a sweet tooth and barley sugar?"

"Telling *Gerald!*" she shrilled. "Gerald! You son of a bitch!"

The Prince picked up a vase from the dining-room table. For a wild moment she thought he was going to throw it through the great glass windows. He thought better of it and set it down, gently, as if it were priceless. He took a deep, calming breath. "I'm sorry I tricked you. I simply didn't know what else to do." He reached out his hand and carefully, gently, touched his finger to her cheek.

Millie recoiled, cringing away, and saw the answering flinch in his eyes.

Her stomach spasmed. She raced to the bathroom, awash in wave upon wave of dizzying nausea. She hung over the toilet, retching shamefully, uncontrollably, crying at the unbearable humiliation. Her body jerked spasmodically, joltingly, as she cried, heaved and gasped for breath all at the same time.

A warm hand pressed firmly against her forehead, and another at the nape of her neck, bracing her against the jarring movements. "Go away!" she yelled between spasms. "Just get the hell out of here!"

The Prince withdrew his hand. Out of the corner of her eye,

Millie saw his trouser legs moving away from her. She heaved, violently.

The bracing hand at her forehead returned, with the addition of a cool damp washcloth at the base of her neck.

She waited for a few moments to be sure the heaving had stopped. Then she stood up, shakily.

"All done?" James asked cheerfully. Millie nodded. He put his arm around her shoulders, drawing her to the door. She shrugged it off, defiantly, and staggered rather drunkenly to the couch.

"Be right back," James said and disappeared. Millie collapsed into a fetal ball of misery. She pressed her face against the back of the couch. Her body felt sore, as if she had been beaten, and her stomach ached.

A hand gripped her shoulder, turning her forcibly around. "Here. Drink this," James said. She shrugged the hand away, refusing. "Drink it right now!" snapped the ex-naval officer.

Millie didn't move. He waited. "What is it?" she asked warily, her voice muffled in the couch.

"Turn around, and you'll see," he coaxed.

Millie swiveled around and sat up. She leaned back against the arm of the couch, her legs curled under her.

James leaned over her with a steaming mug in his hands. "As my old Nanny used to say, there's no misfortune so great a nice cuppa won't make you feel better."

"Your old Nanny was a horse's ass!"

"That too," the Prince agreed cheerfully. He handed her the cup and stood over her, his gaze unwavering, until she sipped at the sweet lemony contents. "That's better," he said, and walked away.

He returned with a plate of honeyed toast. He set it down on the coffee table and rocked back on his heels, staring at her until she gave in and bit into a piece of toast, unwillingly. Satisfied, James sat down on the couch. "You're such a stupid clot," he said genially. "I can't think why I love you so much."

"Don't start that again!"

"Don't you start! You're not so fucking blameless yourself, Millie."

Millie slammed the toast down. "I'm not the one who—"

"Shut up, Millie!" the Prince stood up, livid. His voice whip-cracked, and she shrank back as if from a blow. "The last I knew of you, Goldsworth had told you where the loo was. I couldn't figure out what in hell had happened." His eyes held hers implacably. Millie stared back at him, and he was the first to break away. He turned his back on her. "After all, there was always the chance that you . . . simply didn't want to see me anymore. Between the rabid press corps and the reception and all that, I thought perhaps you had been frightened away. Which is something *I've* been afraid of from the first." He laughed, joylessly, and turned to face her. "But then I got your note, and I knew."

"Knew *what?*"

"I couldn't imagine what had made you cut me off like that. Even if what I had feared was true, I could *not* understand why you didn't say goodbye. I turned it over and over in my mind endlessly. That night was not the best of my life," he said tonelessly.

"You looked pretty good on television."

The Prince's temper snapped. "What the fuck did you expect?" he shouted. "What would you have me do? Bleed for the cameras? Haven't you learned anything at all? It's enough you made me make a scene in the hallway."

"*I* made you!"

"All right!" He paused for a moment to collect the shreds of his composure. "And then, when I got your note, I knew. I started to think logically instead of . . . I knew you were eating your heart out, and that—"

"How?"

"First," he ticked off on his fingers, "in that whole note, you sounded like an imbecile. I knew instantly that whatever it was was something outside. Not between you and me. Secondly, there were no flights leaving La Guardia to the Bahamas that afternoon." He crossed to the couch and sat down, facing her. "By the way, Millie, I've been meaning to tell you. If you ever run away from me again, and I pray you never will—" he grinned impishly at her, *"don't* pick a Commonwealth country." Millie jerked her head up in surprise. He nodded at her, his face mingling triumph and satisfaction. "I checked every passenger list of every plane going into the goddamn country. I know the names of every film crew in the place. I know the precise whereabouts of every thirty-five-, sixteen-, and eight-millimeter camera in the area." He laughed. "I'm probably *still* getting reports on my desk."

"I forget sometimes, about your power."

"Well, don't. And, as regards Hester Marling . . ." He stood up, abruptly, and walked over to the window. He peered out silently, hands thrust deep in his trouser pockets, then said quietly, "She will regret this, I promise you." His voice was unemphatic, without color. "I am not a vengeful man, but this I promise you." When he turned to her, Millie saw that his eyes were cold, ruthless. Millie felt her mouth go very dry. She started to speak, and he cut her off. "The Right Honourable, the Countess of Rossbourne will never again be alone in a room with me for as long as I live. She will not have the privilege of private conversation with me. Anything she has to say will not be heard."

Millie turned this over in her mind. If Lady Hester Marling had been dealt one trump card in her life, it was her access to the future King of England. And she had lost it. It was that simple. She looked up at the Prince, and he knew that she had understood.

"If I had known she was in the loo at that time," he said grimly, "I would have understood straightaway. But the ladies' cloakroom is one place I have difficulty keeping track of events. As it is, looking back on all this, I see I made two mistakes. No, one mistake," he corrected, "and one thing I'm ashamed of."

Millie stared into her teacup, not wanting to prompt him.

"The mistake was . . . perhaps I should have been more open with you. I could have avoided all this if I had let you know all along what I was doing. What I intended. But I couldn't. I was afraid to . . ."

Millie looked at him, and then away. "Why?"

"Because you weren't ready. I knew—or at least I was afraid—that, if I let you know too early what I had in mind for us, and what goes with it, you'd pack up your bags and run. Which is not an unreasonable response," he said wryly.

"But that's not—"

"Hear me out!" James said fiercely. "You're right. That's not all of it. Part of it is that I'm just not used to . . . sharing myself with another person. I've already let you see more than I've ever shown another human being. I feel as if you've penetrated every barrier that I've ever set up. And I need those barriers if I'm to survive."

"What were you ashamed of?" Millie asked softly.

"The thing I'm ashamed of is that . . . that what David did . . ."

He faltered, and then forced himself to continue, "that when I saw your parents, I was shaken." He fell silent. "I'm not a snob, I don't think," he said after a while.

"No, you're not."

"I think that what shook me so much is, not that I found them . . . distressing, but that she looks a little like you. A very little. And, if I'm to be perfectly honest, I have to say that I could not see myself with them. It has nothing to do with wealth or with social class or anything," he said passionately. "Please believe that."

"I do. I know. And I'm sorry," Millie said helplessly.

"You're sorry! *You're* sorry? I never meant to. . . I never meant you to know it. I never wanted to hurt you, and it must hurt."

"The only thing that hurts me in all this—that hurt me," she corrected, "—is that you let it matter. It's something I can't help, and there isn't much I can do about it."

"I know. And to my credit," James said bitterly, "I have to say that it only lasted about fifteen minutes. The minute I saw you again, I knew."

"That's when you came to pick me up for the weekend! You looked like shit!"

He nodded, shamefaced. "But just for a short time, Millie. After that it never bothered me again. Except as a card in the game."

"There you go again!"

"Well, it *is* a card. It's a factor we have to deal with if we're to. . . " He broke off.

Millie looked at his face and was suddenly afraid. "I don't want to talk about this anymore. There's no need to go over and over—"

"Oh, yes, my dear Millie!" He sat down next to her. He put one tentative hand on her knee. Millie didn't push him away, but she didn't look up at him either. "We shall go over and over this until I'm finished. Is that understood?"

Millie stared down at her lap, stone-faced. The Prince chose to take this as acquiescence. "Now, then. Do you know why David came down from Newport the other day?"

"For the Queen's reception."

"Balls! He came down because he saw that all his efforts, all his stratagems and all his talking hadn't worked. And do you know how he saw that?" Millie shook her head, unable to meet his gaze. "He saw that during the weekend. He saw it every time he looked at me.

He saw that I love you. And that I wasn't hiding it. He *knew* that, when the time came, I would bring you out in the open. Despite everything. That I was orchestrating it. I was preparing the way, and I was letting *him* know."

Millie met the Prince's stalwart gaze. "That was the second reason!"

The Prince nodded approvingly. "Now you're thinking, Millie."

"And that's why you said Peter Goldsworth had done you a favour."

"Right again. Although at the time I wasn't sure it was he who had done it. I knew that someone had gotten on to David, but it could have been any one of a number of people. Don't you think," he said quietly, "that, if I didn't want the Marlings to know how I felt about you, they wouldn't have known? Don't you know me even that well yet?"

Millie toyed with his hand, thinking furiously. She was suddenly overcome by a tingling irresistible feeling of sleepiness. She opened her mouth and yawned mightily.

The Prince smiled at her, amused. "Crying makes one tired." Millie dropped her head to his shoulder and, thus sheltered, rested. James brushed his lips against her hair. He pulled her to him roughly, crushing her against his body. "Ouch!" Millie complained sleepily.

"I'm sorry," he whispered and relaxed his grip only a little. "Remember the other night, when I told you the best thing I'd ever done?" Millie grunted, rubbing her cheek against the smooth cloth of his shirt. "I lied," the Prince said, "the best thing I've ever done is you."

He tilted her chin up and placed his mouth, warm and moist, over her lips. He kissed her gently, very gently, and then with a sigh of relief, clamped his mouth on hers, sucking voraciously, drinking from her lips as if they held all the sweetness and all the mystery of the cosmos. "And I don't mean to lose you," he said, when he found himself able to pull away.

He stood up and scooped her into his arms, lifting her as easily as if she were a child. He set her down on the bed, smiling to himself as she yawned. He pulled her T-shirt over her head and sat down next to her, gathering her against his chest. Millie twined her arms around his neck and kissed the tender hollow above his collarbone. "I'm glad," she said simply.

"Not half so glad as I." He pushed her down on the bed and unzipped her shorts. He slipped them and her panties away in one swift movement, and buried his face against her bare belly. He lay still for a while, glorying in the touch and the taste and the scent of the body he had thought lost to him. Millie, understanding, ran her fingertips lightly over his hard-muscled back, caressing his neck and his hair, and waited.

She felt his hot, licking tongue thrust, hard, into her navel. Her clitoris, as if connected by an unseen thread, clutched convulsively. She sucked in her breath involuntarily and smiled, as the Prince looked up at her, his own smile gleaming with ownership.

He put his hand between her legs and felt the satin, dripping wetness. He thrust his fingers inside her, brutally, carelessly, and she felt her vagina contract against his hand. He withdrew his hand and traveled a thread of moisture over her belly, up to her breast. With fingers moistened with her juices, he found her nipple, massaging it, pressing down, circling the point against the palm of his hand.

"James," Millie sighed. If he answered, she was beyond hearing. She reached down and drew him up to her face, wanting him inside her, unable to wait any longer.

When he entered her, she trembled, shivering uncontrollably, caught in the grip of a nameless, violent emotion. The Prince waited, his body poised above her. His hands and his mouth gentled her until she quieted. She looked into his eyes, meeting his clear gaze. "It's all right, beloved," he murmured and began to move. "It's all right, my darling."

When he slipped out of her, spent, Millie found that she was crying. He cupped her face in his hands and licked the tearstains away. Then he kissed the place where they had been. "I wasted two whole days!" She wept with the intensity of a child mourning the irreparable loss of his first, magical balloon.

"Don't worry. Don't cry, my darling. There will be plenty more."

"How?" she sobbed. "We only had two weeks."

He rolled off her and lay on his side, facing her. "Come home with me to England. Come to my country, where I can take care of you."

Millie turned her head to face him. "Nobody's ever taken care of me before."

"I know. And I would like to, if you'll have me."

Millie turned away and stared up at the ceiling. "I've thought of that. I've thought of just . . . picking up and going. But I can't."

"Why not? Is it your job? Come after the shoot. I'll send a ticket for you."

"That's part of it, but it isn't all."

"What is?"

"If I went with you," she said slowly, "I'd become another Mrs. Keppel."

"Another *who?*"

Millie grinned at him. "Mrs. Keppel."

"Who on earth is this buggering Mrs. Keppel? What's she got to say to anything? Not another relative, I hope. At least not one of mine," he concluded, having run through a lengthy list in his mind.

"Indirectly," Millie said impishly. "Mrs. Keppel was the lifelong mistress of Edward the Seventh. How come you're not up on your family scandals?"

"I'm afraid my reading has been more informative than escapist," the Prince returned, hitting the nail on the head.

"Anyway, she was sort of an open secret. Everybody knew but they didn't acknowledge it. Or her. At the end of his life, when he lay dying, his wife, the Queen, broke with a lifetime of silence, of forbearance, and called Mrs. Keppel in. To comfort him. And to say good-bye. I think that's the bravest thing I ever heard of."

Millie turned back to the Prince. "If I went with you, and I love you so much, I'd become another Mrs. Keppel. I'd take an apartment somewhere, and I'd work, and I'd wait for you, whenever you could come. For as long as you wanted to come. I'd watch you marry and have children, and I'd read about you in the papers." Millie sat up abruptly, resting her head on her bended knees. "And I'd be grateful," she murmured, her voice muffled. "I'm trying to save myself and not do that. Please help me not do that, James."

The Prince pulled her back down, so that she lay across his body. He looked steadily into her eyes. "That's not quite what I had in mind. I'd like us to get married."

Millie drew in a breath and held it. "Can I see Sherwood Forest?" she asked stupidly.

James laughed. "Darling, I *own* Sherwood Forest." He hugged her to him. "You can have the whole bloody place if you like."

For a giddy space of time Millie sailed on the wave of his bouyant confidence and, listening to the high, sweet siren call, believed. "How can we?" she asked finally.

"I'll make it happen," he said simply. "You're my mother, my twin. You're part of the furniture of my mind. You don't think I'd let anything separate us now?"

Millie looked at the Prince, afraid more for him than for herself. He's so *sure*, she thought.

"Do you know what I've never owned?" he asked.

Millie quickly ran through, and discarded, the various possibilities. First editions, private jets, priceless art; anything that money could buy, he could have. "I give up."

"A latchkey."

"A what?"

"A door key. I've never opened the door to my own home. There's always someone there to open the door for me. Someone who's *paid*."

"I never thought of that. But you have the other one instead," Millie said, thinking of the tiny gold key that unlocked the secrets of the boxes.

"I know. But I want *you* there, waiting for me, Millie, or I for you. I make marvelous hot toddies," he cajoled, "and I solemnly promise to have one waiting for you whenever it's cold and nasty. And I want lots and lots of children. Small, dark-haired, lissome girls like you. And at least one son, an heir."

Millie looked down into his eyes. "I, James, Prince of Wales, do solemnly swear by Almighty God that I will be faithful and bear true allegiance to Her Majesty the Queen, her Heirs and Successors, so help me God." The measured phrases, recalled from God knows what half-forgotten television program, rolled off her tongue.

James looked at her, astounded. "How on earth do you know that?"

Millie shook her head. "I have no idea how. It just popped into my head."

James chuckled. "Do you realize I swore allegiance to myself?"

". . . Her Majesty the Queen, her Heirs and Successors," Millie repeated, delighted at the absurdity. She rolled off him and sat up. "What would you have been if you—"

"If I had a choice, you mean? I don't know. I don't think about that very much. I could easily have been a university don, living a life of secluded academia in Cambridge or somewhere."

"No. You have the intellect but not the . . . repose."

"Or perhaps a musician."

"A musician!"

"Yes. I used to play the cello. And very well, too, I might add," he said modestly. "But I gave it up, I didn't have the time or the concentration it requires. I couldn't just be a dilettante, fooling about. My grandmother says I would have been an explorer, searching out primitive tribes in the wilds of South America, or wherever there are still wilds left. I would have liked that. Peter Goldsworth has often said that I should have been an actor. Gone on the stage. Peter," he said softly, "I wonder why that should hurt. He was only doing what he thought was right."

"And Lucy, too . . . "

"Yes. I'm not surprised. They're two of a kind. There are people like that. They see things in black and white instead of in color. And they tell those of us who do see things in color that *we're* the one's who are crazy. Still," he hugged her to him, joyously, "we really do owe Goldsworth a vote of thanks. In a way, he did what I was trying to figure out how to do. He brought it out in the open. The cocksucker!"

"I could never understand why that was such a bad thing to be," Millie said plaintively. And listened, as for the first time in a long while, she heard the Prince's ringing, boisterous laughter fill the room.

"I love you, Millie, even if you are a stupid twit!"

"How long . . . when did you first know?"

"Early on. I'm very astute. I think it was that first day when you threw Galileo back at me." He covered his breast with his hand dramatically. "My heart went pitty-pat."

"Galileo? That's all it took? Galileo?"

"I guess that's all."

"And, by the time I spilled the coffee on you, you were a goner, I suppose."

"No," he said seriously. "Way before that. I used to watch you, laughing and talking with Gerald and Morty and whats'ername, that nice wardrobe lady."

"Gracie."

". . . and working and concentrating and being so sweet and funny."

"So you *were* watching me."

"Of course. And I thought, I've always been on the outside, looking in. I'd like to be on the inside, looking out for a change. I think it's time."

"They'll never let us, James," she said sadly. "It'll never happen."

The Prince jumped out of bed and, naked, paced the room. "They have to! This can't keep happening once a generation. They can't let it!"

Millie got out of bed and sat on the couch so she could watch him pace. "You're not talking about abdic— what he did?"

"No. That was different. That whole situation was grossly mishandled. Besides, I have parents who are on my side. I have a *monarch* on my side. Which is something he didn't have. I don't think his mother—or his father, the King—gave a fuck about his personal happiness. My parents, my mother, does. My happiness is very important to her. She's my mother before she is my Queen. She might not like that," he said with a wry smile, "but it's true." He paced the floor, vibrating with intensity.

Millie lit a cigarette with shaking hand. "Give me one of those, will you?" James said.

"But you don't smoke! You *hate* smoking!"

"Quite right," said the Prince, lighting up, "it's a filthy pastime. And there were other factors involved," he continued in the donnish tone of a professor discoursing on a particularly dry subject. "It had little to do with the fact that she was American. Half the peerage at the time had married Americans, and citizenship can be changed. Even as regards her divorce, or divor*ces*, I should say," he corrected with some displeasure. "It has always seemed to me that there were other options—or at least the possibility of other options. Whether they were fully explored or not, I don't know. But it always seemed to me that it had more to do with personality, with character—hers and his—than with anything else. She was brassy and arrogant, and she flaunted her power over him. She ground their noses in it, and they despised her for it."

He turned to Millie. "But everyone likes you, Millie," he said softly. He turned to the windows and, parting the drapes a little, peered out. "And it had to do with his . . . shortcomings. This is very hard for me to talk about."

"You don't have to . . ."

He turned back to her. "Oh, but I *do!* I have to make you understand. Apparently he was the most marvelous Prince of Wales. He was radiant and debonair, and he had the ability to say the right thing at the right time. He *touched* people. But it was all surface. When the time came for him . . . " The Prince's voice sank to a hoarse whisper, " . . . he sort of fell apart.

"Nobody takes it with equanimity," he continued. "My grandmother told me that, when my mother was small, she begged and begged for them to have another child, a boy, so she wouldn't have to do it. And her father, my grandfather, when it came his turn, was filled with a . . . holy trepidation. But the difference is that he, who never dreamt that he would have to ascend the throne in his brother's place, drew upon whatever strengths, whatever resources he had in him. And overcame. And flourished. Perhaps the difference is in the two women. His wife, my grandmother, is . . . a life force. She is the most loving, the most understanding, the most giving of creatures. The other . . ." He faltered, unable, at the moment, to pronounce the name. "The other acted on him like a drug. She debilitated him. She encouraged whatever was lackadaisical and undisciplined in him. Toward the end, so I've been told, he neglected his duties entirely. He left state papers lying around, and, when he returned them, late, they had rings on them. From cocktail glasses. And no signature. He hadn't even read them."

James sat down on the couch next to Millie. He looked at her, letting her see his face, at once naked and taut with effort. "That's why I'm the way I am. I have no leeway, Millie," he said passionately. "You have to come to me. I'll do all I can to make you comfortable."

"Where would we live? In Bucking. . . in the palace, with the others?" Millie found it hard to bring out the words.

"We can. We don't have to. I have a house in Kent. I never go there. It's too big for me alone."

"How big?"

"Eighty-three rooms," James said and grinned at the consternation on her face.

"Are you telling me the truth?"

"Well, there could be eighty-two or eighty-four. I didn't count them myself, you know."

Millie looked around at the small, bright apartment, where at least she was free to walk around naked and go to the fridge when she felt like it. "Then it becomes like it was for us in the Sherry. You sort of make a nest in one or two rooms, and you know that, when you step out of them, there are strangers there."

James looked at her sympathetically. "You'll get used to it."

"Yes, I will," she said determinedly. She took the unsmoked cigarette stub from between his fingers and put it out. "Would I still be able to work?"

"You could," James said, "if you were anyone but the Princess of Wales. Someone else, further removed could get away with a lot more. Both Tony Snowden and Angus Ogilvy, for example, kept on with their jobs after they married into the royal family. It can be done if you marry someone far enough removed from the succession. Then you can get away with it. But the Queen couldn't be identified with any venture of a commercial nature. It wouldn't be fair to the competitors, for one thing, if you worked for one company and not another. And it wouldn't be . . . seemly. I imagine that you could do an occasional documentary on some boring, safe subject, like the stately homes of England or a program explaining the meaning of Christmas to schoolchildren." Millie looked at him, and he caught himself. "No, you wouldn't do that. Do you know anyone in England?" he asked abruptly.

"Not a soul."

"Well, you know me, and that's enough."

"That's more than enough. If I have you, and our family, that's all I need. Can someone who isn't . . . Protestant, become Queen."

The Prince slowly shook his head. "Can you—do you think you could convert?" he asked, knowing the answer.

"I don't see how I can. And my children, they would be . . . "

James looked at her, his eyes steadfast. "Yes. Your son will be head of the church, as I will be."

Millie returned his gaze, chilled beyond measure. "It won't work," she said, looking into a landscape of desolation.

The Prince stood up. "I can't stand it anymore." He turned away and strode into the bathroom.

Let him be, Millie thought. It's not easy for him either. She rested her head on the back of the couch. She was empty, barren of all emotion, as if the loss she feared above all others was not a possibility, but a certainty, not in the future, but here, in the present, and she had to learn how to bear it.

"Millie!" James called from the bathroom. "Where are your pliers?"

"My what?"

"Your pliers. This blasted cistern's been dripping all night, and I can't stand it anymore!"

Millie found the Saks Fifth Avenue shoebox that held her tools and joined the Prince in the bathroom, still laughing.

"What's funny?" he asked absently, rummaging through the tools.

"Nothing. What's a cistern?"

"Well, what do you call it?" He had taken the top off the toilet tank and, elbows deep in the water, adjusted something mysterious inside. "There. That'll hold it." He dried his hands on a towel and hung it up neatly. "Millie, do you know what a morganatic marriage is?"

Millie shook her head. The Prince took her hand and led her to the couch, his face intent, concentrated. He sat down next to her and immediately jumped up again, pacing as he talked. "A morganatic marriage is when the king marries, and his wife renounces, a priori, all claims to his rank, fortune and in this case to the succession, for herself and for any issue of the marriage."

Millie's heart leapt with joy. "Perfect! That's the answer! I don't care about any of that." He looked at her severely, and she wondered if she had spoken too quickly, dismissing his birthright with facile ease.

"It's not that simple. It's quite . . . shameful. Someone once said that the instrument of morganatic marriage should by rights begin: 'Whereas the King, against all advice, wishes to marry a woman unfit to be Queen, and whereas we, his councillors, have been unable to dissuade him . . .' It's not that simple, and it's never been done in my family."

"What would happen then?"

"The crown would pass, after me, either to Helena or to her eldest son, Patrick. He's two." James laughed, and his laughter was uncharacteristically harsh. "Poor bastard. He'll thank me for it. Although it's not so bad. They fly flags on your birthday and give you gun salutes." He grinned at her.

"But can you bear to do that, James. Turn the succession away from your child."

"Yes!" he returned, instantly and vehemently. "I've thought this over. I've turned it every which way from Sunday, and I've decided it's no contest. Look, I won't ascend the throne for another thirty years, God willing. We're talking about something that will happen well into the twenty-first century. And my son will consider himself fortunate. He will have you for a mother."

Millie leaned over and kissed him. He accepted her kiss, and then broke away, shaking his head. "But that still doesn't solve all our problems."

"No it doesn't. It doesn't solve the problem of our children. Of what they will be."

"That's not what I meant. I'm not worried about us privately. We can work out anything we have to work out between us. If that's the price, if it means that we don't have to be apart. But this does solve a major problem. You would not be the mother of the heir to the throne, responsible for his education and upbringing, both secular and *religious*."

"What you're saying is that I wouldn't be Queen, and I wouldn't have to convert!" Millie said joyously.

"Not so fast," he said grimly. "*I'm* still going to be head of the church one day, and I will be marrying out of my religion. That's one. Two is . . . I don't know that I have the right to contract a morganatic marriage. At least not without the consent of privy council and the Archbishop and the bloody union of ice-cream vendors for all I know. And, even if I could get their consent, it's not as simple as all that. It will be a jolt for the country. Which has already suffered a jolt of this nature. I don't know that I can do that. People's sensibilities count. In the end, that's all there is to this whole thing. That's what it's all about. It's metaphysical; it's emotional, not logical. I will still be seen as making an alien marriage. And you will be seen as an alien. Even if we did it the other way and you gave up everything, your country, your friends, your work and your religion, a good proportion of the people would still be outraged."

He paced in silence for a few minutes, as if gathering courage. He turned to her, his eyes forthright, shining with the bravery of a man who has mastered many challenges, but perhaps none so difficult as the one now before him. "The problem of your parents, Millie. I'm not even remotely equipped to deal with that at the moment."

"I could say I'm an orphan," she joked weakly.

The Prince looked his displeasure at her. "They haven't the slightest idea of how to handle the situation—the ceremonials, the role they will be called upon to play. They will be manipulated by the press, and their most innocent remarks will be featured on the front pages. They, and we, will be laughingstocks."

Millie nodded silently. There was nothing she could say. His dispassionate analysis had not been bought without pain. And, of course, he was right.

He sat down next to her. "Let's look on the bright side. At least you're not Catholic," he said cheerily. Millie looked at him blankly. "I'm barred by statute from marrying a Catholic. It's an old law, left over from a time when there was a lot of anti-Catholic feeling in the country. It's a law we must change, because it's ugly. And it's not fair."

He jumped up, the force of his emotion propelling him into action. "It's not fair! It's really not fair!" He paced the small space, head bent, hands clasped behind his back.

"I'm the only man on earth who is not allowed to marry romantically. And yet I live in the same world as all of you. I read the same books, see the same films. I read John Donne and listen to Cole Porter. And, through it all, what's the best, the most sublime thing that can happen to one? What's the thing we all search for and pray for? We—*I* live in a society that values romantic love above all else. What else is the music and the poetry and the dreaming all about? I wouldn't have cared if it had never happened! If I had never met you, I would have given in, eventually, and married some sweet, brainless, properly ancestored girl—God knows they've been shoving them at me since I was twelve—and the more brainless the better, so I wouldn't have to pay too much attention to her. And I would hope that she wouldn't talk very much. Not like you, Millie," he grinned at her, "you talk all the time." He sat down next to her and took both her hands in his. "Now that it has happened, I'll never give you up. I promise you, Millie."

Millie flung herself into his arms, clutching at him desperately, clinging to his body with all her might. "James, don't leave me. I can't imagine not having you with me. I don't want to be alone again like I was!"

He shifted her onto his lap and cradled her, stroking her hair and her face. "Hush, hush my love. I'll make it happen. You'll see. You'll do your shoot, and in the meantime I'll work it out. I'll make it so you'll be comfortable and they will accept you. I must! And I can." He tilted her chin up to look into her eyes. "Do you believe me?"

Millie nodded.

And so they sat, through the few remaining hours of that long night.

Chapter XII

"I'll send a car for you," the Prince said, in the small foyer of her apartment. "Oh, ta!" as she handed him his emblazoned sweat shirt. "I'd hate to lose that!"

"Are you sure you should? Send a car for me?"

James laughed, and kissed her lightly. "Millie, when are you going to stop doubting me?" With another light kiss, he was gone.

When Millie climbed into the glossy Cadillac limousine, carrying the garment bag that held her gown, she smiled, both with delight at seeing Lady Cilly sitting in the back seat and with the recognition of another of James's neatly executed masterstrokes.

Cilly hugged her warmly. "I'm glad to see you, Millie. Ooooh, may I?" as she saw Millie's garment bag. She unzipped it and peeked inside. "That's gorgeous. It'll look smashing with your tan. Let's go get our hair done."

"I wanted to, but it's Friday, and we don't have appointments. I didn't make one because, up until last night, I didn't think I was going."

Cilly leaned forward. "Kenneth's," she told the driver. She sat back, grinning at Millie. "We'll tell them we're goin to the Prince of Wales's ball. You'll see how fast we'll get appointments."

Millie laughed. "I never would have thought of that."

"You will," Cilly said and something changed in her face.

"Did James . . . say anything to you?" Millie ventured.

Cilly shook her head. "No. But I know that whatever went wrong between you has been put right. I'm very glad about that. Actually, I'm more than glad. I'm grateful. I've had custody of Dilly these past two days, and it hasn't been easy." She grinned her impudent, flippant smile. "If you've never seen a very controlled person go slowly, quietly bonkers, you've missed a treat."

"Did he tell you what happened?"

"No. Prince James doesn't talk about things like that to anybody, I don't think. No, the thing was that he suddenly got very, very quiet. James has a temper. He blows up occasionally at his staff, especially when there's some stupid screwup that could have been avoided. But for the past two days he has been exceedingly gentle with everybody. Frighteningly gentle. As if he couldn't bear to inflict even the smallest portion of his pain on anyone. Scared the shit out of me, I can tell you. And, of course," she grinned wickedly, "he suddenly developed this avid interest in the Bahamas . . ."

Millie leaned back against the seat, enjoying Cilly's bright friendship, the unaccustomed luxury of a chauffered limousine, the happy anticipation of the ball, and the buoyant sense that all was right with her world.

"You look perfectly splendid!" James said, coming into his bedroom.

"I do, don't I," Millie said shamelessly. "And I'm not even dressed yet. I just had my hair done."

"Well, I like it," James said decisively. Her short dark hair had been done in a style similar to that she wore every day, but with that extra sleekness, that every-wayward-tendril-just-happened-to-fall-this-way look that is the hallmark of expensive coiffeurs. "I'm buried in meetings," James said, taking her in his arms. "But perhaps . . . " He unbuttoned her blouse. "I could sort of . . ." He put his mouth to her breast and dropped a quick, sucking kiss on each nipple, ". . . disappear for a while."

"Not a chance. This cost me fifty dollars and two boring hours."

He dropped to his knees in front of her and unzipped her pants. She held his head in her hands, laughing, as his mouth traced a persuasive line from her waist to the top of her soft, curly pubic hairs.

"Are you quite, quite sure?" He murmured, pressing his lips against her.

"Positive."

"All right. You win." He stood up.

"I'm not entirely sure you could call it winning," Millie pointed out, laughing up at him. "Hey! What's this?" She picked up a thick book from his nightstand. A bookmark held his place about two-thirds through.

The Prince looked a bit bashful at being caught out. "It's Graetz's *History of the Jews*. Why? Isn't that the right one?" He attempted to brazen it out.

"It is. It's the classic. I was just surprised all of a sudden—"

"It's a subject I know so little about. And I've had a lot of time on my hands these past few days."

This time, when the interrupting knock came at the door, Millie thought, smiling to herself, that the Prince escaped with rather more alacrity than usual.

Millie hummed softly as she shucked off her clothes. Clad only in her bikini underpants, she applied herself to the task of putting on her makeup. She was just at the finishing stages when Lady Cilly called cheerily through the door. "May I come in?"

Lady Cilly wore a chiffon, halter-topped gown the color of clotted cream, which fell in soft folds from the empire waist to the floor. The monochrome color scheme emphasized the fairness of her skin and hair, making her look like a particularly graceful, animated camellia. "Small tits," she said enviously. "You never have to bother with a bra."

"Well, I guess that's one of the advantages." Millie smiled to herself.

"Where's James?"

"Still in meetings."

"That's all right. He can change clothes in nothing flat." Cilly looked around at the black-and-gold opulence of the dressing room. "This place gives me the willies. Although, you at least have swans. I've got flamingoes in mine."

Millie laughed. She put down her mascara and turned to Lady Cilly, who sat in a black-and-gilt chair, smoking a cigarette. "I'm glad

James has a friend like you. You're the first person I've met who's normal around him."

"Nobody's normal around Prince James. It just isn't in the cards. There're just degrees of more and less. Perhaps his family is. They're very much— it's sort of them against the world. I suppose it has to be. But, of course, that's not enough when you're an adult. Your parents and sisters and brothers, I mean."

"James wants us to get married." Millie said abruptly and watched Lady Cilly's face very carefully.

Cilly nodded thoughtfully. "I'm not surprised."

"Did he tell you, the other night? Before our . . . "

"No. But I have eyes, don't I? I saw it right away. I saw it the minute he introduced us. I know James very well, and he looked . . . different."

"He was always good-looking!" Millie objected hotly. Then, catching herself, smiled shamefacedly.

"Of course, he's good-looking," Lady Cilly smiled, conceding the point. "But he looks different just the same. And so do you. You both radiate this kind of . . . celebration. You look like you have a conspiracy going. A conspiracy to commit happiness. So I'm not surprised." She threw her arms around Millie and kissed her on the cheek.

Millie hugged her back, gratefully. "You're the first to know."

"I do like you, Millie. I think you're perfect for James. I hope you two get away with it."

"James thinks— no, he *swears* he can. Do you think he will?"

Cilly hoisted herself up on the counter, heedless of her delicate gown. There was no trace of flippancy in her face, and her gray eyes were thoughtful. "If it was anybody but James, I mean another person in his position, I would say he hadn't the foggiest. But James is . . . special. The country lucked out with him, and they know it. Some of the previous heirs to the throne have been a sorry lot—and may well have included Jack the Ripper." She grinned at Millie. "Look what they have in James. He's got a brilliant mind, a disciplined mind. He's got more energy than six people. But it's more than that . . ."

Cilly fell silent. Whether she was organizing her thoughts or debating the wisdom of continuing, Millie didn't know. She contemplated her mascara and waited.

"It's easy for people to think," Cilly began. "It's— they look at James, and they see someone who has, and accepts as his due, the best of everything. The best the world has to offer. He is, or will be, one of its richest men. He mixes with heads of state, with the cream of society. There is no event that would not be honoured by his presence. All doors are open to him. He actually does all the things that most people only dream of doing—safari in Africa, fishing in Iceland. He has every imaginable luxury, at least the ones he wants. He has never worn an article of clothing that wasn't custom made for him. But what they don't see is that James . . . what he had to pay for it all. James made himself, by an act of will, into the person he is today. Into a worthy monarch, a leader. He reshaped his entire personality, went against every natural inclination . . ."

"I didn't know that. I thought it all came to him naturally."

"No. It took enormous determination. James is very dogged. He won't give up on anything until he's mastered it—or should I say conquered it. The entire country has watched him grow up. You may have noticed," she said drily, "that he has about as much privacy as a goldfish. I think they realize, however subliminally, that he did it for them."

"But what did he do?"

Cilly smiled. "I'll give you an example. When James was young, he was sort of chubby and uncoordinated and not very good at sports."

Millie thought of the lean, hard-muscled body entwined with hers every night. "But today he's—"

"That's the point. He made himself, by sheer effort, into an athlete. Not because that in itself was necessary—although England certainly does revere its athletes. But I think that was just the outward manifestation of the other. It didn't come easily to him. The only things that came easily to him were things of the mind and of the spirit. Contemplative things. All the rest he acquired for himself. At no small cost. Did you know that he plays the cello?"

"Yes."

"Well, he was very good at it. Under other circumstances he might have made a career of it. He's played several different instruments. No one realizes that he's really quite musical. What they see is someone who's charming on a dance floor and goes willingly to the opera. And he paints."

"Really?"

"Watercolors. The most marvelous, sensitive, fey watercolors. I think that's where he puts the dreamy side of him today. He doesn't show them to very many people. He just paints them and sticks them away in a closet."

"I didn't know that," Millie said sadly.

"But the point I'm getting at is that James, by nature, is—was— very shy, very private and quite introverted. All through his school days he was . . . I remember him as being frightfully serious. And quiet, and a little tentative. He didn't speak much, but he used to watch people a lot. And often he looked . . . worried, and hesitant. He seemed like the last person on earth to grow up and make speeches and carry out more than a thousand public engagements a year . . . and be a leader."

"It's hard for me. I only know James as he is today. I can't imagine him any other way."

"It happened all at once. When we were about sixteen. Suddenly he blossomed. I think it was then that he came to terms with things. All at once he was confident, outgoing and very sure."

"Maybe he just grew up?"

"No." Cilly smiled, a smile of infinite poignance, and more than a little regret. "I hadn't seen him for several months. We were both away at school. Then he spent the weekend at my parents' estate in Devonshire. And suddenly he had it. It was there. The incandescence, the indomitable control. And not the least, the ability to command. To hold every eye on him. But from that time on, there was always this . . . this tinge of a wild, splendid, mad gaiety just under the surface. As if, in one hidden corner of his mind, he stood aside and watched himself, and found the whole thing utterly hilarious. It was as if he had thought, all right, that's what you want me to be, that's what I'll be. I'll do it better than anyone has ever done. But you can't stop me from keeping one small private place to myself. And, in that place, James is laughing.

"It's most un-English and very appealing. They'll think twice before they take a chance on losing him."

"That's out of the question," said Millie. "He wouldn't do that, and I wouldn't let him. There are things that neither one of us can swallow."

Cilly looked at her for a long moment. "I'm glad. Because if he did, it would be . . . bloody. But that's why I say that James has a chance. He has a lot of power. Not because of his rank, but because of *him*. Because he's beloved. James is gold! And they know it. What's more, he's very, very tenacious. He always has been. Only this time, he'll be fighting for his life."

"When I say things like that, people say I'm being melodramatic."

"Nonsense. If he loses this one, it's curtains for him, as far as any personal happiness goes. And he *knows* it. Don't forget, once he marries, he's had it. Divorce is absolutely out of the question. There is no circumstance on earth under which he could get divorced. He doesn't have the option to remain single, and a string of extramarital affairs—that just wouldn't appeal to him."

Cilly fell silent. "I'll tell you what else is in his favour," she said after a moment, "his grandmother." Millie looked at her inquiringly. "His grandmother has lived through this twice. She has seen the devastation it can cause."

"Twice?"

"James's aunt. The Queen's younger sister."

Millie nodded. The Princess who had many years ago renounced her first, and perhaps only, love, because her religion and her position prohibited her from marrying a divorcé, was today herself divorced. The lines of bitterness and disappointment had drawn her once-pretty face into something very different. "I forgot about that," Millie said.

Cilly smiled. "I'll bet James hasn't. I don't remember too much about it. I was very young at the time, and I'll bet James doesn't either. But he's very close to his grandmother. She's the one single person that he really bares his soul to. She's very special, and there's something very special between them. There always has been, from the time he was very small. His parents were away a lot, and she was always there. When he was miserable at school, I know that she was the only person who— I think she's the only person who has seen James shed tears."

Not so, Millie thought. Not anymore.

"She understands sacrifice," Cilly continued, "perhaps better than anyone. I've often thought that she was the only other person who really, truly understood the magnitude of what James did. What I was telling you about. Everybody else more or less thought that he had grown out of an awkward stage and heaved a big sigh of relief. But his grandmother, when she looks at him, you can see that she understands."

"Will she help us?"

"I don't know that for sure. She—all of them . . . are very dedicated. They have a tremendous devotion to duty and all it stands for. None of them think it was meant to be easy. Every one of them has made tremendous personal sacrifices. But she loves James very much. No one really knows if things would have been different if his aunt had married the other chap. But they might have been. The whole thing is a heartbreak—and maybe, if you're lucky, an object lesson. His grandmother, who sees first hand what happened to her youngest daughter—she has *got* to wonder. I would, if I were in her place. At least James can say, 'Look, you've tried it the other way twice, and it hasn't worked. You've wound up with wasted, broken lives. Don't, for God's sake, make the same mistake again!' Don't underestimate James, Millie."

Millie's heart flared with hope. "Are you saying he'll win, Cilly?"

Cilly waited several long moments before answering. "I don't know. I honestly don't know." She looked at Millie's face. "Knowing James, I'd say he has a chance. Maybe a good chance. I'll tell you something, though. If James doesn't marry you, I don't think he'll care *who* he marries."

"Don't say that, Cilly. I didn't like either half of that sentence."

Cilly smiled. "Nevertheless, it's true. If it doesn't work, you're far better off than he is."

"The whole thing was such a surprise to me. I've only known him for two weeks. Not even. And it seemed like the minute I saw him, things started . . . spinning. I sat there in the studio watching him, knowing in my heart that he was watching me. It took me a long time to believe it. Even after I had a hard time believing it was real. What on earth do I have in common with the Prince of Wales!"

"Bullshit!" said the peeress. "People don't fall in love based on things like that. It's all—God knows what it is. Chemistry. Pheromones. People fall in love with someone who answers something in their souls. If people fell in love based on rank and shit like that, James would have been married a long time ago to some drippy European princess or a duke's daughter and have a nursery full of little royal children. The fact that they haven't succeeded in marrying him off yet—and believe me, they've been trying—I've always felt that James had trouble . . . reconciling himself."

"Cilly, I'm so scared. What if he doesn't . . . what if he fails?"

Cilly slid off the counter. She put her arm around Millie's shoulders. "I'll tell you this. He'll try like hell. And James is very good at . . . he knows all the complexities and all the convolutions of the world he lives in. He's pulled off a lot of things in the past. He was the first Prince of Wales to go to public school or take a University degree, and all those other firsts I have trouble keeping straight in my head. Flying jet planes and submarines and—"

"But none of that is the same as marrying a Jewish girl from the Bronx, is it?" Millie looked into the sympathetic gray eyes.

"Here. Put your dress on, honey. It's getting late." Cilly helped her on with her dress, a strapless, elegantly severe column of peau de soie in the palest of shell pinks. "See! I knew it. You look all shiny. Pale pink and golden tan. If I so much as look at the sun I fry." Cilly found her high-heeled sandals, her beaded purse and the wispy shawl that went with the dress. Then she put her arms around the smaller girl. "Don't look like that, Millie. It'll be all right."

"Cilly, you're just . . . you're terrific. You're the best person."

"Of *course*," Cilly smiled.

And all at once, James was there. His flamboyant energy and his lighthearted laughter brightened the room, banishing the shadows. "Look at you two. I'm dazzled! All this perfection is somewhat inhibiting." He put his hands on Millie's bare shoulders. "Dare I kiss you?"

"Always," she said and reached up for his kiss.

He turned to Cilly and took her hands in his. "Has she told you, Cilly? Are you happy for me?"

And this time it was Cilly who responded, "Very, James." And there, on the tiled floor of the dressing room, she curtsied to him. When she rose, there was no trace of the laughing twinkle in her face. "I'm very happy for you, Dilly." She raised her mouth to his and kissed him.

"Thank you, Cilly." He held her in his arms for a moment, then broke away. "Get out of here, you two. I've got about three seconds to shower and change."

In the large drawing room-cum-office of the suite, a tuxedoed man sat at one of the desks, looking a little lonely and obviously waiting for them. He rose when they came out of the Prince's room. "Good evening, Miss Myerson. Good evening, Lady Cecilia."

"Where's Goldsworth?" Cilly demanded. And Millie recognized the junior equerry. For the life of her, she couldn't remember his name.

Nameless Equerry looked a little uncomfortable. "I'm to accompany you to the ballroom. His Royal Highness specifically instructed—"

"Righto," Cilly said. "Let's get on with it then, shall we?"

Millie, as in a dream, stepped into the ballroom and into a fairyland filled with music, with the scent of perfume and heated bodies and flowers. The crystal chandeliers clustered overhead threw off glints of light that caught on precious stones and satin and bare shoulders. She paused on the threshold, thrilling to the sight and the sound and the scent. There was an air of charged glamor, of high, sweet excitement, a sense of being transported, for the space of one evening, out of time, to a legendary world of swords and pageantry and diamonds, of flirtation and romance and intrigue.

The women, gorgeously gowned, jewels at their ears and throats, sparkled against a masculine backdrop of black and white, dotted here and there with the brilliance of full-dress uniform. There was a muted buzz of many languages being spoken at once, and Millie spotted, among the Balenciagas and Balmains and Givenchys, a woman dressed in a silk sari shot with silver. Her skin was the color of tea held up to the light, and a black caste mark dotted the center of her forehead. Here and there were tall, imposing Africans in national costume, some turbaned, one man even plumed. Their jewel-encrusted robes worn over flowing white linen eclipsed the more sedate Western men with their brilliance.

"The entire bleeding diplomatic corps is out tonight," Cilly observed in her ear.

"It's fabulous!" Millie said, looking around.

"Let's get a drink," replied the veteran of a thousand such nights.

Nameless Equerry cleared his throat meaningfully. "Perhaps

not," Cilly said. "Perhaps we should do the honors first."

At the far end of the room, two identical flags were crossed on the wall, the crimson Welsh dragon on a field of green and white. Between them, taking pride of place, was an enormous Union Jack. On a raised dais, Prince James, flanked by the portly ambassador and his wife, greeted his guests.

"This'll go fast," Cilly said. "It's not conversation, like the other, it's curtsy, bow, say hello and move on."

Millie examined with fascination the burly Scotsman, who, in company with his gowned and tiaraed wife, made his obeisance to his young prince. He wore formal Highland evening dress, a black velvet jacket, frilled white shirt and a kilt. He wore a cummerbund at his waist, and a dirk peeked out from the top of his checkered stockings. His wife wore a sash of the same plaid crossed over her green lace evening gown and a clump of heather at her shoulder.

Cilly followed them. "Good evening, Sir Ivor," she said nicely. "Good evening, Your Royal Highness." She dropped James a quick, light curtsy, and, as she turned away, Millie heard her murmur, with no change in her demure expression, "I'll see you later, when I've got a bloody drink in my hand."

"I'll look forward to that, Lady Cecilia," James responded decorously. James, looking tall and imposing in his white tie and tails. A periwinkle-blue satin sash crossed his breast, running from his left shoulder to his right hip. From a lighter-blue silk band under his collar hung an ornate, four-pointed cross with a sapphire at its center.

Millie smiled at the ambassador, who shook her hand and assured her once again, rather wistfully, that she was a charming girl, and moved to stand in front of Prince James.

His tan face split with his wide grin when he saw her. Instead of shaking his offered hand, Millie lifted her arms and sank to the floor, executing a deep, perfect court curtsy, the formal homage of a subject to her sovereign. She held it for the briefest of moments, then inclined her head and rose, in a swirl of pink peau de soie, to face him.

The Prince threw back his head and laughed, a laugh of pure joy, of release and of understanding. "Well done, my darling. Well done!" He extended his hand once again, and this time she took it. He held it between both of his for a long moment, and then, his eyes sparkling, handed her on to a somewhat puzzled Mrs. Ambassador.

Millie shook her hand, smiled and turned away. She found herself enfolded in Lady Cilly's hug. "You'll do," Cilly told her. "Now you really rate a drink! You may as well, they won't let Dilly off till after the toast to the Queen."

"Here we go," Cilly said later, as waiters passed through the crowd with trays holding shallow-mouthed, long-stemmed glasses of champagne.

A microphone was placed in front of the ambassador, and he obligingly blew into it, to see if it was live. It was. The guests lined the room, forming a horseshoe shape around the dais. Millie, bred in the New York City subway system, grabbed Cilly's hand and engineered their way through the crowd to the front row, a few feet away from the Prince.

"I'll keep my remarks brief this evening," the ambassador chuckled, "for I know it's not me you want to hear." He then went on to speak at some length, expressing his pleasure at having the Prince visit him in his exile in service of his country and his dismay that the visit, all too short, had seemed like but a day. He might rather have wished to have seen more of His Royal Highness, but, he understood, duty will always come before pleasure.

"They breed them like that," Cilly whispered. "If you're not a crashing, prosing bore, you can't be an ambassador. It's a rule."

Finally he said, "And I give you, His Royal Highness, the Prince of Wales."

James stepped to the microphone and waited gravely, until the prolonged applause had died down. "I cannot tell you how much I have enjoyed my visit to your country," he began. "What I have found here has enriched my life beyond measure. I am grateful to you all for your hospitality and your courtesy." His face was unreadable, devoid of all emotion. "During my stay here, I have received many gifts, all of them valuable, all of them appreciated, and not the least of which was a frog named Kelev."

Millie felt a hard, burning lump rise in her throat. The Prince paused. He swallowed and then continued. "Some of them I will carry back to England with me, and I shall treasure them forever. And for that, I thank you most deeply."

He waited for a moment, and, when he continued, his voice was husky. "Let me conclude by saying that I shall never forget you." He stretched out his arm and raised his glass. "To the Queen!"

Prince James's eyes found Millie's and locked. He alone of all the people in the room did not drink from his glass. "To the Queen!" he repeated. His voice, resonant, assured, rang through the room. He raised his glass once again and deliberately, and ever so slightly, tipped it to Millie.

Millie's heart turned over in her breast. James brought the glass to his lips and drained it.

The Prince, heedless of the people who milled around him, set down his glass and walked directly to Millie. As he reached her, the band started to play, and she walked into his arms.

They circled the room, oblivious to the other dancers, sailing on a sea of melody, floating, adrift, and they hoped never to make landfall.

Tears burned against Millie's eyelids as she recognized the words to the song the band was playing.

> *If you go away, on a summer day,*
> *Then you might as well take the sun away*
> *All the birds that flew in the summer sky*
> *When our love was new and our hearts were high . . .*

She wondered if James knew the words. She was afraid to look at him, and then she did. His face was impassive, austere. His eyes glinted with unshed tears.

> *When the day was young and the nights were long*
> *And the moon stood still for the nightbirds song . . .*

She looked away, and beyond caring, rested her cheek against his chest. The Prince did not stop her.

> *But if you stay, I'll make you a day*
> *Like no day has been, or will be again.*
> *We'll sail the sun, we'll glide on the rain*
> *We'll talk to the trees and worship the wind.*

She moved with him, the words to the haunting Jacques Brel melody playing in her head.

If you go away, as I know you must,
There'll be nothing left in the world to trust
Just an empty room full of empty space
Like the empty look I see on your face.
I'd have been the shadow of your shadow
If I thought it might have kept me by your side.

James rested his face against her hair. She turned her head to look at him, and marveled at his complete composure. Millie touched her lips, lightly, secretly, to his cheek and found, to her great surprise, that it was wet with tears.

But if you stay, I'll make you a night
Like no night has been, or will be again.
I'll sail on your smile, I'll glide on your touch
I'll talk to your eyes that I love so much.

The music came to an end some seconds before they realized it. Millie looked up at him speechlessly, unable to trust her voice. She felt his inner stiffening as, with a heroic effort, he schooled himself to his normal reserve. "I can't stay any longer," she whispered. "I'll wait for you. I'll be in your bedroom when you're ready."

He nodded and turned away to his duty.

* * *

"Who the hell is responsible for that!" the Prince snapped, later in his bedroom. He ripped his shirt open, scattering little pearl buttons all over the carpet.

Millie followed his glance and saw what had upset him. Some well-meaning soul, in an excess of romantic zeal, had left a chilled bottle of champagne and two crystal flutes on the nightstand to mark the Prince's last night in New York City. Millie climbed out of bed and walked into his arms. "It's just an ordinary night," she said, "just an ordinary night."

James fingered the gold chain that rested in the hollows of her throat. "I've been meaning to ask you all evening. What do the letters say."

"It's my name, in Hebrew. Malka."

"Malka," he repeated, tasting it on his tongue. "That's pretty.

Does it mean anything? What does it mean?"

Millie smiled up at him, anticipating. "It means 'queen.'"

James fell back on the bed, laughing so hard he rolled off it on to the floor. "Millie," he gasped, "nobody ever listens to me!"

The glass coach, which had carried England's royal brides for over a century, rolled to a stop in front of Westminster Abbey.

Millie got out, careful of her billowing satin train. She paused for a moment, looking up at the venerable spires and the brilliant blue sky. Gerald, elegant in his morning coat and striped trousers, smiled at her and gave her his arm. Together they walked up the steps and entered the Abbey.

The massive cathedral, lit by white candles in silver candelabra, was filled to overflowing. Millie glanced up at the galleries and saw that they, too, were lined with rows of smiling people.

Peers of the realm, ermine-robed and coroneted, watched as Princess Sarah, smiling shyly, moved slowly down the aisle. Her jonquil-yellow gown was the exact shade of the flowers she held at her waist.

Millie felt a tug at her elbow. She looked down and saw her nephew Danny. "I'm wearing a skirt!" he said indignantly.

Millie straightened one of the ruffles on his shirt and smoothed the collar of his black velvet jacket. "A kilt, Danny. The Balmoral Tartan. You remember about that."

"My name is Sarah, too," her niece said and picked up the ends of Millie's flowing train.

Millie glanced down at her bouquet. Hidden among the white roses and lily-of-the-valley was, she knew, a sprig of myrtle grown from Queen Victoria's bridal bouquet, in accordance with Royal tradition.

High up in the ancient walls, the regimental trumpeteers of the Welsh Guards raised their silver trumpets and sounded a fanfare, heralding the arrival of the bride of their commander-in-chief.

Millie started down the aisle on Gerald's arm, her head proudly raised, the diamond tiara, gift of her prince, glittering and winking in the gloom of the cathedral.

She looked down the long, long aisle. In the distance, the Prince, tall and regal in his scarlet uniform, waited for her.

"You look beautiful," Gerald said. And, even though he hadn't spoken, she heard him.

298 /

"All the rest was only a trial," Lord Marling smiled. "You know about trials, don't you, Millie?"

"You are our daughter," the Queen said.

"And very lovely she is, too," echoed the smiling Duke. "My son knows what's what."

"Welcome," said the Queen Mother. "We know you love our James."

"I do," Millie said silently. "I do."

She reached the Prince and stood at his side. She looked into his eyes, and they were joyous and eager and grave.

They turned and faced the Archbishop, magnificently robed and mitred. "Who giveth this woman in lawful wedlock?" he asked.

Gerald stepped forward. "I do."

The Prince turned to face Millie. He took her hand, and, in flawless, perfect accents, he repeated the ancient Hebrew marriage vow. "Harei at mekudeshet li betabaat zo, kedat Moshe veYisrael." He slipped the wide gold band on her finger and repeated. "With this ring, I consecrate you unto me according to the laws of Moses and Israel."

"Mazal tov!" came the full-throated cry from the peers of the realm. "Mazal tov!"

The Prince took her in his arms. She raised her lips to his. "It's all right, my love," he whispered. "You couldn't come to me, so I came to you."

The organ sounded the crashing notes of Mendelsohn's "Wedding March," and the Prince, proud and smiling, started down the aisle with Millie on his arm.

They paused in front of the radiant Queen and the debonair, smiling Duke. Together, as one person, they made their obeisance. The Prince bowed, deeply, and Millie, in a sea of white lace, swept to the floor in a curtsy.

The trumpets pealed once again, and every bell in England rang, as Millie and the Prince, hand in hand, stepped out into the brilliant sunshine. The cheering, waving throng blurred mistily in front of Millie's eyes. Her smile, tremulous and radiant, and the Prince's—brilliant and glowing with triumph—held all the splendor of the magical day.

Millie awoke to find her pillow wet with tears—and not of joy.

* * *

"Say good-bye to all these people now, Millie," the Prince said. "You won't be seeing them again today." The only outward sign of his iron control was a certain flatness of expression and a darkening of the blue of his eyes.

Millie steeled herself, determined to match his offhand manner, if only not to threaten his hard-won equanimity. It's good practice for you, she thought. You'll need to be able to do as he does.

She glanced around the sitting room that had been her home for the past few days. Everything had a strange, oppressive tinge to it. I know what it is, Millie thought. It's— everything is filtered, like the ones they put in front of a camera, when they have to block out the sun to match a shot from a gray, cloudy day.

She walked over to Peter Goldsworth and, smiling, put out her hand. Bear him no malice, she thought. And don't worry about him. James is watching him.

"It's been very nice knowing you, Miss Myerson," the equerry said and smiled soberly at her.

You can never tell what he's thinking, Millie thought, and turned to Matthews, the press secretary, whose first name she had never learned.

"It's been my pleasure, Miss Myerhoff," he said blandly. And grinned broadly.

Millie returned his smile and moved to Ian MacCrae. "Thank you for everything," she said to the detective.

The stolid Scotsman looked down at her. "You're a good lass. See that you look out for yourself." Millie reached up to kiss his cheek and saw that his face was creased with emotion.

She threw her arms around Lady Cilly. "Take care of him, Cilly."

"I can't. He's far too much of a handful for me. You'll just have to do it for yourself." Cilly hugged her. "I'll see you very soon, Millie. I know it."

Goldsworth cleared his throat. "It's time we left for the airport, sir."

"Right. Make sure I've got the Rolls," the Prince said, and thereby fulfilled his promise, made almost two weeks ago in a taxi outside Des Artistes.

The silver Rolls Royce waited for them at the curb, flying the two national flags and the crimson, gold and blue standard that proclaimed the identity of its passenger.

Millie settled herself on the gray suede seat, thinking that it smelled like a new handbag on the first day you buy it.

James climbed in next to her. He pressed a button, and the glass partition rose, cutting them off from the driver and MacCrae, sealing them in a private, mobile room.

Millie sat next to the Prince, her hand in his, silently looking out the tinted glass window. She ventured a glance at him, and saw that he was doing the same. "You'll sleep in your own bed tonight," she said.

He nodded. "Actually it'll be tomorrow morning before I get there. Because of the time difference."

"How do you travel?"

The Prince's laughter rang out. "Millie, how will I manage without you? Who will ask me all these endless questions? What do you mean how do I travel? What do you think? Alitalia? British Airways!"

"No, I meant do you sit with everybody or what?"

"We take the whole first-class compartment. Otherwise every time I close my eyes, somebody'll be at me."

He dug into his pocket. "Millie, I have something for you. I don't know whether I should give it to you, you ask so many pesky questions . . ." He grinned at her and handed her a small blue-velvet jewel case.

"What is it?"

James broke up. "There you go again!"

I'll miss his laughter, Millie thought. She opened the case. Inside was a gleaming gold pendant on a slender thread of chain. It's abstract shape suggested a stylized leaf. Its lines, some curving and some angular, had an esthetic grace. In the center was a flowing lower-case initial "M." "It's beautiful," she breathed.

"Turn it over."

Millie touched her fingertips to the pendant and carefully turned it over. The pendant, when viewed from the reverse side, was the three-feathered device of the Prince—and the Princess!—of Wales. "James, you can't mean me to wear this!"

"Are you telling me I'm the sort of person who gives people presents he doesn't mean them to wear? What kind of bloke do you think I *am?*"

He gathered Millie into his arms and kissed her forehead, chastely. "Wear it with discretion for the time being. A short time."

His voice broke. "A very short time, I promise you, my darling."

"I love you, James," she whispered.

And with a final kiss, and another quick brush of his lips against hers, he turned away and stepped out of the car.

Millie threaded the gold chain through her fingers and watched as the Prince strode away. *And please win, James.* She sent the unvoiced plea to his retreating back.

Prince James ignored the clamoring reporters and ran lightly, swiftly up the steps to the plane.

When the door slammed shut behind him, the Rolls Royce turned and started back home. Millie looked down at the pendant in her hand. *"Ich Dien,"* she read, "I serve," and was suddenly very cold.

Epilogue

The cab pulled up in front of CC&G. Millie paid the driver and got out. She stood for a moment outside the studio, heedless of the wind that nipped at her stockinged ankles and whipped up eddies of the nameless detritus that blankets New York City streets. The sun fought mightily to break through the clouds and succeeded only in shedding a pale, milky-yellow light. Please God, she thought. If I get this one, it'll be number three, and I'm on my way.

She pushed open the door, carefully avoiding the cracked glass. Her business this time was on the second floor, which held the executive offices, and she ran lightly up the stairs and walked rapidly down the corridor.

"Hey, Millie! Hold it a sec, will ya?" She turned and saw Gerald loping down the corridor toward her. "Jesus! You move like a bunny rabbit!" He handed her a copy of the early edition of the *New York Post* and watched her intently as she read it. His bony face was wrinkled with concern.

The front page had a screaming headline: "IT'S OFFICIAL! PRINCE JAMES TO MARRY!

Buckingham Palace announced today the engagement of His Royal Highness, the Prince of Wales, to Lady Pamela Bronnington, daughter of the Duke and Duchess of Newberry.

The thirty-three-year-old Prince released the following statement: "There are very few occasions in one's life when one is able, at one and the same time, to give pleasure to oneself and to others. It is my privilege to share with all of you, my family and my countrymen, the great joy which is in my heart today.

"It is difficult to express in words just what one feels at such a moment. My cherished hope is to follow the shining example set me by my parents and create a secure, happy family unit, and give you, one day, an heir, who will serve you as wholeheartedly as I do.

"I ask you all, on this, one of the happiest days of my life, for your blessings."

The entire bottom half of the page was given over to a picture of Prince James and his fiancée. They stood next to each other, shoulder to shoulder, a decorous six inches between them. Lady Pamela wore a simply cut wool dress and a string of pearls. It was difficult to tell from the photograph what color her hair was, but it appeared neither very light nor very dark. Her smile was warm and she had an air of innocence and an appealing simplicity.

Be sweet with him, Millie thought. *Give him kisses and laughter and tumbling, merry children.*

She handed the paper back to Gerald. "I knew about this. I've known about it for a long time." She smiled at his sigh of relief.

"Okay, cupcake. See ya. Good luck!" he called over his shoulder.

Millie opened the door to the conference room. George Gilhooley sat at one end of a long table, and four men flanked him at the sides. There was an empty seat at the foot of the table, and Millie took it. It didn't occur to Mr. Gilhooley of the gracious manners to introduce her.

"About time," he said.

Millie set her attaché case on the table and looked around the room, while Gilhooley did twenty minutes on the fact that she was six minutes late.

A tall, curly-haired man sat perched on the credenza against the wall. Everything about him was rumpled, his unruly, shaggy hair, his striped polo jersey, his corduroy slacks, even his socks. Everything except his face, which had strong, angular features, and his eyes, which were sharp.

Millie ventured a smile. He eyed her expressionlessly in return.

And then, just as Millie was sorry she had ever bothered, he smiled back, a smile of challenge, with just a hint of complicity.

Millie turned her attention back to the proceedings. "Look, Mr. Gilhooley—George," she said, cutting him off in mid-tirade, "I'm here to discuss directing a two-hundred-fifty-thousand-dollar documentary. I think we can dispense with any further discussion of my tardiness."

I liked that, she thought. You did that very well.

Gilhooley looked at her, pissed. "I don't even know what you're doing here, Millie. You don't have enough experience, and I personally don't think you can handle it."

"Then what *am* I doing here?" Millie asked bluntly.

"We got a phone call about you," he said sourly. "A very strong recommendation. From someone called Rupert Gallagher at Thames Television."

Millie suppressed the spurt of laughter that welled up in her. Thank you, Cilly, she thought. And thank you, James . . .

"As you know," Gilhooley continued, in his inimitably pompous manner, "the BBC, in conjunction with PBS, is preparing a half-hour documentary on prerevolutionary architecture in New York City. CC&G is the production company, and we're interviewing directors. No decision will be made today, Millie. We're being very careful about this. We're going to talk to a lot of other people and—"

"No, we're not." The man slid off his perch on the credenza. "I have neither the time nor the inclination to sit about interviewing clods when I've just decided. The matter's been settled. Miss Myerson here is going to direct the piece."

I never thought people's mouths really drop open, Millie thought, looking around in amusement. The man walked over to her and put out his hand. "H'lo. I'm Jason Hiller. I'm the producer of this piece, so, when I say something, they all have to listen to me." He grinned at her. "Everybody calls me Jay," he added in his clipped British accent.

Millie shook his hand. He's adorable, she thought. "Thank you," she said primly. "I'm very much looking forward to it. I'll do my best, and you won't be sorry."

"I better not be. For your sake. I'm not a very patient chap. When my directors give me grief, I don't waste time discussing the situation, I simply bash their heads in." He waited for her laugh, and then turned abruptly and left the room. His entourage, still stunned, gathered their wits and scurried after him.

"I'm very glad things turned out this way," Gilhooley said. "I always knew you could do it." He smiled weakly at her and chased after the rest of the contingent.

Millie picked up her attaché case. I wonder if he's Jewish, she thought, smiling to herself. I wonder if he likes kids.

She left the conference room and walked briskly down the corridor. It's a good thing I'm making some money. I'll have to take a few months off, at least.

Millie glanced down at the suit jacket that hid the safety-pinned waist of her dirndl skirt. And smiled again, a delicious, secret smile, as she felt the first, swift thrust of the heir, kicking inside her belly.